Waters of Marah is a different kin
toward wholeness through the tr
read by a very gifted storyteller.

Rand...
Christy Award-winning au...
of *Oxygen* and *Premonition*

Sylvia Bambola has once again touched a deep place in my soul with her writing. In *Waters of Marah*, Gloria Bickford realizes that lonely people feel the cold more keenly than others. As she learns to ease her loneliness by obeying Christ and reaching out to those in need, her life blossoms with warmth and meaning.

Hannah Alexander
Author of *Hideaway, The Crystal Cavern,*
and the Healing Touch series

Sylvia Bambola captures glimpses of the human heart with poignant realism. A stimulating and inspiration read that will make you want to cheer!

Kathy Herman
Author of The Baxter series

Realistic and compelling—a coming-of-age story rich with compassion—*Waters of Marah* satisfies the soul.

Lyn Cote
Author of the Northern Intrigue series

Sylvia Bambola pulled me from the first words into Gloria Bicford's struggle for independence, her search for love and finding illusions, and her groaning to stretch her faith. I felt in the hands of a skilled writer who knew every nook and cranny of her character's interior being.

Janet Chester Bly
Author of *Hope Live Here*
and twenty-seven other books

Waters of Marah

SYLVIA BAMBOLA

MOODY PUBLISHERS
CHICAGO

Also by Sylvia Bambola

Tears in a Bottle
Refiner's Fire
A Vessel of Honor

Scripture taken from the *Holy Bible, New International Version*®. NIV®. Copyright © 1973, 1978, 1984 by International Bible Society. Used by permission of Zondervan Publishing House. All rights reserved.

Scripture quotations marked KJV are taken from the King James Version.

Published in association with the literary agency of Alive Communications, Inc., 7680 Goddard Street, Suite 200, Colorado Springs, Colorado 80920.

Library of Congress Cataloging-in-Publication Data

Bambola, Sylvia.
    Waters of Marah / by Sylvia Bambola.
        p. cm.
    ISBN 0-8024-7905-7
    1. Parent and adult child—Fiction. 2. Conflict of generations—Fiction.
3. Mothers and daughters—Fiction. 4. City and town life--Fiction.
5. Problem youth--Fiction. I. Title.

PS3552.A47326W37 2004
813'.6—dc22

2003020044

1 3 5 7 9 10 8 6 4 2

Printed in the United States of America

Dedicated to my brother Bud—Who was there when I needed him.

Dedicated to Sue—More than a sister-in-law. A dear friend who taught me about dictionaries and so much more.

Acknowledgments

SPECIAL THANKS TO James Joyce, Detective, Suffolk County Police Department, retired, Doctor Philip Mantia, and Carol Wheat, (NYS Social Services, MAPP [Model Approach to Partnerships in Parenting], MSW) for fielding my numerous questions.

Also in researching eco-terrorism and various issues of environmentalism, I found the following books to be especially of value: *Eco-Scam* by Ronald Bailey, *The Skeptical Environmentalist* by Bjorn Lomborg, *Ecoterror: The Violent Agenda to Save Nature* by Ron Arnold, and *Undue Influence* by Ron Arnold. To say these books were an eye-opener would be an understatement.

And last of all I want to thank: Michele Straubel, my editor at Moody Publishers, and Andrea Christian, my agent. And finally, my husband, Vincent, and daughter, Gina, for reading my raw manuscript and offering corrections and comments.

I am blessed to have such support.

AND WHEN THEY CAME TO MARAH, THEY COULD NOT
DRINK OF THE WATERS OF MARAH, FOR THEY WERE BITTER: . . .
AND THE PEOPLE MURMURED AGAINST MOSES, SAYING,
WHAT SHALL WE DRINK? AND HE CRIED UNTO THE LORD;
AND THE LORD SHEWED HIM A TREE, WHICH WHEN HE HAD
CAST INTO THE WATERS, THE WATERS WERE MADE SWEET.

~❧ EXODUS 15:23–25 KJV❧~

Chapter One

DO NOT STARE AT ME BECAUSE I AM DARK,
BECAUSE I AM DARKENED BY THE SUN.
MY MOTHER'S SONS WERE ANGRY WITH ME
AND MADE ME TAKE CARE OF THE VINEYARDS;
MY OWN VINEYARD I HAVE NEGLECTED.

—⊛ SONG OF SONGS 1:6 NIV⊛—

THE MINUTE SECURITY BECOMES more important than your dreams, you're in trouble. Gloria Bickford nibbled the cuticle of her thumbnail. At least that's what Tracy kept telling her.

But dreams rarely come true.

Gloria felt her cuticle tear, then absently picked up a napkin and swaddled her thumb. It was easy for Tracy to dispense wisdom, as though it came from the *Encyclopedia Britannica.* Tracy had green eyes and red hair. People with green eyes and red hair ruled the world. Or at least the world she knew.

But hadn't God *promised?* Hadn't His promise come to her like a sword of fire, piercing deep into the secret place where she guarded her dreams?

She glanced at her thumb—a digit of importance and dignity reduced to a comical pig-in-the-blanket. *What a disgusting habit.* On that, both she and Mother agreed. But it was the only thing. How long had she been doing it, anyway? Mutilating her fingers? She couldn't remember, it had been so long. Maybe she didn't want to. The habit was too frank a revelation. It showed that her courage was as fragile as a sparrow's egg. Would it shatter if Cutter fought her decision? She pictured his face, with its sneer. She of all people knew what lay behind it. Still . . . there could be no backing down. And she couldn't let anyone change her mind, either.

Not even Mother.

Gloria released the napkin, watched it fall from her thumb and float to the floor. Then like nomads, her fingers roamed the tabletop, arranging the green ceramic salt-and-pepper shakers her mother had given her, aligning the small stack of paper napkins, removing a dried leaf from the philodendron that her mother swore spewed spider mites and fungus into the air. Finally, her fingers rested on the edges of the green jute place mats her mother had bought from Wal-Mart.

Green. She hated it. No, not really. She loved it in grass, on hills, on trees, but not in her kitchen. Peach, cream, now those were her colors. But Mother liked green.

What was she going to tell Mother?

The phone rang and Gloria jumped, yanking a place mat off the table. She stared at the black cordless, which looked uncomfortably like the head of a snake.

Ring. Ring.

Gloria twisted the jute in her hands.

Ring.

If she didn't answer, her mother might worry and come right over. Her hand lunged for the phone, toppling the shakers. Out of the corner of her eye, she saw a chip fly into the air and land near her feet. *Oh, great. How was she going to explain that to Mother?*

"I can't believe what I just heard from Mrs. Press!" The sharp voice drilled Gloria's eardrum like a corkscrew, then pierced the brain, producing an instant headache. "You think husbands grow on trees? What in the world were you thinking? Sometimes, Gloria, you don't have a brain in your head."

"I've been trying to tell you I'm not interested in getting married, Mother."

"Why do girls who have few prospects always say that?"

Gloria's hand tightened around the phone. "What good are prospects if they're the wrong ones?"

"You want to be alone forever? It's no picnic, believe you me. Ever since your father died . . . well, it's no picnic. You think I want the same for you?"

"Mother—"

"Don't underestimate the value of security. That should be your goal. And you almost had it too. Virginia . . . Mrs. Press and I just about had it arranged, but then you went and said something stupid and spoiled it all."

"But I don't love him, Mother."

"Since when has that stopped anyone from getting married? You think most people getting married are in love? If they were, why do half of them end up in divorce court?"

"I could never marry someone I didn't love."

"Gloria, wake up and see things for what they really are. You think because I was a beauty queen I had it easy? How many times do I have to tell you beauty pageants aren't all that different from real life? Everyone's trying to create perfection. To win something. But sooner or later the Preparation H wears off, and the bags begin to show. That's what you've got to learn. Everyone's got bags, Gloria, or sweaty feet, or . . . But you live with it. A wise woman closes her eyes and lives with it."

"Mother . . . honestly . . ."

"It's certainly nothing like those romance novels you read."

"Didn't you love Daddy?"

"Maybe I shouldn't have named you after Gloria Swanson. How was I to know you wouldn't have any looks at all? That you'd turn out to be—"

"I'm sorry I disappointed you."

"No use crying over spilled milk. No use crying over something we can't change. Though heaven knows I've tried. Tried to teach you all the tricks I've learned over the years. But you still can't apply makeup to save your life, and your hair . . . why do you *insist* on frizzing your hair?"

"I like my hair this way."

"You only like it because I don't. You've made it a war between us."

"No I haven't. Why can't I have my own—"

"Like I said, no use crying. I learned long ago life isn't pretty. But we all have to walk down that runway, Gloria. Do our acts, strut our stuff. We have to do the best we can with what we've got. And when you don't have a lot, you can't be choosy. You've got to settle. Though Cutter Press is hardly a booby prize. For heaven's sake, he's loaded! You'd never have to worry if there was money in the bank when you wrote a check. And that's nothing to snub your nose at. Security, Gloria. That's what you should be looking for. Believe me, plenty of women would jump at a chance to marry Cutter. All things considered, he's far more than you have any right to expect."

Gloria had already opened the cabinet near the refrigerator and removed a box of Domino sugar cubes. She flipped up the top, plunged in fingers, and pulled out a perfectly shaped cube and placed it on her tongue. Now she stood by the counter letting the cube disintegrate, letting the crystals crumble and float and sweeten the bitter taste that had filled her mouth. She couldn't remember when she first started using Domino cubes, but she was ten when her mother caught her and gave her a lengthy lecture on tooth decay and cellulite. Gloria covered the mouthpiece of the phone before she bit into the last of the chunks, then swallowed.

"You're all I've got in the world. I love you, and I only want what's best. But you've got to cooperate, Gloria. Give me a little help here. You've got to shake those cobwebs out of that head of yours and face facts. With your limited assets—"

"Mother, *please*, can't you leave me something?"

"You've got to take what comes along."

Gloria was back by the table and picked up the salt shaker. For a moment she felt like smashing it on the floor. "Looks and brains aren't everything."

"Try telling a man that. No, Gloria, you've got to stop fooling yourself. The only assets you have are youth, and you're not getting any younger—"

"I'm only twenty-eight."

"And you're a hard worker. For some men, that's enough. They're just looking for a wife who'll keep a nice house and put meals together."

"You mean like a maid?"

"And fortunately, Cutter Press is one of them."

"But I want more, Mother. I have hopes . . . dreams . . . I want to be loved." She looked at the gold-framed photo on the coffee table of Tracy and Tucker holding margaritas and each other and smiling, as though they also held the whole world in one of their Velcro pockets. Then she thought of the picture of just Tucker—taken on the sly from Tracy's castoffs. She had cut

13

that one, trimmed it around the edges so it would fit in her wallet, then wedged it between her driver's license and VISA like a guilty secret. She wondered if most people carried secrets in their wallets, or only those who led small lives. Small lives didn't require large secret spaces.

"I want someone to love me for myself. Can't you understand that?"

"But you already have that. *I* love you. You're my daughter, for heaven's sake. Why are you looking for the whole pie, Gloria? Be content with one slice."

Gloria felt her chest constrict, felt the oxygen being cut off from her lungs as if someone had just shoved a plastic bag over her head. "I need more," she whispered.

"I've got a pan of chicken tarragon sitting right here on the cooling rack. I made it just the way you like. You know . . . with those little egg noodles? I can't possibly eat it all myself. And I bet you haven't had a thing to eat. Why don't I bring you some? It'll make you feel better, and then we'll talk. You've got the jitters, that's all. I was nervous too, before I married your father."

Gloria placed the salt shaker carefully on the table and sat down. "Please don't bother. I'm not hungry, Mother."

"Nonsense. You're too thin as it is. The last time I saw you, you could barely keep those new green pants I bought you from falling off your waist."

"You bought them a size too big, Mother. I keep telling you I'm a—"

"We can't have you looking like a scarecrow at your own wedding, now, can we?"

Gloria didn't bother pressing the off button but just laid the phone on the table. The dial tone droned like a muffled air-raid siren, warning her that soon the bombardment would begin. She slid as far down into the chair as she could without falling off and thought of God's promise.

~❦ ❦~

Gloria lay on the couch surfing channels, trying to forget her mother's visit and the last three grueling hours she had endured. She stopped when she saw Big Bird and Kermit the Frog. She couldn't remember the last time she had seen Sesame Street. Big Bird was listening to Kermit sing "It's Not Easy Being Green." She wondered why Sesame Street was on so late, then realized it was a documentary on children's programming. Suddenly, Gloria began to cry. Actually bawled like a baby. Frogs. She hated them.

But was that anything to cry about?

~❦ ❦~

Gloria faced the mirror, brushing her teeth with the new generic toothpaste she had bought from Sam Hidel's grocery and thinking how incredibly late it was for her to be going to bed. In the background she kept hearing the word *frog*—as if a voice were calling from a distant street or trickling through the air vent of a large high-rise.

Frog. Frooog.

She was sure it was her imagination and concentrated on making small circular motions with the Oral B. Her teeth were so perfect it was impossible to tell she once had an overbite.

Frog. Frooog.

Gloria shook her head. All these years, and she still had trouble understanding what an overbite had to do with frogs. But the kids at school had seen a connection. She had hoped the teasing would stop after she got braces. Then she had hoped it would stop after the braces came off. Then she stopped hoping.

Frog. Frooog.

Gloria rinsed her toothbrush and slipped it into a twelve-ounce paper cup tucked in the corner of the vanity. Even after she turned out the light, she stood in front of the mirror listening and wondering why she wanted to start bawling all over again.

You hear a thing long enough, and you begin to believe it.

Gloria counted ten names on the list. Nine doctor offices and one hospital. She pulled out ten glossy cream folders from the slotted bin in front of her and spread them over her desk. A garnet logo cut the folders in half: *Medical Data Corp.* Gloria ran her fingers over the slightly raised lettering. Verdana, 36—a good choice—clean, bold, but with a hint of class. She would have used burgundy, though, in mirrored letters behind the garnet to make it more striking.

If it were up to her.

Tracy said she had a keen eye for color. A flair. And Gloria suspected it was true. She could put colors together better than some, but she'd stop short of calling it a flair. Though the yearbook editor *had* allowed her to design the cover of her senior yearbook—huge navy letters, mirrored in tan—their school colors, all placed on a solid background of Cape Cod gray. Nobody had ever done that before. And everyone said it was one of the best covers they ever had.

Gloria smiled and slipped the *Company Overview* into a folder pocket, followed by five different product information sheets. Too bad her mother's best friend didn't own a print shop instead of a medical software company. She'd much rather be doing layouts, creating balance between objects and text, coordinating colors, choosing fonts, cropping photos.

"That's right. The Medical Management System is compatible with nearly all network architectures and hardware platforms, including Novell, Windows, AIS, and OS/2."

Tracy was making her pitch in the next cubicle, and just by Tracy's voice, Gloria knew she'd have to add another folder to the pile.

"Naturally it supports EDI standards . . . yes, state of the art, no other practice management system touches it. What? . . . oh, no problem. We can automatically back up your files off-site . . . sure you can outsource billing and claims processing . . . right . . . and create your reports in any format . . . oh, it's soooo easy . . . ."

Gloria could tell by the sound of Tracy's voice, the way it rose and fell, then vibrated in the air like a musical note, that Tracy was getting ready to close the deal. The skin of Gloria's arm prickled. It was like listening to Andrea Bocelli sing *Il Mistero Dell'Amore.*

Tracy was an artist.

Sometimes, Gloria called her a *con* artist, but that was only when she was miffed or—God forgive her—excessively jealous. But Gloria had learned to live with her jealousy just as some people live with asthma. It was a chronic condition that needed medicating, and calling Tracy a con artist now and then was part of that prescription.

When Gloria no longer heard Tracy's voice, she peered around her cubicle. There she was, with her headset draped around her neck, coming straight toward her. Gloria didn't know why Tracy bothered wearing the headset because she never used it. Instead, Tracy always held the phone. Said it was more personal that way.

If Tracy was anything, she was personal.

And that was the core of Gloria's jealousy. It didn't come from meanness or any desire to see Tracy hurt. It had more to do with heroes and admiration and wanting to be someone you were not.

Someone else entirely.

Because Gloria, on those rare occasions when she was allowed to speak to a customer—to relay a message or take one —*always* used a headset. And that said a lot.

"So like I was saying"—Tracy breezed into the cubicle, acting as though nothing had interrupted their conversation begun an hour ago—"you've got to get out of town."

"I don't know. It seems so . . . so drastic. Don't you think?"

"You want to marry the Monkey?"

Gloria choked. "Of course not!"

"Then you've gotta get outta here."

"I don't know. Sometimes I think about what it would be like getting away and living somewhere else. Starting over. And the thought makes me feel . . . well, like Mother says menopause makes her feel—all sweaty and cold at the same time. Sometimes I actually think God wants me to go. I get a sense, deep inside. Then I think, what if I'm wrong? What if I'm not hearing God at all? That's when I start second-guessing myself. I mean, wouldn't that be like running from my problems?"

"Well, kiddo, I can't tell you what God wants. I'm not into that. But I know one thing. If you stay here, your mother'll talk you into it. She always has—talked you into doing exactly what she wanted. In your gut, you know I'm right. How long did she work you over last night?"

"Three hours." Gloria shoved the *Company Overview* so hard into a folder she crumpled it and had to pull it out.

"See what I mean? She'll never stop until she gets her way.

I've seen her do it a million times. Now add the Monkey and Virginia Press to the mix. You don't stand a chance, Gloria. Not with the three of them working on you day and night."

"You've got to stop calling him 'Monkey'. It's so . . . so . . ."

"True?"

Gloria covered her mouth to suppress a giggle, but it came out anyway.

"It's good to see you laughing." Tracy squeezed Gloria's shoulder, then picked up one of the finished folders. Her face lit up when she scanned the familiar contents, and Gloria wished she loved her work as much.

"Promise me you'll think about it. About moving."

Gloria wadded up the crumpled *Company Overview* and tossed it into the small oval pail by her desk. "I don't know. This is where I grew up, went to school. I've never lived anywhere else. And you know how I am . . . with people. It's hard for me to make friends. For heaven's sake, Tracy, I've only had two friends in my life. Sherry Laneer, and she went away to college and never came back. And you."

"Three."

"Huh?"

"You've had three friends. You forgot Tucker."

Gloria felt heat rush to her face. Any minute now her cheeks would look like the burners on her stove when she fried chicken. She avoided Tracy's eyes. "That was long ago. We were kids. And he was only nice because of you."

Tracy's voice rang with laughter, full, rich, and contagious. From the corner of her cubicle, Gloria saw heads poking out from behind other gray Velcro-like partitions that divided the room into eight equal workstations. She quickly ducked back behind hers and put a finger to her lips. "Shhhhhh!"

"You still have a thing for my big brother, don't you?"

Gloria thought of Tucker's picture hidden in her wallet. *Silly, pathetic Gloria.*

"Yes. Yes, you do! Look at your face!" Tracy hopped up and down on her perfect size six feet, just as she used to do when cheering after a touchdown. "Now, why didn't I see that? What was I wearing, blinders? But it all makes sense now. The way you get so quiet when I talk about Tucker. The way you look at his pictures on my mantel but never touch them, like they're a shrine or something. The way you *never* ask about Tucker or talk about him unless I do. If nothing else, that should have tipped me off." Tracy smacked her forehead with the palm of her hand. "I can't believe I didn't see it. And I can't believe you've kept it from me for so long. You fox."

"The thing I don't like about you, Tracy, is the way you jump on something and gallop away. I haven't seen Tucker in years. And we're not kids anymore."

"Well, you can start seeing a lot more of him if you want to. You know how we keep in touch? Talk a lot and—?"

"You *didn't* tell him about me and Cutter? About this mess, did you?"

"What? I'm not supposed to tell him about my life? My friends? About what's happening in Appleton? Silly goose. Of course I told him. He knows everything. And he wants to help. He even told me he'd give you a job and that he'd let you rent one of his apartments—at a discount. It's practically all set. You've got no excuses left."

Gloria felt the fire leave her cheeks, as though Tracy had just doused her with a bucket of ice water. "You shouldn't have done that . . . involved Tucker. I had no idea you were telling him about me, about this mess. You had no right."

"Nonsense. What are friends for?"

Gloria suddenly felt the same tightness in her chest, the

same trapped, suffocating sensation she always felt when talking to her mother. Only it was Tracy. *Tracy.*

"What's the problem?"

Gloria shook her head. Tracy was her best friend. She loved her. She relied on her. Only . . . she wished she wouldn't be so manipulating.

"Gloria?"

"I'm . . . upset. Okay. I just wish you had consulted me before involving Tucker, that's all."

"For heaven's sake, why? I've been wiping your nose forever."

The remark felt like a slap. "That's hardly a nice way of putting it."

"Oh, come on, kiddo. I didn't mean anything. This is me, your best friend. Since when can't we talk? Gee . . . I've never seen you so . . . touchy. Come on. Give. What's the problem?"

Gloria looked at the little wooden plaque hanging on the one solid wall of her workstation. In the bottom corner was a bird sitting on a leafy branch. Above him the words: "This is the day the Lord has made, let us rejoice and be glad in it. Psalm 118:24." She had bought it at the Christian bookstore near her apartment. She loved that Scripture and looked at it often. It reminded her that if nothing else she could rejoice in the fact that Jesus made this day, this very day she was in now, this very second she was inhaling or exhaling or blinking her eyes. It was usually enough to make her smile. But not always.

"C'mon. What's the problem, Gloria?"

"Well . . . Tucker's a man now. An important man who's done something with his life."

Tracy laughed. "Don't get all googly-eyed. Tucker's not some icon on the front page of *Fortune.* He owns property and a development company. That's all. He's been lucky. Maybe luckier than most. And, okay, he could become a *multi*millionaire if everything goes right with this new project he's working on. But that doesn't change the fact that he's still plain old Tucker. The same Tucker you used to squirt with the hose and bury in the sand and smush peanut butter into his hair."

"Maybe so. But I just don't want . . . that is . . . well, I'd hate for him to see what a nothing I still am after all these years."

Gloria felt Tracy's hand on her head; felt the small nimble fingers stroke her brown curls like a mother might stroke the head of a distraught child.

"Can't you see how impossible your situation is? The Monkey . . . ah . . . Cutter's got a mean streak. You've seen it all your life. Remember that bird he stole from you? You never saw it again. Alive. And how about the time he broke your finger when you beat him at marbles and won his yellow cat's-eye? And then there's the time he made a laughingstock out of you at—"

"Okay. Okay. You made your point."

"The *point* is that even now he can wilt a person with a titanium backbone. He'll chew you up, Gloria. You know he will."

"I . . . suppose."

When Tracy left Gloria's side and perched her bottom on the desk, Gloria saw that all-too-familiar look and knew it would be hard getting her off the topic of Cutter.

"You see the way he treats people," Tracy continued. "He doesn't say hello. Talks to everyone like they're idiots. He even talks down to Stue Irving. *Stue Irving.* And you know what a genius he is."

Gloria laughed. "He's only a genius because you're interested in him. But he's smart. I'll give him that."

"And Cutter's getting worse. Ever since he went into that real estate deal, you know—the one Sadie Bellows told me was a doozy of a problem—he's been so stressed. I wouldn't be surprised if one of these days he exploded like a microwaved egg.

And that's not all. Sharon Lamston—you know, the one in Patient Billing—she said a few accounts have canceled because of some environmentalists putting pressure on them . . . though she didn't have any details . . . so I don't get the connection . . . but—"

A shadow fell across Gloria's desk, and when she looked up into Tracy's face, she knew instantly that Cutter Press was standing behind her. Tracy gave the headset around her neck a twist, then handed Gloria the Medical Data folder.

"Make sure you get this one right out to that doctor's office."

Gloria nodded and watched Tracy slide off the desk. She didn't watch her leave the cubicle, though. She didn't want to turn around.

"She's some talker," said a deep, raspy voice. "I guess that's why she's top banana with the customers."

When Gloria heard Cutter's footsteps come closer, she slid down in her chair. When he came up to her desk and actually leaned against it, she shoved her pinkie in her mouth and began nibbling her cuticle.

"I'd like to talk to you." The statement sounded like a command. "But not here. Say, in ten minutes? I have to stop by Patient Billing, then I'll head back to my office."

Gloria nodded, her pinkie clenched between her teeth. She felt like a jerk. Why did he always put a knot in her stomach? *Just like her mother.*

~⊕ ⊕~

Gloria watched the red pulsating hand of her Timex tick away the seconds and closed her eyes. She thought she smelled hay—sweet, pungent, clean—then visualized Clive McGreedy's barn, with the long pruning shears and sickles and axes and shovels and rakes hanging on hooks along one wall. She saw herself walk into the barn to check the litter Little Sandy had suspended her rat-catching duties to have, the very same barn where Little Sandy's mother, Big Sandy, had begun her own career of rat catching. Gloria saw herself reach into the box Clive had given Little Sandy and pick up her favorite kitten, a tiny orange ball of fur with white markings on its feet that looked like booties. Then she heard voices . . . Cutter's voice first, then the others. She watched herself turn and look at him, leading the pack as usual. He was wearing duck boots in the middle of summer, and it wasn't even raining—his camouflage pants tucked into the boot tops. On his head was his "field" hat, an olive green cap purchased from an army surplus store. In those days Cutter dressed like a commando.

"Kiss the frog and make a princess. Kiss the frog and make a princess." A sing-songy chant rose up and filled the barn.

Even now, Gloria squirmed as she pictured Cutter's face suddenly next to hers—could almost feel his wet, sloppy lips as he completed his commando mission, then she watched herself kick him in the shins. In those days, she still kicked boys' shins. But that was before they got to her. All of them.

"Did she turn into a princess?" one of the boys yelled.

"Oh, yuck . . . look, she's still a frog," another cried.

"Did you want to throw up?" said the one closest to Cutter.

The memory of Cutter wiping his mouth on the dirty edges of his olive green tank top, then spitting into the hay, still made Gloria sick. She remembered just standing there, hoping they wouldn't hurt Little Sandy's kittens, and thinking she just had her first kiss. Mother had told her not to be a pest and come to McGreedy's barn. Had told her to stay away from the "tick-infested" animals. Mother had specifically instructed her not to touch the cats because the fleas would jump onto her new clothes, and she'd bring them back to her nice clean house, and then what was she going to do? But Gloria had disobeyed. And she had been properly punished—humiliated by Cutter Press and his friends.

That was the first time Gloria actually believed God saw everything.

When Gloria opened her eyes, the Timex told her ten minutes had passed. Cutter would be waiting, but so would God. She needn't be afraid. This wasn't McGreedy's barn, and Cutter didn't have a rabble of friends to impress. Still she sat. Head knowledge could be so shallow.

How nice if Tracy would burst into the cubicle and tell her all was well, that Cutter was no longer a problem, that she could go about her business as usual. How many times had Tracy come to her rescue? Too many. That was obvious.

"I've been wiping your nose forever."

Gloria mumbled a quick prayer that sounded wooden and graceless, so unlike the lyrical prayers of those church ladies in her prayer group. It still astonished her that God ever bent His ear to listen to her poor supplications. But the wonder of it was that He did. And more times than she could count.

It seemed He listened this time too, because she found herself rising from her chair and taking one step after another until she had walked out of Telemarketing, past Accounting, Product Development, Customer Support, and Patient Billing, down a separate hallway that passed the cafeteria and rest rooms, past Marketing and Sales, until she finally stood in front of Sadie Bellows's desk.

"Mr. Press has asked to see me," Gloria croaked, then cleared her throat.

The attractive secretary looked up, took a sip of coffee

from a mug that said "I'd rather be sleeping," then puckered her lips. "I don't know if this is a good time. I'll have to check."

Gloria watched Sadie open a black appointment book and sluggishly drag one long lavender nail through the scribble that was her handwriting. Then Gloria watched Sadie shift her weight to the arm resting on the desk, as though the strain of sitting up was too great. But the shift made Sadie's scoop-neck blouse dip lower than was appropriate for office wear, and Gloria saw why many in the office called her Behemoth Bellows. Gloria looked away and wondered if the rumors about Sadie and Cutter were true.

"Doesn't look like he's got any appointments now." Sadie swiveled her chair to the side and crossed her long shapely legs, showing off her three-inch lavender heels with rhinestone clips. "I guess you can go in."

Gloria quickly smoothed down her white oxford shirt and walked toward the closed office door. She could count on three fingers the times she'd been to Cutter's office. The irony of her coming now—being summoned like a geisha—in order to reject a proposal that would make her mistress of Medical Data made her smile.

Behind her, Sadie Bellows's high-pitched voice added to the comedy as she spoke to Cutter through the intercom. The conversation produced shuffling noises behind the office wall. Gloria would have laughed if she weren't so nervous. She knocked softly and opened the door when she heard a gruff, "It's not locked."

The sight of Cutter sprawled behind his maple desk and throwing darts into a board made Gloria think of her little plaque. *This is the day the Lord has made.* Yes, and He was master of it, even of this very second. And He was master even in Cutter Press's office.

Her eyes quickly took in her surroundings. The medium-sized desk, the small filing cabinet, the pine bookcase, and two black leather director's chairs hardly filled half the room and made it, with all its empty space and blank walls, look as though it was in the early stages of renovation. But Gloria knew better.

Virginia Press ran a tight ship.

Gloria clamped her hands together and stared down at her scuffed brown pumps, then shifted awkwardly on her feet, waiting for an invitation to sit. Cutter continued throwing darts.

Why didn't he say something?

"Yesterday you claimed you weren't interested in my proposal, but I've been wondering if you've changed your mind?" Cutter looked up. For a second he almost looked friendly. "Ever since we were kids, all I've heard from my mother . . . and yours . . . is how someday you and I were going to get married. I know you've gotten the same pitch."

Gloria nodded and eyed the chair. Her knees had begun to shake. "Mind if I sit?" she found herself saying.

Cutter waved his consent, and Gloria eased herself into one of the director's chairs. When he threw another dart, she noticed he wore his Appleton High ring. Why not the one from NYU? Cutter had picked a college as far removed from this small town as possible. She never expected him to come back. Nobody did.

"Your mother and mine have been working on this a long time. We both know that. And maybe there's some wisdom in their collective madness. We're used to each other. Know what to expect. We wouldn't be two awkward strangers trying to occupy the same house. We have a lot of history, Gloria, the two of us, and that's an advantage."

Gloria shoved a pinkie into her mouth. The only history they had was the kind she didn't want repeated.

"On top of that, you'd be well cared for. I'd see to it you

never wanted for anything. These things should be weighed, Gloria, given proper consideration and examined fully in the light of today's world. I'm offering you comfort and security."

Gloria's stomach felt like a beach—huge waves crashing against sand. She couldn't answer. She couldn't say a single word. All she could do was remove her pinkie and shake her head.

"*No?* Mind at least telling me why? It's not like you to buck your mother. I hadn't expected you to . . . well, never mind. Just tell me why."

"I don't love you." There. She said it.

Cutter laughed. "Well, certainly not. I never thought you did. I hope you don't think . . . I mean, you can't seriously believe I love you either?"

"Actually, I never thought about it, one way or the other." Gloria twirled the little gold friendship ring around her finger, the one Tracy had given her when they were ten.

Again Cutter laughed. "Well, at least you're honest. And I can't say I don't like you. You're a decent sort. Anyway . . . now that we've got that settled, about our feelings for each other, just tell me if there's someone else."

Gloria wanted to put her hands over her ears and shout, "Stop it! Stop this mad conversation! Stop making a fool of yourself and me." Instead, she said, "Why do you want to marry someone you don't love?" Had she offended him? His face was a blank, so she couldn't tell. There was no way she could stop now. It was an opportunity, perhaps her only opportunity, to enlist Cutter's aid in squelching this thing. If they banded together, maybe they could talk some sense into their mothers. She took a deep breath.

"If rumors can be trusted, you have plenty of female admirers. So why pick someone who's not interesting? I'm not even your type." Gloria folded her hands tightly together, anchoring them to her lap. "I mean . . . not that I even know what your type is . . ."

For the first time, Cutter put down his darts. A slow smile brightened his dark, brooding face. "Your pluck comes as an unwelcome surprise." Cutter rose to his feet. "But you've been honest, and that deserves equal honesty. You had it right. You're not my type. But that could be to your advantage. After we're married, I'd continue my . . . friendships. There would be no need to bother you, if you understand me. You would run my household, for which you'd be well compensated."

Gloria suddenly saw him in his commando suit, still trying to humiliate and insult her in McGreedy's barn. She glanced at his feet, half expecting to see duck boots. "It doesn't take a marriage license," she said, her voice snapping like a twig. "Around here, maids can be hired for minimum wage."

"You're not making this easier, Gloria. You think I want to do this? You think I want my mother picking my wife?"

"Then why are you letting her?"

"Because!"

Gloria braced herself for the cursing she suspected would follow and heard nothing but an exasperated sigh.

"Look. I said I'd be honest, so I will. At the least, you deserve that. Mother wants me to marry. Said I have to settle down before she'd even think of turning over the rest of the company to me. She said it would be a wedding present. I've paraded a dozen women past her, and she didn't like one of them."

As Cutter paced behind her, Gloria thought of Sadie Bellows.

"Mother called them floozies. Can you imagine anyone using that word in this day and age? Finally, we had it out. She said I needed someone stable. Someone I could count on. Someone I could trust. That's when your name came up. She said I needed the stability you'd give me. That you'd settle me down. She said all these years she knew you'd make the perfect wife. And that if I ever wanted to take over the company for real, I better see it that way too. These old crows—your mother and mine—have been cooking this scheme up for years. You know that. Only, it's finally come to a head."

"But we don't have to give in."

Cutter returned to his desk and sat down. "I *need* this company." He looked like a raging bull with his dark saucer eyes and flaring nostrils, and by the way he lowered his head and almost pawed the desktop with his hands. "Something's come up . . . a real estate investment . . . then those crazy environmentalists . . ." Cutter picked up a dart and flung it at the board. "What difference does it make? It's enough that you understand I'm offering you a business deal. We'll both benefit from it."

Gloria shook her head. "I'm sorry about your problems, but I can't help. I *won't* help." She wondered if he was going to fire her now.

"What have you got to lose? It's not like you've got guys crawling all over you with rings in their pockets waiting for you to say, 'I do.'"

Gloria struggled to her feet, her hands clamped in balls at her side. She hoped Cutter didn't see how much she was trembling. "If that's all, Mr. Press, I'll get back to work now."

She didn't remember walking past Sadie Bellows's desk, or the Marketing and Sales Department, the rest rooms and cafeteria, down the separate hallway, past Patient Billing, Customer Support, Product Development, or Accounting. She didn't even remember walking into Telemarketing and sitting down at her desk. She had been too busy listening to a still small voice repeat the same thing over and over.

Arise, My darling, My beautiful one, and come with Me.

Chapter Two

I WILL GET UP NOW AND GO ABOUT THE CITY,
THROUGH ITS STREETS AND SQUARES;
I WILL SEARCH FOR THE ONE MY HEART LOVES.

~@ SONG OF SONGS 3:2 NIV@~

GOD WAS GOING TO GIVE HER the desires of her heart. The thought made Gloria want to alternately dance in the aisle of the speeding Greyhound bus and cringe under her seat. She felt ashamed of her fear, as though it showed disrespect toward God, as though she didn't believe Him capable of keeping His promise. But in spite of herself, she giggled. She had always thought of herself as plain, boring—a mule instead of an Andalusian. But God could do anything, couldn't He?

Oh, beautiful Jesus, I wish . . .

She thought of Tucker—her guilty, pathetic secret. Surely God wasn't going to give her Tucker? Certainly not Tucker. That would be like believing a mule capable of winning the Kentucky Derby.

The wind whipping past the window of the speeding bus suddenly made a whistling sound.

Frog. Frooog.

Gloria flinched. But God *was* in the miracle business, and miracles still happened, no matter what anyone said. And hadn't she obeyed His leading? Allowed Him to rip the pathetic cling- ing tendrils of her life from the sand dune that was home? He could be trusted. All the church ladies, all those ladies whose Bibles were highlighted in yellows and greens and pinks, and with notes scribbled in the margins, all those ladies who could make up beautiful prayers right from their head, all those ladies who quoted Scriptures as if they had written them, all *those* ladies had told her God was trustworthy. He wasn't a man that He should lie. He was kind. His mercies were new every morn- ing. He was faithful. He had a plan and a purpose for her, and it was for good and not evil.

And she believed them.

Only . . . it would be easier if she had Tracy with her. There was no one like Tracy. Tracy had arranged everything, the new job, the new apartment, the subletting of Gloria's old apart- ment. Tracy had even bought Gloria the bus ticket. There could be no better friend on the face of the earth. It would be hard not having Tracy to lean on when things got rough. And that was the point, wasn't it? *No Tracy to lean on.*

Jesus would have to be her best friend now.

Only, it was hard having a best friend you couldn't see or hear most of the time. The whole idea was overwhelming: relo- cating, leaving Tracy, having only Jesus to rely on. And it was bold and foolish and wonderful and terrifying too. She was making history. So how come those around her didn't notice? How come they looked out windows or slept or traded cookie recipes? Didn't they know that one small, insignificant soul had issued a declaration of independence on one hand and a declaration of total dependence on the other? Didn't they see the wonder of it?

She pressed her face against the window. Outside, battalions of trees stood at attention, as though nature, at least, had taken notice of what she had done and was saluting her for her bravery.

But she was so weak—always falling short. What made her think this time would be any different? That this time she'd make Him proud of her? She couldn't even make her mother proud.

Dear merciful God. Dear Savior. Dear Jesus, I can't do this without You.

Outside, the world flashed past her window and made Gloria wonder if she was ever going to find her place in it. The scenery mesmerized her with its monotony and beauty, its insignificance and grandeur. Green trees, green hills, green-blue skies almost lulled her to sleep. But then suddenly a valley would appear, clean shaven and fresh, and in it, a tiny village, which looked as though it had been dropped by a stork, much like Gloria believed babies were transported when she was still young enough to believe everything her mother told her.

Her mother.

In a matter of hours her mother would know everything. By now, Tracy had given Cutter Gloria's letter of resignation—a polite, grateful letter. But the truth was she had hated her job at Medical Data. She was sure it would fool Cutter. He would never believe someone like her had hopes and dreams . . . could want more out of life than stuffing folders day in and day out. And once he found out she had left her job *and* Appleton, he'd tell Virginia, and Virginia would tell her mother, and her mother would . . . declare war. Gloria hated conflict. It grated against her tranquil nature, her natural desire to live in peace, and placed her in an emotion-filled trench. Made her feel what nice people weren't supposed to feel—hate and revenge and cowardice and revulsion.

She pulled away from the tinted glass and watched a flock of geese fly by, their V-shape formation dipping and bending to the left. If only she were one of them—free and high above everything that troubled her.

❧ ☙

The old Victorian sat like a prim spinster beside a large gnarled maple. A recent overhaul—which included a shored-up porch, freshly whitewashed clapboards, new wood shutters painted hunter green, and a new wood Pella door, also painted hunter green—made the house look years younger. A wreath of dried flowers, mostly pink hydrangea and baby's breath, hung on the front door. Underneath it, large brass numbers told Gloria she was finally at her destination: 352 West Meadow Drive, Eckerd City.

She stepped from the cab and let the cabbie help her with her luggage. She had compressed everything she valued into two Duralite suitcases. The rest of her belongings, Tracy was storing.

"I'll take them as far as the door, then you're on your own," the cabbie said, huffing along the sidewalk and up the three porch steps. "Nice neighborhood. Not like some. Leastways, you won't have to carry pepper spray in your purse. You don't want to be in some parts of Eckerd when the sun goes down. Almost getting as bad as them really big cities."

Gloria watched the cabbie return to his car and drive away, then she pulled the two keys from her purse that Macy Pierce, of Pierce Real Estate only a mile away, had given her. Macy didn't handle Tucker's properties, but she had held the keys for Gloria as a favor to him.

Gloria inserted the fat gold key into the Baldwin lock. It opened with ease, and she stepped into a hallway that made her think of Grandma Quinn's house. A Queen Anne armchair in the corner invited those wearing boots to remove them before going farther. Cream lace doilies, smelling of lavender, covered soil marks on the arms and headrest. A wooden coatrack, with a single baseball cap dangling from one of its arms, stood like a sentry beside the chair. Pictures of men, women, and children in antique frames covered the walls of the hall like a family gallery. For a fleeting moment, she felt safe. When the moment passed, she gripped her keys and headed up the steps.

Gloria finished hanging the last of her skirts in the closet, snapped the suitcase shut, and pushed it under the bed. She could hardly contain her joy. She would have been content with a one-room apartment. But this . . . she felt like a sixteen-year-old who had been promised her father's old Ford and had gotten a new BMW instead. Her BMW had three rooms and a bath—twice the space she had had in Appleton.

And so beautifully decorated.

She wandered from room to room, hardly able to take it all in, and stopped by the lace-covered window in the living room. From it, she could see the sidewalk and, across the street, a row of Victorians clustered like old maids on a bench. Only three maples dotted the landscape, tenaciously sprouting through concrete, a memorial to kinder days when Eckerd was more suburb than city. But the trees gave Gloria comfort, made her almost feel as if she were back on Grandma Quinn's street.

It was all so perfect, she wanted to shout for joy. And she did, in a manner of speaking, as she poured out a stream of praises to God. Her heart felt like the fountain in the Appleton Mall, whose water kept spilling over and over and over three tiers of huge marble dishes shaped like lily pads. Those church ladies certainly knew what they were talking about.

God was good.

Only twice had she felt this spiritually high—once while sitting on Mother's clean berber rug and reading *The Practice of the Presence of God* by Brother Lawrence. She had decided right then and there she wanted this Jesus who Brother Lawrence talked about—this beautiful, tender Jesus who spoke to humble cooks as though they were friends—and had invited Him into her heart. Her second spiritual high occurred the day she moved out of Mother's house and into her own apartment. Gloria had never thought that possible, but God made a way where there was no way, had put a backbone where there was no backbone, had walked beside her every step of the way. Just as He would on this new journey.

Now Gloria's mouth moved of its own accord, forming words of thanksgiving. And just when she thought her praises were finished, she started all over again.

"Thank You, Jesus. Thank You. You're so wonderful and kind, so thoughtful . . ."

It was between these outbursts of praise that she heard it, so softly at first she nearly missed it. But then it came again, and again—little muffled sobs. She stood perfectly still, trying to determine the direction of the sound. She moved from the living room into the kitchen, where the sound was strongest, and put her ear to the wall. It was unmistakable. Someone was crying.

Suddenly, Gloria heard a man curse, then a crash, as though something fell to the floor. She held her breath, her ear to the wall, afraid to move, afraid she would make noise and let them know she was on the other side, listening. She stood absolutely still, not moving a muscle, until she couldn't hear anything more, then she crept away.

She found herself at the door of her apartment, standing there, wanting to look out and not knowing why. With an impulsiveness that was foreign to her, Gloria finally yanked it open. The Victorian house had four apartments on the second floor, two on either side of the hall. Suddenly, a man in a gray pin-striped suit charged out of the apartment next to hers, slamming the door behind him. He gave Gloria a searing look, then rushed down the steps and out the front entrance.

Gloria leaned into the hall, half expecting to see the door open again. When it didn't, she closed hers and walked back into the kitchen. Hesitantly, almost shyly, she put her ear against the wall. She could still hear them, those soft muffled sobs. She slid down onto the floor, ignoring the cold hardness, and hugged her knees. After a while, she let her forehead drop. She could hear the low, almost whimperlike sobs even without holding her ear to the wall. She sat there a long time, feeling guilty for listening, yet unable to move, as though connected to the person on the other side.

"The place is a dream. I can't thank you enough, Tracy." Gloria's eyes scanned the far kitchen wall, grateful that Tracy's call had finally forced her from her post, where she had sat listening for the past hour.

"I'm glad the phone's working. I told Tucker to make sure it was up and running today."

"Another thing I need to thank him for . . . to thank you both for. How am I ever going to make it up to either of you? The rent's got to be twice what I'm paying. Maybe more. Only,

I can't afford pride right now, so I must humbly accept your brother's charity."

"No charity, kiddo. He's happy to do it, for old-time sake, and because I told him if he didn't I'd never speak to him again."

"Tracy! Now I'm really embarrassed. I can't believe you're forcing your brother to—"

"Yes, you can. You know how I operate. But it's no big deal. I'm only glad I was able to get you out of town before your mother and the Monkey finally did it to you."

"Speaking of which . . . how did it go?"

"I believe the earth moved. Only once and just a little. But I do believe when Cutter read your note there was a slight tremor beneath Medical Data. The Monkey actually read it in front of me, as though he knew all along what it was going to say and wanted me near for questioning."

Gloria giggled and began nibbling her thumb. "What did he say?"

"At first he didn't say anything, just turned the color of the Appleton fire truck and glared. Then he asked me if I had anything to do with it. Of course I said no. That's when he started acting like the primate we both know and love."

"I hate it when he curses and yells."

"Oh, he didn't do that. He was actually calm and polite. Told me if he ever found out I lied, he'd fire me on the spot."

"Oh, Tracy, that's terrible! You can't afford to lose your job. You've got more credit cards than the entire student body of Appleton Community College." She heard her friend laugh. "I'm really really sorry. I shouldn't have let you help. I can't bear the thought of you getting into trouble because of—"

"Stop worrying. I'm his number one telemarketer, remember? He's not going to fire his meal ticket. The Monkey just likes to hear himself talk."

"Tracy, I really *wish* you'd stop calling Cutter that."

"Why?"

"Because . . . because it's too cruel, even for Cutter."

"Oops, your halo is showing. That's the one thing that really irks me. I still don't understand why you started going to church. As if you're not mealymouthed enough. How am I ever going to get you to stand up for yourself if every Sunday someone's brainwashing you to 'turn the other cheek'?"

"It's not like that. It's all about Jesus . . . a relationship with Jesus."

"I don't care what you call it. At this rate, you're going to stay a doormat forever."

Gloria thought of what God had already done—how last year she was living with her mother in Appleton, and now here she was in Eckerd City. *Stay a doormat forever?* Even Gloria's timid heart knew Tracy couldn't be more wrong. The thing that puzzled her was why couldn't Tracy see it?

"I don't like arguing with you," Gloria finally said. "Let's just drop it."

"See? See what I mean? You've got to stand up for yourself, kiddo. If you believe in something, don't back down."

"There's no point in fighting. I can't remember a time my arguments ever changed your mind. Besides, I'm exhausted . . . and I need to go shopping . . . get some groceries. Let's talk about it another time, okay?" She heard Tracy sigh.

"Okay. Go shopping. But call me tomorrow after work. I want to know how your first day at the job went. Are you nervous?"

"What do you think?"

"Not to worry. I told Tucker to be nice."

Gloria suddenly felt irritated. She didn't know why, exactly. Maybe it had something to do with Tracy bullying Tucker into helping her. Or maybe it was because Tracy seemed to think Gloria couldn't do *anything* without help. "I wish you hadn't done that."

"Oh, you're welcome. Think nothing of it. And call me tomorrow. I want to hear all about the job. Actually, call anytime you feel like talking. You know I'm here for you."

⁓◑ ◐⁓

Gloria pulled a beige sweater over her head, fluffed her short, frizzy hair, then grabbed her purse. If she wanted to eat, she needed to get to that grocery Macy Pierce told her about before it closed. Gloria had already penned a short shopping list. For a while, until she got on her financial feet, she'd have to watch every penny. Buy smart. So frozen dinners were out, and canned soup and stew, pasta, eggs, and bread—the things that could stretch into a week's worth of eating for a minimal cash outlay—were in.

She had already decided she'd make an omelet for dinner. She'd pack it with plenty of onions and peppers. Maybe even put in a little cheese to give it some body. She'd certainly make it large enough to have leftovers for breakfast and use that extra time to find her way to the new job tomorrow.

Tomorrow.

Her stomach did push-ups. She had to blot tomorrow from her thoughts, use some sort of mental whiteout because she couldn't afford to think about it right now. First, she had to get through today. She had to concentrate on settling in, stocking her refrigerator, getting used to the neighborhood. Even now, the enormity of trying to find the grocery just made her want to go to bed and pull the covers over her head. She'd have to walk streets she never walked before. See people she had never

40

met before, people her family and relatives had never even heard of. Who was there to vouch for them? To warn her of the pervert, the scam artist, the moocher?

"Oh, God," she whispered into the silent room, her heart beating a little too fast. "This is all so scary."

The sudden knock on the door made her heart beat even faster.

Never talk to strangers.

What good was that advice when everyone in Eckerd was a stranger? Gloria crept to the door with her purse. "Who is it?"

The knock grew louder.

"Who is it?" Gloria repeated.

"Your neighbor." The words sputtered in the air like a warped CD.

Gloria opened the door ever so slightly, barely able to see the thin, pale girl through the tiny crack she had made. When her mind told her it was safe, Gloria opened it wider and saw that the girl was jumpy, agitated, almost as if her shoes were wired to a 20-amp fuse. It frightened Gloria, and for an instant she considered closing the door without a word. Then the thought hit her—*maybe this was the voice on the other side of the wall*—and she relaxed a bit, enough to take in the designer jeans, the white Tommy Hilfiger shirt, the blue espadrilles, the quarter-inch gold neck chain—things that said "cool, in control." But the twisted mouth, furrowed forehead, and swollen eyes said something quite different.

Gloria couldn't explain why she suddenly had an overpowering desire to run. Maybe it was for the same reason people ran from her. The girl was obviously unhappy. No one liked being around someone who was unhappy. It was one thing listening to sorrow through a wall but quite another seeing it face-to-face.

"I was just on my way out," Gloria said, raising her purse slightly as proof, while avoiding the girl's eyes.

"Oh . . . sorry . . . I didn't mean to intrude." The girl took a step backward.

"Was there something you wanted?" Gloria said, hoping the girl would say no and just go. She didn't want to be unkind, or unfeeling, or any of those things that kept people at a distance. Only her plateful of problems was too full to fit in anyone else's. Maybe when she got settled, when she got her new life together, she'd try to make friends with the girl.

Maybe.

Gloria stepped out into the hall. For a minute, the girl looked as though she was going to cry, and Gloria held her breath.

"I was hoping . . . that is . . . I was wondering if you had . . . well . . . any milk I could borrow."

Gloria smiled with relief. "No. I've just moved in. There's nothing in the fridge. Actually, I was just going out for groceries. I'd be happy to pick up an extra gallon."

"Oh, no. No. Don't bother."

The girl tossed her hair. It was long, shiny, and straight, like a model's Gloria had seen on the cover of *Glamour*. It made Gloria feel ugly in her short, frizzy perm.

"It'll be hard enough getting all your packages up those stairs."

Gloria watched the girl pick at her gold chain with a polished red nail. Her mouth was no longer twisted, but her eyes had narrowed like little laser beams and cut into Gloria's conscience.

"You don't need me adding to the load. Sorry I troubled you."

With a sigh, Gloria closed and locked her apartment door, then watched the girl spin around, almost as if she were doing a pirouette, and head toward her own apartment. "Please let me get you that milk. It's no bother, really." The girl laughed a coarse sort of laugh, which sounded almost insane to Gloria, and opened her apartment door.

"It was only a thought. I really don't need it now."

And before she disappeared, she gave Gloria a look that made her shudder. She had seen that look before, on the face of one of Grandma Quinn's friends when she told Gloria her family was putting her into a nursing home. It was a look of utter defeat.

"Honest. I don't mind," Gloria said as the neighbor's door closed.

Why should she feel guilty?

She sprinted down the stairs. Why should she feel sorry for a girl who looked like a model? Sorry for someone who had handsome, executive-type men, angry or not, streaming from her apartment? Was it Gloria's job to comfort every girl who had a quarrel with a boyfriend? It hardly seemed fair to expect that from someone who couldn't even get blind dates. Who, in fact, had never had a boyfriend in her whole life. No. It just wasn't fair. And no one could expect that. But even as she thought it, Gloria knew she was wrong.

God had expected it.

—◦ ◦—

The first thing Gloria noticed was that all the garbage cans along Pratt Parkway were bolted to the gray concrete sidewalk. Only the inserts could be removed. Gloria stared in amazement. In Appleton people didn't even bolt their doors.

Welcome to Eckerd City. Garbage theft capital of the world.

Gloria clutched her purse tightly under her arm. If garbage pails weren't safe, what then? Somewhere she had heard of purse snatchers coming right up and ripping bags off people's shoulders. And what about those nimble-fingered pickpockets who could lift wallets without raising the slightest alarm? But that wasn't in Eckerd City. *Was it?* No, that had to be L.A. or New York. She was glad she had nothing valuable in her pockets. Only the purse. That was the thing. She'd keep it close.

A steady stream of people bustled past. "Excuse me," she kept saying as they bumped her. After a while, she felt foolish, then angry. Then she felt invisible.

Out of the corner of her eye, she saw a kitten, a little orange ball of fur with white booties for paws. It looked as though it was limping, and Gloria followed it, without thinking, when it turned into a narrow alley. A dozen cardboard boxes, stacked in threes, hugged a doorway. Near them, a pile of black plastic bags formed a pyramid. Gloria assumed it was a delivery of some kind and watched the orange fluff disappear behind the bags.

"Here, kitty, kitty." She moved the bags, then almost frantically fumbled among the boxes. "Here, kitty, kitty." She didn't know why she felt this urgency. Why it was so important to find the cat. Maybe it had something to do with her neighbor, with that look—that look of an old desperate woman in those young eyes.

Oh, beautiful Jesus, why can't I be more like You?

Gloria placed three cans of chunky beef soup in one of the two kitchen cabinets that weren't full of dishes, then slid two pounds of linguine alongside them, followed by salt, pepper, a jar of sauce, a box of Domino sugar cubes, and a bag of peanuts—she had decided to buy one treat a week, just to keep from feeling deprived. The last thing she put away was the philodendron spilling over a white two-inch ceramic pot. She positioned it carefully on the small kitchen table and wondered how her other plant was doing, the one Tracy was tending for her. She had had that one for a year. Had bought it when it could fit in the palm of her hand. A year of pruning and fertilizing, of watering, of tender care, had made it outgrow two pots. She fluffed the waxy leaves of her new philodendron. This one was even smaller than her first one had been when she bought it. She shouldn't have splurged. Been so frivolous. But after not finding the kitten in the alleyway, she felt a need to connect with something living.

Why couldn't she stop thinking about that girl next door?

It was good to be back in the apartment. The shopping trip had been a nightmare. Coming out of the alley, she had lost her bearings and had to ask three different people for directions. She was sure the last person she asked was a stalker or serial killer or pervert because his eyes kept looking at different parts of her body. She was afraid he might follow her, but he didn't. At least not that she saw. But the whole experience had made her feel uncomfortable and had given her a headache. Now, all she wanted to do was lie down. But she couldn't, not until she made the one phone call she had been dreading all day.

Gloria poured herself a glass of water. Her mouth felt like a gravel driveway, and drinking half the glass didn't make any difference. She paced the apartment a full five minutes, mentally composing what she'd say. Oh, what was the use? Even if she came up with something brilliant, it would get shot down. As she walked slowly to the phone, she remembered reading in her Bible how God's strength was made perfect in weakness.

She was sure it was true. At least she hoped so.

The phone felt clumsy in her hand, and her fingers behaved more like thumbs. Somehow, she managed to dial the familiar number and waited in some suspended place, where people don't breathe or blink, until a voice said, "Hello."

"Mother, it's me. I just wanted—"

"Gloria! Where in heaven's name are you! I've been paralyzed with fear ever since Virginia called and told me you had quit your job and *left town*. How could this be? How could you do this . . . to me . . . to Cutter . . . to all of us? And without a word. You nearly killed me. What were you thinking?"

"I'm sorry, Mother. I didn't mean for you to worry."

"*Worry?* That doesn't nearly cover it. I don't know how I didn't have a stroke or seizure, or . . . or something, with all this stress. My arm's been hurting for hours, with shooting pains to my wrist, you know, like when you have a heart attack? I was actually considering going to the hospital, but I didn't dare leave the house in case you called. But never mind that now. I *can't* believe you did this."

"Mother, this is something I had to do. Try to understand."

"I'll never understand how you could do such a thing. *And without a word.* I can only blame Tracy. This has her fingerprints all over it. It's something that little fiend would cook up. Even you wouldn't do something this stupid on your own. But never mind that. You've got to come home. Tonight. Right now. I'm sure if you explained it to Cutter and told him how sorry you were, he'd give you your old job back. I don't know about the other thing, the wedding I mean. The way you've acted, Cutter might not want you now, and I can't say I'd blame him. I still can't believe you'd do such a foolish thing. What were you thinking? Sometimes, Gloria, you don't have a brain in your head."

"It was the only way—"

"Never mind that now. You can explain it when you get home."

"I'm not coming home, Mother."

"Don't be ridiculous. Of course you are."

Gloria bit into her thumb. "I'm *not* coming home."

"Gloria, I know there're two sides to a coin. And I've given it some thought. Maybe I pushed too hard. Okay. You've made your point. If there's going to be a wedding, we'll all have to slow down a bit. Give you some room. The ball's in your court now, and you have to be reasonable . . . show some intelligence. What do you say?"

Sirens blared in stereo through the closed window and made Gloria leave her spot in the kitchen. She let the phone dangle in her hand as she peered through the lace and watched two squad cars and an ambulance pull up to the curb in front of the house. Within seconds, the sidewalk was full of uniformed police and paramedics.

"What's going on, Gloria? What's happening?" Even with the phone at arm's length, Gloria could hear her mother's frightened voice.

She put the receiver to her ear. "Hold on, Mother." Then she placed the phone on the end table and opened the window. The police were already out of sight. She heard their voices and feet on the porch, then heard them go through the front door. She held her breath, wondering where they would go next, and almost fainted when she heard their feet racing up the stairs to the second floor.

Oh, God.

She watched the paramedics pull a gurney from the back of their ambulance, snap it into an upright position, and run with it to the house.

What was happening?

She sucked air like a goldfish.

"You still there? Gloria? Answer me!"

47

Gloria brought the phone to her ear. "I can't talk now, Mother. I'll call you tomorrow."

"Tomorrow? Wait . . . that's it? No explanation? Not even your address or phone number?"

"No." Gloria hadn't planned on saying that, but she was too rattled, too distracted to talk anymore.

"This is ridiculous. You can't mean that, Gloria. You've got to stop this and—"

"I'm fine. I just wanted you to know that so you didn't worry. I'll call tomorrow." With that, Gloria hung up the phone and flew toward the door. Her hand went to the knob, then recoiled. She was afraid to confirm what she already knew, so she just stood at the door, listening to the commotion on the other side. When she heard someone shout, "Call the coroner," she slowly opened the door, ingesting the scene a half inch at a time, like a child taking medicine through a dropper.

The door of the adjoining apartment was open, and two uniformed police loitered nearby. Everyone else was inside. When one of the officers saw Gloria, he walked over, his holstered nine-millimeter Glock bouncing against his hip, his left shirt pocket covered by a solid silver shield, indicating his status as patrolman.

"You know this lady?" he said, jerking his head toward the open apartment.

"No. I . . . just moved in today." Gloria slumped against the doorjamb. "What happened?"

"Suicide. Pills, it looks like. Not sure yet. I don't know what's with you young people. You'd think you had the world by the tail, had everything to live for. I don't get it. And this one was a looker too. But she must've had second thoughts, because she called 911."

Gloria pressed her hand against her queasy stomach. "Is she . . . dead?"

The officer gave her a puzzled look. "I said it was a suicide, lady." He looped his thumb over the thick black utility-like belt that held, in addition to his Glock, two clip cases, a handcuff case, a holster for mace, and a ring for a nightstick. "She waited too long. She should've called sooner. Young people today. I don't get 'em."

Gloria shrank back into her apartment and closed the door. How could this happen? How could this terrible thing happen?

Her first instinct was to call Tracy. She found the phone and punched in the numbers, then hung up before it could ring. No. She didn't want to talk to Tracy. Tracy would tell her not to sweat it. That there was nothing she could have done. It wasn't her responsibility.

It wasn't *her* fault.

Gloria carefully placed the phone back in its cradle. Then she walked to the bedroom and picked up her Bible from the nightstand. She carried it to the kitchen, pressed to her chest, and sat down on the floor against the wall. She heard muffled voices and scuffling feet, and pictured the strange, unhappy girl lying cold and lifeless on the gurney. Still hugging her Bible, Gloria rested her head against the wall. She should never have come to Eckerd City. Never have left home.

She listened to the noise that continued to filter through the wall, then closed her eyes, trying to squeeze back the tears.

You expect too much from me, Lord. You expect too much.

Chapter Three

STRENGTHEN ME WITH RAISINS,
REFRESH ME WITH APPLES,
FOR I AM FAINT WITH LOVE.
⟿ SONG OF SONGS 2:5 NIV ⟾

WHAT WAS HE GOING TO THINK when he saw her after all these years?

Gloria dabbed the corners of her mouth with a tissue, trying to remove the last bit of Strawberry Ice lipstick that had been too quickly applied by a shaky hand. When she reapplied it, she accidentally smudged it with her thumb and had to rub it off. When the third application didn't look any better, she bent over the sink and washed her mouth.

She'd forget about the lipstick.

With a spiked styling comb, Gloria forked her short, frizzy hair. She had tried using the little round styling brush with the pink rubberlike tips to get the frizz out, but it didn't do any good. Even wetting her hair, then wrapping it around the brush, and blow-drying it until her scalp felt as if it were on fire hadn't helped. After a half hour she gave up and accepted the fact that this was a bad hair day. A very bad hair day.

But why today, Lord? When I so wanted to look my best?

She sighed at her reflection in the mirror. Tucker would certainly be disappointed. She hadn't changed much in the eighteen years since she'd last seen him. She was still nothing to look at.

Once Tucker had actually complimented her eyes, called them "mysterious." Gloria batted her eyelashes and felt the lashes of the upper lids stick to the lower. It took her a second to separate them and make them stop looking like a solid clump. Too much mascara. She wasn't used to wearing it. Maybe she'd take that off too.

Her hand went for the jar of cream and stopped in midair. The mascara did make her look a teensy bit better, made her eyes larger, and yes, maybe even a *little* mysterious.

She'd leave it.

After all, she was starting over. She could step out of character if she wanted, wear lipstick and mascara if she wanted. Her mother had been hounding her for years to use makeup. Gloria grabbed the tube of Strawberry Ice and reapplied it for the fourth time.

Her mother, the beauty queen.

How had a beauty queen ended up with such a plain daughter?

She capped the lipstick and tossed it on the dresser. Then she picked up Estée Lauder's *Beautiful,* gave it two quick squirts: one aimed at the hollow of her neck right below the Adam's apple, the other at her left wrist. This was her favorite perfume. She only used it to mark the special occasions in her life. Maybe that's why after three years the bottle wasn't even half empty. But things were going to be different now. God had promised.

She put the bottle back. Who was she kidding? Makeup. Perfume. No matter what she did, she'd never make herself look like someone who should be named after Gloria Swanson. She needed to get a grip. Stop all this hyperventilating over Tucker. God never promised her Tucker. Tucker was beyond her reach. Way beyond. She'd do well to remember that.

Even so, she couldn't stop her stomach from fluttering like the wings of a hummingbird. She wiped her clammy hands on a towel, then looked at her watch. She'd given herself an extra hour so she could have time with the Lord and time to dress without rushing. She wanted to be prepared spiritually for whatever came and . . . yes, she admitted it, she wanted to look nice. Okay, extra nice. But time had gotten away from her, and now she'd have to hurry if she wanted to make that bus.

She grabbed her purse and opened it to make certain the bus schedule was inside. Then, after one more wistful glance at the mirror, Gloria left the apartment.

The bus was already at the stop when Gloria arrived, and she barely made it on before the bifold doors closed.

"Sixth Avenue," she said, fumbling in her purse for money. "How much?"

"A buck seventy-five."

"Will the bus stop near Pratt Towers?"

The driver smirked. "It did yesterday."

Gloria's fingers scrambled inside the black leather purse, pushing aside keys, a small notebook, two pens, Tic-Tacs, a bottle of aspirin. Finally, she found her wallet and quickly pulled out two dollars.

The driver looked at her sideways. "Exact change only." His

brows were arched in a superior scowl, as though he were tired of having to deal with bumpkins who didn't know the first thing about mass transit. "It's there in black and white." One finger pointed to a small sign taped to the dash.

Gloria's hand plunged back into her purse and frantically felt for change. "I'm sorry. I only have bills." She felt her cheeks burn.

"Can't make change. Against regulations. You'll have to put in two dollars and call it a learning experience."

Gloria shoved the money through the slot of the large plastic receptacle and bit her lip. Why did he have to talk so loud? Now everybody on the bus knew she was from out of town—a yokel. The woman in the front seat was already eyeing her strangely.

Gloria closed her purse, then looked for a place to sit. There wasn't any. Even the aisle was crammed. As the bus lunged forward, Gloria lost her balance and careened into one of the standing passengers, a man holding a twenty-ounce Styrofoam cup. The force of Gloria's body impacting his sent the cup flying into the air and his coffee swirling, like little waves, around her head. Miraculously, most of the coffee ended up on the floor behind her. She sighed with relief and was about to extend her apologies when she noticed that one wave, at least, had washed upon her shore. There, in the middle of her starched white cotton blouse, in a spot just above the V of her beige vest, was a coffee stain the size of her hand.

"Sorry," she said, staring helplessly at the offended gentleman.

Tucker was sure to be impressed now.

Pratt Towers was not what Gloria expected. It was massive and seemed to rise like a giant glacier right through the concrete sidewalk. She had always thought Medical Data large and sprawling with its five acres of land. But it was one story and looked like a dollhouse compared to this building. But the thing that made Gloria tremble, the thing that made her want to turn and run, was the way Pratt Towers glowed and shimmered as the sun hit the endless blue-tinted windows stretching twenty-seven floors skyward, making it look like some strange pagan temple.

She took a few steps backward, her mouth open, her hands knotted tightly around the straps of her purse.

Oh, God.

She felt someone bump into her, then someone else, then heard cursing.

"Hey, watch it, lady. Watch where you're going."

Gloria mumbled her apologies, took several deep breaths, and walked toward the entrance. Inside, a large marble fountain, twice the size of the fountain in the Appleton Mall, splashed water over the heads of three chubby angels and cascaded off the lily pads they held in their hands. Ficus trees and flowering hibiscus spiraled out of huge terra-cotta pots and stood, like guards, next to teak benches. From where Gloria stood, she saw a dozen storefronts lining both sides of the mammoth tile walkway.

A mall?

She glanced at the signs: Williams Sonoma, Laura Ashley, Gucci—stores that sold merchandise she couldn't afford. Merchandise she'd only heard Tracy talk about. The feeling of alienation came over her again. In a million years, she'd never fit in.

A steady stream of people passed her, all headed for elevators and for somewhere high inside the mammoth glacier. But as far as the first-floor stores were concerned, nothing seemed open, so that ruled out ducking into one of them and asking directions. She looked for a directory and spotted a huge gilded frame hanging by the entrance. It took her a minute, but she finally found what she was after: Mattson Development Company—Mattson Real Estate—sixteenth floor.

She rode silently in the corner of the elevator, happy that two dozen bodies hid her and her coffee-stained blouse. No one spoke. Not even a "good morning." Only two people nodded to each other in recognition. In Appleton, this many people in this little space would create a stereo of dialogue.

Everything was so different here.

By the time the elevator stopped at the sixteenth floor, only a dozen people remained. Two got out with her and passed without comment. Gloria stopped and gawked as the elevator closed silently behind her. Mahogany paneled walls met highly polished black granite floors. In the center of the hall hung a huge crystal chandelier that looked as though it belonged in a Viennese palace. A large, highly polished gray granite slab, propped by a mammoth brass hand, stood directly under the chandelier. Chiseled gold letters on the granite read: Mattson Enterprises. On either side of the massive hallway were glass-and-brass doors with letters etched into the beveled glass. The door to the right read, Mattson Real Estate, the door to the left, Mattson Development. Gloria gasped.

The entire sixteenth floor belonged to Tucker.

Tracy said he was doing well, but this . . . this was over the top. Tucker must be richer than either one of them thought.

Much richer.

Gloria bore left and entered Mattson Development Company, where the receptionist sat at a semicircular desk in the middle of the large anteroom. Her jet-black hair was perfection itself—high gloss and turned under in a long pageboy and looking like an ad for Lady Clairol. Her lipstick was applied without a hint of error, and her mascara looked so natural that Gloria had to look closely before she could see the faintest suggestion of overapplication. She wore a two-piece blue twill suit and white silk blouse, a thin gold chain, and little gold earrings shaped like knots.

But the receptionist had more than good looks. She had poise and self-control, and allowed Gloria to stare without comment. Only after a respectful interval did she speak, and when she did, it was in a clear, pleasant voice and with perfect diction. Gloria felt herself shrivel, like one of those Shrinky Dinks in an oven.

"How can I help you?" A smile, not too wide, but not too stingy either, crinkled the receptionist's face.

"I have an appointment with Tuc . . . ah . . . Mr. Mattson."

The receptionist's eyes rested on the large coffee stain on Gloria's blouse, then took in the long khaki skirt and slightly scuffed brown pumps. Her lips never moved a centimeter. "And your name?"

"Gloria Bickford." Gloria watched the receptionist scan her computer screen.

"Yes, here you are. Your appointment was for eight." The receptionist glanced at her leather-strapped Bulova.

"I know I'm late . . . I'm sorry . . . but . . . I wasn't sure what floor you were on and—"

"Mr. Mattson has instructed me to let him know the instant you arrived." With that, the receptionist picked up the phone and spoke softly into it. Seconds later, a man wearing a herringbone double-breasted Hickey-Freeman suit came from one of the offices. Every Christmas, when Tracy bought her brother ninety-dollar silk Hickey-Freeman ties, Gloria would chide her. But now, Gloria could see clearly that Tucker belonged in fourteen-hundred-dollar suits and ninety-dollar ties.

"Gloria!"

Gloria sucked air as she watched the tall, handsome man come toward her. Tucker always photographed well.

But, oh my, he looked so much better in person.

In one simultaneous motion, he lifted Gloria several inches off the floor and gave her a hug; something six-foot-two men can do easily. "It's good to see you."

"It's good to see you too." Gloria felt her cheeks burn, felt perspiration bead between her fingers. She hoped she wouldn't do anything stupid, like get her Strawberry Ice lipstick all over the collar of his expensive gray silk shirt. For a second, she wished she had left the lipstick off.

Tucker released her and made Gloria cringe when he began looking her up and down.

Oh, merciful heavens, what did he see? C'mon, Gloria. What *could* he see? Only the frog that never did turn into a princess.

"You still remind me of Annie Hall," he finally said with a smile. "Or . . . maybe with that hair, Little Orphan Annie."

Gloria shrugged, not quite knowing what to make of his comment. "Some of us don't have as much to work with as you do. You look *fabulous.* Like . . . like something out of a magazine." She gnawed her lip, wondering if she should have said that and resolved to say as little as possible from this moment on. It had only taken her two minutes to make a fool of herself.

But he did look wonderful.

She suddenly felt more shame than ever over her own looks.

"Tracy's been calling every hour for the past two days. 'Don't do this; don't say that.' Suggestions, she calls them. You know, the usual Gestapo tactics. If you're unhappy, she's going to kill me. So *please*, like it here or at least lie to Tracy and tell her you do."

For the first time, Gloria actually wanted to strangle Tracy. "I'm sorry. I wish Tracy hadn't done that."

Tucker's arm folded around Gloria's shoulder as he guided her toward his office. Out of the corner of her eye, Gloria saw the receptionist looking at her, the smile still on her face. Then Tucker closed the door and gestured for her to sit. She eased herself into a plush leather armchair and looked around. The surroundings made her even more uncomfortable. She had seen lavish offices in movies, but nothing to match this. Raised mahogany paneling covered the walls. A massive mahogany desk with intricately carved animal-looking legs dominated one end of the room. At another end, wall-to-wall barrister cases held books and statuary that looked expensive. An exquisite leather couch and two chairs sat near the bookshelves. Off to the side was a tremendous horseshoe-shaped room divided into three distinct parts: a fully stocked bar, with crystal stemware hanging from a glass rack; a complete kitchen with stainless steel appliances; and a dining room with a table that sat twenty, comfortably, for meals or conferences.

Against the last wall was a door, partially ajar, through which Gloria saw a fully tiled bathroom and shower. Next to the bath was another door, wide open, revealing an elaborately decorated bedroom that looked as if it went on forever and was probably the size of Gloria's entire apartment. She guessed it contained another bathroom as well.

She glanced at Tucker, then looked behind him at a Lladro the size of a fish tank. Why had she come? Why had she allowed Tracy to impose on her brother like this? What right did she have to be here? What could she possibly do for this man that he couldn't hire someone else, no, a dozen someones, to do for him, and better? She fiddled with the straps of her purse. "I'm really sorry about this. I mean it. I never wanted Tracy to impose—"

She stopped when she heard rich laughter. She remembered that laugh. It was warm and jolly and made you want to think up more funny things to say just to hear it. Only problem was, she hadn't said anything funny.

"I'm *glad* you're here. It'll be nice having someone in the office I can trust."

"Ah . . . that's nice of you to say." *Trust?* What did he mean? Was he trying to tell her something was wrong? That something was amiss in his office? No. Hardly that. He was way out of her league. He lived and worked in a world she knew nothing about. Why would he want to confide in a silly nobody?

"I'm happy to be here, and I'll do my best for you," she said, looking up from her lap in time to catch a glimpse of something very sad in Tucker's eyes just before it disappeared.

The rest of the day, Gloria spent with Elizabeth Price, Tucker's secretary. Gloria figured her own title was the assistant to the administrative assistant, if labels meant anything, which they didn't as far as she was concerned, because no one gave her one anyway, other than "Beth's helper."

One thing she was happy about, though, was that no one made a fuss. It would have embarrassed her if they had.

For a while, Tucker's hug in the hall generated speculation and some rumors, but they quickly died when everyone learned Gloria would be Beth's helper. She was far too low on the food chain to produce any real interest. And office gossip settled on the erroneous supposition that Gloria was some distant relative in need of a job. And everyone knew how odious relatives could be. For now, Gloria let the error ride.

Her duties paralleled this image and consisted largely of filing and making photocopies, especially copies of endless applications to Eckerd City Department of Planning and Development. Other minor duties broke the monotony. Twice she was asked to fax something over to the construction trailer at The Estates site, and once she was even permitted to call the site itself and leave the name of an electrical subcontractor. All in all, an uneventful first day.

So when it was quitting time and Gloria began preparing to go home, she was surprised to find the receptionist suddenly standing by her desk, the stock smile creasing her face.

"Mr. Mattson has asked that I take you shopping."

"Shopping?"

For the first time, the receptionist looked uncomfortable. "Mr. Mattson has asked . . . that is . . . he would like me to take you shopping for some clothes."

Gloria rose from her desk, clutching her purse. "I . . . don't understand."

"Mr. Mattson feels . . . that is . . . he would like me to help you pick out a few outfits. Of course, he will pay all expenses. He has asked me to assist you in this, in picking out . . . appropriate office attire."

"*Appropriate* office attire?" Gloria looked around to see if anyone was hearing this. When she saw one of the draftsmen duck into a nearby office, humiliation bit like a venomous snake. How could Tucker insult her like this? If he thought she looked that bad, why hadn't he come to her privately? But to do this . . . to send an employee . . .

There were other ways of calling someone a frog without actually saying it.

"Mr. Mattson said he implies no disrespect. He understands,

not being from Eckerd City, you're unfamiliar with our office dress code. He . . . Mr. Mattson hopes you'll accept his offer in the spirit in which it is intended. He knows you have left most of your clothing behind and, therefore, to ease any hardship and remove all inconvenience, he'd like me to purchase a few things. He said he would have explained all this himself if he hadn't had to leave unexpectedly for The Estates."

Gloria bit her lip. *Show you have some backbone.* Show Tucker and this receptionist and Tracy and all of them that you have some backbone. Walk right out that door, right out of this glacier of a building—this pagan temple—and right out of Eckerd City. She clutched her purse and walked past the receptionist.

But to where?

Gloria's heart dropped and her steps slowed, and before long, the receptionist was at her side, and Gloria was thinking about how the sweat rolling down her armpits was going to soil the new clothes she'd be trying on.

"Where . . . are we going?" Her voice was deadpan, her eyes welling up in spite of her resolve.

"Look, I'm going to be honest. I don't really like this."

Gloria looked up and saw the receptionist twisting one of her gold-knotted earrings around and around in her ear.

"This is embarrassing for me, but if I don't take you, I'm going to hear about it. Mr. Mattson doesn't like it when his instructions aren't followed to the letter."

This didn't sound like the Tucker she knew.

"And don't take it personally. He's done this before, with other girls. He has an image to maintain. When clients come in, he wants all his employees to look the part."

Gloria frowned. "What part?"

"Successful. He wants them to look like employees of a successful company."

This had to be sexual harassment. Surely it violated her civil rights . . . or some rights. But what was she going to do about it? What *could* she do? She owed Tucker, big time. Her apartment was dirt cheap. Her job, though it may be less than she had hoped for, certainly paid top dollar.

What was it they said about payback?

Gloria forced a smile. "Who am I to turn down a free wardrobe?" The words tasted like chalk.

The receptionist seemed relieved. "There are a few shops downstairs I think you'd like, and after that we could go for a bite to eat."

Gloria nodded slowly, as though her skull contained a thousand-pound weight.

"We could make it fun," the receptionist said.

Gloria shrugged. She knew neither of them believed that for a minute.

"By the way," the receptionist said, with her perfect smile back on her face. "My name's Jenny Hobart."

"I'm Gloria Bickford," Gloria returned, realizing as she said it that Jenny already knew her name. How much smaller could she feel before the evening was over?

～❦ ❦～

"Hey, kiddo. I called to find out about your first day at work. I've been trying to get ahold of you for hours. Where've you been?"

Gloria, still clutching her purse, tossed it on the kitchen counter. "I just got in."

"It's nearly ten o'clock. Don't tell me my brother's got you working OT already?"

"No." Gloria glanced at the living room floor, where half a

dozen bags lay scattered over the carpet where she had dropped them.

"Well, I guess it's safe to assume you weren't out on a date."

"Yes, it's safe to assume." Gloria tried to keep irritation from seeping into her voice.

"Oh, I get it . . . my brother took you to dinner. Good ol' Tucker. I knew he'd come through. 'Course that might qualify as a date."

"*No.* I didn't go to dinner with your brother." Gloria opened her purse and pulled out the bottle of aspirin.

"Have pity! Don't keep me in suspense."

Gloria filled a glass with water and uncapped the Bayer. "Tracy, I really don't want to get into it right now, okay? I'm upset and might say something I'll regret."

"What's the matter? What *happened?* You can't leave me hanging in suspense like this. I won't be able to sleep a wink. I'll lie awake all night thinking of terrible scenarios—worrying about what horrible trouble you've gotten yourself into."

"It's nothing like that." Gloria popped two aspirin in her mouth and took a swig of water.

"What are you doing? You got one of your headaches?"

"Yes. And I feel lousy. And I'm tired. And I'm dying to get out of these panty hose. It's been a long, long day."

"Okay, kiddo. You win. Just tell me one thing. How was it seeing Tucker after all these years? Did your stomach ride the Cyclone?"

Gloria banged the glass on the counter. "For heaven's sake, Tracy, this isn't grade school. And Tucker and I aren't playing tag anymore in your backyard. And if you want to know the truth, right now I'm really annoyed with him."

"With Tucker? No kidding? What did he do? Parade you around and introduce you to everyone as his boyhood pal?"

"No . . . it was worse." Gloria walked into the living room and stood by the pile of packages. "He really embarrassed me, Tracy. And I'm . . . really, really mad at him."

"No! I don't think you've ever been really, really mad at anyone, except maybe Cutter Press. You've got to tell me what he did. Otherwise for sure I'll never sleep tonight."

"He . . . well, he bought me new clothes." Gloria heard an explosion of laughter. "I don't think that's funny. Sometimes you have a sick sense of humor."

"It's hysterical, kiddo. Absolutely hysterical."

"It was humiliating, if you want to know the truth." Gloria eased herself onto the couch and slipped off her shoes. "How would you like a receptionist to come up to you and tell you that her boss has instructed her to take you shopping for *appropriate* office attire?"

"I only wish. You lucky stiff. So what did you get?"

Gloria poked one of the bags with her foot. "Three Ann Taylor suits, five blouses, a couple pair of slacks, two dresses, three pairs of shoes."

"Boy, my brother outdid himself. I told him to get you some clothes, but I never—"

"*You* told him?"

"Gloria, let's be honest. I've been trying to get you to change your look for years. You dress like a geek, for heaven's sake! I thought a little image change would raise your self-esteem, be good for morale."

"But . . . but the receptionist said Tucker has done this before. That he has done this for other girls in the office."

"Well, who can say? Tucker has always known how to treat the ladies. But in your case, he did it because I asked him. And because he knows I'm a pain-in-the-neck sister and would never get off his case if he didn't."

"I can't believe you did that! How am I ever going to pay him back? You think I want to be somebody's charity case?"

"I told Tucker you'd feel that way, and he said he had planned on giving you a relocation bonus and would take it out of that."

"Relocation bonus?"

"Yeah. Companies do it all the time when an employee relocates in order to take a job."

"You think I'm stupid! Executives may get a relocation bonus, but not a file clerk. You've put me in a bad situation. You shouldn't have interfered."

"I've been interfering all your life. This is me, your backbone, remember? I don't know what you're getting so hot about. I was just trying to—"

"You're starting to remind me a lot of my mother, you know that?" Gloria said, and then she did something she had never done before in her life. She hung up on her best friend.

Gloria removed all the tags from her new clothes, then hung them on wooden hangers. When she was finished, she stripped off her long khaki skirt, her beige vest, her coffee-stained white blouse, her beige panty hose, and tossed them in the corner like some shameful thing. Then she slipped into her pajamas. She was too wired to sleep, even though it was way past her bedtime. She knew she'd be sorry in the morning, but she needed to stay up a while and unwind. She was still fuming about Tracy. Tracy had to be just as mad because she never called back. Gloria was sure Tracy would never see, never in a million years see anything wrong with what she did. And Gloria would follow the customary pattern and do what she always did whenever they had a fight.

She'd apologize.

But it was the comparison she had made between Tracy and her mother that bothered Gloria. She shouldn't have said it. It was cruel. *But it was true.* She could see it so clearly. Tracy was a manipulator just like her mother.

Gloria curled up on the couch, then surfed channels, stopping at the eleven o'clock news. An apartment house in Eckerd's poorer section was blazing, and a beautiful female reporter stood in front of the flames, talking about the fate of the displaced families who lived there.

Displaced. That's how Gloria felt. Displaced, with nowhere to go. She had only been here two days. Hardly time to generate a fair assessment, but so far Eckerd City was not the paradise she had hoped for. Her apartment was new, her job was new, but she was the same plain, boring Gloria. Even Tucker thought so.

She wanted to cry when she relived the humiliation of having to follow Jenny, the receptionist, around the store and pretend she was enjoying herself. What was going to become of her? Was God going to be able to make good on His promise? Look what He had to work with. Who could blame Him if He couldn't deliver? Then everyone, including her mother, would all say, "I told you so."

Gloria pictured her mother's face, with her beautiful high cheekbones, her short perfectly straight nose, her flawless skin, all of which made her look like one of those dolls that collectors liked to set in the middle of their beds. She wasn't going to call her mother tonight, and that made Gloria feel bad because she knew her mother would worry. And she wasn't calling because she was too tired or didn't want to hear the nagging. She wasn't calling because when her mother started her tirade, when her mother tried to make Gloria come home—tonight . . . tonight she might not say no.

Chapter Four

SHOW ME YOUR FACE,
LET ME HEAR YOUR VOICE;
FOR YOUR VOICE IS SWEET,
AND YOUR FACE IS LOVELY.

~◉ SONG OF SONGS 2:14 NIV◉~

GLORIA NEVER EXPECTED TO BE in Pratt Towers on Saturday. But here she was standing outside Curls & Things, muttering to herself and trying to decide whether or not to go in. Jenny Hobart had told her this was *the* place to go for a great style and cut. But at the time, Gloria was still embarrassed and angry over her forced shopping expedition and made it obvious to Jenny the advice was not welcome. Now Gloria couldn't believe she was actually here.

Compliments abounded in the days following her wardrobe change and, it seemed to Gloria, people began to treat her differently. By Friday everyone had stopped calling her "Beth's helper" and called her "Beth's assistant" instead.

A definite elevation in status.

Gloria had tried to be spiritual about the whole thing. *Life and death are in the power of the tongue.* That had to be the reason why all these compliments, all these positive affirming words, had given her new strength. But could she really be that shallow? Attaching so much importance to trivial compliments about her clothes? Maybe it wasn't that spiritual after all. She pictured herself as a tomato plant with all her floppy branches suddenly given stakes to lean on. A puny self-image propped up by sticks? Is that what this was?

Oh, how shallow was that?

And Tucker? She still needed to confront him. There was no way she could just let this go without a word. But he had been out of the office all week. What must he—this secret lover pressed so tightly in her wallet—think of her? And what was she going to say to him, anyway? She'd have to give it some thought, maybe write a few ideas down on paper, then practice so when the time came, she could speak coherently and not bumble along like Miss Boiler, her sixth-grade teacher, who now had Alzheimer's. Tracy never had to think about what she'd say. It was always there, ready to roll off her tongue like packaged pastries off an assembly line. It didn't seem fair that God gave some people everything and others so little. Gloria was sure He'd explain it all to her someday. Only thing was, by then it wouldn't matter anymore.

And somehow that brought her to the question of a new hairdo. She couldn't get over the notion that changing her hair would say to Tucker she approved of what he did, or rather of what he made Jenny do, when she still was very, very angry.

The toe of her new Nine-West shoe tapped against the ceramic floor as she watched people enter the salon. The beauty business. How she hated it! In a sense, it was a privileged place only for the beautiful. So why was she even here? More staking? More attempts to extract a few paltry compliments like the last bit of toothpaste out of a tube? *Silly, silly Gloria.* She felt embarrassed, then angry, then rebellious. And why not? Why shouldn't she lay claim to any hope, any infinitesimal hope of improving herself? Why should the world only belong to those with green eyes and red hair? There were plenty of plain, uninteresting people in the world. Surely, the world was big enough for even them. And why were people like Tracy so special, anyway?

Maybe because people like Tracy didn't agonize over something as silly as this. They just did it. If Tracy were here now, she'd say new clothes needed a new hairdo and then she'd drag Gloria in.

Life was so simple for the beautiful.

They were back on speaking terms now—she and Tracy. Gloria had finally done what they both knew she would. She had called Tracy and apologized. Only this time it had taken her two days to do it. Gloria couldn't remember it ever taking that long before.

Yes, if Tracy were here, Gloria wouldn't be agonizing. Tracy would make the decision for her. Tracy was always making decisions for her.

Or Mother was.

How silly that a grown woman couldn't make up her own mind about such a simple thing as getting a haircut. Still, Gloria held back, tugging at her new black slacks and wondering why she had gotten so dressed up just to stand outside a beauty parlor. When a lovely woman came out sporting an attractive hairdo, Gloria knew what she had to do. How could God give her the desires of her heart? How could He bring her love and happiness if she didn't give Him more to work with? No, it was only right that she did her part. Make a few changes. Help Him along.

With a defiant tilt of her jaw, Gloria walked through the salon door and stopped just before she reached the white Formica counter. The first thing that struck her was the smell—an odorous mix of perms, dyes, and hairspray all wafted through the air, bringing with it memories of long hours spent at the beauty parlor with her mother. How many times had she sat in the chair dreading for the beautician to finish, dreading to see that familiar look of disappointment on her mother's face? And afterward, how many times had she sneaked upstairs to her room and cried into her pillow?

No. She couldn't go through with this.

But before Gloria could turn and walk out, the tall, well-groomed woman behind the counter stopped her.

"May I help you?" One manicured hand gestured for Gloria to step closer.

Gloria looked past her, at the posh surroundings, the large potted plants that were everywhere, and the oversized workstations that contained, along with the usual tools of the trade, white insulated coffee pitchers, creamers, sugar bowls, white paper coffee cups, and miniature cake pedestals containing assorted pastries under glass—little snacks for the elite clientele. She was definitely out of her league. How could she do this without blowing the budget?

"Is there something I can do for you?" the receptionist repeated, sporting a wide smile.

"I don't have an appointment or anything," Gloria stammered. "Maybe I should come back another—"

"We take walk-ins. And one of our operators is free. Is this for a cut or—"

"A total makeover." Gloria picked at her frizzy hair, still not sure if she'd stay. "But I don't know what I want . . . I mean what I'd look good in. "

The receptionist nodded thoughtfully. "I understand. But that's not a problem, not with Imaging." Her perfectly manicured nails fluttered in the direction of a large monitor behind her. "It's a computer program that'll show you what you'll look like in any hairstyle. Just the thing to help you take that big step."

First, Gloria had to put on a wide black headband that covered her hair. Then she had her picture taken with one of those digital cameras. After that, she spent forty-five minutes skimming through a database of almost three hundred hairstyles. From these she picked out twenty, which Tina, the hairdresser, then superimposed over Gloria's photo. The style they both agreed on was straight, parted on one side, short and layered in the back, with longer sides that covered her ears and came to soft points in the middle of her cheeks. It was a drastic departure from Gloria's perm.

Tina called it chic. She also said it would make Gloria *beautiful.*

After the shampoo girl washed Gloria's hair, Tina straightened then cut Gloria's hair. While Tina worked, Gloria kept her eyes closed, like someone who had been promised a wonderful surprise and told not to peek until it could be delivered.

Beautiful.

Had Tina really used that word?

Gloria felt her excitement build, then teeter like a too-tall stack of folded clothes. *Oh, God, don't let me be disappointed. Again.*

She was getting too old to cry into her pillow.

Snip. Snip. Snip. Things were serious now. The rubber was hitting the road. Gloria held her head as if her neck had been packed in concrete. She had seen movies like this, where the plain girl gets a makeover and becomes a dazzling beauty, surprising everyone. Tina said she could make Gloria beautiful. And she had to know. Didn't she? After all, this was her trade. *Right?*

But what if Tina used that word all the time? Told all her customers they were going to look beautiful when she was trying to talk them into something new? Gloria's heart suddenly felt dull and heavy, like a bag of rocks sinking to the bottom of a river. Beauticians always exaggerated. Always tried to make their customers feel good. She had seen enough of that when she used to go with Mother.

Gloria felt her head bob in the direction where Tina was pulling and cutting, pulling and cutting, almost in time to some tune she was humming. It didn't sound familiar, but it was happy and upbeat. Tina must be pleased with her work. Gloria felt a new surge of hope. Maybe, just maybe Tina knew what she was talking about.

"Open your eyes."

"You finished?" Gloria said in a tentative voice, eyes still closed.

"No, but I gotta blow-dry, and I want to show you how to do it for yourself."

The white cape, draped around Gloria, hid her hands. She tightened them into balls. Then, slowly, as though waking from a coma, she opened her eyes and looked into the mirror. She had had a perm for so long that at first she was shocked by the straight hair falling over one eye and lying against her cheeks as if she were a wild child without cares or inhibitions. She stared and stared and stared, and suddenly, right there in that chair, Gloria saw something she had never seen before. Right there, surrounded by the smell of hairspray and styling gel, with Tina's big hips bouncing to an unknown tune and with her hair dryer blowing hot air across Gloria's neck, Gloria had an epiphany.

All these years she had used her looks to punish her mother.

If she couldn't be a Gloria Swanson her mother loved, she'd be a homely dullard her mother despised. So, she had refused to wear makeup and began perming her own hair. What better punishment for a beautiful mother dissatisfied with a plain daughter? After a while, those mandatory trips to the beauty parlor had stopped.

Gloria studied her face in the mirror. Why had she been so foolish? All this time she could have looked at a face more suitably framed, like now, softer and with a forehead not so high. She watched with silent admiration as Tina worked her hair with the dryer and brush, pulling here, fluffing there, until finally Tina was through and stepped back and let Gloria survey the finished results.

Gloria bit her lip with pleasure. For a long time she sat in the chair grinning stupidly, but she didn't care. She had never looked so good.

"Wow, Tina. You did a great job," she finally said.

"I told you I'd make you beautiful."

Gloria felt her heart sink again and bent over to retrieve her purse from the floor. She might look better than she'd ever looked, but one tenable truth had emerged from this mad, happy Saturday adventure. She was never going to be beautiful.

Gloria studied the selection of Pepperidge Farm cookies, then finally picked up her favorite—Milano. She held the bag for several seconds, then put it back. After what she spent on her hair today, she didn't dare buy anything that wasn't on her list of essentials—and that meant only milk, bread, eggs, and dental floss. Everything else would have to wait until next payday. It also meant she was going to walk home from the West Meadow Market instead of hopping the bus. Right now, every penny counted. Besides, it was only a little over a mile from the apartment.

When she passed the produce, a cucumber rolled off the pile of other cucumbers and landed on the floor in front of her. She swung her basket around it, refusing to pick it up. It repulsed her. For years Mother had made her put cucumber slices on her eyes, as if that would accomplish anything. Why did her mother torture her like that? Torture them both with her unrealistic expectations? Maybe it was wrong to be so hard on Mother—especially after her recent epiphany. *Let he who is without sin cast the first stone.* That's what the Bible said. Maybe she needed to view this whole thing with more compassion. She was about to go back to where the cucumber lay and pick it up, then stopped. Could one little sentence of Scripture erase a lifetime of hurt and disappointment? Mother had tortured her for years. It was only natural to feel some resentment. She wasn't one of those concrete statues you see outside a Catholic church. You could gouge them all you wanted, and they wouldn't feel a thing. And she wasn't one of those ladies at the Appleton Full Gospel Tabernacle either. Her Bible had only a handful of notations.

If only she were like one of those dirty, scribbled chalkboards in a high-school classroom, and after coming to the Lord, His big, mighty hands just erased everything that went before. But things didn't get erased. They got forgiven, but they didn't get erased. There was still the residue you had to deal with. Gloria wondered why that was. Why words and deeds could follow you around like a stalker. Especially when the Bible said we were new creatures after coming to Christ.

Why did she still feel like the same old Gloria most of the time?

She left the cucumber on the floor and headed for the dairy aisle. When she got there, she slipped a half-gallon of milk into her cart. She didn't see where she owed her mother anything. Her mother's tongue had nearly shriveled up every ounce of spunk and sparkle in her. Nothing she ever did pleased her. Weren't mothers *supposed* to love their daughters? If Mother really loved her, then Gloria could have looked like anyone, anyone at all, even Mrs. Potato Head, and it wouldn't have mattered.

Gloria suddenly stopped when a box of Bloombuster caught her eye. Sam Hidel's Grocery in Appleton never carried this stuff. She had seen it the first time she came to West Meadow Market but still couldn't believe it, couldn't believe that right here, in the middle of a food mart, were all these odds and ends she normally could only get from a nursery: small and medium-size plastic and clay pots, miniature digging tools, small boxes of fertilizer, a flat of philodendrons. She poked the box of Bloombuster with her finger. Wouldn't it be something if they had this stuff for people? To mix up like a gallon of Kool-Aid and sip throughout the day until their spindly barren selves could burst into bloom. Into big beautiful ones.

Why did she have to look like Gloria Swanson before her mother could love her?

Gloria found the dental floss and bread, then headed for the checkout. After all, how many people in the world looked like Gloria Swanson? She scanned the faces in the long lines and felt justified. Not one woman could claim a resemblance. She felt added satisfaction when she spotted a woman at the end of the line who looked a lot like Clive McGreedy. Gloria smiled to herself as she tried to squeeze past her and ended up grazing a girl's leg with her basket—a lanky teen with stringy hair.

"Sorry," she said, looking up in time to see the girl take a box of linguine from the end-cap display and slip it under her shirt. Their eyes met, and Gloria saw the fear. "You should think about that," Gloria whispered, hardly believing her nerve.

The girl looked away, as though she hadn't heard.

Now, what was she supposed to do? Just when Gloria decided the answer was "nothing," she felt a check in her spirit. But the check was outshouted by her own inner voice. *This is not your business.*

Her mother was right. She couldn't help all the strays of the world. The girl eased past Gloria's basket and headed down one of the aisles. Without thinking, Gloria followed. The girl scurried along the aisle, then suddenly with lightning speed, the girl's hand reached toward one of the shelves and pulled something off. A second later, it was no longer in her hand.

Where in the world was she putting this stuff?

Gloria quickened her pace and reached the girl at exactly the same time as a man in a short-sleeved blue shirt. On his pocket "West Meadow Market" was embroidered in little white letters. She dreaded what was coming and held her breath.

"You need to follow me," the employee said. "The manager wants to see you."

"Why?" The girl cocked her head in a challenge.

Gloria was behind her and saw the sudden droop in the girl's shoulders.

"You better come quietly. No point making a scene."

The girl suddenly whirled around as though she might make a run for it and crashed right into Gloria's cart. "Oh, there you are," she said, stepping so close that Gloria saw the panic in her young eyes. "I was wondering where you went. This man wants me to come with him." The girl pointed to the West Meadow Market employee. "Maybe you should come too."

Gloria's mouth dropped. *What was she talking about?*

"Who's she?" the employee said, looking as confused as Gloria felt.

"My sister. I've been helping her shop." Her eyes pleaded with Gloria.

Strange thoughts enter a person's mind when witnessing a robbery. And stranger ones when implicated in one. Gloria's first thought was who in the world would she call if she was arrested? The next thought was of that poor, limping, little orange kitten that disappeared into the alley her first day in Eckerd City.

"Ah . . . did you get the linguine?" she found herself saying.

"Yes." The girl hiked up her shirt and pulled the linguine out of something tied around her waist, something that looked like a cloth utility belt. "And here's the crackers and pack of sardines you wanted." Gloria and the employee watched silently as the girl emptied all the pouches. "Oh, and here's the Hersheys with almonds."

"Put it back," Gloria said.

"*What?*" The girl turned white.

"Put the chocolate back. It'll give you pimples and rot your teeth." Gloria didn't know why she said that, except that's what her mother used to tell her every time she had wanted a candy bar.

"Well . . . okay." The girl threw the rest of the things into Gloria's cart and tried to head toward the candy aisle, but the man caught her arm.

"You think I was born yesterday? I know what's going on here . . . what you tried to do."

"Prove it." The girl knocked his hand away, then lifted her shirt a few inches. "There's nothing here. Nothing on me. It's gonna be your word against mine."

When the employee shot a glance at Gloria, the young girl

laughed. "You think my sister's gonna testify against me? Fugheddaboutit."

Perspiration beaded Gloria's forehead.

Aiding and abetting? How many years was that?

Gloria swiped at her damp hair. She hadn't wanted to get involved. And now she was. She glanced at the employee, at the muscles that made his short sleeves look too tight, at the tattoo on his forearm of a skull with a snake coming out of one eye. Hardly someone you wanted to tangle with. What if he made a scene? What if he marched them *both* to the manager's office? What if he called the *police?*

What was she going to do?

Gloria's fingers curled around the cart handle like the talons of an eagle as she began pulling her basket backward, away from the two strangers who were trying to claim so much of her.

Even when they both said, "Where're you going?" she turned her cart in the opposite direction and continued on her way. And when the employee followed her and barred her progress with his body and asked her again where she was going, she responded in a voice that didn't sound like hers at all.

"To the checkout and pay."

When he didn't stop her, Gloria knew she was going to make it out of the store without being arrested. But he watched her get in line. Watched her unload her basket. Watched her bag the eggs, milk, bread, dental floss, the linguini, sardines, and crackers. All the while Gloria watched *him* out of the corner of her eye. And finally, when Gloria left the store, she knew he was watching her go.

As she stepped through the door of the market into freedom, she couldn't help but wonder what her beautiful Jesus was thinking about all this. She stood trembling as the sun drizzled warmth on her head like balm. What if she were stepping into one of those small dark cells she'd seen in a prison movie where the sun never shines? How could she have been so stupid? How could she have allowed such a young girl to manipulate her so easily? How long was she going to allow everyone to lead her around by the nose?

Sometimes, Gloria, you don't have a brain in your head.

"Can I have my things now?" The girl slipped beside Gloria.

"You had some nerve involving me! I . . . we could have been arrested." She gave the girl an angry glance and saw her shiver. Was it the thin shirt, or was the girl still frightened? "It's a miracle we both made it out of there."

"It was no big deal." The young girl laughed, but Gloria saw the relief on her face. "C'mon, I need my things."

"Wait until we turn the corner. I don't want anyone to see." Gloria twisted around so she could check out the grocery store entrance and half expected the muscle-bound employee to be walking behind them. She was relieved to see only an elderly couple. When she turned, the girl was still shivering. "You should have a coat on. It's chilly."

The girl shrugged.

Gloria's mother would never have allowed Gloria to go prancing around town dressed like that at her age. If it was cold, she always made sure Gloria had her warm coat or mittens or hat. What was wrong with this girl's mother? What was she thinking? Obviously not enough about her daughter—the little thief.

As they rounded the corner, the girl stepped in front of Gloria. "I gotta go. So just gimme my stuff, okay?"

"Actually . . . it's not your stuff. I paid for it, remember? And a 'thank-you' would be nice."

For the first time, Gloria noticed the five toe rings on bare sandaled feet that looked almost blue from the cold, the little rosebud tattoo under the girl's collarbone, the string of silver pierced earrings lining her left ear and almost hidden by brown stringy hair. *What was this girl's mother thinking?*

"Can I have my stuff?"

"My goodness. Didn't your mother teach you *any* manners?" Gloria saw the lips twitch, saw the eyes darken, eyes that looked like an old lady's eyes. She shouldn't even be talking to this girl. She didn't want to get involved. But those dark brooding eyes made Gloria shudder. They reminded her of . . . "Look. I'm sorry I said that, about your mother. You can have your things but just think about what you're doing. Okay?"

The girl put out her hand as though she wanted to shake. "Mom did teach me manners. Thanks for your help. The name's Perth."

"Perth?"

"Yeah, after Perth, Scotland. That's where my grandfather was born. Cool, isn't it?"

Almost reluctantly, Gloria took Perth's hand. It was rough, like a laborer's hand, with broken cuticles and dirt crusting the fingernails. "This doesn't mean we're friends. I don't like what you did in there. And I'm sure your mother wouldn't like it either if she knew."

Perth shrugged. "You changed your hair."

"What?"

"Your hair . . . I like it. The other way made you look like a geek. You know . . . bad. Like you didn't care about how you looked."

Gloria glanced at Perth's unkempt hair and wondered that Perth couldn't apply this insight to herself. "I've never seen you before. What do you know about my hair?" She reached into the bag and pulled out the linguine.

"I saw you, the last time I was here. I was luckier. Mr. Busybody in there didn't catch me. I got away with a week's worth of stuff."

Gloria handed her the pasta. "You're playing a dangerous game. You may think it's fun and exciting now, but when they send you to reform school, you'll wish you never started this."

Perth threw back her head and laughed.

"Look, it's your life." Gloria's hand dove back into the bag just as the October wind whistled past them, lifting Perth's stringy hair and flimsy cotton shirt. Gloria watched Perth shiver. "I just thought I should say something. You're the one who involved me in this, remember?" *What was wrong with this girl's mother?*

"You think this is for kicks, don't you?"

"Isn't it?" Gloria pulled out the box of crackers and the tin of sardines and handed them to Perth.

Perth shrugged. "Why should I bother explaining? You've already figured it out. Took one look and made up your mind. I can see it on your face. Juvenile delinquent. That's what you're thinking. Right?"

"Are things so bad you have to steal?"

Perth began stuffing the groceries into the pouches hidden beneath her oversized shirt. "Everything's relative. Right?"

For the first time, Gloria noticed how thin Perth was. How even the utility apron and the goods in the pouches didn't make her look overweight. After a moment's hesitation, Gloria dug into her purse and pulled out a ten-dollar bill.

"Here." She shoved the money into Perth's hand.

"I knew you were all right . . . that you had to be nice . . . just by looking at you." Perth curled her fingers tightly around the bill. "Thanks. This'll help."

Gloria frowned. It was hard pegging the girl. There was sweetness and vulnerability and even innocence. But juvenile delinquent still headed the list. "Well, take care of yourself. And try not to get into trouble." Gloria readjusted the bag of groceries, then wrapped her gray sweater tighter around herself against the cold wind. "And next time you see me, please don't tell anyone I'm your sister." With that, she began walking away.

"Hey . . . where you going?" Perth scampered after her like a puppy, her toe rings catching the glint of the sun and making her foot sparkle. "What's your hurry?"

Gloria quickened her pace to be on her way.

"Now look who's being rude. I asked you where you were going."

Gloria crinkled her forehead trying to look irritated. "I thought you were in a hurry."

"Yeah, well . . . it just hit me that having a sister might be nice."

"Don't think I'm giving you any more money."

"I wasn't thinking that, exactly. I was thinking more about how it's not so great being an only child."

"Well, if you were my sister, right now I'd probably smack you."

Perth giggled. "Isn't there some Chinese proverb or something that says if you do a good deed for someone you become responsible for that person?"

Gloria stepped up her pace. So did Perth.

"I think there is . . . a proverb, I mean, and well . . . you should consider it."

Gloria stopped suddenly, her fingers almost ripping into the brown paper bag. "Stop being silly, Perth, and go home. And stay out of trouble."

Perth's face knotted up like a child who had gotten separated from her parents and was lost in a giant mall somewhere.

Oh, please don't start crying now.

Gloria shifted the bag to her other arm so she couldn't see Perth's face and darted past a man and woman pushing a stroller. Perth followed.

"I don't eat much and I'm real neat. I don't have any bad habits and I don't do drugs."

Gloria flipped the bag away from her face. "For heaven's sake, haven't you been enough of a nuisance?"

That must have done it, because Perth slowed her pace. "Yeah . . . well . . . I'm sorry I said you looked like a geek . . . you know . . . before. I think your hair's really cool. And thanks for helping me back there. And for the money."

When Gloria turned around, she saw Perth jerking her thumb behind her. "I guess I'll go that way."

Surprisingly, Gloria didn't feel relieved. "There are agencies that help people who need it . . . Social Services . . . something. You should check it out."

Perth nodded. But Gloria could tell by the expression on her face she wouldn't.

"How old are you, anyway?"

Perth smiled and backed away. "Old enough."

"Well . . . stay out of trouble."

Perth waved, then turned and sprinted away.

Gloria remained fixed on the sidewalk, watching the wind catch Perth's shirt like a sail and take her farther down the street. She wondered if she should go after her. But already the young girl had crossed the intersection and disappeared into the crowd. There was nothing for Gloria to do but turn and head home.

The mile back to the apartment seemed more like two, and Gloria argued with God all the way. Perth wasn't her responsibility. Why should she feel guilty? It wasn't Gloria's fault that Perth was a delinquent. Surely God couldn't expect Gloria to bring her home? No telling what trouble that would cause. Perth was a total stranger. Maybe psychotic. Dangerous even. And her apartment was large, but not large enough. After all, Gloria only had one bedroom. And what was Perth . . . fourteen maybe fifteen? A minor. There had to be a slew of legal ramifications. One couldn't just take in a minor without the proper consent.

And why had God allowed this situation, anyway? Hadn't He promised her the desires of her heart? Hadn't He promised her love? So far all He'd given her were problems, and plenty of opportunities to be humiliated and embarrassed. Nothing at all what Gloria had expected.

Chapter Five

I WILL SEARCH FOR THE
ONE MY HEART LOVES.
SO I LOOKED FOR HIM
BUT DID NOT FIND HIM.
— SONG OF SONGS 3:2 NIV—

SUNDAY MORNING GLORIA WOKE UP feeling as though she
had upholstery stuffing for brains. She was groggy, befuddled,
and couldn't focus. At first she thought it was the beginning of
a headache, but she soon realized it wasn't a physical thing but
a spiritual disconnect. All yesterday, after coming home from
the West Meadow Market, she had been irritated with God. She
realized she was still irritated.

Could one get irritated with God? She wondered if that was
blasphemy, then wondered what the church ladies would say if
they knew her angry feelings right now. Maybe they never got
angry. Maybe they were like those sports pros who had entered
The Zone—but a spiritual one where you were always on a high

and could do no wrong. If that's how it worked, then she knew the trouble. She wasn't a pro. She hadn't been at it long enough. She was still stumbling and tripping like an amateur.

But it seemed so easy for those church ladies. Every week they had talked about answered prayer—how God had answered this and how God had answered that—as if He were the pizza delivery boy bringing their orders as fast as He could.

Not fair. There were other prayers too—cancer, lost jobs, children on drugs—still waiting to be answered, and yes, she had seen their tears. Sometimes those ladies cried too. She really did have to be fair.

And when she put it like that, did she have any right to be angry? Did a clay pot have the right to be angry with the potter who made it? She had read that only last week and liked it right away, liked the symbolism. A clay pot. Now, that was something she could understand, could relate to.

But how could a clay pot like her ever really be angry at her beautiful Jesus? After what He did? After hanging there on the cross for her, for silly plain Gloria, and whispering her name. And after coming into her heart when she had asked.

She picked up her Bible from the nightstand and opened it. She needed to get her thoughts centered on Him again. Set her priorities straight. For over an hour she read. But concentrating was difficult. So was finding relevance in places and times so far removed from her own. She was in Eckerd City. She needed help now.

Oh, why is it, sweet Jesus, that sometimes You're so real to me, so real I can almost feel Your fingers laced in mine, and other times I'm tempted to believe You're just a figment of my imagination.

She returned her Bible to the nightstand, then rose from the bed and pulled the Yellow Pages from the drawer. Her fingers flew down the list of churches in the area. What she needed was like-minded people. Yes, some fellowship with other believers. She scribbled down the names of several churches she would visit, one at a time, in the coming weeks. *Don't forsake the fellowship of the believers.* One of the church ladies had told her that.

That's what she needed, fellowship.

She carried the list into the living room and plopped on the couch, staring at it. Yes, but what she needed most was fellowship with *God.* She folded the paper and dropped her head.

"Oh, Jesus, why are we so at odds? Why can't I feel Your fingers now? Or hear Your sweet voice?"

She sat that way for a long time, feeling depressed and out of sorts, then suddenly her heart burned within her. She was the one at odds. He was as He always was. Patient, kind . . . inscrutable. *How unsearchable are Your ways?* He knew what He was doing even if Gloria didn't. She closed her eyes.

"I want to follow You. You know I do. I don't know why I'm so difficult. I don't mean to be. I don't mean to bungle the situations You put me in. I'm sorry I keep letting You down, keep disappointing You. But sometimes . . . sometimes You disappoint me too. And then I get scared. I think You're not there. I think You don't love me. I think everything but the right thoughts. Please forgive me. I *do* trust You. Oh, why can't I be more like You?"

~◆ ◆~

After breakfast Gloria tidied up the apartment and showered. Then she dressed and went for a walk. West Meadow Drive was quiet, with only the sound of a lone bird chirping high up on a branch. The maples were changing color, and fallen leaves had collected around the trunks. Soon there'd be no chirping, no colored leaves. She felt the loneliest in winter. That's when nature mocked her with its frozen air and frozen ground. Who was there for her to share a fire with, or a cup of hot cocoa? Who was there for her to share a blanket and a movie on a lazy afternoon? The world had plenty of fires and cocoa and blankets and movies to spare, but never in her house. *Never in hers.* And people all alone felt the cold more keenly that than others. She knew what she was talking about. She had spent enough winters alone. But maybe this year would be different. After all, she had God's promise hanging out there in the air. And maybe the first good snowfall would bring it down and wrap it around her shoulders.

As she rounded the corner to her right, the street became livelier. Cars sped along the four-lane highway that only a few years ago was called West Meadow East but was changed to Pratt Parkway after Hugo Pratt sank his millions into Eckerd City. Slowly, Gloria began to forget about winter and let the buildings catch her fancy instead. Several were five stories, most of which had a store on the first floor and who knew what on the others. Apartments probably.

She stopped at the florist's window to admire the half-dozen dried arrangements—table centerpieces and wreaths mostly. She strolled by Pierce Real Estate. Next came the law office of Smith, Smith, and Tobias. It looked as though it had to be at least a hundred years old by the wide floor planking she saw through the window.

Then she passed E-Z Printing and chuckled at the hideous brochure in the window. The colors were all wrong: green and yellow, a visual counterpart to the irritating fingernails on a blackboard. And look at that text and artwork! What a mess—totally lacking in balance and eye appeal. She shook her head and continued walking.

Before long she spotted West Meadow Market. She had

come with no purpose in mind other than some exercise and fresh air. So she was surprised when she suddenly found herself looking around with an excessive degree of alertness.

What was she hoping to see?

Perth?

Gloria stopped in her tracks. The thought was at once ridiculous and mad. What if Perth were here? What would Gloria do? Invite her home? Gloria put her hand to her thumping heart. She had already explained to God why that couldn't happen. But . . . hadn't she just told Him she *trusted* Him? Hadn't she just asked for His forgiveness for messing things up? Hesitantly, and with a sense of dread, Gloria scanned the street, the sidewalk, the Market entrance. No sign of the skinny, foolish girl. Gloria was relieved. As she turned to head back home, she realized she was something else. She was sad.

Gloria couldn't believe how fast Monday was going. Another hour and it would be time to head home. In some ways she didn't want it to end. The day had been a heady one. More than five people had complimented her hair. A lot more. But she had stopped counting when Mr. Simms, the middle-aged head of accounting, and a man rumored to have an eye for the ladies, came to her. He was the fifth person to come over, and he told her how attractive she looked.

Attractive.

Now that was a word no man had ever spoken to her before. It had almost made her dizzy, had almost made her want to swoon like one of those heroines Tracy was always reading about in her historical romances. But Gloria had not fainted. She didn't even stutter. She had simply smiled, thanked him, and looked at the clock. 10:46 A.M. She believed she'd remember that time, along with the date, for months to come.

The one obvious missing entry was Tucker's. He was back in the office but had yet to say a word, even though they had been in each other's company twice: once in the giant hallway earlier that morning when everyone was streaming in from the elevator, and once when he stopped by Elizabeth Price's desk and she happened to be there. Gloria was sure he'd notice her new hairdo, and since he had paid for the lovely navy Ann Taylor suit she wore, she figured he'd at least remark on that, too. She had been keenly disappointed when he didn't. She was embarrassed by it now and could hardly believe she had actually done it, but earlier that day she had even walked by his office, four times, with no purpose in mind other than to catch him coming out of his door and hopefully elicit his response. But she never did catch him, and now, when she thought about it, she knew she had acted like a fool.

Why was she so silly when it came to men? After all these years she should have learned something from Tracy. Now, there was a girl who understood men, who could handle them like a trainer handled a horse. That's because Tracy had lots of experience. "Relationships," Tracy called them. And that's what Gloria thought they were until recently, when she heard them called by another name, *fornications*. She learned that from the Bible ladies when one of them talked about her daughter living with a man. Later, after the Bible study, Gloria had gone home and checked it out herself. She read every passage that had the word *fornicate* or *fornications* in it, thirty-nine in all, just to get the proper handle on it. Not that she had ever been tempted. For twenty-eight years, temptations of this type had not plagued her at all. Not until Eckerd City. Not until the first day she saw

Tucker, all grown up and in the flesh. And that was the problem, wasn't it? The flesh. Oh, how it can tantalize.

And now it was too late to go that route because of Jesus. How could she? With His hand in hers and all? But maybe if she had listened and learned from Tracy *before*, well, maybe she wouldn't be worrying about winters anymore. And even as it passed her mind, Gloria knew Jesus couldn't have liked that thought one bit.

Now, when she saw Tucker walking toward her with a smile that looked like a toothpaste ad, a smile that had always sold her, even when she was ten, Gloria tried to remember some of the harsher warnings against fornication.

"I've been meaning to talk to you all day." Tucker came up beside her and pulled at her arm, indicating he wished to put more distance between them and Beth Price, who sat at her desk only inches away.

Gloria felt her face flush. She also felt everyone's eyes on her. The office would be buzzing about this. In the short time she had been here, Gloria had learned it buzzed about everything.

"If I hadn't had those problems at The Estates, I would've taken you out last week."

Gloria looked at the handsome face, watched his lips move, heard the words float past her ears, and still couldn't believe them.

"I thought it would be nice to reminisce, talk about old times. Laugh over our wicked childhoods."

"You must have no memory left at all," she croaked. "My childhood was dull."

Tucker put his face close to Gloria's, almost like a tease. "I never found you dull. Not a bit."

"That's nice of you to say." Gloria folded her hands behind

her to hide her perspiration-soaked fingers. Had she heard right? Had Tucker actually said he had wanted to take her out? Of course Tracy had to be behind it, had probably threatened to put the screws to him. But just the same, Gloria was pleased . . . and flattered. "If you really want to relive our past, I'd be happy to oblige."

"How about tonight?"

"Tonight?" Oh dear, what would she wear? "Ah . . . sure . . . tonight's fine."

"Then meet me in front of the parking garage in an hour."

Gloria nibbled her thumb and nodded, hoping she didn't look too eager. At least she didn't have to worry about what she'd wear.

When he walked away she tried to act natural, as though nothing had happened, as if the ground beneath her hadn't suddenly cracked open because of an earthquake named Tucker. She avoided Beth's eyes and pretended to sort papers for filing. The next hour was going to be the longest sixty minutes of her life.

～❦ ❧～

When Tucker pulled up in his red Camaro, Gloria thought she'd die from happiness. All her life she had watched girls being driven in cars like this by handsome men. She had never ever dreamed that someday she'd be one of them.

As she pulled open the door, a quick glance told Gloria no one was witnessing her triumph, and that disappointed her. Even so, she almost leaped into the front seat, as though afraid Tucker might change his mind and drive off without her.

The gray leather interior felt like down, it was so soft, and made Gloria hold herself as if she were wearing stays. How could she wrinkle such exquisite leather? She turned toward Tucker in time to see him flash a huge smile, and away they went.

He was going far too fast for her taste and darting from one lane to the other. She wanted to tell him to slow down but didn't dare. He'd think she was a nag. Or figure out that she was boring, after all. And she couldn't have that. This was a dream come true, sitting in a sports car next to Tucker. There could be no sour notes to spoil the lovely sonata she hoped would play itself out this evening.

When Tucker switched lanes for the hundredth time and nearly grazed the fender of a black Toyota, Gloria dug her nails into her palms. "So, where are we going?" Maybe conversation would take her mind off Tucker's driving.

"First the Tomb—for a few drinks—then to dinner. You like seafood?"

"Love it. But . . . Tucker, I don't drink. I mean, I drink—naturally everyone drinks something—but not alcohol. I don't drink alcohol. I thought you knew. I mean . . . since Tracy tells you everything. You don't mind, do you?" Gloria wiggled in her seat with embarrassment. *Why had she said that?* Maybe because she didn't want him to think she had become a religious nut or something just because she knew Jesus.

"What I meant to say is . . . well, I don't mind going with you, but I just thought you should know, that's all. I didn't want it to be awkward . . . later." Her elbow dug into the seat back as she tensed. Tucker's magnificent leather no longer seemed important.

"Relax. Don't tie yourself in knots. You always were the serious type. You've got to let down a little, Gloria. I don't care if you drink or not. Just as long as you don't mind going."

Tucker took his eyes off the road, and Gloria thought she

was going to have a heart attack. They were moving so fast the cars on either side of them almost looked parked.

"You don't mind, do you?"

"No! Not at all." Gloria's palms ached from the pressure of her nails.

"I can't tell you how glad I am you're here. How important it is to me to have you in the office. I trust you, Gloria. And I need someone around who I can trust. You can be my eyes and ears, especially when I'm away. You won't mind doing that for me? Being my eyes and ears?"

"I'm . . . not sure I understand. Your office seems efficient. I haven't met anyone who didn't seem capable of doing their—"

"Remember the time you nursed that pathetic little bird . . . what was it? . . . a finch? . . . back to health? A broken wing, if memory serves me right. Your mom was really ticked. Said birds carried germs and that you shouldn't waste your time. But you did it anyway. And that bird finally got better and flew away."

Gloria watched Tucker out of the corner of her eye. She didn't want to stare at him head-on. He had on his I-want-to-sell-you-something smile, and Gloria had the feeling she'd buy no matter what it was. Even so, she wanted to correct him, to tell him that bird never flew away, that Cutter Press had killed it, but she didn't have the heart.

"Anyway, when I saw what you did with that bird, I think that's when I fell in love with you—when I saw that you could take something broken and fix it or at least try. I only wish we had stayed friends after my parents split up."

"You moved away," Gloria said in a near whisper. She was shaken to the core. *That's when I fell in love with you . . . fell in love with you . . . fell in love with you.* Words, Gloria. Just words. *Poor, silly Gloria.*

"Yeah, Dad got me, and Mom got Tracy—his-and-her

dolls. But if Tracy and Mom had been the ones to move to a new town instead of me, I wonder if things would have turned out different."

"What do you mean?"

"I could have used a friend like you after the divorce. But Tracy got you instead."

"But you had your sister. You and Tracy are so close."

"No, not then. In those days I still believed everything Dad said. And Tracy was the enemy, or rather she had gone over to the enemy, meaning Mom, and my twelve-year-old mind just lumped them together. I didn't understand all the other stuff that had gone on—Dad's women, his gambling. I used to think the divorce was all Mom's fault. I guess in a way, I'm still trying to make it up to Tracy."

The Camaro came to a screeching halt, making Gloria grind her teeth. She looked out the window, wondering why they had stopped, and saw a sprawling two-story building with a façade that actually looked like the entrance to a tomb. "I never realized how hard the divorce was for you."

"Ancient history." Tucker laughed, and it sounded canned. "And, hey, I wanted to reminisce without turning the evening into a wake. We're supposed to be having fun, remember?"

She was about to say that if they were really friends they could talk about anything, only right then Tucker suddenly pulled onto the paved driveway leading up to the Tomb entrance. For a second Gloria thought he was going to smash into the giant, boulder-looking door. But it was made of molded plastic and swung open to a parking garage below the club. By the look on his face, Tucker seemed to love it, all of it, the molded plastic, the way it made strange, eerie noises when it opened, like the kind you'd hear from the sound track of *The Mummy*. But Gloria thought it was just plain silly.

Gloria was having trouble hearing Tucker over the blaring music, but she could see, by the foolish grin on his face, he wasn't saying anything important. They had been at the club for hours. It began filling up shortly after they arrived, like water in a tub. Now bodies spilled over into every nook and cranny of the two rooms that constituted the Tomb. Many people who had stopped after work were still here, and Gloria wondered if they didn't have someone waiting for them at home. Maybe there were a lot of lonely people even in crowded bustling Eckerd City.

From the beginning, the bartender catered to Tucker. He called Tucker by name, shared inside jokes, knew without being told that Tucker drank Black Label cut in half by water. It was the same with many of the people who bellied up to the bar. They knew Tucker's name, shared inside jokes. Before long, Gloria decided everyone knew Tucker.

It had been fun, even heady, meeting people one right after the other whom Tucker knew. And it had been fun, even heady, when they accepted her into the group. She had never been accepted into a group so easily. Tracy always had to bully and cajole in order to get Gloria in one, and even then the accept-ance only lasted as long as Tracy was present. Being with Tucker obviously carried weight. But in this dark, silly place filled with Egyptian paraphernalia and a full-size figure of Boris Karloff dressed in rags, nobody questioned her right to be included.

It had also been fun listening to Tucker rehash the "good old days," the times he and Tracy and she had gone exploring in the woods by old man Griffin's house. The times they went trout fishing in the stream a mile out of Appleton and finally caught "Bubba." The times she and Tracy helped Tucker glue together his Skyhawks and Furys. The time they all built Fort Apache in the backyard and how Tracy couldn't get over Gloria's skill with a hammer.

It had been fun listening to the stories of Tucker's business conquests. Of how he had graduated from college with a hundred dollars and parlayed it into a business worth over a million and possibly multimillions in the near future. It had all been fun for the first two hours.

After that, she had stood back, just watching. He was smooth. Handsome. *So very handsome.* He had a quick wit. Made people laugh. Made them eat out of his hand, even. Made them want to hang around him, as though his words were dewdrops that refreshed their own dry lives. Gloria guessed Tucker had what people called "charisma." Tracy had it too, but not like Tucker.

He was in a class all by himself.

And *she* was with him. That made her feel special. She couldn't remember the last time she felt special.

But by the third hour she was antsy and hungry. Tucker was drunk. But not noticeably. She wanted to leave. He didn't. He was starting to tell the same stories, the same jokes to different people as they stopped by his place at the bar. And in between it all was talk of business or politics. Clearly, his thoughts were far from the dinner he had promised. She tried filling the gap with peanuts and pretzels, by telling herself she was lucky to be here. Lucky that Tucker cared enough about her to even want to spend an evening with her. That he was having so much fun, dinner no longer mattered. But she knew it was a lie. By the time Tucker drained his fifth drink, she could have been anyone. A stranger on a stool.

Before Tucker could order another scotch, someone cranked up the music to a maddening level, and Gloria knew she couldn't stay any longer.

"Tucker." She tugged at his arm, trying to get his attention. "Come on—"

"Dance? Sure I'll dance with you." He pulled her off the stool and began dragging her toward the dance floor.

"No, Tucker, stop. I don't want to dance. I want to go home."

Tucker continued propelling them forward, then staked out a small spot on the crowded dance floor. Before Gloria knew what was happening, he pulled her close, then snapped his arms around her like a trap.

She smelled his liquored breath; felt his body move to the loud, pounding music; heard him click his tongue in time to the beat. His eyes closed as though he were far off on an alien world.

Bodies all around her moved to the mad, sensuous rhythm of the music. She could barely see their faces, it was so dark. She struggled to free herself, but he held her too close, too tight, forcing her body to move with his. She felt repulsed by this violation, this disrespectful intimacy. She also felt moved. Instinctively, she knew she was feeling what the crowd felt. It was alien and dark . . . erotic and irreverent, but it made her blood flow and gush like an unrestrained flood.

She put her head against Tucker's chest, against his $135 Hickey-Freeman white twill shirt, not even worrying about lipstick stains. A thousand other women had felt like this before. Women all around her were feeling it now. But she never had. She could see why there was so much fornication, why people filled their need to be loved in the wrong way. To be held like this . . . to move in such a way. Even when it was a lie, it was powerful. She had dreamed about this. Of what it would be like to be in Tucker's arms. She knew it meant nothing to Tucker. But to her, it meant so much. To her—plain, boring Gloria—it meant so very, very much. Only . . . it wasn't what she had expected.

She felt Tucker's hands move down the length of her back, felt them pull at her. Then she felt a check in her spirit, a need to break free and flee this place, but the music . . . the music had grabbed something deep inside her and wouldn't let go.

Oh, God, I have to get out of here.

She felt his mouth on her neck, felt tiny kisses that both tickled and made her shiver. "Jessica, I could dance with you all night."

Jessica?

His grip slackened as his mouth reached her shoulder, and she was able to wriggle free. She clamped her hand tightly around his arm and pulled him back to the bar.

"Tucker, I'm leaving." She picked up her purse. She had already decided she wouldn't let him drive her home. She'd get a cab. "Thank you for a lovely evening. I'll see you in the morning."

Tucker glanced at his watch. "It can't be ten!" He shook his wrist, then checked his watch again. "It's ticking, so it must be. I don't know what to say except I'm sorry. You've got to be starving. Let me take you to dinner."

Gloria looked at his empty scotch glass and shook her head. "Thanks . . . but I'd rather go home. I'm tired."

"Out of the question. I promised you dinner. Besides, you want me to get chewed out? You know what *Tracy* would say?"

Gloria's anger rose. Quite frankly she didn't care what Tracy would say. It was sounding like a broken record. She was about to tell him so, when two people she had never seen before came over to Tucker. There was an explosion of greetings and laughter, handshakes, and the order to the bartender for "another round." Then Tucker slipped into an easy dialogue, and Gloria could tell it was going to be about Eckerd politics.

In a flash, she darted behind the couple and tried to squeeze through the crowd. As she did, someone's drink spilled all over her beautiful new Ann Taylor suit. But she didn't stop. She maneuvered through the maze of bodies, then out the door. She couldn't believe she was actually walking out on a man, a man whose picture she'd been carrying in her wallet for over three years.

Sometimes the dream was better than the reality.

Gloria paid the cabbie and wondered how she was going to stretch the few dollars she had left until payday. With the cost of her new hairdo, Perth's groceries and the extra ten Gloria had given her, and now this cab fare, she was way over budget. She'd have to be very careful, or she wouldn't have enough money to take the bus to work for the next four days. That meant no coffee from the machines and no chocolate-covered donuts with sprinkles on Wednesday when the Donut Delight man came to the office.

She fumbled in her purse for her keys and wondered if Tucker was still at the club. How was he ever going to get home? Maybe she shouldn't have left him. Maybe she should call someone—someone who would go to the Tomb and take him home. Beth Price? Mr. Simms? No. That would create too much office gossip. She knew of no one else.

Lord, please get Tucker home safely.

She was still shaken by Tucker's behavior . . . and hers. Tucker had a lot of pressure, a lot of responsibilities. What was her excuse? She was sure she had disappointed her beautiful Jesus tonight, though He'd probably never say so.

She'd change, make herself an egg, then spend some time

with the Lord. She needed that now. Time with Jesus. Time to sort things out, about herself. About Tucker. She wondered what Tracy would say if she had seen how her brother acted tonight. With all those scotches. But he could hold his liquor. That was obvious. And when he had finally gotten drunk, he wasn't sloppy or loud. He was . . . Gloria inserted her key into the door, knowing she didn't want to think about how he was because that would make her think about how she was. But she'd bring it to the Lord, talk to Him about it, and maybe, if He said it was okay, she'd talk to Tracy about her brother. On the other hand, who was she to talk to anybody about anything? The first time out with Tucker and she had made a complete fool of herself. Oh, how was God ever going to be able to give her the desires of her heart when she couldn't even manage one small evening with a man?

When Gloria turned the doorknob, she heard the bushes near the porch rustle. She hesitated, listened, then decided it was nothing. A squirrel or bird. She was about to go in when she heard it again, this time accompanied by a voice.

"Don't be scared. It's just me."

Gloria turned to the direction of the voice. "Who's that?" The light from the streetlamp reached partway onto the porch. When a figure emerged from the shrubbery, Gloria saw it was a girl.

"Never figured you for a party animal. But I can smell you from here."

"Perth?"

The girl went around the side of the porch and slowly walked up the steps. Gloria thought she heard her groan.

"You really stink. You musta had a blast."

Gloria's mouth dropped, as though she were seeing an apparition, only hers was wearing green sweats and a string of sterling silver earrings on her left ear. "What are you doing here?" she finally asked.

"Waiting . . . for you."

Gloria's first thought was to call the police, but when Perth turned toward the light, she saw Perth's swollen lip and the shadow of a bruise on her left cheek. *"What happened?"*

"Nothing."

Gloria backed closer to the light, taking Perth with her. "It looks like someone hit you."

Perth shook her head. "Nobody hit me. I had an accident. It's nothing. But I was thinking maybe I'd stay the night. What do you say?"

"I'd say you're crazy. Your parents will be frantic. No matter what trouble you've gotten yourself into, you must go home and tell your parents."

"You still have everything figured out, don't you? Right away you're sure I got into some kind of trouble."

Gloria tried to calm herself, tried to pray and ask God what He'd have her do. Tried to remind Him she only had one bedroom. "Did you report this to the police?" She didn't know what else to say.

"You've got a one-track mind. Sorry I bothered you."

Perth began walking away, and when Gloria grabbed her arm, she heard her groan. "What's wrong?"

"Nothing."

Gloria turned Perth's arm toward the light, then gently lifted her sleeve. There was a large bruise above her elbow. "We're not going to get anywhere until you tell me what happened."

"I fell. Okay?"

"If you want my help, you'll have to do better than that."

"I was trying to get my dad into bed, and I fell and hit my face and arm."

Gloria pulled the sleeve back down when she saw Perth shiver. "What's wrong with your father? Why did you have to help him?"

Perth kicked one sneaker against the porch step. "He was drunk. You satisfied?"

Gloria's head began to ache. She hadn't eaten anything since lunch, except for those handfuls of peanuts and pretzels at the Tomb. She was hungry and tired. And now she was saddled with a troubled teenager. But how long could she continue standing out here like a burglar trying to pick the lock of Perth's mind? Better to get her inside, calm down, and try to figure this out. "Come upstairs. I'll make us an omelet and we'll talk." *Sometimes, Gloria, you don't have a brain in your head.*

She turned to Perth and gave her a firm look. "That's all I'm promising. Food and conversation. When I say go, you go. Is that understood?"

Perth nodded her head and smiled.

"How in the world did you know where I lived?" Gloria asked as she opened the door and let Perth go in ahead of her.

"I saw you by West Meadow Market Sunday and followed you."

"I never saw you."

"I know. That's the way I wanted it."

Gloria knew she should be angry, should say something harsh, but she couldn't think of what, so she just directed Perth up the stairs and finally into her apartment. Inside, she flicked on lights and kicked off her new heels. Then she directed Perth to one of the two chairs by the kitchen table. In the light she was able to see Perth's face more clearly. The girl's lips were badly swollen and her left cheek puffy, discolored.

"You hungry?" Gloria plopped her purse on the counter before opening the refrigerator. She hardly knew Perth, but already she knew enough not to press her for more details. She'd give the girl some room, let her loosen up. And when she did, Gloria would decide what to do next.

She pulled out the carton of eggs, the container of milk, and a package of cheese. She didn't have the energy to make anything fancy. A simple omelet would have to do for the both of them. She cracked two eggs in a bowl, then turned to Perth. "In case you didn't know, I'm on a budget and can't afford to make food for someone who's not going to eat. So before I crack any more eggs . . . are you hungry?"

Perth had been sitting quietly in the chair, as though relieved to be safely inside, and savoring her good fortune. From her seat, Perth could see the living room, and Gloria watched as the young girl devoured everything with her eyes.

"Perth?"

Perth turned and smiled, then winced with pain and brought her fingertips to her swollen lips. "I had a few crackers earlier. I could eat something if you're offering."

Aside from the cooking noises, the apartment was quiet. Only when Gloria brought two plates of steaming eggs to the table and placed one in front of Perth did the young girl speak.

"It looks good."

Next, Gloria put two large glasses of milk and a few slices of buttered toast on the table, then sat down. She bowed her head and said a simple prayer of thanksgiving. When she was finished, Perth began shoveling food into her mouth.

"You one of those churchgoers?" Perth asked between bites.

Gloria thought Perth was eating amazingly fast for someone with a lip the size of a hot dog but said nothing, only nodded.

"Not surprised. You seem like one of them."

"One of them?"

"Yeah. Most church people I meet are real nice. Real helpful."

Gloria's eyes narrowed. "Don't try to manipulate me, Perth. I've already told you you can't stay. You're here for a meal only. As soon as I can figure out what to do with you, you're leaving. Understand?" Even though Gloria could see that it hurt, Perth smiled anyway.

"Now, don't get mad, but you *are* nice. And I'm not trying to get anything from you. Okay?"

Gloria ate her omelet and watched Perth eat hers. She had decided Perth reminded her of Maggot Mary from the sixth grade, a transient who had only stayed at Appleton Elementary for five months and never came back. The kids swore Mary had maggots in her pockets from carrying rotten vegetables when she and her family harvested the local farms, but Gloria never saw any. She remembered feeling sorry for Mary, but not because the kids teased her. The kids teased Gloria too. And not because she was plain—so plain that nobody ever mentioned her plainness, as though Mary didn't even have a face. But it was not having a home, and the need to move from place to place to find work that bothered Gloria. Even Gloria had a home, could stay in one place where she knew what time Sam Hidel locked his grocery at night, and that the Full Gospel Tabernacle had two Sunday services, and that the mayor's first name was Wilbert, but everyone called him Bert because he hated the name Will even more than he hated the name Wilbert.

But Mary had taught Gloria one thing. There was always someone worse off than you.

"How old are you, Perth?" Gloria asked, spearing the last piece of her omelet.

"Seventeen." The teen ripped into the whole wheat toast and flinched. Crumbs fell down the front of her sweatshirt as she eyed Gloria. "Surprised? I bet you thought I was younger.

Everyone does. That's cause I have no shape. Well . . . practically. That's it, right?"

Gloria suppressed a smile. She had had a figure much like Perth's when she was seventeen. Had only moved up one size from her first bra, while most of her classmates had moved up three. "No . . . it wasn't because of that," she said slowly. "It's your face. You have a young face."

"Yeah. Well, I guess it won't look so young if I keep falling on it. Mom used to call me clumsy. Guess she was right. I'm just glad I didn't break my nose. I worry about that . . . breaking my nose. It's kinda stupid, I know. I shouldn't worry about something that stupid. It's just that if I ever were to break it I don't know what I'd do, 'cause we don't have the money to get it fixed."

"Does this happen often? With your father, I mean?"

Perth shrugged. "Dad drinks sometimes. He can't help it—"

"You shouldn't make excuses for him. That doesn't help anybody." Funny how it was easy to be wise when it came to other people's problems.

"You still think you know it all, don't you? But you don't know anything about my dad. He's not like that . . . he's not like what you think. He's really kind and nice and . . . and . . . he never used to be like this." Perth hung her head. "He's changed a lot. Sometimes I can't stand watching him hurt, so I go out, somewhere . . . anywhere. I've just got to get out, get away. I can't take seeing him like that. I sleep on the street a lot then. But I feel guilty. I don't like leaving him. I never know what will happen. I should be there for him, but I can't. Not all the time. Maybe . . . maybe it's because I'm scared he's gonna die right there in front of me, or that I'll wake up in the morning and find him dead on the couch. It really eats at me. Sometimes I think I'm going crazy."

"What about your mother?"

"I don't have one. Not anymore."

Gloria felt an odd, lonely feeling. "How about friends? Can't you stay with them?"

"I don't have any friends. It's easier that way. No questions. No explanations."

Gloria had the biggest urge to put her arms around this unhappy, friendless girl. Instead, she pushed her empty plate away and folded her hands on the table. She hoped she looked calm because she felt an anger rage inside her that wanted to vent itself by watching the police drag Perth's father, the child neglecter, the drunkard, to jail. "Maybe you should call the police."

"No way!" Perth put down her fork. "You think I'd do that to my dad?"

"You can't continue like this . . . running from home, sleeping on the street. The police can contact the right agency. Get both you and your father some help."

"You don't understand. You just don't understand."

"Then explain it to me."

Slowly, Perth picked up her fork and began pushing the remaining food around on her plate. "He never used to drink . . . that is, not like this. He'd have a few beers once in a while. But never like this. Then Mom had a stroke. A bad one. She was in the hospital a long time . . . with an IV, a respirator, heart monitor, you name it. The insurance paid some of the bills, but Dad had to pay the rest. He said it wiped out all of his savings . . . which was supposed to go for my college, in case I was ever able to get into one. Anyway, I didn't care about that. I just wanted Mom to get well and come home." Perth snorted. "You gotta be careful what you wish for. Mom finally came home, and two days later she had another stroke and died."

Gloria brought her hand to her mouth. "I'm . . . so sorry."

"Yeah. Everybody's 'so sorry'."

Gloria leaned over the table as far as she could. "I *am* sorry. But, Perth, that doesn't excuse what your father's doing. He has no right to neglect you. Not now, not when you need him most."

"He can't help himself."

"Perth, stop it. Stop excusing—"

"He's in so much pain all the time. That's why he drinks."

"You're in pain too. You've lost someone you loved too. But you don't get drunk."

Perth glared at Gloria, then cursed. "You're really stupid, you know that? You think my father drinks because he lost my mom? Yeah, he was wrecked—we both were—but that's not why he drinks. He drinks because of the pain. It's so bad I hear him crying sometimes. And I've never heard Dad cry—except when Mom died."

"What pain are you talking about?"

"He's got bone cancer."

Gloria sank in her chair. *Cancer.* That's how her father had died. She remembered how bad he was at the end, so doped up because of the pain. "Aren't the doctors giving him anything?" she said. "And what about radiation and chemo?"

Perth shook her head. "He's had all that. There's nothing more the doctors can do. The cancer's inoperable. He's on pain pills, but sometimes the money doesn't last till the end of the month. We don't have much. We've sold everything. Even our nice house. We live in a basement now. And the unemployment checks only stretch so far. If Dad runs out of his medicine, there's no money to get more. Then he'll pick up a cheap bottle of booze and use that. What do you expect him to do? He can't go without anything. The pain's too bad."

"You said he had insurance. It has to pay some of the—"

"Dad lost his insurance when he got fired. When Mom was in the hospital with the stroke, he took so much time off, his boss fired him. He didn't even know he had cancer then. He's not one to complain, but I'd see him taking a lot of aspirin for the pain in his legs and arms, in his back. He said it was because he was working too hard. When he found out what it really was, the cancer was too far gone. But he did what he could. Paid for the chemo and radiation and doctors' visits by doing odd jobs. But he's too sick now, too weak, and in too much pain. And unemployment barely covers the rent and utilities and medicine. I do what I can. I baby-sit and clean apartments for food money, and when that's not enough I . . . steal."

Gloria put her elbows on the table and cradled her head with her hands. "What happens when unemployment stops?"

Perth looked down at the table without saying a word.

"There's got to be an agency that can help."

Perth shook her head. "Dad won't go. He's afraid the state will take me away and put me in a foster home or something. I won't be eighteen for six months. He's trying to hold on till then. I know when I turn eighteen, Dad's just gonna give up and die."

Gloria studied Perth's face, studied the tearless old eyes. Was this an act? She had seen Perth in action before. Had seen how quick she was on her feet. How easily she could lie.

"Are you telling me the truth, Perth? Or is this all a story?"

At first Perth looked stunned. Then she looked angry. When anger gave way to sadness, Gloria had her answer. "I'm sorry. But I had to ask."

"Yeah."

Slowly, Gloria reached over and covered Perth's hand with hers. "I can't even begin to imagine what you've gone through. And I can't believe a company could be so heartless as to fire an employee for taking off to visit his sick wife."

"Yeah, well Dad said Tucker Mattson was just looking for a reason to fire him, and when Mom got sick, he finally found it."

"*Tucker Mattson?*" Gloria felt her blood rush to her toes.

"You should see how white you look. Don't tell me you know him?"

"I work for him," Gloria said, her voice like vapor. Tucker might not be all she had originally thought, but surely he was fair-minded and professional? Surely he wouldn't knowingly do something this heartless to one of his employees? There had to be an explanation.

"Maybe your dad was mistaken. He was under a lot of pressure with your mother being sick, and he was sick himself. Maybe he can't remember things anymore . . . or maybe what he remembers isn't really the way it was. I know you don't want to face that possibility, but it could be true. Maybe Mr. Mattson had a good reason for firing him. Maybe your dad just wasn't doing his job."

Perth snorted with laughter. "My dad's the best foreman there is. Everyone says so. Eckerd's been popping its seams for years, with all the construction going on. At one time, Dad had so many job offers he used to tell Mom he should put them all in a hat, close his eyes, and just pick one. Everyone wanted him. He has a good reputation in this town. A year ago, he went to work for Mattson Development, to head this new la-de-da Eckerd Estates. Mom and Dad used to talk about it a lot before she got sick. Dad always used the best contractors, followed code to the letter. But Mattson wanted him to cut corners. Do stuff Dad didn't want to do. I don't know the whole story, only that Mattson and Dad argued all the time about it."

Gloria shook her head. "I don't believe it."

"Well, believe it," Perth said sarcastically. "You're working for a crook. That's what Dad called him. A crook."

Chapter Six

SOMETIMES, GLORIA, YOU DON'T have a brain in your head.

Gloria tucked the covers carefully under Perth's shiny pink chin and gently pushed aside a clump of damp hair. The teen looked as if she had been plunged into a sink and rubbed over a washboard a dozen times with her squeaky-clean hair and skin still rosy from the shower. She looked so young and innocent, so childlike. The cotton floral pj's Gloria had loaned her added to the picture—the way they hung at the shoulders, the way the sleeves kept catching Perth's thumbs whenever she moved her hands. So did the talc—hidden under the nightclothes and coming visible only around the collar, where it formed a pale ring under Perth's chin and made her smell like a freshly powdered baby.

But Perth *was* a child, a child forced too early, too abruptly, into the unsympathetic world of adulthood. And Perth's face said she was glad to be a child again, to receive care instead of giving it, even if it was only for this one night.

You don't have a brain in your head.

Yes, yes, I know, Gloria's thoughts answered the phantom voice that had been whispering in her ear for over an hour. *But what was I supposed to do, let the girl sleep in the streets?*

She gave the covers a final pat, then said, "Good night." When she saw Perth's swollen lips part in a smile, when she saw that look, that old-woman's look in Perth's hazel eyes swallowed up by youth and hope, albeit only for a moment, Gloria finally silenced the voice.

"You're really phat, you know that?" Perth said, closing eyes heavy with sleep and curling like an inchworm on the couch.

"Fat?" Gloria laughed. "Most people say I'm too thin."

"No . . . *phat*—cool, neat."

"It's just for one night. Remember that."

"Yeah." A clump of hair fell across Perth's left cheek, then her breathing settled into a slow, even rhythm.

Gloria resisted the urge to push the newly fallen strands of damp hair from Perth's bruised cheek and flicked off the lamp on the end table instead. Then she quietly tiptoed to her bedroom, knowing that Perth was already asleep.

Gloria collapsed into bed, omitting the flossing, the night cream, the one hundred brush strokes to her hair. It had been a long, long day. Her tortured body refused to move another inch. Refused even to let Gloria pull the covers around her shoulders. So she lay there like a cadaver and closed her eyes. But instead of sleep, her mind formed its own insurrection by bringing up topics that could occupy hours. What was she going to do about Perth? And what about Tucker? Could he really be the crook Perth had called him? And what about her mother? She hadn't called her in days.

Not now. Go to sleep.

She concentrated on her breathing, listened to the sound of air being drawn into her nostrils, felt her chest heave upward, then the sound of expelling air, then felt her chest retracting. Finally, her breathing began to slow—as though air wasn't the important thing anymore. It seemed she barely breathed now and could feel herself slip into an ethereal vapor, weightless and floating. And then a voice. Oh, what a voice—sweet like maple syrup poured over freshly fallen snow—calling, calling her name.

"Gloria."

She couldn't open her eyes, even though she tried with all her might.

"Who the Son has set free is free indeed."

Gloria tried again to open her eyelids, but they felt like they had been stitched shut.

"I've led captivity captive."

Gloria had a sense of someone sitting on her bed and tried to rise up, but her body remained suspended in the place of twilight and shadows and refused to obey. "Jesus?" she said, but couldn't hear her own voice, couldn't open her eyes, couldn't lift her head, which remained denting the pillow like lead. She prayed that the sweet gentle voice would go on forever or at least until she could respond.

"Fear not, I am the Potter, you are the clay." The voice sounded almost like laughter now—happy, lilting, tender laughter, so tender she wanted to weep. *"And you are fearfully and wonderfully made."*

She heard herself gasp, then struggled to sit up, to open her eyes, to see the face of the tender lover who sat so near. By sheer willpower she moved her arms that felt like anchors at her side and propped herself on the pillow. Then fighting the pull on her eyes, that horrible, horrible pull on her eyes, Gloria finally squinted them open.

"Jesus?"

Had she been dreaming? No. It was too real. Surely it was no dream.

"Jesus?" she called out again into the darkness and was answered only by the thumping of her own timid little heart.

∽❦❦∼

She had put it off long enough. Now she couldn't think of any more excuses. Slowly, she dialed the phone, then swiped at the toes of her old scuffed brown pumps with a paper towel. She had two blisters on her right foot and three on her left from her new shoes. Today, she'd give her feet a break and wear the old ones. While she listened to the phone ring, Gloria buffed both shoes, then impatiently tossed the soiled towel into the tall kitchen garbage pail. Where was Mother? Gloria glanced at the clock. She rarely left the house this early.

"Hello?" a sleepy voice finally answered.

"Mother! Thank goodness. I wanted to call before going to—"

"Gloria, is something *wrong?*"

"No, not at all." How silly that both of them jumped to a worrisome conclusion. She must be more like her mother than she thought . . . or wanted. "Did I wake you up?" Even now she found no easing of her nerves. Her mother was an early riser, except when she was sick. "You feeling okay?"

"Yes, I stayed up late. Watched one of those old Gloria Swanson movies."

"Oh . . . well, sorry to be calling so early, but I wanted to get you in case it's late when I come home—"

"You really frightened me for a second. I mean, you *never* call. What am I supposed to think? I had you mangled somewhere, or your apartment robbed, or—"

"Mother, I don't have much time. I'm on my way to work and just wanted to say hello."

"Well, you've said it."

"And to tell you I love you." Gloria pictured her mother with those multicolored sponge rollers in her hair, with her satin Victoria's Secret loungewear, her matching two-inch high heel slippers trimmed with feathers.

"Well . . . you sure have a funny way of showing it. Leaving without a word and—"

"Mother, *please* let's not go over this again." Gloria bit into her thumb. "I want us to be friends."

"Friends you can find on the street."

"Can't we call a truce?" Gloria glanced at her watch, then slipped on the jacket of her chocolate-colored suit. "Can't we be civil?"

"Gloria, I didn't start this. You always think I'm the difficult one."

"I never said that."

"You don't have to. You don't know what it's like being a mother. Just wait till you have children and walk the floors at night, dry their tears, bandage their cuts. Wait till you pour everything you have into them, teach them all you know . . . just so they can leave you. Just wait . . ." Her mother's voice broke.

"I'm sorry if I've hurt you. But I'm not a child anymore, Mother. I think you need to understand that."

"You always were difficult, Gloria. But I suppose if I were to compare you to Tracy . . ."

"Mother, I want you to take down my phone number and address—"

"Do you have any idea how embarrassing it was to tell Virginia that I didn't even know my own daughter's address or that I couldn't call you when I wanted because I didn't have your number?" Gloria heard a rustling noise and knew her mother was next to the junk drawer, the one with the screwdrivers and hammer, the pack of red thumbtacks, a roll of garden string, pads of paper, and tons of untried recipes from *Better Homes & Gardens* she was saving for when she got off her perpetual diet. It was the only space in the house allowed to be a mess.

"You ready?" Gloria said when all was quiet. "Yes."

Gloria rattled off the information. When she was finished, she looked at her watch. "I've got to run, Mother. It's late."

"When will you be home?"

"I'm not sure."

"How will I know when to call?"

"Call whenever you want. If I'm home, I'll answer." After Gloria hung up, she slung her purse over her shoulder, opened the cabinet door where she kept food, then quickly pulled two Domino sugar cubes from the box and flew out the door.

Gloria clutched the edges of her suit jacket and brought it tighter around her chest. The sky overhead, what she could see of it, looked like the gray ash left in a fireplace after a nice blaze. A cold front had come in from Canada and now laid in a trough across the entire United States, covering Eckerd City. People at work had been talking about it for days. This was just the beginning, they said. Winter in Eckerd this year was sure to be a beaut. Then came the talk about global warming and how eventually everyone was going to crisp up like French fries, so they might as well enjoy a few cold winters here and there.

Then Mr. Simms, the married man with the eye for the ladies, the one who had begun stopping by Gloria's desk every afternoon before his three o'clock break, had said not to put too much store into global warming, since less than thirty years ago the National Academy of Sciences echoed what many scientists for the thirty-five years prior to 1975 believed—namely, that we were on the threshold of another great ice age. Mr. Simms claimed that since global warming became all the rage, more and more scientists were buying into it to get their share of the funding dollars. Gloria didn't understand how Mr. Simms, an accountant, knew so much about climatology, but the topic hadn't really interested her, and she had spent the time thinking how it was getting too chilly to walk the streets in just a suit. She had made a mental note to ask Beth Price the best place to get a bargain on outerwear, then tried to calculate how many weeks it would take to save enough money for a trench coat.

Now, as she braced herself against the cold autumn Eckerd morning, she thought maybe she wouldn't bother with the trench coat after all. Her beige cloth winter coat was shabby and too thin for the kind of winter they were talking about. She'd need something new, something heavier. And that would take priority over a trench coat.

Her brown scuffed pumps clicked against the smooth concrete sidewalk that was starting to feel familiar beneath her feet. Familiar. Not quite the same thing as comfortable, but still, familiar was good. Gloria suddenly felt a strange euphoria, a giddiness that actually made her smile at the first passerby. She noticed, with amusement, that all the garbage pails leading to the bus stop were still there. None had been ripped from their bolted platforms during the night. And she didn't feel as afraid as she normally did. What was Pratt Parkway, anyway? Just a street like any other. Only maybe wider, busier. People on Pratt Parkway were doing what people all over the country did, indeed all over the world—dressing for work, opening their shops, preparing for one more day. They had family and friends and problems, like everyone else.

We all have to walk down that runway, Gloria.

The bus had already pulled next to the curb, and the last person was getting on. Gloria quickened her pace but felt no anxiety, no panic that it would pull away without her. Rather, she felt so free, like a puff of steam escaping from a boiling kettle. Free to rise and rise and rise. The exhilaration was so new that Gloria didn't quite know what to make of it. Freedom. Didn't she just read about that? Or hear something about it . . . it was so familiar . . . Familiar.

Her foot hit the first step of the bus just before it jerked away from the curb.

"I told you before, this bus don't wait for nobody," the bus driver growled.

In almost one motion, Gloria leaped up the second step of the moving bus, then dropped her exact change into the slot box.

"Beautiful day, Mr. Norton," she said, ignoring the scowl on the driver's face.

Gloria bounced along Pratt Parkway, thinking about Perth, about the pile of bedding folded neatly on one end of the couch where Perth had left it. She still couldn't believe she had let the teen spend the night. But Perth had been true to her word. She was neat, quiet, and had no obnoxious habits that Gloria could detect. She had left early for school, to do homework before class began, with only a piece of toast and small glass of milk for breakfast. Maybe Gloria shouldn't have said she was on a budget because she had to practically stand on her head just to get Perth to take the toast and milk. Perth wasn't such a bad kid. She was nice, actually.

But if Perth showed up tonight, what was Gloria going to do?

Gloria would just act natural. Pretend nothing was wrong. That she hadn't left Tucker at the Tomb last night. That he hadn't been too drunk to take her out to dinner. That Perth hadn't called him a crook. She'd just go to her desk and do her job as though it was a normal day.

The first person she saw was Jenny Hobart, who looked less than perfect this morning with that pinched forehead.

"What's wrong?" Gloria asked, stopping at her desk.

Jenny pointed to Tucker's office. The door was closed. "He came out a second ago . . . yelling." She gave Gloria a worried look. "I like to stay far away when he gets like that."

Gloria walked down the hall toward her cubicle, thinking it was going to be another long day. Before she could even put her purse in the large side drawer of her desk, Beth appeared.

"He's been asking for you for the past ten minutes. Says he wants to see you, *immediately.*"

Gloria's pumps tapped awkwardly against the highly polished granite floor. How quickly courage became the coward. Only a minute ago she had felt so confident, so carefree. Now look at her—palms sweating, tongue glued to the roof of her mouth like a glob of peanut butter. She purposely slowed her pace, giving herself time to rehearse what she'd say. *I'm sorry I ducked out on you. I should have let you know, but you were having such a good time I didn't want to tear you away from your friends.* All half-truths. She felt her stomach lurch. *Okay, lies.* Jesus couldn't be too happy with her right now. Even so, she rehearsed her script yet again as she opened the office door.

But the instant she saw Tucker, huffing and puffing like a steam engine around that outrageous office of his, Gloria's mind went blank. It took all her strength to keep from sticking one of her fingers into her mouth.

"For years Tracy's been telling me how good you are with colors and design, so take a look at these and tell me what you think." Tucker tossed a folder across the desk. "I just want an honest opinion before I go blowing my top with Precision."

Hesitatingly, Gloria picked up the folder. It was heavy brown matted paper—and reminded her of the grocery bags in Sam Hidel's store—with white glossy letters that read "The Estates" on the first line and "Phase II" on the second. Courier, probably 40 or 42. The folder opened like a notebook with flaps on both sides that contained pullouts. From the left flap, Gloria withdrew a sheet of white paper that listed six different models, with a descriptive blurb under each. At the end of the description was the price. The right flap contained another paper with a small layout of each of the six models. The flaps themselves were covered with information about The Estates, and on the back of the folder were two pictures: one, a smiling couple holding tennis racquets, filled the top half of the back; the other, a map of the area and directions on how to get to The Estates, filled the bottom.

"You *really* want to know what I think?"

"I thought I already said that." Tucker fingered his silk tie, looking irritated.

"Well, then . . . in a word—terrible."

"Exactly!" Tucker slapped the desk with his hand. "Beth tried to tell me it was fine. That it did the job. But I want it to do more. I want people to get excited when they see it. I want them to think *wow*. This . . ." He gestured toward the open folder with disgust. "This thing is dull as dirt."

Gloria shuffled her feet. "Maybe . . . I'm wrong. If Beth thinks—"

"She didn't design it, so relax. No one's blaming her. But Precision Printing is going to get an earful. I paid plenty for those idiots to create this horror."

"Didn't they submit proofs?"

"Yes." Tucker's face reddened, just as it used to when he'd mess up one of his fighter models because he failed to read the directions. "But I was at The Estates when they came and I gave a verbal okay. They've done plenty of jobs for me before. I figured they knew what I was looking for." He laughed. "Now who's the idiot?"

Gloria could see his anger fizzle, like the last dregs of an Alka-Seltzer. It made her hopeful that he wouldn't mention last night.

"Take a seat." Tucker pointed to the empty leather chair.

Without a word Gloria sat down. *Oh, boy, here it comes.*

"If you were designing this folder, what would you do?"

Her tongue suddenly felt like a beached jellyfish, all spread out and helpless. This was not the question she had braced for. "Well . . . ah . . . first I'd have to know more about The Estates. Is it on a golf course? Are they houses or condos? Any swimming pools? Tennis courts? You know . . . things like that."

Tucker picked up an acrylic ruler, the kind that had little

odd-looking shapes engineers used to alter floor plans, and began tapping it on the desk. It made Gloria think of the times they used to play school. Tucker was always the principal. Even back then, he wanted to be top dog.

"It's a retirement community, very upscale. Six different models of houses, all facing a huge man-made lake. And yes, there are tennis courts, a swimming pool, clubhouse, the works."

"Well, then . . . I . . . guess I'd put the money into a neat folder cover—three- or four-color, coated stock—maybe show a lake, a sunset, a small sailboat. Below that, *The Estates* in gold foil."

Tucker's eyes stared past her, expressionless, refusing to yield any reaction. *He probably hates the idea.* She swallowed, then continued. "Ah . . . then I'd add two or three glossy pages inside. I'd sprinkle it with pictures of people riding bikes, maybe a grandfather with his grandchildren fishing, people swimming in a pool. And the text would talk up the advantages of living in a community. Maybe I'd start with something like, 'Come home to The Estates,' since a lot of retired people may not have family close by and need that sense of belonging . . . that sense of home."

She wished Tucker would say something. Only his eyes spoke, telling her he was listening, that he was taking in every word. "Then . . . well . . . I guess I'd keep the back flap and use six . . . no, seven pullouts. Six would be large, maybe twenty by fifteen folded in fourths, gloss coated and also in color, maybe two-color—one pullout for each of the different models. It would have the name of the model, the artist's rendition of the home, the specs. The seventh pullout would be a single sheet of paper . . . maybe blue or green, with the names of each model, square footage, taxes, and price. This way, the price sheet can be changed without much cost."

Gloria couldn't think of anything more to say, so she just stopped talking. But she felt good. Inside, she felt really good. *Tucker was asking her advice.*

"Maybe you should start designing some of my PR pieces."

Of course he was kidding.

"For the money I paid Precision—it frosts me. You certainly couldn't do any worse. I was on the phone with Precision for over an hour telling them what I wanted. And here, in only minutes, you've grasped the concept perfectly. So what do you say? Want to try it? Do a few of the marketing pieces? If they're good, I'll give you more. You'll still work for Beth, but I'll add to the mix, and in time, who knows, this could be a whole new career path for you. I'll even throw in a nice raise. Maybe even a new title. I think this'll be good for you, Gloria, good for both of us. What do you say?"

"I . . . can't. I don't know QuarkXPress . . . that's what most of the printers use now to design camera-ready material."

Tucker laughed. "So learn it. Beth can book you into a class. But for now, this morning, in fact, I want you to go to Precision and have them design exactly what you've just described. Beth can give you some blurbs about The Estates. Don't leave Precision until they have it right, then bring me back a copy for final approval. Tell them if they want my business, I need these folders tomorrow or in forty-eight hours at the latest."

Gloria's color drained. "You want *me* to tell them that?"

"Yes." Tucker tapped his ruler against the desk impatiently. "And, Gloria . . . let me say again how happy I am you're here. I knew you'd be good for this company. Good for me."

Gloria bit her lip. This was all a tad overwhelming, frightening even, but one nice thing—Tucker didn't seem angry about last night.

Gloria walked the half-mile to Precision Printing instead of taking a cab, as Tucker suggested. Her funds were low, and besides, she'd be too embarrassed to hand Beth a voucher for cab fare. She had never walked this far down Sixth Avenue before.

She stopped at the corner of Sixth and Montgomery to get her bearings, right where Patty's Palace, an upscale department store for women, took up half a block. When Gloria first heard the name Patty's Palace, she thought it sounded more like a bordello than a department store. Then someone told her about its tainted past, about how Patty Fabrio, a former mistress of Hugo Pratt's, was promised a palace by Pratt. He kept his word and built it right on Sixth Avenue. Now it was a place where you could buy fifty-dollar French panties and bras and a whole bunch of other expensive items from around the world. Patty Fabrio was dead now, along with Hugo Pratt, but the Palace had been incorporated and was still going strong.

Oh, the things you heard in an office.

What would the office start saying about Gloria, she wondered? When they heard she was going to start designing marketing materials? Would they call her a no-talented upstart? Or worse? Well, let them. She was used to meanness, to being called names. It didn't hurt like it used to.

She finally stopped in front of a large building with marble scrollwork and a brass-and-glass door, and overhead, chiseled in marble, the name Precision Printing. Beth had called Precision the premier printer in Eckerd City. How did Gloria have the audacity to come into a place like this and start giving orders?

Oh, Lord, please help me.

With a folder of The Estate blurbs tucked under one arm,

her purse dangling from another, and a stomach in knots, Gloria pulled on the solid brass handle that looked like a lion's paw and stepped inside. The first thing she noticed was how clean it was. Not filled with the boxes and clutter she saw through the E-Z Printing window on Pratt Parkway. The next thing she noticed was that it looked more like an office than a print shop. Ten oversized desks, each separated by brown partitions, filled a large room. An HP computer sat on a stand near each desk, and on the desktop: a scanner, laser printer, and an ultrathin nineteen-inch monitor. The shop was amazingly quiet, and Gloria decided that the actual presses had to be on another floor.

A young man sat at the first desk, his hands, like crabs, scurrying over the keyboard. She cleared her throat, then in a calm voice asked him if she could see the manager.

Mr. Smallie was tall, dark, and not very handsome, but he had a smile that instantly put Gloria at ease. He ushered her into his office, which turned out to be moderately sized, sparsely decorated, and well lit. A room, which Gloria could tell, was actually used for work. He gestured for her to take a chair while he himself remained standing.

"What can I do for you, Miss Bickford?"

In one breath she blurted out the problem, then watched him push aside several sketches on his desk and stretch out his hand for her folder. Without a word, she handed it to him and watched as he spread it across his desk. Along with The Estates blurbs, the file contained the folder Precision had made for Mattson Development.

"I see what you mean," he said after a significant silence. Then he left the room and returned a few minutes later. "I just spoke to our new man. He's actually in training and shouldn't have been given this job. But all our veterans were swamped, and it . . . well, it was just one of those things. Tell Mr. Mattson,

Precision always stands by their work. This time I'll make sure one of our senior designers handles it."

Gloria straightened in her chair, not liking the disadvantage of the tall Mr. Smallie standing over her. "Actually, Mr. Mattson has asked me to design it. I only need someone to lay it out in Quark."

"I'm afraid that's impossible. We either work with camera-ready material, or we do the designs ourselves. Mr. Mattson knows that."

"Mr. Mattson was very emphatic. I am to do the design." Gloria rose from her chair. "But if that's not possible, Mr. Mattson will look elsewhere."

"Sit down, Miss Bickford. Please."

Gloria watched Mr. Smallie take his own seat, then followed suit. She balled her hands so he wouldn't see them shake. *Please, God, don't let me blow this.*

"You could do a rough draft, then bring it to us in a day or two, and we could work off that."

Gloria shook her head. "Mr. Mattson would like the new folders within twenty-four hours." She watched Mr. Smallie tent his fingers, watched his cheeks balloon as he exhaled.

"Even if by some miracle we could get the new design camera-ready today and print it tomorrow, the ink wouldn't be dry enough to collate and staple the folders."

Gloria leaned closer to the desk. "I see your problem, and I'll tell Mr. Mattson his request was unrealistic. I'll tell him it'll be forty-eight hours before the job can be done."

Mr. Smallie gathered up the scattered papers and neatly placed them in Gloria's folder. "Yes . . . I suppose forty-eight hours is doable. I suppose I don't need to point out our policy stating customers must proof all work before it is printed. Had Mr. Mattson done that, it would have saved headaches on both sides."

"I'll personally see that Mr. Mattson approves the new design. Only . . . forty-eight hours is not much time. Maybe I should get started with the design."

"Yes . . . the design. I suppose, for Mr. Mattson, we could make an exception. Just this one time. Seeing how we botched the job. But just this one time."

Would wonders never cease?

Gloria nodded and noticed that Mr. Smallie's smile had disappeared.

Gloria could hardly believe she had a copy of the proofs in her hand and was heading back to Pratt Towers before closing. If Tucker hadn't gone to The Estates and was still in the office, and if he approved, then Mr. Smallie's presses could start running the job tomorrow. She couldn't believe how happy she felt. All day she had worked with Precision's top graphic designer. Had guided the designer in moving text, inserting photos, creating clipping paths and Beziers boxes, selecting fonts, points, Pantone colors for coated stock. Gloria had never had such a wonderful day, had never enjoyed her work so much. It was as if God had given her a taste of what work could be like—*should* be like.

And the folder was *beautiful.* She was proud of it and hoped Tucker would like it too. But the strange thing was she didn't really care. It was enough, truly enough, that she liked it.

Now how odd was that?

She whispered praises to God as she walked briskly down the street. There wasn't anything He couldn't do. Not one thing. The joy she felt made her want to get right down on her knees on the Sixth Avenue sidewalk in thanksgiving. But she kept walking, weaving in and out of the crowd like a ribbon in a young girl's hair. Even when the crowds got thicker and people began bumping carelessly into her, Gloria kept her joy. And when she finally looked up and saw Pratt Towers looming large and intimidating in front of her, her heart didn't even shrink. Through the doors and into the elevator she walked, suddenly realizing that for the first time she didn't feel the least bit scared entering the building.

Gloria didn't have to hear Tucker say it, she already knew by his face that he was pleased. He held up the proofs, one at a time, whistled, smiled, nodded his head, then looked at Gloria and grinned.

"Starting today, you've got yourself a new job description —Communications and PR."

Gloria turned white. *"Communications?"*

"Relax. I'm talking newsletters, flyers, that sort of thing. You'll take that whatever-it's-called course—"

"QuarkXPress."

"Right. Then I'll give you some projects to do. I'm looking to do a massive campaign—make The Estates a household name. Get the price I want by creating demand."

A slow smile spread across Gloria's face. *Oh, Jesus, could this really be happening?*

Gloria couldn't believe she was sitting across from him in this very expensive restaurant eating *fiori di zucca ripieni di salsiccia,* zucchini flowers stuffed with sausage, but Tucker—after viewing the proofs of the new folder and after Gloria had called Mr. Smallie with the approval—had insisted they go for a bite.

Though last night was never mentioned, Gloria was certain it was on Tucker's mind because he stressed they would go directly to the restaurant with no stops in between. And before dinner, he hadn't even ordered a cocktail, and dinner didn't include wine. She wondered if they'd ever talk about it, then realized Tucker probably remembered little of the evening. She finally decided to forget about it too.

She put one of the flowers into her mouth, tasted the Parmesan cheese and garlic, the rich extravirgin olive oil, and closed her eyes. She had never tasted food like this. Had never been in a restaurant like this, or sat across from a man like this. Even if she was nothing at all to Tucker, she was grateful. During her time at Precision Printing today, and now, eating Tuscany food, Gloria didn't feel so plain, so boring.

"You did a good job on that folder. I want to thank you again."

Gloria opened her eyes and frowned. Any minute now she was sure someone was going to wake her up and tell her it had all been a mistake; that she had to go back to being just Beth's assistant because she wasn't qualified for anything else. Certainly not for "Communications and PR."

And it was true.

"Gloria? Something wrong?"

Gloria shook her head. "What things do you think you'll want me to do first? In PR, I mean." She needed him to validate her, needed to reassure herself that it was for real.

"I was thinking a little monthly or biweekly newsletter. Something we could put in libraries, food stores, community centers—something that gives regular updates on The Estates, how it's progressing . . . What? You don't like it?"

Gloria was stunned how easily Tucker could read her. "Well . . . it's rather self-serving, don't you think?"

"That's the point, isn't it? Otherwise, why bother?"

With a big swig of iced tea, Gloria washed the last remnant of Parmesan cheese and garlic from her mouth, then braced herself. Already she sensed that bucking Tucker was a little like playing Russian roulette. Sure, there was an element of excitement, and it certainly got the adrenaline going, but you never knew when the bullet would come. But she was starting to like giving her opinion—liked the freedom in saying what was on her mind. "What you really need to do is something more community minded. Discuss what's going on at The Estates—the book clubs, the theater excursions, the barbeques." Gloria knew about these kind of retirement community activities because of Grandma Quinn's friends. "You know, 'Life at The Estates,' and maybe open a few of them to the public for one night so they can get a bird's-eye view of what a retirement community is all about. Even those who aren't old enough to be interested have parents who might be. It would give them a chance to see it firsthand. Maybe take away the fear of selling their house and changing their lifestyle." *Like Grandma Quinn.*

Tucker's face brightened. "That's good. That's *really* good. This is going to be better than I thought." Absently, he ran his finger around the rim of his water glass, then stopped and looked at her strangely. "I suppose we could use the newsletter to perform other community services. That would be good . . . a good thing to do."

"I suppose so," Gloria said slowly, not liking the look on Tucker's face. "What kind of service did you have in mind?"

"The Estates butt up against a wildlife preserve. So does the land stretching twenty miles east of us, paralleling Eckerd City. The environmentalists are concerned that too much building is going to disrupt the preserve, especially building in The Lakes area. Maybe our newsletter can talk about that issue, about the importance of the preserve and keeping a balance in nature, and what builders can do to help. And maybe it can talk about rethinking the development of *all* of that land. Maybe suggest that some of it be set aside."

Gloria couldn't quite put her finger on her feelings. Exhilaration? Yes. Tucker was discussing his business with *her*, asking *her* opinion. And that made her head swim. But the other feeling? What was that? Misgivings? What did he mean, "rethinking the development of *all* of that land"? Whose land was it, anyway? His? Hardly. More likely a competitor's. Look at him, so excited, so aglow with righteous indignation. Maybe Tucker cared about the community and the environment. Maybe he cared about the people in his city. And maybe he only cared about Mattson Development.

She let Tucker talk on, in that excited way of his, with his hands making circles in the air and little whooshing sounds, wishing she had the nerve to call him on it, wishing she had the nerve to bring up the subject of Perth's father, wishing she could really talk to him like a friend. Instead, she said nothing. Giving her honest opinion on a flyer was one thing. This was something entirely different.

As soon as Gloria unlocked the door of her apartment, she heard the phone ring. She really should get an answering machine. That way, the machine could take the calls when she wasn't up to doing it herself. She debated whether or not to answer, then remembered her promise to her mother. *Call whenever you want. If I'm home, I'll answer.* Well, she'd have to revise that commitment.

She walked slowly toward the phone, secretly hoping it would stop ringing by the time she got there. When it didn't, she reluctantly picked it up.

"Yes?"

"Is that any way to answer a phone?"

Gloria took a deep breath. "Hello, Mother." Tomorrow she was definitely getting one of those inexpensive answering machines at Wal-Mart.

"I've been calling you all night. It's so late to be coming home. I was worried."

Gloria slipped off her shoes. "I was having dinner with Tucker. A working dinner they call it. Tomorrow I'm getting an answering machine, so if I'm not here or it's too late to take a call, you can leave a message."

"You mean you're going to make me talk into one of those silly contraptions?"

Gloria heard her mother choke. "Only if you want to, Mother."

"I suppose that's a convenient way to screen your calls. To weed out the undesirables. I only hope you don't include me in that group."

"Of course not, Mother. But sometimes I get home late, like now. It's after ten and I'm exhausted. It's not always convenient talking on the phone."

"I suppose you're trying to tell me I shouldn't have called you so late. But you stay out till all hours. Make me worry all night. Make me call every half hour, thinking you're lying dead in an alley somewhere, and then you get annoyed because I'm calling a little late."

"I'm not annoyed at all, Mother. Only tired."

"Well, when are we going to talk about this situation? About you coming back to Appleton?"

"Not tonight, Mother. It's late and my alarm goes off very early in the morning."

"Gloria, we need to get this settled."

"It is settled, only you don't want to accept it."

"There's always room for discussion—for viewing other sides to get the right perspective."

"You mean *your* perspective, don't you, Mother?"

"I only want what's best for you."

"Then let me go and get some rest. We'll talk another time. I love you. Sleep well." Gloria hung up the phone. Any minute now it would ring, and it would be her mother, mad as a hornet. Would she answer it? She hadn't quite decided, when the phone did ring. It rang and rang and rang. Gloria stood rooted to the floor staring at it. When it finally dawned on her that her mother couldn't come over if she didn't answer it, she turned and walked toward the bedroom.

Gloria had just finished getting ready for bed, when there was a knock on the door. She glanced at her nightstand clock. 11:20. The first person she thought of was her mother, then laughed. It was impossible to get from Appleton to Eckerd City in an hour, even for someone as enterprising and determined as her mother. But if it wasn't Mother, then who could it be? Who would come to her door at this hour?

The knocking continued. "Who is it?" Gloria asked when she got to the door, her full weight pressed against it, as though afraid whoever was on the other side would force his way in when he heard her voice. "Who's there?"

"Miss Dobson, from downstairs."

Only a few days ago Miss Dobson had introduced herself

and welcomed her to the neighborhood. Then told her all about her two dogs: Mark Antony and Cleopatra, and about her insomnia.

What could she possibly want?

Hesitatingly, Gloria opened the door and saw the attractive older woman wrapped in a terry-cloth robe.

"There's a young girl downstairs knocking on the door, trying to get in. Been knocking for twenty minutes. I went to the door and told her if she didn't stop I was calling the police. I told her that through the door. No telling what folks are up to these days. You've got all kinds prowling the streets. So I told this skinny thing to scat, and she said she was here to see you. I say, 'At this hour?' She says to please get you. Well, I sort of felt sorry for the poor thing. Like a stray kitten, if you can picture her, all huddled against the door—hungry and cold looking. So I told her I'd check with you. I figured that's the least I could do as a God-fearing woman. Says her name's Bert. Now, what kind of name is that for a girl, I ask you? Unless, she's not a girl. But she looks like a girl to me. You know any girls named Bert?"

Gloria nodded. Who else could it be but Perth? But she didn't want to see Perth now. Didn't want to deal with her. Reluctantly, she stepped into the hall. Like it or not, this stray kitten had picked her. The only problem was, she didn't want to have to keep it.

Chapter Seven

LIKE A LILY AMONG THORNS
IS MY DARLING AMONG THE MAIDENS.
~◉ SONG OF SONGS 2:2 NIV◉~

IT HAD BEEN A GRUELING WEEK, and Gloria felt as if she were back in Appleton High. Not that she hadn't liked school. She loved it actually, even though she had only been a C student who had to work for everything she got. "You're like Clive McGreedy's old mule," her mother used to say. "You just keep at it until you get it done." It was true. Gloria wasn't afraid of hard work. But she wondered why it was that a mule worked so hard, only to be led back to an empty barn and forgotten. Nobody ever made a fuss over a mule. There was another reason she had never cared for her mother's callous comparison. McGreedy's mule was short and ugly with a nubby coat that looked like a worn-out chenille bedspread. The comparison certainly contrasted Gloria and her mother. If she was McGreedy's mule, then her mother was Sam Hidel's Andalusian, the prize Spanish stallion that had fetched dozens of ribbons and gold cups for Sam.

Not that she was bitter. No. She didn't think she was bitter. Although Jesus might say otherwise. But she just wished she understood the why of it. Why God had made her the mule and not the Andalusian. And why her mother never let her go to college. "You're just not college material," her mother said, and that was that. But Gloria knew plenty of kids with GPAs barely above hers who had gone. She would have liked that—college. Even if it meant studying twice as hard as anyone else.

And she could have done well. She proved it by taking a three-week QuarkXPress course in one week. She was sure it cost Tucker a fortune because it meant one-on-one instruction. That thought had added to her pressure of doing well. But she was determined to show Tucker his trust had not been misplaced. She worked diligently in class during the day, then took the 345-page manual home nights so she could read and reread sections that gave her trouble. She even made lists of questions to ask the instructor the next day. Sometimes she had ten questions or more.

By the end of the course, her instructor had pronounced her his best pupil all year. Gloria had harbored feelings of pride and hoped Jesus didn't mind.

Now, heading for Pratt Towers, Gloria was anxious to test all her newly acquired knowledge. There were still three hours left in the workday, and Gloria planned to use them creating templates for the newsletter. Throughout the week she had thought a lot about the design, had envisioned the masthead, the position and size of the company logo, the number of columns, the font. Everything that would bring it together in a visually appealing promo piece.

Tucker had insisted on talking regularly and staying in the loop, so Gloria had met with him three times in the past five days. He wanted her ideas. He gave his. He even had text for her—little interesting stories of people at The Estates that Beth Price had put together. He also had a piece for the *What's New in Eckerd* column that served as a type of community affairs section. But he had not told her the exact nature of the piece, except that it involved The Lakes area and the environmentalists.

The last time he had spoken to her, he had been very excited. Almost too excited. Gloria couldn't understand why a small newsletter was so important. And if it was, why was Tucker assigning a novice to do it? The whole thing seemed like one of Grandma Quinn's thousand-piece puzzles that just lay on the card table in little sections until she got tired of it and put it away. That's what Gloria had finally done. Put it away. There was no use in fiddling with it any longer. She had been given a promotion and a chance to do something she loved. What was it they said about looking a gift horse in the mouth?

She had a new purpose in life, a new significance swelling inside her she had never felt before. Now maybe she could do something useful. Really contribute. Surely all this had to be part of God's plan? Eckerd City, Mattson Development, the QuarkXPress course? It seemed so clear. God was building her up. She was going to be somebody. Somebody worthy of being loved.

Still . . . with all that was going on, Gloria couldn't understand why God was allowing Perth to claim so much of her time. In the past five days, she had come over twice to sleep. Gloria had been meaning to discuss this with Jesus, but with her Quark course and Perth, there hadn't been time. Obedience was essential, she knew that. But she couldn't see how Perth figured into the equation. Maybe it was just a lesson in patience.

Because as far as Gloria was concerned, Perth was a rather large intrusion into her life, and the sooner she could be rid of it, the sooner she could be about the Father's business.

Patience. Yes, that had to be it.

⚜ ⚜

Gloria stepped into the elevator, clutching her Quark manual and Stuart Hall spiral filled with notes. She paid no attention when a man in a pin-striped suit stepped in with her. She simply took her usual place in the left corner. The barely discernable motion of the upward pull and the quiet sedate interior made her realize how tired she was. Tonight she'd get to bed before twelve. Catch up on her sleep.

As the elevator glided upward, Gloria's attention was drawn to the man in pinstripes. His back was to her, but even so she saw how antsy he was, shifting from one foot to the other, smoothing down his already perfect hair, tugging at his jacket. She tried ignoring him, but soon she felt fidgety too. She took deep breaths to relax, but they must have been too loud, because the man turned, as though she had disturbed him.

Oh, no, it can't be!

She was glad her back was braced against the wall. Even so, she barely managed to keep her mouth from yawing open like a hinged door. This man, this fidgety little man, was the very one she had seen coming out of her neighbor's apartment.

What was he doing here?

The elevator stopped twice before reaching the sixteenth floor. People got on and off, but the nervous man remained. He had moved to the side and was separated from her by a woman with large permed hair. Even so, she could still see him, and she watched as he repeatedly fingered his collar or hair or jacket.

140

When the elevator finally stopped at the sixteenth floor, he stepped out.

She had heard the cliché about how small the world was and never gave it much thought. Until now. Only she couldn't believe it. Maybe things like this happened in Appleton but not in Eckerd City. Not in great big Eckerd City.

Who could he be coming to see, anyway?

She didn't have to wait long for the answer. She watched Jenny Hobart's fire-engine-red lips smile at the man, then watched her pick up the phone and say something in that quiet, perfectly enunciated way of hers. And even before Gloria reached the tiny cubicle next to Beth's office, she saw Tucker appear, walk over to where the man stood, and shake his hand. Then the two disappeared behind closed doors.

Gloria felt the veins in her temple throb as she plopped the manual and notebook on her desk. Jessica Daily—that was the name of the poor girl who had died in the apartment next to hers. Miss Dobson had told her that, along with the fact that the police had officially declared it a suicide.

As she booted up her computer, she thought about how she and that nervous man were probably the last two people to see Jessica alive. *Forget about it, Gloria. Just forget it.* She eased herself into her chair and watched the monitor brighten, then moved the mouse on the pad and absently clicked icons. Jessica Daily. Jessica Daily. The name began pulsing in her mind in sync with her throbbing temples. Jessica, Jessica, Jessica. With a start, Gloria remembered that was the name Tucker had whispered into her ear on the dark, crowded floor of the Tomb.

Jessica, I could dance with you all night.

Had he been talking about Jessica *Daily*? Gloria suddenly felt sick. What was the big deal? Even if it was the same girl— so what? Why should it bother her? Before she knew it, she shut down her computer and gathered her things. Then, without a word to anyone, she left the office.

~⊕ ⊕~

Gloria's head rested against the smudged window of the bouncing ECM bus as it sped down Sixth Avenue, away from Pratt Towers. The avenue was congested with cabbies and cars, and up ahead two construction trucks partially blocked the road, causing a traffic jam.

Silly Gloria. Silly, silly, Gloria. Why did she run away like that? Was it because she had put a face to someone Tucker might have loved? *C'mon, Gloria, aren't you over Tucker yet?* Or was it seeing that man again—of being reminded of the horror that someone as young and beautiful as Jessica Daily had taken her own life. Whatever the reason, her running out of the office seemed so foolish now.

She looked down at the traffic, at the cluster of men who stood near the construction trucks pouring smoking asphalt into a pothole. The sidewalk around them was crowded with people bustling by the gleaming graystone buildings. No one seemed to notice the carved stone doorposts or the ornate lintels of gray, veiny marble grapes or rushes or animal faces that decorated the entranceways. There was nothing like that back in Appleton. This city was just too big, too complex. She felt like such a bumpkin.

Silly, silly Gloria.

~⊕ ⊕~

The breeze played with Gloria's sleek brown hair as she walked slowly down West Meadow Drive. She was starting to

142

feel better. She was certainly glad to be here, on familiar, comfortable ground. As she passed one stately Victorian after another, she thought about Grandma Quinn and wondered what she was doing. Did Grandma miss her? Grandma's mind wasn't as sharp as it used to be. She was starting to forget things. Maybe she had forgotten Gloria altogether. No. That was silly. Almost as silly as running out of the office. Grandma Quinn was still sharp. Sometimes. Gloria really missed her, though. She wished she could call her, but Grandma never wore her hearing aid, so it was useless to try. Maybe she'd write Grandma another letter. A nice long one. She'd like to tell Grandma Quinn about Tucker and Jessica, about that man in the pin-striped suit, and see what she thought of it all.

Grandma Quinn had plenty of wisdom to spare. It was Grandma who first told her there was a God she could trust. Grandma had come to trust Him shortly after joining AARP, hardly in time to make any impact on Geraldine Quinn. Maybe if her mother, maybe if Geraldine had known the Lord, things would have been different. Maybe Gloria wouldn't be walking the tired streets of a tired neighborhood two hundred miles from Appleton, feeling confused.

Gloria pictured Grandma Quinn's face, with its chubby cheeks, red as Macoun apples. Grandma's face made you want to eat pancakes or egg noodles or strawberry jam. It also made you feel loved, just by a look or turn of the head or a smile. Even before Jesus, Grandma seemed to have a heart as big as Appleton. And everybody loved her too. But since Jesus, there was no end to that love or to Gloria's trouble, because that's when Mother stopped seeing Grandma Quinn, and that's when Mother had forbidden Gloria to see her too. "She's not right in the head," Mother would say, "not a fit example for a child."

Gloria had only been thirteen. A time when a girl could really use the love of a grandmother.

Gloria sighed. It was comforting to know that no matter what was happening in her life she still had the love of Grandma Quinn and Jesus. Only it would be nice if one of them were walking alongside her now, at least in a way she could see. When she saw Miss Dobson coming toward her in a white lace-collared blouse, gray cardigan, and linen gray slacks, pulled along by two shih tzus on red leather leashes, Gloria couldn't help but smile at God's sense of humor. Miss Dobson looked nothing like Grandma Quinn with her tall, stately figure, her gray-brown hair that looked frosted and fell in soft waves over her head, with her coordinated outfit and prissy dogs, but there was something comforting about her just the same, some hint of love brewing behind the aging green eyes and pink glossed lips.

"Hello, Miss Dobson."

Miss Dobson nodded and smiled and pulled her two "babies" to a stop. "She's here again." She gave Gloria an anxious look, then tried to rein in the two dogs straining against their leash.

"Who?"

"That child, that spindly young thing, Bert. At least it's not some ungodly hour of the night. Thank heavens. Scares a person almost senseless having someone pound on the door like that. In my day, young ladies would never think of doing such a thing. But what can you expect from a girl named Bert? Land sakes, those parents should be horsewhipped. Naming a girl Bert."

Miss Dobson turned from Gloria to make kissing noises to her dogs. When she did, Gloria caught a whiff of her gardenia perfume and wondered if her bottle wasn't three years old like Gloria's and not even close to empty. Was that why she had taken to wearing it while walking her dogs?

"She's so puny and all, that Bert," Miss Dobson said, turning back to Gloria. "You have to feel sorry for her. I didn't have the heart to chase her away. Leastways, this time she had the decency to come before dark."

Suddenly, one of the dogs tugged so hard it choked on its rhinestone collar and began coughing. Immediately, Miss Dobson slackened the leash, said her "good-byes" to Gloria, then continued down the street with her dogs, tidy and neat and in control of her world.

Gloria sighed. She was sighing a lot these days, almost as much as Hester Owens in seventh grade. Kids used to call her Hester the Pester because of her annoying sighs and because they couldn't come up with anything else that rhymed. Gloria sighed again. *Gloria the Pester.* Well, as long as she gave God control of her life, things wouldn't be the tidy, neat package Gloria was looking for. She had to understand that. It would always have its surprises and interruptions. It would always have its Perths. It was a picture she had not considered before, and one that disturbed her. But what was she going to do? What could she do? Leave Jesus as if He were a disappointing blind date? Who else had the words of eternal life?

She passed one of the maples heading toward her house. Curled-up leaves still clung tenaciously to the overhead branches, stretching to catch the late-day sun. Nature was always twisting and turning itself just to catch the light. How many times had she seen flowers turn from their natural arrangement to a new position facing the sun?

"What would You have me do, Lord?" she whispered, feeling her own little heart twist and turn within her. "I find Perth an inconvenience. There's got to be somebody who can help her more than I can. And honestly, Jesus . . . I don't want to stretch myself for her. I know You want me to be honest. Don't You?"

The wind rustled the leaves in the branches above her, shaking some free to float to the ground by her feet. She stepped over them, not wanting to crush them, and felt silly. If you got right down to it, the only purpose this old maple had was to serve its Creator and others with its fall beauty. When considered in that light, then the leaves were rather noble things. She stepped over the last one.

Noble things.

Not like her. She rarely thought about serving her Creator or others—honestly speaking. In fact, she rarely thought of serving—period. She suddenly pictured a barefoot Cinderella washing dishes in a dingy cold kitchen. Was that her concept of service? If it was, then she must be the most selfish of creatures. *Oh, Jesus, why can't I be more like You?*

She heard a dry leaf crunch beneath her foot. When her life was over, would she weep over her lost opportunities to serve God?

"I don't want to stretch myself for Perth," she repeated in a whisper. "But I don't want to live a life of selfishness. I *am* willing to be made willing. Help me, please, because I can't do it on my own."

Perth was sitting on the steps of the porch with a dreadful look on her face that made Gloria shudder.

"What's wrong?" Gloria watched tears stream from Perth's eyes.

"It's Dad . . . I think he's . . . dying . . . I mean I think he's going to die . . . soon. And I don't know if I can handle that. I mean . . . I really thought he'd last until I graduated. You know? Guess he just can't hold on anymore. I don't know how I'm going to handle . . ."

Gloria sat next to Perth and put her arm around her shoulders. Perth didn't have that pink scrubbed look anymore. She smelled and looked old and worn and grungy with her stringy hair and dirty jeans and oversized shirt. For a second, Gloria's eyes rested on Perth's shirt as she wondered if beneath it lay a belt laden with stolen goods. She resisted the urge to ask. "Do you have any family you could call? An aunt, uncle?"

Perth shook her head and brushed her eyes with fingers hosting dirt and who-knew-what-else under the nails.

"A close family friend?"

Again Perth shook her head.

Gloria gave Perth's shoulder a gentle shake. "You've got to think now. Surely your mother and father had a few good friends? Certainly *one* good friend you could call?"

"Dad had plenty of work buddies, but my mom was his best friend. My mom and I . . . we were his whole life."

"Then you've got to call an ambulance and get him to a hospital."

Perth crusted like two-day-old bread. "No! I promised Dad I wouldn't do that. There's nothing they can do except hook him up to machines; keep him alive when he shouldn't be. He didn't want that, and I promised. *I promised!*" Perth burst into tears.

"Okay. Okay." Gloria held the girl, one hand stroking her stringy brown hair. She was an awkward novice, totally unschooled in reaching out to others, and didn't know what to say, so she said nothing. She let Perth cry and continued holding her and stroking her head, hoping that was enough and knowing it wasn't nearly enough. *Oh, God, You have to help this girl.* And even as she offered up her silent prayer, she knew God had already answered it, in part, anyway. He had given Perth Gloria.

"What do you want me to do?" Gloria said after a while.

Slowly, Perth raised her head, her moist eyes wide like that of a doe caught in the headlights of a car. "I . . . was hoping you would help me."

Gloria's heart twisted and turned, and for a second she fought it. Finally she nodded. This is what God wanted—for her to reach out and help Perth. It was what He expected. She knew that as surely as she knew that without Grandma Quinn's love these past many years Gloria wouldn't have made it either. But what of her own heart's desires? She felt them being stepped on and crushed like that dried leaf on the sidewalk. But God wouldn't do that to her. It made no sense. Not after His promise. "What do you want me to do?" she repeated.

"Can you come home with me? I'm scared to go by myself. I'm scared I'll find him . . . dead."

Gloria rose to her feet and walked toward the front door. "I'll change and then we'll go."

In a flash, Perth was beside her, through the door, up the stairs, and into Gloria's apartment. Gloria headed for the bedroom and shouted for Perth to grab something to eat out of the refrigerator, but Perth just shouted back she wasn't hungry. Quickly, Gloria changed into a pair of jeans and T-shirt, not even bothering to hang up her brown Ann Taylor suit or put away her new brown Italian leather heels. She just left everything where it landed, then grabbed her purse, an apple, and Perth and raced out the door.

It was going to be a long weekend.

Gloria couldn't believe the smell. Vomit and body odor, mingled with the musty apartment air, almost made her gag. She tried not to cover her nose or make any retching noises for fear of upsetting Perth. Perth was already strained to the limit.

148

Quickly, Gloria assessed the room. Against one wall was a nine-teen-inch TV on a metal stand; against the opposite wall, a couch flanked by two metal folding chairs. Gloria saw a mound of bedding on the couch and headed toward it, navigating the empty bags of chips and gin bottles littering the floor like debris on a beach. Her hand reached for the blanket and stopped. What was she going to find? *Oh, God.*

Slowly, she pulled back the covers and saw only a cheap gray-and-blue striped sofa—the kind made up of six removable foam cushions, and not very comfortable for sleeping. She heard Perth gasp.

"He . . . he was here when I left." Perth began racing through the tiny apartment calling out as she went, "Dad! Dad!"

Gloria followed her into the kitchen, which was more of an alcove than a room. It consisted of one small refrigerator next to a small gas stove next to a four-foot-long countertop with a tiny stainless steel sink. The sink was piled high with dirty dishes. A Cheerios box sat on the counter, with stray Cheerios scattered around like bird droppings. Above and below the countertop were two cabinets, their doors open.

Next they went to Perth's room, where a twin box spring and mattress rested on a brown metal frame. The white sheets looked clean, but they had come untucked, leaving the mattress exposed. Gloria saw foam rubber protruding from a rip on the side. The only other furniture in the room was a four-drawer dresser against the far wall. Even so, there was barely enough room to get around. Through the open door of the closet, Gloria saw Perth's and her father's clothing crammed together. On the floor, against one wall, were neat stacks of shoes and books. But no sign of Perth's father.

Perth flew past Gloria and headed for the bathroom.

"Dad!" Perth's voice was high-pitched, shrill. She collapsed against the bathroom door.

Gloria gently nudged her aside and looked at Perth's father sprawled on the floor, unconscious and facedown in a puddle of vomit.

"Is he . . . dead?" Perth asked.

Gloria bent over the body, looking for signs of life, and saw his back rise in a shallow breath. "No." She turned to Perth. "Go fix your bed. It'll be easier to care for him there."

"Yeah . . . okay . . . sure." Perth disappeared.

Gloria pulled a towel from the rack, wet it, and began washing the vomit and blood from his face. It took a long time because she had to kneel down to wash him, then get up to wash the towel. She got up and down a half-dozen times before Perth returned.

"Okay. It's ready." Perth's voice sounded like a whisper.

"We'll move him to the living-room floor and change him there."

"Change him?"

"He's got vomit and blood all over his shirt, and he's . . . wet." Gloria watched Perth's eyes travel along her father's pants legs and saw Perth blink back tears when she realized they were wet with urine.

"I . . . think he's got a clean pair of pajamas in the dresser," Perth mumbled.

It took a while, but the two of them finally managed to lift the sprawled man up under his armpits and half drag, half carry him to the living-room floor. It took both of them to remove his wet clothes, do a sponge bath, then put on a mismatched pair of green-checkered and brown-striped pajamas. They struggled to get him into Perth's bed, and finally they succeeded by rolling him, like a sack of potatoes, onto the mattress.

The indignities suffered by the sick and helpless were many. Gloria had seen them firsthand. Had seen her father spoon-fed like an infant, had seen the dribble wiped from his mouth, had seen the catheter carry his urine from his body and into a plastic bag strapped to the end of the hospital bed, had seen his hospital gown open at the back, exposing thighs and buttocks no longer muscular and firm but thin—so thin you could see the bony protrusions of the pelvis—and covered by sagging yellow skin after his liver failed. She prayed Perth would be spared these sights, that God would be merciful and swift.

"He looks so peaceful, like he's asleep," Perth said, looking down at the unconscious man, relief written on her face.

Without a word, Gloria retrieved the two folding chairs from the living room, then placed one on either side of the bed. A second later, Perth was sitting down, her father's hand pressed between hers, soft murmuring sounds coming from her mouth. Gloria left the room, and for the next hour busied herself cleaning the small apartment, and never once thought about Cinderella.

~◊ ◊~

Gloria didn't know how long she had been sitting in the room with Perth, saying little, just watching the man's chest rise and fall, each time expecting it to be the last. The whole scene was uncomfortably familiar. Expecting death, wanting it or wanting the release it brings, but dreading it too. After what seemed like hours, Gloria finally rose from her chair. "Do you have a Bible?"

Perth nodded, went to the little four-drawer dresser she shared with her father and opened the top drawer. She came back carrying a small leather-bound King James. She handed it to Gloria.

"It's Mom's. She used to read it a lot. When we sold our house and moved here, Dad said he just didn't have the heart to part with it, even though he never used it himself. But it meant so much to her . . . to my mother."

Gloria carried the Bible to her folding chair and sat down. She wished she had known Jesus when her father was suffering like this. She would have liked to talk to him about her beautiful Savior. He would have listened too. At least she thought he would. But she didn't know Jesus then, so she hadn't told him. She had only sat in a chair like now and watched him slip away, little by little, until finally she was the only one left in the room. But maybe Jesus had introduced Himself. Maybe Jesus had bent over and whispered into her father's ear one night. Maybe during one of those long, lonely hospital evenings, he and Jesus had gotten acquainted. *Oh, how her heart hoped that was so.* With a sigh, she flipped to the Gospel of John and began reading in a soft, clear voice.

"'In the beginning was the Word, and the Word was with God, and the Word was God . . .'"

Friday night they took turns. One slept on the couch while the other sat by the bed. Sometimes both of them would be in the room: Perth holding her father's hand and Gloria reading the Gospel of John. Saturday morning Gloria gave Perth money to go to the small grocery around the corner and buy bread and cold cuts. When she returned, they ate bologna sandwiches and stared quietly at the walls. The rest of that day and night, and all Sunday and Sunday night, they followed the same routine, with the only exception being that sometimes Perth would read aloud from the Bible instead of Gloria.

At eight o'clock Monday morning, Gloria called Mattson Development and took her first day off. At 8:30 Perth's father, Stue Christopher McGregor, age fifty-nine, without ever waking up, departed for parts unknown. Only once before his death did he make any sound, a moan, when Gloria asked him if he wanted to accept Jesus. She had taken that as a hopeful yes and prayed the sinner's prayer—twice, because the first time she had forgotten the part about confessing he's a sinner—even though she knew Perth's father was in no condition to confess anything. Even so, Gloria threw them both on the mercy of God. Who knew what last-minute thoughts passed through the mind of a dying man? Repentance, confession, acceptance—all could be part of it.

And only once before his death did Perth think he moved—a slight twitch of his fingers—and that was after she had squeezed his hand. Perth later told Gloria that she believed with all her heart it was his response to her squeeze.

Did people see and hear what they wanted when watching a loved one die? Maybe. Gloria wasn't sure. All she knew was that she hoped and prayed Perth's father had accepted the Lord. When he moaned at just the right time, it was just as easy to believe he was asking her to pray with him as it was for her to believe he was moaning in pain. Because one thing she hoped with all her heart, one thing she wanted desperately to believe was that God was right there with every dying person who didn't know Him, giving them one last chance, one final invitation to the banqueting table. She didn't know how that stacked up with proper Appleton Full Gospel theology, but for her father's sake, she wanted desperately for it to be true.

Still, aside from the moan and the moving fingers, Perth's father had slipped quietly into eternity without the opportunity to say "good-bye," and Gloria could tell it grieved Perth deeply.

But Perth had said her good-byes. Throughout all those long hours of sitting by his bedside, she had stroked his hand, told him she loved him. She had even tried being brave by telling him she'd be all right, that she wasn't frightened about him leaving her. But it was all a lie. Gloria saw the deep terror that lay behind Perth's eyes like a bandit ready to claim her as hostage.

Gloria had been the one to call information and get the number of the nearest funeral parlor, Avery Funeral Home. She talked low into the phone, wanting to spare Perth as much as possible and explained what had just happened.

"When can you pick up the body?" she asked, feeling as though it was all surreal, as though she had just asked FedEx when they could come and pick up a carton of Medical Data folders.

"I'm sorry, very sorry, Miss Bickford. We just can't do it."

"You mean you can't come today?"

"I mean, we can't come—period. It's the law. When someone dies at home, someone who wasn't under a doctor's care, the police must be notified."

Gloria peeked through the open door of the bedroom and watched Perth rock back and forth in her chair. "*Why*, for heaven's sake?"

"I'm sorry, very sorry. I know how difficult this is, and I'd like to make it easier, but I can't circumvent the law. An autopsy is required in all cases such as yours."

Gloria hung up and quickly dialed 911, then as calmly as possible told the woman on the other end what happened. When she finished, she let out a big sigh. *Gloria the Pester.* Now, how in the world was she going to tell Perth that her father would have to undergo yet another indignity, that his body would have to be probed and examined? She sighed one last time, then headed for the bedroom.

Perth was still crying when two squad cars pulled in front of the building, their sirens blaring, their red strobe lights casting eerie shadows along the gray sidewalk. In seconds the apartment was full of large blue-clad bodies smelling of Old Spice and tobacco. But throughout the questioning, Gloria was proud of Perth, of the way she handled herself and answered question after question that stretched for almost an hour. "How long was your father sick? When did your mother die?" On and on the questions went.

Gloria suffered with Perth, cringing at the sometimes personal details that would find their way into an impersonal report —the pain, the gin, the passing out, the discovery on the bathroom floor, the vomit, the blood. The young blond officer with freckles felt bad too. Gloria could tell by his face, by the way he apologized whenever Perth began to cry, then the way he kept clearing his throat, as though he needed a spoonful of Robitussin. Finally, when the questioning was over, Gloria came up alongside Perth and spirited her into the kitchen on the pretext of wanting to find that nice officer something to wash away the tickle in his throat. Gloria didn't want Perth to see the coroner's men place her father in a body bag and tag it like something that belonged in a Home Depot warehouse.

"Soon as the autopsy's done, we'll release the body," the blond officer said when Gloria and Perth walked into the living room empty-handed. "How can we reach you?" There were only two men in the apartment now. The coroner's men had left, and so had the backup.

Perth stared vacantly. "Well . . . I guess you can call me at my sister's." Gloria cringed when Perth pointed to her.

The young officer studied Gloria then Perth. They looked

nothing alike, and Gloria wondered if that had occurred to the officer as well. Maybe she should just tell him the truth, get everything out in the open, let the police take Perth to Social Services and put her into foster care. At least Perth would have a decent roof over her head, and meals. She watched the young officer turn to his buddy and shrug.

Gloria was about to open her mouth until she saw the panic on Perth's face. She rubbed her temples instead and avoided the officer's eyes.

"Anyone gonna tell me the phone number?" the officer said, looking from Gloria to Perth.

This wasn't right. This wasn't how God wanted Gloria to handle things. To let others manipulate her. And what about Perth? He couldn't want Perth to continue lying and manipulating others, either. God was more than capable of sorting this out. Of doing the right thing.

"I'm not her sister," Gloria said, watching Perth crumble to the couch. "I'm a friend. And I'm willing for her to stay with me." *Had she really said that?* It was too late to stop now. "It's not necessary to drag Social Services into this, is it? I mean, by the time they get all the paperwork sorted and place her somewhere, she'll be eighteen—that's only six months away. Then she'll be able to stay wherever she wants, anyway. So what's the point?" Gloria smiled at the officer and tried to look mature, like someone capable of caring for a teenager who had lost almost everything and who would probably need serious counseling before it was all said and done. She reached for Perth's hand. "She's been through a lot. What purpose will it serve if she gets bounced around when I have a job and a nice apartment and can take care of her?" *Oh, Jesus, how will I ever be able to take care of her?* "Why not let her stay with me until she graduates?"

The officer scratched his head. "It sounds reasonable. And

Perth seems to want to go with you. So I guess that'll be okay for now. I see no reason to take her out of an environment she's comfortable in, not when there's a responsible adult willing to assume the role of caretaker. And if it were up to me, that would be the end of it. But it's not. I have a report to fill out. And in that report I have to say she's a minor and that you're not a relative. So that'll mean Social Services will have to be notified. The final decision's gonna be up to them. But I'll put in a good word for you." He smiled, showing big white teeth covered with those new-fangled plastic braces, his freckles looking like specks of cinnamon in the dim light. *He was only a boy, younger than her.* How did he handle so much responsibility?

"So . . . she can stay?"

The officer nodded. "If I get that phone number." Perth rose to her feet and let out a yelp, then sank into the couch, covering her mouth. "'Course I'll need your name and address too, and where you work."

Gloria rattled off the information, then settled on the couch next to Perth. She was beyond exhausted. If only she could go home and sleep for a week. But there was too much to do. They'd have to cancel the basement apartment and try to sell what they could. And then there was the funeral. How were they going to manage that? Where would the money come from? Her temples began to pound as thoughts of what had to be done whirled around and around like snow in a blizzard.

Oh, God, how am I going to take care of this girl when I can barely take care of myself?

～❦ ❦～

Tuesday morning Gloria called Mattson Development and took her second day off. Then she picked up where she had left off the day before. Monday she had argued with the apartment manager, trying to get Perth a refund for vacating two weeks before her rent was due. He wouldn't budge. But Gloria won a small victory, in that he agreed to purchase the entire contents of the apartment for 250 dollars. He was now calling it "furnished" rooms and planned to up the rent for the next tenant. But it saved Perth and Gloria the hassle of getting rid of what they both knew, for the most part, was junk.

So Tuesday they only had to sort through Perth's father's clothes and personal items. Already two bundles lay on the floor of the living room, one for the church, the other for the trash—the trash bag being the biggest. Perth cried off and on as she went through everything item by item. In the end she only found, aside from a few family snapshots, two treasures worth keeping: her mother's Bible and her father's yellow hard hat with a little emblem of an American flag stuck to the side. Before he died, Stue Christopher McGregor had sold virtually everything he owned.

After the last of Stue McGregor's belongings were sorted and bundled, the two of them went to Avery Funeral Home and made arrangements. There would be no wake, no flowers, no limos, no funeral procession. Only a simple burial in the nearby cemetery. And even for this, the director wanted $1,150: $500 for the plot in West Eckerd Cemetery; $450 for a plain, unlined pine casket with rope handles aptly named Econoslumber; $150 for the driver to get the casket to the cemetery; and $50 for an additional person to help him get the casket and hydraulic lift out of the hearse and to the grave site. Perth's deposit of $250 still left a balance of $900, and after a lot of soul-searching, Gloria found herself offering to pay that amount out of her jealously guarded savings account—an account that had taken Gloria three years of scrimping to build up. In one day it had crumbled like the Parthenon.

Perth cried and told Gloria she'd sell her jewelry—her five sterling silver toe rings and eight silver earrings she wore on a single ear—as partial payment, promising to pay the rest in installments. And Perth cried one other time when she actually saw a model of the Econoslumber—a cheaply constructed casket that looked more like an oversized crate for shipping apples. The rest of the time she bore up well.

The whole unpleasant scenario finally concluded when Perth agreed to let the funeral director place a notice in the obituary column of the *Eckerd City Review* and *EC News*, Eckerd's two main newspapers.

After they left Avery, they packed up Perth's belongings. That project took several hours, but finally they crammed everything into a cab and locked the basement apartment for the last time. Then they headed for the old Victorian on West Meadow Drive.

By the time they finished lugging everything from the cab to the apartment, the entire living room looked like Pompeii, only this Pompeii was smothered by stuffed black garbage bags and jeans and shirts and sweaters and blouses and shoes instead of ash. The first problem to smack Gloria between the eyes was her meager storage space. Where were they going to put all this stuff? Well, they'd find someplace. And it wouldn't be forever. Eight months and school would be out.

School!

"Will you have to transfer schools?" Gloria watched Perth dump a pile of clothes, still on hangers, onto the couch, then push strands of stringy brown hair behind her ears.

"I guess."

"What district is this?"

"Same one I transferred out of when Dad sold the house. We lived in a Victorian about two miles from here." A slow smile broke over Perth's face. "New Field High. It would be nice graduating with my friends."

"I thought you didn't have any friends."

"I don't. Not at my new school. Never bothered to make any. I told you why."

"But you have friends at New Field?"

Perth grinned. "Sure."

"Then why did you lie? Why did you tell me you didn't have any friends you could go to?"

"Because they're not that kind of friends."

Gloria gave her a harsh look. "Perth?"

"Because . . . I was too ashamed. I didn't want my old friends to see what had become of me . . . how I lived."

Gloria pushed past the large black plastic bags and the clothes and shoes, and grabbed Perth's arm. "C'mon. Comb your hair and let's go."

"Where?"

"To get you back into New Field."

Gloria sat across from the principal, watching him shake his head and look sadly at Perth. *Please, Jesus, let Perth get back into this school. She's going to need her friends now.*

"So sorry to hear about your father. We knew how sick he was by some of the things he shared when he withdrew you. We've all been worried. You had started doing well, and we thought that you might consider college. How are your grades at Jefferson?"

Perth shrugged. "Not too good. Actually . . . terrible. It's been hard studying, getting assignments done. You know? But I can make them up. I'll work real hard and——"

"That's not the problem. The problem is you have to be living in the district."

Perth's face beamed. "I am." She rattled off her new address. "I'm staying with her." Perth pointed to Gloria with pride, as though she were pointing to Albert Einstein or Madame Curie.

"A relative?"

"My sister." Perth's face colored when Gloria gave her a harsh look. "Well . . . she's *like* my sister."

Quickly, Gloria introduced herself and explained how the police were allowing Perth to stay with her until Social Services had a chance to check things out. When the principal looked hesitant, Gloria gave him the name of the policeman so he could verify her story.

Finally, the principal placed his palms flat on his desk and smiled. "Naturally, I must corroborate all you've told us, but we'll allow you to matriculate while we're sorting everything out."

Gloria felt an overwhelming desire to jump up and kiss the scholarly-looking gentleman with the curly white hair and metal-rimmed glasses, but she restrained herself. He was nothing like Miss Pritchard, her high-school principal. With Miss Pritchard, everything was politically correct and by the book. No exceptions. Some said she had her eye on the state legislature, but a brain aneurysm took her before that could be proved or disproved. Not many people came to her funeral, not even all those petty politicians she used to spend so much time with. Gloria was embarrassed to admit it, but she hadn't gone, either. Kids always had an inner sense of who loved them and who didn't.

"No need to penalize you, Perth, for the confusion in your

life right now. We'll do all we can to help you make your transition back to New Field. You want to start Monday?"

"How about tomorrow?" Perth said, looking like the kid whose nose had been pressed against the candy store window and now was finally asked to come in for free samples. "I'd rather be in school than just sitting around."

Gloria silently blessed her beautiful Jesus. Everything had gone so well, so smoothly. There was no doubt about it; *Jesus could still part the waters.*

When Gloria awoke to muffled sobs, she was sure she was dreaming. Then she remembered Perth was sleeping on the couch and rose quickly, not even bothering to put a robe over her yellow cotton pajamas, and tiptoed into the living room. She stood near the couch listening, and when she heard little muffled sobs again, she moved closer. Her eyes were accustomed to the dark, so it was easy to see that the mound on the couch was moving, not moving really but rather quivering, as though it were on one of those vibrating beds in a cheap motel.

"Perth? Are you all right?" Gloria stood quietly, waiting for an answer. When one didn't come, she tiptoed around to the front of the couch. With a gentle motion of her hand, she felt for a spot where she could safely sit and eased herself down. Then without a word, Gloria drew back the covers that were pulled over Perth's head. For a long time Gloria sat quietly stroking Perth's hair, remembering all the nights she had cried on a big down pillow right after her own father had died. And she thought of all the times she had wished her mother or Grandma Quinn or someone kind and tender would sit by her bed—sit and stroke her head while the pain in her puny little heart worked its way through her eyes.

"I'm sorry." Perth's voice finally broke the silence. "I didn't mean to wake you."

"It's not important," Gloria whispered.

"You don't . . . have to stay with me. You've gotta be exhausted. I don't want to keep you up."

"Shhhh. It's all right. You just sleep now. Just go to sleep." Gloria rubbed Perth's back, then stroked her hair, and felt Perth gradually relax, felt her breathing become shallow. Still she didn't leave. What lay ahead for this poor child who had no one in the world to love her?

No one to love her.

What a sad sound those words made, like the sound of a train pulling away from a station with everyone in the world on it except you who was left standing on the platform. Perth didn't even have Grandma Quinn or Jesus. Gloria sat beside Perth for a long time, and only when she was sure Perth was asleep did she leave.

Gloria didn't like the *Mattson Newsletter*. Only half of it was filled with Estate news. Then came an article on the Environmental Protection Agency and another one on the importance of preserving the environment. The last article was the one that really bothered her. It sounded like the rantings of a madman. The ending especially startled her. "With human beings gobbling up all the natural resources like so many insatiable Pacmen, we could conceivably wake up facing not another ice age or deadly greenhouse effect but a total destruction of nature in general and Homo sapiens in particular. In light of such critical scenarios, any means of turning the tide would be valid—the proverbial end justifying the means. It is not time for those who love the earth to be squeamish."

It was not the newsletter she and Tucker had discussed.

She checked with Beth Price to see if there wasn't some mistake. But Beth insisted Tucker had given her the environmental pieces himself. Gloria had no choice but to use them. The worst part was that she had to put her name to it as editor.

She needed to speak to Tucker, tell him her concerns, but he was at The Estates and would probably be there for the rest of the week. All the things she wanted to discuss with him were beginning to mount up, forming a pile that was getting as high as Pratt Towers.

Gloria felt Perth sink into her shoulder when the attendants positioned the plain pine casket near the grave site. They stood at a distance, waiting for the two men from Avery Funeral Home to complete their somber task and signal their readiness. Already, dozens of mourners had trickled into the area and formed little black and navy and brown-clad clusters around the grounds.

"Your father had a lot of friends," she whispered into Perth's ear.

Perth raised her tear-streaked face and smiled. "Everyone liked Dad, but . . . I never expected this."

Gloria couldn't help but notice the sun slice through the overhead branches and dance on Perth's dark hair, on both of their black dresses, on the dark ground around them, as though God was reminding her that all was not darkness and shadows. She tightened her grip on Perth's shoulder. But things did seem dark and shadowy. Nothing was as it should be. Her life was more complicated and difficult than ever. Her job was going in a direction she wasn't sure she liked. There were things about Tucker that puzzled and disturbed her. Her savings were being depleted at an alarming rate, and now with Perth to look after, the likelihood of them going down even further was strong. On top of that, what did she know about being a "big sister"?

One of the men from the funeral parlor gestured with his hand that everyone could come forward and pay their last respects. Gloria wished she had brought her Bible to read something for Perth's father one last time.

As Gloria led Perth to the casket, she felt the tension in Perth's back, heard her sigh, then choke back a sob. Then she watched Perth fling the single mum she had picked by the cemetery gate onto the plain brown casket with rope handles, which told everyone the person inside had left this world with nothing of worth save the one throwing the flower.

Then a curious thing happened. People began to line up and file, one by one, past Perth, stopping to say a few words of sympathy, and many pressed an envelope in the palm of Perth's hand. Later, when Gloria and Perth got back to West Meadow Drive, Perth opened the envelopes and counted out five thousand dollars, mostly in cash, and gave Gloria nine hundred of it. Gloria remembered the time under the tree with the sun dancing and felt ashamed.

Chapter Eight

HOW BEAUTIFUL YOU ARE, MY DARLING!
OH, HOW BEAUTIFUL!
YOUR EYES BEHIND YOUR VEIL ARE DOVES.
~❦ SONG OF SONGS 4:1 NIV ❦~

THEY WERE EVERYWHERE, with their angry faces and angry words and angry placards, and somehow Gloria felt responsible. Everyone in Eckerd was talking about it—about the horde that had descended upon the city like the army of Genghis Khan to do battle with wicked, decadent industrial technology. "Stop Urban Sprawl," "Earth Killers," "Down with Technology," "Beware of Big Business," and on it went. And no one knew what triggered the angry response, why the environmentalists had picked their city to descend upon almost like a biblical plague.

But Gloria knew why. It only surprised her that no one else could figure it out.

Or maybe they didn't want to.

"You think all this fuss has anything to do with Tucker's articles?" she said to Beth Price after hours of working up the nerve to ask, after hours of preparing herself for the answer. Beth had a gutsy, hard-boiled side, and Gloria could always expect a straight answer.

Beth sat behind her desk, her normally neat chestnut hair disarrayed as though she just woke up from a nap. Her desk was crowded with papers and folders, with in and out boxes, with a computer keyboard and monitor, and stapler and pens and pencils, a plastic tray of paper clips, rubber bands, whiteout—all no-nonsense stuff except for the one small picture of her husband hugging his golf bag, and for the mug with the big red heart that said *World's Best Wife.*

In spite of her obvious harried state, Beth put down her folder and looked up. These days it seemed as though Beth took Gloria more seriously. Everyone at Mattson Development did. In less than a month, Gloria had gone from Beth's helper to Communications and PR Troubleshooter. That was her official title. Though Gloria still wasn't sure what it meant.

"I mean, those articles, especially that one on The Lakes, could rile anyone. 'Technology and urban sprawl should be considered Public Enemy Number One and Two, and should be dealt with in the harshest terms if we want to preserve alive our children.' What's that all about?"

Beth fingered the cameo broach pinned to the throat of her high-collared blouse. "I realize that to you the *Mattson Newsletter* is a big deal, but in the scheme of things, it's really small potatoes. Nobody takes it that seriously."

Gloria thought Beth looked nervous, the way she kept glancing at the picture of her husband, then at the mug. "I hope you're right," she said, meaning it because the whole newsletter thing still mystified her. And when she tried talking to Tucker about it, he'd go into a spiel about how happy he was to have her here, how happy he was that he had someone he could finally trust.

It's hard to confront someone after a buildup like that.

She kept telling herself it wasn't pride that kept her from confronting Tucker, that it wasn't because it gave her pleasure to have Tucker confide in her, trust her, put her on a level that required respect and admiration and, perhaps, yes . . . even envy from other employees at Mattson. And, of course, it wasn't because she still loved Tucker. How could she? That would be like her mother saying she was in love with Errol Flynn or Tracy saying she was in love with Elvis. Ghosts, phantoms, shadows of reality. No. A thousand times no. It was too absurd to have any validity. The reason she avoided confrontation was because she couldn't afford to rock the boat, now that Perth was with her, now that she had another mouth to feed. But inside, Gloria knew it was all a lie.

"I only hope you're right," she repeated, and that would have ended it, except just then Aldo Simms from Accounting came in and asked what they were talking about. As department head, he could do that, come into Beth's office basically at will. When Beth told him, Gloria was sure he'd burst out laughing, but he didn't. Instead, he walked over to her as he had been doing lately —like a mouse about to eat a piece of cheese—and stopped deep inside her comfort zone.

"So, what do you think, Aldo?" Gloria asked and watched him backpedal. Everyone called him Al. When people wanted to irritate him, they called him Aldo, a name he hated.

"I must say I was shocked when I read it. Rather inflammatory, to say the least."

Gloria watched Aldo scan her body, starting at her face, then down her neck, over her blouse, down the length of her skirt to her ankles, then back up again. His eyes lingered on her legs. When she was twelve, Cutter Press told her she had the best legs he'd ever seen. She felt bad, now, about socking Cutter in the eye years ago, even though he had ended the compliment, "on a frog." But that's what she would like to do now to Aldo, punch him in the eye, maybe both eyes, so he'd stop looking at her as though she were some appetizer on a plate.

"Of course, with these people, you have to be careful," he continued, finally drawing his eyes back up to her face. "They're usually backed by deep pockets, and when angered they can go the distance."

"What do you mean?" Gloria asked.

"Just hang around our new friend, Spencer Jordon, and you'll find out."

Beth grabbed one of the folders and sent her husband's picture crashing to the floor. Gloria had never seen Aldo Simms rattled, but he was now as he glanced at Beth and began edging toward the door.

"I don't think it's wise to be at cross-purposes with Mr. Mattson," Beth said, retrieving the picture, now marred with what looked like spider webbing over the glass. "This new PR campaign is important to him. If you have a problem with it, I suggest you both take it up with him."

Gloria was really puzzled now. A minute ago, Beth had told her no one was taking the newsletter seriously, but obviously she had been wrong. Obviously, Tucker Mattson was.

"This is just conversation. I didn't mean anything. You know how I like to get in there and mix things up. Just talk. Nothing more. Sorry I mentioned . . ." Aldo Simms was already by the door, his pink well-manicured fingers grasping the white painted frame. "I was just trying to be friendly, that's all," he said, then disappeared.

Beth placed the photo back in its proper spot, ignoring the cracked glass, then turned to her computer and opened a Lotus file, as though she were alone in the office, and began pounding her keyboard. Gloria liked this woman, had from the first time she met her, in spite of Beth's often abrupt manners and her often obvious lack of friendliness. For some reason it didn't intimidate Gloria one bit, and that told Gloria there was something kind and decent and tender in Beth Price's interior. Gloria would have liked to drop the issue so as not to bother Beth further, but it had taken Gloria so long to get up the nerve to talk about the newsletter she was loath to stop now.

"I just wish I understood why Mr. Mattson has taken such an interest in the environment," she pressed. "It would make my job easier."

"Your job seems easy enough."

Gloria could hear the scorn in Beth's voice. Even for Beth this was a bit much. Beth could be abrupt, but Gloria had never known her to be cruel. It made Gloria think that Beth was upset over the newsletter too. "My job's easier than I expected. But I suppose that's because I don't know the whole of it yet."

"Well, I'm sure I don't know." Beth turned her head to the side, giving Gloria a quick glance, her gray roots visible on the crown of her head. "We've never had a 'troubleshooter' before. But then Mr. Mattson has a tendency to create jobs out of the air when he needs to."

Bitterness. Yes, there was definitely a touch of bitterness in Beth's voice. "Ah . . . like what kind of jobs?"

Beth flicked her hand impatiently in the air. "It was another young girl—a while back. Just forget it."

From the side, Gloria saw Beth's lips pinched tight, saw worry lines deeply groove her forehead, and wondered how many times Beth had watched younger women being given creative new jobs. "I don't blame you for resenting me," she said softly, making Beth's head swivel in her direction.

"I . . . don't resent you. Is that what you think?" Her cheeks suddenly looked deeply rouged.

"I know I'm not exactly 'troubleshooter' material, that I don't fit the image."

"Noooo."

"And I'm not as knowledgeable as you are about the construction business. Not even close. So I could see why in your eyes and everyone else's I'm underqualified and maybe undesirable—"

"Now, don't go putting words in my mouth."

"But I'm willing to work hard. I'm willing to learn. And I have a real chance of doing something with this job if . . . well, if you and I could be friends. I could learn a lot from you if you'd let me."

Beth rotated her chair. "I guess you have some character, after all."

"*After all?*"

"Don't go there."

"Why not?"

"Because, quite frankly, I don't want to hear it from Mr. Mattson after he blows your nose and wipes your crybaby tears. He's already told us it's important that you like it here."

Words could still hurt. After all the cruel words Gloria had heard in her lifetime, they could still hurt, like bullets piercing her tender vulnerability. Even with the bulletproof vests she'd tried wearing over the years, they still somehow managed to find a soft spot. "I'd like to know what you meant by that. Whatever you say will stay between us. I promise."

For several seconds Beth stared into space, her lips forming a little puckered O, almost like Grandma Quinn when she was mulling something over. Finally, Beth put her elbows on her desk and tented her fingers. "What do you expect people to think? You waltz in here looking like something out of a cartoon one day, then a few days later, you have a new wardrobe and hairdo and look like some high-powered exec. Everybody knows who bought you the clothes. And everyone knows that you don't get a fancy schmantzy title and a salary that pays . . . more than mine . . . when you have practically no experience unless . . ."

Gloria felt her face drain like the radiator of her last car that rusted out and left her pinching pennies for six months. So that was it. The office no longer thought she was some pesky, distant relative in need of a job. They thought she was . . . And that explained Aldo Simms's attention too, his silent innuendos.

Oh, Jesus, how could this be? She resisted the urge to run to the ladies' room and have herself a good cry. Then she thought of Tracy and nearly laughed. Wouldn't Tracy howl if she heard how everyone took Gloria for a loose woman, a kept woman? Even so, her heart ached. How she would have loved to be linked romantically with Tucker, but not like this. Not like this!

"Believe me, it's not what you think," Gloria said, moving closer to Beth's desk. "It's not at all what you think. Mr. Mattson's sister is my best friend. We grew up together. And Tracy, Mr. Mattson's sister, she's the one who put her brother up to buying me the clothes. She thinks I looked like a nerd. She's been telling me that for years, and well, you saw the way I looked. You saw the way I came in here the first—" Gloria stopped when she heard Beth chuckle.

"I know all about Tracy. I've taken enough of her phone calls." Beth leaned closer to Gloria. "She can be a tyrant. 'Make sure Tucker calls me *immediately.* Tell Tucker I'm *ticked* he didn't call. Find him *now* and put him on the phone.'"

Gloria smiled. "That's Tracy."

"So how long have you two been friends?"

"Forever."

Beth nodded slowly. "That explains a lot." She picked up her *World's Best Wife* mug and took a sip of whatever was in it, her eyes peering at Gloria over the rim. "My first suggestion would be to get a job description. You can't succeed if you don't know what's expected."

"But it's a totally new job." Gloria could see something in Beth's eyes—a mix of kindness and friendship and sadness and anger—all there floating in a swamp of other emotions she couldn't identify. And something had just happened between them. She could see that too. "Nobody knows my job description, or exactly what I'm supposed to do. Except . . ." She saw a hint of mischief explode, like little kernels of Pop Secret, in Beth's eyes.

"That's right. You'll have to ask him."

Gloria nodded.

"And don't let him put you off, either. He does that. Sometimes gives vague instructions and expects you to fill in the blanks, and then he's disappointed when it's not right. You're the troubleshooter, remember? You might as well get some practice." Beth winked and returned to her computer, leaving Gloria feeling more satisfied than the very first time she wrote *Communication and PR Troubleshooter* after her name.

When Gloria saw the lean, nervous-looking man coming out of Tucker's office, she stopped in her tracks. This was the second time she had seen him at Mattson Development. Only today he wasn't wearing his pin-striped suit. She bent over the water fountain so he couldn't see her face, then from the side, she watched him stop briefly at Jenny Hobart's desk, then go out the glass-and-brass door.

Instead of going to Tucker's office as she planned, Gloria headed toward Jenny. This whole thing was getting silly. Why should she be afraid to ask questions? Relieve her mind? Grandma Quinn always told her, "No question is stupid. That's how you learn." *Exactly.* How else was she going to learn what connection this thin, nervous man had to Tucker Mattson?

Jenny Hobart was busy typing something into her computer, the air around her smelling like Grandma Quinn's flower garden. But her forehead was pinched and her lips, painted Rose Apricot—a color so attractive on Jenny that Gloria bought it too—were set in a hard, thin line.

"What's *wrong?*"

Jenny shrugged. "Nothing."

Jenny's eyes suddenly misted, and Gloria was sure she was going to cry. "It's that bad, huh?" Gloria moved closer to Jenny's desk.

"No." She blotted the corners of her eyes with her fingertips, Rose Apricot slicking her nails. "It's . . . it's actually good. I mean, it's something good for me. And I should be happy. I mean . . . I *am* happy."

"Well, what is it?" Gloria had never seen Jenny so miserable.

"I haven't told too many people this, but . . . I've been trying to break into television. I've been sending my head shots to agents. I'm not a *real* actor, I know that. I've had enough drama coaches spell it out to my face. But I thought commercials might be the thing. I photograph well and thought I could do those soap or shampoo or toothpaste things, you know, where I didn't have to say anything, only splash water on my face, or toss my hair or smile."

"But you speak beautifully."

"You think so?" Jenny pulled on her left ear, then began twirling one of those gold-knotted earrings she wore so often. "I've had lessons. Tons of them. But my coaches told me that speaking well doesn't mean you can act. They said I had no spontaneity. That I couldn't emote." Jenny shrugged. "They're right. I'm okay as long as I don't have to talk. But once I open my mouth, I turn to wood. I don't know why."

"Is that the good news?"

"Good news?" Jenny drummed the desk with her perfectly manicured nails.

"Yes, you mentioned that something good had happened."

Jenny's Rose Apricot lips thinned again. "Well . . . I've made a really good contact. Actually, Mr. Mattson has made it. When he interviewed me for this job, he saw on my résumé that I had done summer stock, and that's when I told him about my aspirations. I thought I should be honest and let him know, just in case something came up quickly. I thought it was only fair. Anyway, a week or so ago, Mr. Mattson's friend, Spencer Jordon, came to town, and Mr. Mattson introduced us. It turns out Spencer . . . Mr. Jordon, knows an agent *personally.*"

"Really?" Gloria became uneasy. It was the second time today she had heard that name. Who was this Spencer Jordon, anyway?

"Yes. And he promised to hook me up."

"And did he?"

"Not exactly. Spencer said the agent wants more head shots and a more comprehensive résumé and that he'll explain it in more detail when he sees me tonight."

"Why do I get the impression you're not happy?" Gloria felt almost silly, consoling a girl with Jenny's looks, with her obvious experience with men, with her promising future, but Jenny *did* look unhappy, and out of everyone at Mattson Development, Jenny had been the first person who had really been kind to her.

"I'm happy. Only . . . we went through this last time, and I had hoped . . . that is . . . actually I had hoped I wouldn't have to see him again."

"Why?"

Jenny looked around, as though making sure no one was listening. "First off, he's high-strung—so fidgety and nervous he actually makes *me* nervous. And he was a little . . . you know, expectant."

"What do you mean?"

"You *know*. Expectant. Mr. Mattson told me to be nice to him, but I wasn't prepared to be that nice."

Gloria blushed when she finally got Jenny's meaning. "I don't know what to say. I haven't had much experience with men." She stopped and laughed. "Actually, I haven't had *any*, unless you count my prom date, which Mother arranged, and a date with Tracy's distant cousin, which I swear she paid him to go on."

Jenny started laughing too, and her forehead smoothed as though an iron had just steamed out the wrinkles. "I don't believe that for a minute. You're really so attractive, and you've got a head on your shoulders. Much better than mine, anyway, especially for business."

Jenny couldn't really mean what she was saying. *Don't be silly, Gloria.* "Listen, why don't you just tell him to forget it?"

Jenny sighed and cradled her face in her hands, looking so like a commercial for lipstick or mascara or nail polish or shampoo —any one of which she could have sold to Gloria on the spot. "I suppose I could tell him to forget it . . . only, I don't want to make Mr. Mattson mad. I've already told him and Spencer that

I'd go tonight. I suppose one more night won't hurt. I'll be very businesslike and make sure he keeps it that way too. Only, I hope this is the last time. I hope he doesn't need to come see Mr. Mattson again, because then it'll be hard to say no if he asks me out."

"Spencer came here?" *He's high-strung—so fidgety and nervous he actually makes me nervous.* "He was here?" Gloria already knew what Jenny was going to say.

"Yes. You must have seen him. He was at my desk just before you came over—the one with the brown suit and . . . hey, you look a little funny, Gloria. Anything wrong?"

Gloria shook her head. "Who is he? I mean . . . what brings him here?"

"He's some bigwig in the EPA, the Environmental Protection Agency, and I'm not sure why he keeps coming. But he's been here a lot, and I know that Jessica used to take him out whenever he was in town."

"Jessica?"

"Yes, Jessica Daily. She used to work here and—"

"Jessica Daily worked *here?*" When she was little and the boys teased her so unmercifully, Grandma Quinn claimed that the techniques of boxing could be applied to verbal conflict as well. And one of the things she told Gloria to watch for was the sucker punch. But it was too late. When Jenny nodded, Gloria felt as if she had taken the big one right in the breadbasket.

"Actually, Jessica used to have my job. Then she got that promotion, and that's why they had to hire me."

"What was the promotion?" Gloria's voice came out like a croak.

"I don't know. Marketing, I think. But they say, aside from Beth Price, Jessica was Mr. Mattson's right-hand man . . . ah . . . woman."

When Gloria got home and found Grandma Quinn's letter waiting for her in the white metal mailbox, she tore it open and read it right there on the sidewalk.

Dear Pumpkin,

Maybe I shouldn't call you that anymore—with you being so grown up and now living in a big city and all. But habits are hard to break, so indulge a poor old lady. You do know I still see you with pigtails and braces instead of how you are now. Maybe because I saw more of you in those days. Or maybe old age just naturally makes a body gravitate to the past, 'cause, don't you know, after a certain age the mind convinces you that life was better in the good old days. In any case, you're grown now, twenty-eight. I know, because I mark it down in my family notebook, all your birthdays. I say, 'Well, Pumpkin had another birthday, and she's such and such an age.' I do that right next to the date. I've got everything there, in my little book, so when my mind goes, all these memories, all these times and events and special occasions will not go with it.

My stars, how time flies. Sometimes I have to pinch myself to see if I'm still here and not smack-dab in the middle of the Milky Way, where your grandpa always said was the residence of heaven itself. I've been thinking about him more these days. And sometimes, when I start feeling a little down or a little faded-out like my favorite blue polka-dot dress that's been hung out on the line once too often, don't you know I start looking for Jesus' beautiful face? And Zack's too. To be honest, I look for Jesus' face first, but I'd never tell Zack that for fear of hurting his delicate pride. He was always one to get his feelings hurt at the drop of a hat. But I expect he knows that anyway, about Jesus, I mean.

Well, I was tickled pink when I got your letter. You, my little Gloria, in a big city. I still can't get over it, even though this is the second letter you sent me from the big city, so I know it must be true. And I guess you've got yourself some big city problems too. But, Pumpkin, don't you know that Grandma can't sort them out for you? I wish I could. I surely wish I could. But why do you think Jesus went to all that trouble getting you out of here in the first place? He wanted you out of Appleton and away from the Quinns, and I do mean mostly Geraldine—and I'm not saying that to be cruel. The balm of Gilead covered that hurt long ago. But to be fair, I gotta put myself in the mix too, because as sure as God made little green apples, I'd want to just roll you up on my lap and hug and kiss you, and cook and bake all your favorites just to help you get through this, but obviously Jesus has a better plan.

Sometimes, Pumpkin, it's just gotta be you and Jesus, and nobody else.

I guess I can say one thing, though. I think you've overrated Tucker. You have a tendency to do that with people. It's all or nothing with you. Either someone is all wonderful in your eyes, or you have no use for them at all. But, Pumpkin, people are just not like that—not all one way. They're mostly somewhere in between.

I'll keep you in my prayers. You are already in my heart.

Grandma.

After reading the letter, Gloria went inside and sat on the couch in her gray Ann Taylor suit and tummy control panty hose and black Italian leather shoes that pinched the big toe of each foot—longing for just one of Grandma Quinn's hugs or kisses.

~♦ ◈~

The next morning when Gloria asked Jenny Hobart how it "went" with Spencer Jordon, Jenny became flustered and started talking about the weather. Then, for no reason at all, she got up from her desk and headed toward Accounting. And Gloria thought it was strange that Jenny never once looked her in the eye.

For a while now, Gloria knew she needed to confront Tucker. She had spent a lot of time talking to Jesus about it, especially after Grandma Quinn's letter. She had asked Him to go before her as He always did. But it took another three days before Gloria got up the nerve to ask Beth Price to block out time on Tucker's calendar. Then another two days passed before the appointment rolled around. Throughout that time, Gloria rehearsed what she would say. It reminded her of her My Fair Lady fiasco, when Tracy forced her to try out for the part of Professor Higgins's housekeeper in tenth grade. Roberta Hatcher, a ninth-grader, finally got the part because Gloria could never remember her lines.

Now, sitting across from Tucker, all she could do was stare at his highly polished, expensive desk, her lines forgotten like that housekeeper's name.

"I'm really pleased with your newsletters, Gloria. They're snappy looking—cutting edge. I like that. But I guess that's not why you wanted to see me."

Gloria tore her eyes from the carved legs of the desk and looked squarely at Tucker. *I hope you paved the way, Jesus.* "Actually, that's one of the reasons. I'm worried about the tone of the newsletters. Those articles you've been dictating to Beth are really . . . controversial, and I think they're stirring up a lot of antagonism. Every day in town, there's a fight between one of the environmentalists and a local. Yesterday, some man got his jaw broken because he told a picketer to go back where he came from. And the day before, someone spray painted 'tree killers' on the front of Precision Printing in big red letters, then smashed that beautiful glass door."

Tucker absently flipped through his leather planner. "Yes. I've heard all that, Gloria, but what does that have to do with me? With our newsletter? You can't seriously be blaming all the protest over the future development of The Lakes on my articles?"

"Yes . . . actually I do, and frankly, I can't see any difference between building The Estates and building in The Lakes area."

The smile on Tucker's face evaporated. "Since when are you such an authority on the environment?"

"I've been doing research." After her conversation with Beth, Gloria began researching the radical environmental movement, groups like Terra Firma, who called themselves the Guardians of Earth—the group behind the current picketing in Eckerd—and it wasn't a pretty picture.

Gloria took a deep breath. "Did you know this group, Terra Firma, actually has an Eco hit list? They make a joke of it, but it's a list of people they consider enemies. One of them actually was pipe bombed and—"

"I'm not paying you to research Terra Firma or any other group." Tucker's face was fierce, his nostrils flaring. He reminded Gloria of Clive McGreedy's wild stallion. "And I don't pay you to question my tactics or motives, either."

"My name goes on that newsletter. And I can't be party to—"

"Party to *what?*"

Gloria swallowed hard. "Is this a scam, Tucker? This whole environment thing? Are you trying to keep other builders from building on The Lakes because of your project at The Estates?"

She had heard it said that a person under extreme stress can see his entire life flash before his eyes. For one brief second, it was Tucker's life Gloria saw flicker across her retinas—as she pictured a wild stallion pawing the ground and trampling everyone who got in his way. Then it vanished, like bubble bath mist, and only a smile remained on that handsome, chiseled face.

"You're going to make a good troubleshooter. And actually the more I think about it, the more I approve of you digging around, asking the right questions. Yes . . . that's good . . . I need that. Because those are the kinds of questions other people might ask, and then you'll have just the right answer to give."

Gloria ignored his toothpaste smile. He wasn't going to sell her anything this time. "What answer is that, Tucker?"

"The truth. That Mattson Development isn't afraid of competition. We're the best builder around. We'll stack up our houses against anyone else's. And dollar for dollar, we'll beat the competition every time."

"And this sudden interest in the environment?"

"I live here, Gloria. This is my home, my city. I care about it. I want to safeguard it for my children and grandchildren."

His smile got wider and suddenly Gloria felt herself being drawn like a little metal shaving pulled by a magnet—another minute more and she'd just drop right into that mouth of his and disappear forever. What had happened to all her resolve?

"And . . . I've got a friend in the EPA who asked me to alert the public about the problems with developing The Lakes. Friends do things for each other. Remember?"

His eyes held Gloria suspended, and she didn't know which was more dangerous, his smile or those eyes.

Oh, silly, silly Gloria.

He broke the spell by looking at his watch. "I've got to cut this short. I know I was supposed to give you more time, but something's come up."

It always does. Gloria nodded and rose from her chair, then almost jumped when Tucker's fist whacked the desk.

"I don't know why I didn't think of this sooner! What you need is to see the big picture. Really see what Mattson Development is all about. How can I expect you to do any real PR when you haven't even seen one of my developments? I'm taking you to The Estates. Now, how does that sound?"

Gloria nodded, feeling annoyed by his patronizing manner, and by how smoothly he had gotten out of giving any solid answers to her questions.

"Good. I'll let you know when. Probably next week sometime."

Then Tucker rose from his chair, and Gloria knew she was being dismissed. It was almost like being in Cutter Press's office. Without a word, she turned and walked out the door.

Chapter Nine

MY DOVE IN THE CLEFTS OF THE ROCK,
IN THE HIDING PLACES ON THE MOUNTAINSIDE,
SHOW ME YOUR FACE, LET ME HEAR YOUR VOICE.
—SONG OF SONGS 2:14 NIV—

"YOU'RE NOT MY MOTHER!"

Gloria stood within inches of Perth in a face-off that had
been weeks in the making. "No. But this is my apartment, and
I won't have you coming in at all hours of the night."

Perth flipped her brown hair over one shoulder. It was shiny
and clean and sported two cornrows on either side of her temples. Behind her, the coffee table was cluttered with textbooks
and notepads, pens and a backpack. On one end of the couch
was her bedding, neatly folded. A gray sweatshirt draped the
armrest at the other end. Out of the corner of her eye, Gloria
spied Perth's new white Reebok sneakers tucked under the coffee table and glanced down at Perth's bare feet. Mother would

never have allowed Gloria to stand on a cold kitchen floor without shoes or slippers or at least socks. She bit her tongue. Beth Price had been giving her pointers on handling teenagers. "Pick your battles," she had said, "then go the distance." She looked again at Perth's feet, with their silver toe rings that made her look like one of those Burmese dancers. And wouldn't Mother just die if Gloria ever came home wearing those? *Forget about it, Gloria.*

"I don't see why you're getting so upset. I go to school all day, waitress half the night, do homework the other half. When am I supposed to have fun?"

"On weekends. Not school nights. It was after three when you came in last night. You'll not do it tonight!" Gloria had been praying about this all day. She had to be sure her objections didn't spring from buried jealousy or envy. After all, she had never had much of a social life, and it was possible to resent someone who did. But she had talked to Jesus about that and was comfortable with her stand. Perth needed boundaries. And this was Gloria's apartment; she had the right to make rules.

Gloria watched Perth's lip quiver. She was still so vulnerable. Still cried herself to sleep. It wasn't easy being the adult, scrambling for answers and caring enough to see it through when you thought you'd found one. There was no manual. No step one, step two thingy she could follow. She watched Perth toss her hair again in defiance. "Why is this so important?" Gloria asked, trying to soften her voice, trying not to sound so confrontational, which almost made her laugh because of the irony of it. From Peewee Herman to Attila the Hun, at least in Perth's eyes. "What's the big deal?" she repeated.

Perth shrugged. "You wouldn't understand."

Gloria clamped on to Perth's arm and pulled her into the kitchen, then gestured for her to take one of the chairs. Quickly, she began making two cups of chamomile tea, a ritual she had started with Perth when they needed to talk. She put three cubes of sugar into Perth's cup, just the way Perth liked it, and fought the temptation to say anything about rotting teeth or pimples. It was almost frightening the way she sometimes sounded like her mother.

When everything was ready, Gloria joined her. "Now, won't you please tell me why lately you want to go out, after a long hard day, and party till three?"

Perth blew across the steaming cup, then sighed. "I'm not very pretty, you know."

Gloria covered her mouth so she wouldn't laugh. She had thought Perth to be quite pretty.

"Boys never pay any attention to me. You can't possibly know what that's like. But I finally have friends again, and I even have . . . well, this one guy, Spike, he's interested. I mean, he kinda likes me. If you can believe it."

Gloria removed her hand from her mouth and nodded. "Kids at school used to call me 'frog,' and the boys would try to kiss me so I'd turn into a princess."

Perth's mouth dropped. "No way! People can be so mean. I can't believe how mean they can be."

"Yes. But that's not the point. The point is we all want to be loved, Perth." Gloria thought of God's promise. Then she thought of Tucker behind his massive mahogany desk. "And I think that people, especially people like you and me, have to be very careful. Because if we want it too much, then love may not come in the right way, or with the right person. Does that make sense?" Gloria couldn't believe she was saying this. Not with the way she felt about Tucker. Not with his picture hidden in her wallet. Oh, what a hypocrite! Had Mother ever said things she didn't believe, either? Or maybe believed but didn't follow? Did parents just say things that sounded right, as she was doing now? What a miserable big sister she was turning out to be! She poked the floating tea bag with a spoon and watched it bob up and down like a bloated vest. "Am I making any sense?" she repeated.

"Yeah. I guess." Perth wrinkled up her button nose and frowned. "I'm not in love with Spike or anything like that. I mean, I don't know if I could ever fall in love with someone named 'Spike'. And he's a little goofy." The frown was suddenly replaced by a smile that went from ear to ear. "Actually, he's *really* goofy. He thinks it's cool eating live bait. Can you believe that? But he usually has to have a couple of beers before he'll do it." She sipped her tea. "Still . . . it's nice . . . I mean it's *really* nice having a boyfriend, even a boyfriend like Spike. I didn't think it mattered so much, but it does."

"I know." Gloria covered Perth's hand with hers. "And if you promise not to come home at three, you can go out—but just this once. Weekdays are for school and work. Weekends you can have fun."

Perth yawned, then stretched out her thin arms and legs. "I'm more tired than I thought. And I don't really feel like watching Spike eat a bag of killies tonight. Think I'll just turn in."

The first thing Gloria noticed when she walked into Mattson Development was Jenny Hobart crying at her desk. It was something you wouldn't see if you were in a hurry, like the half-dozen people that trotted by her. But Gloria wasn't in a hurry. These days she wasn't all that anxious to get to work. Ever since the environmentalists came to town, Gloria had been questioning the merit of working at Mattson Development. Now she moved sluggishly down the hall like a leatherback turtle, watching Jenny's hand dart from her lap and swipe her eyes.

"How's it going?" Gloria asked when she reached her.

The hand clutching a tissue disappeared beneath the lip of the oval desk. "Hi, Gloria."

The puffiness under Jenny's eyes, the deep line creasing the middle of her forehead, the smile that was so obviously forced surprised Gloria. But when she saw the split in Jenny's bottom lip, she caught her breath. Even with her enormous skill with makeup, Jenny hadn't been able to hide it. Gloria pretended she didn't notice. "How are you this morning?" she asked, leaning against the desk like a broom.

Maybe Jenny needed to talk.

Jenny opened a desk drawer and began rummaging inside. "Fine," she said, without looking up.

The morning started out great, then quickly went downhill. For the first three hours, Gloria did those fun things that made Saturday mornings special. She sat at her kitchen table reading a book with her chamomile tea. Took a long, leisurely shower using her new aloe soap. Practiced styling her hair like Doris Day's. After all that, she began cleaning the apartment. Perth was out early, taking the breakfast shift at Phil's Diner for someone who had called in sick. Usually, Perth slept late Saturdays, making it impossible for Gloria to start cleaning before noon. The adjustments required with Perth here were more than Gloria had anticipated. So were the rewards. Happily, Gloria vacuumed the bedroom, then the living room.

Then the phone rang.

"Gloria, I just bought you a bus ticket so you can come home for Thanksgiving."

"Mother?" They had come to a truce of sorts after Gloria had hung up on her. They now kept their conversations superficial, with talk about the weather and town news. Gloria sensed a radical departure was at hand.

"You know what they say—Thanksgiving's the most traveled time of the year. I figured you wouldn't think about it until the last minute when it'd be almost impossible to get tickets. And anyway . . . I wanted to treat you. I know you're on a tight budget."

"That's . . . really nice. But honestly, I hadn't planned on coming home for Thanksgiving." Gloria knew what was coming and pulled the phone away from her ear.

"That's not possible! How could you not want to be with family on Thanksgiving!"

Could Gloria tell her mother she wasn't ready to come home? That she didn't feel strong enough. That the muscles of her inner fortitude were still weak, and that once she was back in Appleton, she might not be able to bear up under the pressure to remain home. For good. And then there was Perth. How could she explain Perth? And even if, by some miracle, her mother didn't faint from the shock of Gloria taking in a "stranger," she didn't want to put Perth under additional strain by making her come to Appleton and get the "Bickford" grilling. Yet . . . how could she leave Perth behind, all alone in Eckerd City?

"Gloria. I'm talking to you."

"Sorry, Mother. But I've made up my mind. I'm staying in Eckerd."

"Just like that? Without even discussing it with me?"

"I see no reason to discuss *everything* with you. I need to make decisions on my own. How else will I—" The phone suddenly went dead, and Gloria knew her mother had hung up.

Okay, now they were even.

She was still thinking about Thanksgiving and her mother when someone knocked on the door.

"Yes," Gloria said, trying to peek through that silly hole that made everyone look like a distorted reflection in a fun house mirror. When she saw Miss Dobson's huge head and little body, she opened the door.

"Land sakes. I do believe they've added extra stairs." Miss Dobson stopped a moment in the doorway, her chest heaving as she tried to catch her breath. She looked perfect, as usual, with her little pearl earrings visible through the clumps of brown frosted-looking curls, and the little corsage of artificial carnations and baby's breath pushed through the top buttonhole of her white sweater. Beneath the sweater was a beige silk blouse and brown linen slacks. "I shouldn't complain. It really is good exercise. Too bad I can't let my babies take a few turns up and down them. But no telling what kind of problems that would cause with the other tenants."

Gloria couldn't imagine what other tenants Miss Dobson was referring to, since Jessica's apartment was still empty. That left only Gloria and the tenant on the first floor, the one Miss Dobson called The Monk because of his Friar Tuck-like bald spot on the back of his head and because he always dressed in brown. He was never home anyway; he worked days and nights, and weekends, as an undertaker.

"Won't you come in?" Gloria invited, opening the door wider.

"Oh, no, no. I just came up to tell you there's a gentleman at the front door asking for you. He says he's a friend."

Gloria's palms became moist. *Tucker?* She wiped her hands on the sides of her wrinkled navy sweats. *Who else could it be?* She couldn't let him see her like this.

"Well? You going down?"

Gloria shook her head, her mind racing. With the way Miss Dobson walked and then the time it would take Tucker to come up, Gloria figured she could change into decent clothes and run a comb through her hair, but that was about all. "Could you just send him up, please?"

Miss Dobson clucked her tongue. "In my day, a lady *never* entertained a man in her apartment. It just wasn't done." Then she bent so close Gloria saw the little hearing aid hidden in one of her ears. "Land sakes. Don't young girls today know anything about feminine mystique—about keeping a man interested?"

Gloria wasn't sure that *Miss* Dobson was the one who should be talking about keeping men interested, but since she didn't know anything about her past, she'd give her the benefit of the doubt. "This man's just a friend, Miss Dobson. It's not what you think."

"Well . . . if you say so. But I'm doing it under protest. I just want you to know that."

Gloria smiled. "Thank you for walking up all those stairs. Maybe someday the landlord will put in a proper intercom system so we can let in our own visitors." *Maybe she'd mention it to Tucker.*

"Oh, land sakes, I don't mind coming up. What else have I got to do?"

Gloria watched the tall, stately woman walk away, then closed the door and ran for the bathroom. Quickly, she pulled off her sweats and put on jeans and a navy T-shirt, then ran a brush through her hair. When she still didn't hear a knock, she pulled out her Maybelline mascara—brownish black—and quickly applied it. She was more adept at makeup now. Her mother would certainly be pleased. When she finished with the mascara, Gloria uncapped the tube of Watermelon Fizz and applied it to her lips, barely able to keep her hand from shaking.

Why was Tucker here?

When she finally heard a knock, she sucked air, held it for a second like a diver about to plunge off the high board, then slowly exhaled while she surveyed her reflection in the mirror. The Costco jeans and T-shirt showed off a nice figure, and with her hair freshly brushed and face made up, she didn't look half bad.

Ready or not, here I come.

"What brings you to this neighborhood, Tuck—" Gloria found herself unable to finish the sentence as she looked into a dark, angry face. She stood rigid, her mouth open like a brick oven, her mind trying to compute the image in front of her. Finally, the dark, muscular man pushed past her and into the living room.

As she closed the door, panic clawed and scratched Gloria's insides like a frantic squirrel trapped in a chimney. She turned to face her visitor and absently stuck her pinkie in her mouth and bit the cuticle. When she realized what she was doing, she yanked it out.

"How did you find me?"

"You should know by now that your mother tells Virginia everything."

"Cutter, if you've come to fight, then I'm going to ask you to leave." Gloria noticed the muscles of his face tighten, could almost hear the grinding of his teeth.

"I came to get some things off my chest." Cutter glanced at the couch behind him, walked over and sat down. "When I'm done, if you want to throw me out, fine."

Silent prayers rose from the depth of Gloria's thumping heart, and immediately thoughts came whirling in her mind like Black Hawks in a firefight. He was on her turf now, and she was no longer in his employ. She'd hear him out, but if he crossed the line, just once, she'd toss him out quicker than you could say Peter Rabbit. She stared down at him, deep into his dark soulful eyes, and knew that for the first time in years, she'd be able to stand up to Cutter Press.

With only an "I'll be back" as an explanation, Gloria left Cutter sitting in the living room and headed for the kitchen. She'd be civilized, she thought, as she poured two glasses of iced tea. Hot tea would be better. Outside, it was cold enough for a winter coat, and Cutter only had on a suit. But hot tea would take too long, and the object was to get Cutter Press out of her apartment as quickly as possible.

She returned with a tray of two frosted floral glasses, a sugar bowl full of Domino cubes, and one spoon. The sugar and spoon were for Cutter. She took her tea plain. Cutter sat and fiddled with his Appleton High ring, making no attempt to help Gloria push aside the books Perth had left, to make room for the tray.

"Help yourself," she said when she finally got everything arranged. Then she settled in the armchair, hoping Jesus wasn't going to listen too closely to their conversation, because she didn't think it was going to be very friendly. "Help yourself," Gloria repeated, gesturing with her hand toward the tall sweaty glass on the tray.

Cutter didn't even look at it. Instead, his dark, expressionless eyes focused on her every move. She curled her legs under her and took a sip from her glass. She wasn't going to say one word to make it easy. She'd just sip her tea and let him start the conversation.

"What brings you to town?" she asked, in spite of her resolve. Later, her beautiful Jesus was sure to ask an accounting of her every word and attitude, and she didn't want to have too much to repent of. It was getting more and more painful to disappoint Him, as though every harsh word or thoughtless act hurt Him directly. She wished He didn't take everything personally. It would make going ruthlessly for Cutter's throat quite impossible if she thought it might be injuring Jesus' as well. "So, what brings you to town?" she repeated.

"Eckerd City Hospital. They're updating their MMS software with Rev 5. It's a big account, and I want to make sure it goes well."

Gloria nodded, as though she knew all about the hospital account, when in truth she had no idea they used Medical Data software. She took another sip of tea just to give herself something to do while she studied Cutter. He looked good. His suit was new—not expensive like the ones Tucker wore, but nice with paper-thin stripes of brown and tan. His shirt was new too. The tips of his collar were still as stiff as tongue depressors. One thing about Cutter, once he got over his commando dress-up days, he took pride in his appearance. But there was something different about him too. Even from where she sat, Gloria could smell Cutter's cologne. She couldn't place the scent —something musky—but she liked it. He had never worn cologne before, at least not that she noticed. But, oh, how stiff he looked, almost like a bronze statue in a park. Was he that angry he needed to keep himself reined in so he wouldn't explode?

Funny how he wasn't saying anything either, just sizing her up too. "So. Did everything go well? With the update?"

Cutter nodded, his eyes still locked on to Gloria, his fingers still twisting his school ring. "You changed your hair."

Gloria leaned over to put her iced tea back on the tray. This was silly. They were both miserable. *Why prolong it?* "Let's not waste any more time. Why don't you just tell me what you want to get off your chest?" She braced herself and was surprised to hear silence. "Cutter?"

Cutter raked one hand through his thick black hair and twisted in his seat. A mustache of perspiration appeared above his upper lip. If Gloria didn't know better, she'd say he was nervous. Finally, he jammed his hand into his suit pocket and pulled out a crumpled paper, then tossed it onto the coffee table. Even with it folded, Gloria recognized it as one of her newsletters.

"Just tell me why you'd write such drivel? Why you'd come down so hard on the development of probably one of the best pieces of property left in the Eckerd area? I'd expect that from someone else, but not you, Gloria. I always believed you had integrity."

Gloria picked up the *Mattson Newsletter* and opened it. She cringed when she saw her name circled in red. "I'm not particularly proud of this. It's not . . . what I had hoped it would be." She shook her head. "No. I'm not proud of it at all. And you probably won't believe me, but I didn't write this stuff. I'm not excusing myself, because I did put it all together, the newsletter, I mean. But I didn't write it."

"At least that's something," he said in a near whisper, as though speaking to himself. His eyes softened, his posture relaxed. Her answer seemed to have deflated some of his anger.

"Why does the newsletter interest you, anyway? Why would you care what anyone wrote about The Lakes?"

"Because I *own* it."

Gloria's swallow felt like a hard-boiled egg going down her throat.

"Me and two doctors at Eckerd Hospital. Friends of mine. But maybe not for long. When the opportunity came to buy, I was the one who convinced them to do it. Told them condo communities were all the rage now, and this area would be the perfect spot for a really upscale neighborhood. But right now, the way things are going, we stand to lose more than we can afford to."

"So this was the real estate deal you were talking about when . . ."

Cutter nodded. "And it was a good investment. Until Tucker got his slimy friends into the act and convinced his pals at the EPA to stir up the loony fringes of Terra Firma. Now injunctions are dropping into my mailbox like confetti. Every agency, you name it, seems to be trying to stop the building at The Lakes. Some of them want to turn it into a preserve. They're checking out the possibility of declaring it a wetland, which is ridiculous. And others are desperately trying to find something that would qualify as a threatened species. They're prepared to do anything . . . everything to keep my partners and me from building. Tucker doesn't want competition."

"Pretty wild accusation, don't you think?" Gloria said, ignoring the fact it mirrored her own.

"Is it? Maybe you should open your eyes, Gloria. Take a good look at the scum you work for." There was a growl in Cutter's voice. "And that part really disappoints me. The fact that you're working for a lowlife like Mattson. But I should've known Tracy had a hand in this. I should've known Tracy would set you up with a job at her brother's."

For the first time since Cutter sat down, Gloria felt fear. "You're not . . . you wouldn't fire Tracy, would you?" Her voice was like vapor. She couldn't bear the thought of Tracy having to pay for being a good friend. Gloria watched Cutter's eyes harden like musket shot, watched him throw back his head the way he did when getting ready to curse. Then she watched him take a deep breath.

"And if I did?"

"Then I'd probably hate you for the rest of my life."

To Gloria's surprise, Cutter laughed. "You already hate me."

"No . . . no, I don't. I just don't like you very much. There's a difference."

When his laugh got louder, Gloria couldn't help it and began laughing too. They laughed and laughed, and when it was finally quiet, Cutter rose from the couch and walked over to the door, his face not so angry or dark. For the sake of etiquette, Gloria followed.

"I've said what I wanted to say. And you took it. Just like always. No . . . not like always. Not quite like always." For a brief second he bent closer to Gloria. "You've changed, and not just your looks. And I like it." Cutter yanked open the door. "You were smart to leave. If I were you, that's what I would've done. There's only so far those old crows can push us before we . . ." Cutter gave Gloria a funny smile and shrugged. "You know what I mean."

Gloria nodded, feeling a strange emotion stir within her, one of kindness toward Cutter. "Have you been able to work out your financial problems?"

"No. Things are just as bad . . . maybe worse. My only consolation is that Tucker's in even worse shape."

"Oh, that's not possible. He's doing so well . . . you should see his office and—"

Cutter burst out laughing, not the same laugh as before. This was sharp, hard. "I guess you haven't changed as much as I thought. You still can't see beyond your nose, Gloria. From what my partners tell me, Tucker owes everybody and his brother, and if The Estates don't come in for him, big time, he'll have to go chapter seven."

"Chapter seven?"

"Bankruptcy. Total liquidation."

Gloria stood in front of the bathroom mirror applying the new Rachel Perry Jojoba moisture cream Jenny Hobart had told her about. She had already exfoliated, using the sea kelp scrub Jenny also recommended. The apartment was silent. Gloria was alone and preparing for bed. Perth was going out with friends after her shift at Phil's Diner, so she wouldn't be home until late. It suited Gloria, after her busy day of cleaning and her draining run-in with her mother and Cutter Press. *Cutter Press.* She still couldn't get over that one. How he just showed up. How angry he was at first. Still, in the end he had proven to be decent enough. But seeing him had rattled her.

Frog. Frooog.

Her fingertips moved in semicircles over her face, covering her forehead, her nose, her cheeks, her chin, then her neck. She liked the feel of the cream. It was light and worked easily into her skin.

Frog. Frooog.

Gloria's hand stopped in midmotion as she listened to that vaporous thin voice coming from a distance. A second later, she continued her ritual. Two weeks ago, Jenny had told her about this cream, and Gloria had been using it ever since. Maybe it was her imagination, but she thought her complexion was creamier, smoother, with more clarified pores. Clarified pores. That was the thing to strive for, according to Jenny Hobart.

Frog. Frooog.

She bent closer to the mirror and giggled. What an imagination she had! Those pores didn't look too clarified to her. Wishful thinking, that's all it was. What was she trying to prove, anyway? As she peered into the mirror, inspecting the bridge of her nose and along both sides of her nostrils where the most unclarified of all the pores hung out, she giggled again when she realized it didn't matter one bit. Yes, she'd try to do the best with what God gave her, but it really didn't matter to her anymore that she'd never look like the Jenny Hobarts of the world. And that realization brought such an infusion of pleasure and freedom she almost felt like a helium balloon.

With a quick twist of her wrist, she screwed the cap back onto the small green jar and turned out the light.

Chapter Ten

ALL NIGHT LONG ON MY BED
I LOOKED FOR THE ONE MY HEART LOVES;
I LOOKED FOR HIM BUT DID NOT FIND HIM.
— SONG OF SONGS 3:1 NIV —

GLORIA WAS DULY IMPRESSED. The Estates' sales office was neatly incorporated in the fully furnished Cambridge, the smallest of six models that made up The Estates repertoire. Magnificent crown molding decorated the space where ceilings met walls. Oak hardwood floors glowed in various shades of honey and brown underfoot. Wallpaper, furniture, window treatments all blended in harmonious, tasteful colors. The attention to detail was exceptional. Nothing had been overlooked. Frosted glasses with fake ice stood on colored place mats next to plates full of fake food that looked so real Gloria's mouth watered when she passed the kitchen table. It was a buyer's delight, a place that perpetuated the dream that even the ordinary could live in the extraordinary, could live in something that looked straight out of *Better Homes & Gardens*.

Gloria watched the faces of the newly arrived couple: of the woman's when she inspected the kitchen with its hanging pot rack and Corian countertops and its sleek state-of-the-art appliances; and the man's when he glanced through the sliding glass doors and spied the huge Garland barbecue with tiled countertop and stainless steel doors that opened to ample storage space.

She looked from the happy couple to Tucker. There was no way Perth could be right. Nor Cutter either. Tucker had gone out of his way to make the Cambridge a dream. And he had told Gloria this was the plainest of the six models. The others were even more spectacular, with double fireplaces, Jacuzzis, swimming pools, lofts, and raised-panel library rooms.

"You like it?" Tucker asked, coming up beside her.

Gloria nodded, wondering why she felt so relieved. What had she expected? A shantytown? Or houses with roofs falling in or beams exposed or frayed wiring?

"I told you seeing this place would give you an idea of what I was trying to accomplish." He took her by the elbow. "C'mon. You need to see the rest of the models. Then the grounds. Before you leave, I want you to love The Estates as much as I do."

For another two hours, Gloria tromped through five different models, each one more stunning than the other. Then they inspected the clubhouse, the tennis courts, the huge man-made lake, the guard shack that looked anything but a shack with its portable TV, desk, armchair, and private bathroom.

Only Phase One was up for sale and nearly 30 percent occupied. Tucker indicated Phase Two would open for purchase in ten days, and at that time the price of each of the six models would go up twenty thousand. Phase Three would see even a bigger price increase, but wouldn't be opening for at least another six months to a year. By sell-through, Tucker expected The Estates to be the most expensive and desirable property in the whole of Eckerd City.

As they walked back to the sales office, Gloria gathered her suit jacket tightly around her. It had started out mild, one of those Indian summer days that looked orange from the sun but had turned grey, and the breeze now had a sharp edge to it. The wind suddenly kicked up, making her shiver, and sprinkled brown powder across the tops of her black leather shoes. In the distance, dirt and dust swirled, like miniature tornadoes, around the three giant Cat excavators with their forty-two-inch buckets prepping Phase Two.

All around, the landscape looked desolate, barren, with only a half-dozen trees visible. Bushes and shrubs surrounded the thirty occupied homes, and greenish brown sod lawns blanketed their grounds, making them look like giant checkerboards. Even so, the vegetation was immature and did little to eliminate the feeling of desolation. The Estates sat on an old potato farm, and in the distance, as far as the eye could see, as far even as the future sites of Phases Two and Three, the grounds looked like a lunar landscape.

"I had planned on bringing in fully grown trees, but it's cost prohibitive. So instead, I'm going to use Royal Paulownia saplings to line the streets. That'll take away some of the starkness." It was as though Tucker had read Gloria's mind, or maybe he had seen it on her face.

"Then, there's going to be several ponds, in addition to the man-made lake." Tucker swept his arm in the direction of the excavators. "Originally, I wanted ten, but I'm thinking of cutting that number in half. Digging the lake killed me with over-runs, so I need to conserve cash."

This sudden money talk felt uncomfortable to Gloria,

unseemly even. She bent down and grabbed a handful of soil, hoping he would change the subject. The dirt looked anemic in her palm, and she wondered if that was why the sod was doing so poorly. Clive McGreedy's soil was always moist, loamy, no matter how far down you went, and loaded with worms that wiggled in your hand when you grabbed a fistful. She knew sod came with its own layer of topsoil, but the soil beneath it still needed to be substantial to encourage the roots to penetrate deep. She tossed the dirt, then brushed her hand clean. "The sod doesn't look good. What's wrong?"

Tucker laughed. Gloria thought it sounded strained. "All the topsoil's blown away."

"You mean like one of those '30s dust bowl farms?"

"Yeah, I guess. This farm's old and wasn't well managed. We'll have to do some serious soil enhancement before we put down any more sod."

In Appleton, Gloria's mother kept a garden in back and was forever complaining of all the money it cost her to get just the right mix of organic matter, clay, and sand for her vegetables and flowers, not to mention the cost of the fertilizer. Gloria wondered how much it was going to cost Tucker to change this dust bowl into the lush green paradise he had featured in his brochures. When she looked at his face, she knew he was wondering the same thing.

Lunch was twin lobster tails stuffed with crabmeat, buttered new potatoes in their skins, and asparagus with hollandaise. Gloria still wasn't over the dust bowl effect and hadn't wanted such an expensive lunch. But Tucker had ordered for both of them, in advance, without consulting her. She wondered why he did that. Lived so extravagantly, then worried about the cost of soil enhancement. Could Cutter really be right? Was this all a house of cards ready to come tumbling down? She couldn't put that much stock in what Cutter said, though. He had his own ax to grind, and over the years Gloria had seen Cutter bend or stretch the truth, like saltwater taffy, when it suited him.

No, she liked what she saw at The Estates. But only partially. And that's what bothered her. She had wanted desperately to sign on, to be able to get behind Tucker 100 percent. She had wanted, once and for all, to dispel both Perth's and Cutter's accusations as utterly groundless. Only . . . Tucker's reference to money didn't sit right. She had never heard him discuss it before. And that too was a puzzlement, since he seemed so anxious for her to be sold on The Estates. Why would he cloud the issue now?

"I don't want you to go home with the picture of a dust bowl in your mind," Tucker said, pulling one of the lobsters out of its tail and slicing into it. "Construction's a messy business. It takes time to get it all right. Delays, hidden expenses, they all make the job harder. But you wait and see. Before long, the ponds will be in, so will the landscaping around the other seventy houses in Phase One, and it'll start looking like paradise. It's just that everything takes time . . . and money."

Gloria nibbled one of her potatoes and said nothing.

"But you agree, Mattson Development builds magnificent homes? You'll give me that, right?"

"Yes, the models are . . . what can I say? Outstanding." Gloria swallowed the last of her potato. "So are the tennis courts and clubhouse. And the landscaping around them is superb. I'm just surprised you didn't follow it up with—"

"The houses?"

Gloria nodded.

Tucker reached into his pocket and pulled out a handful of coins. He sifted through them and placed four quarters on the table. "Let's suppose these quarters represent the total available cash flow for The Estates project. And let's say that the first quarter goes to pay for the land, all three phases, or at least the down payment and the interest on the bank loan for the land, plus attorney's fees, building permits, advertising. The next goes to pay for building the lake, the clubhouse, tennis courts, and the six models, plus their furnishings and landscaping. The next quarter goes to build the houses you actually sell. You figure you can put up twelve maybe fourteen houses for that and still have the last quarter in reserve. Because you won't be adding any more money to the kitty until you actually go to closing. Any money the buyer puts down goes into escrow. I can't touch it. But you figure it's okay. By the time you start your fifteenth house, you should have some closing dates, and that quarter is going to turn into two. Besides, you still have one quarter waiting in reserve, just in case. You should be fine. Right?"

Gloria stared at Tucker, speechless.

"Wrong. While you're busy building your fourteen houses, this last quarter, this one in reserve is being eaten up by delays, overruns, broken equipment, by more PR and advertising. By loads and loads of unforeseen, *unbudgeted* expenses. And then suddenly, that quarter is gone, and so is the one you used to build those fourteen houses. Only now you've got to start on number fifteen, and none of the other houses have closed. But if you don't start fifteen on schedule and delay too long, that creates other problems. Buyers may pull out, word might get out that Mattson can't deliver on time, or worse yet, that there's a problem at The Estates, and then future buyers won't come. You see the dilemma? So what do you do? You go ahead with number fifteen and stretch out payments to your contractors. And as the houses begin to close and money begins to trickle in, you give a little to them so they keep working, but you're always behind, always one step away from someone walking off the job because you can't meet payroll."

Tucker removed his second lobster tail from the shell, then pushed his plate aside without eating it. His eyes looked filmed, clouded, and Gloria could tell he was in some far-off place.

"But it's going to be okay. By the time I finish Phase Three, this scraping will be over. I won't have to worry about money to enhance the soil or put in trees, or . . . I won't have to worry about money for anything. Everyone will be paid off, and I'll be filling my own pockets with lots and lots of quarters. Only, I need time." He suddenly leaned forward in his chair. "And that's where you come in. You're going to buy me that time."

"How?"

"By doing your job. By troubleshooting."

Gloria placed her fork on her plate. "You've never told me what that involves. What exactly do you want me to do?"

Tucker quickly explained what a punch list was, then he told her about the two homes that had fifty items each on the list and how angry the owners were.

"What is the usual number?" Gloria asked, still not understanding her role in all this.

"Ten to fifteen before closing."

"And these people have moved in?"

Tucker nodded.

Gloria glanced at the remaining lobster on her plate and wondered if Perth liked lobster. Maybe she'd take it home for her. Gloria thought it strange that Perth came to mind now. *You're working for a crook.* Or maybe it wasn't so strange. Was this the reason God had sent her here? To Eckerd City? For Tucker? To lead him on the right path? Help him change his ways? Gain his confidence and then tell him about Jesus? And maybe, who knew what could happen in the process? Maybe Tucker would fall in love with her. It wasn't that far-fetched. Well . . . maybe it was, but it also made sense in a strange way. God was always using people to touch other people, to get His plans accomplished. It was all starting to make sense.

"I still don't understand what you want me to do," she said with renewed interest.

Tucker's hands shot into the air along with his frustration. "I *told* you. Buy me some time. Calm these people down. Assure them that all will be taken care of. The last thing I need is for someone to go to the newspapers."

Gloria calmly folded her hands on her lap. If this was going to work, if she was going to accomplish God's plan, then she'd have to be more forceful than she was accustomed to being. "Why me?" she asked, staring down at her cuticles and noticing how much they had healed since coming to Eckerd. It was as though she had entered a whole new phase of her life. *Good-bye old Gloria, hello new.* And in this new life, this new Gloria could dare to believe the fantastic. She could dare to believe that God could give her Tucker—the desire of her heart.

"Why me?" she repeated.

"Because you're honest. People will instinctively see that. And they'll trust you."

Gloria squeezed her folded hands tightly together and looked at Tucker, at his Clark Gable nose, at his large, wide-set dangerous eyes, at his full lips that with just a twitch could do things to her she never thought possible. It was no secret he was capable of making her little heart flutter like the wings of one of those swallowtail butterflies in Grandma Quinn's garden, but never before had he made her head buzz as though a bee had gotten loose in her brain. And that was good because that made her brain kick in, made her gray matter take control of her fluttering heart.

Tucker was using her.

Oh, he said he wanted her to buy time. But what he really wanted was for her to lie. And just how far was she prepared to go? He'd expect her to go the distance. A desperate man would. Maybe Cutter had been right about Tucker all along. The bee buzzed around and around. And if Cutter was right, did that make Perth right too?

Was Tucker a crook?

Oh, foolish, foolish Gloria.

Gloria sat in the construction trailer opposite The Estates foreman and watched a slow smile appear on his face. Most construction crews had any number of men with ponytails— quasi-hippie looking and scruffy. But Don Blaster's short blond crew cut, along with his meticulously clean clothes and his unbelievable physique, made him look like a marine sergeant or one of those Aryan supermen who did Herculean feats by day, then went home and polished pajama buttons. The whole package intimidated her. She had never felt comfortable around men. But now, she was smack-dab in a man's world loaded with testosterone. *Get over it, Gloria.*

"Mr. Mattson told me he was sending over a troubleshooter," Don Blaster said, cracking his walnut-sized knuckles. "It's about time too. I'm tired of people parading in and out of here with one complaint after another. I've already got my hands full with contractors. I don't need this other noise." He wore an unbuttoned plaid flannel shirt over a black cotton T. When she arrived he was out on the grounds talking with his men—no coat, just the flannel shirt flapping in the wind. She wondered why he wasn't frozen. This morning the weatherman said it had dipped below thirty.

Don Blaster pointed to a corner in the back of the trailer where a small pine desk sat piled with papers. "Mr. Mattson told me to give you a desk. You can use that one. He says you'll be here every other day. That's good. That'll give those with complaints a way to vent. And believe me they will. Every day there's something. They drove my secretary away. Actually three. I lost three girls since I've been here. The first one was an idiot —didn't even know how to make photocopies. The others were okay, only they couldn't take the pressure. These people over here have money and are used to getting what they want. Sometimes they're hard to deal with.

"Got a new girl coming next week, and I was worried. Now I can tell her she doesn't have to handle the homeowners. All she's got to do is manage those pouches." His hand flipped in the direction of a corkboard hanging behind his left shoulder. It was covered with stapled pouchlike folders, with each folder marked in bold black manly lettering: Roofer, Framer, Plumber, Electrician, Mason, and a half-dozen more. All macho sounding trades.

Gloria shriveled in her chair. Outside were excavators, backhoes, dump trucks, dozers, graders. Most of their tracks or tires were taller than she was. It was all making her feel the way Cutter and his commandos used to. Testosterone. She just couldn't get away from it. *Get over it, Gloria.*

Don Blaster's hand was still pointing at the folders behind him. "It's not easy juggling all this stuff. Anyway, I guess you can start by going through all those complaints on the desk back there. If you have any questions, come to me. Mr. Mattson said

I was to help. But after the new girl gets on her feet, you can take everything to her. Okay . . . that about covers it."

When Gloria didn't rise from her chair, Don Blaster leaned back in his and began plucking at the loops of his jeans. His face knotted in a frown. Obviously, he was in a hurry to get back to work. Already one of the backhoe operators was standing by the door, letting in all the cold air and gesturing with his hand. With all this machismo stacked against her, for a minute Gloria wasn't sure if she'd hold her ground, but she did. She had one question she needed to ask. She had entered the world of hairy underarms and body odor, of grunts and heaves, and swear words and power. Lots of power. But she had power too. Because sitting right next to her, with fingers tightly lacing hers, was her beautiful Jesus. She cleared her throat. "I understand Stue McGregor used to be foreman here."

The large man squinted at her, his blond bushy eyebrows looking like fur pasted to the ridge of his forehead. "You know Stue?"

Gloria shook her head. "I know his daughter, Perth."

"Sad business. Heard he lost his wife. And just a few days ago, somebody told me Stue had died a while back. That true?"

Gloria nodded.

"Sad business. Didn't know he left a daughter. But I didn't know Stue personally. Just knew him by reputation."

"And what reputation was that?" Gloria held her breath.

"One of the finest construction engineers in this city."

For two hours Gloria pored over the stack of papers on the corner pine desk. Leaks under the sink, loose bathroom tiles, cracked or missing grout, cabinet doors that didn't close, wall-to-wall carpeting that didn't cover corners or closets, missing linen closet doors, paint splatters on tiles, ceiling fans that didn't work. The list was endless, and at one point, Gloria left her desk and discussed some of the complaints with the foreman. He assured her that punch items of this nature were common in any new construction, that they would all be fixed, and that Gloria needed only to fill out a Work Order Request form for each problem and put it in the appropriate pouch. His secretary, once he got one, would book appointments for the repairs. Gloria's only other task was to call each homeowner and tell them that someone would be contacting them for an appointment and that all their problems would be solved.

And they all lived happily ever after.

Her first call took twenty minutes. She listened politely while the woman of the house droned on and on about her cracked ceiling and how they never fixed it right the first time and how the tape and spackle they put over the crack were starting to look like a camel's hump and had cracked all over again.

The second call wasn't much better. One of the toilets didn't flush properly, and the marble saddle between the bathroom and hall was cracked and beginning to lift. Already someone had tripped over it twice. It was a lawsuit waiting to happen. Fifteen minutes into the conversation, Gloria was able to utter her first word since introducing herself. "Sorry." Another ten before she could get in a full sentence. "I'll check and see why they didn't show up."

When Gloria hung up, she flipped the edges of the stack of papers in front of her with her thumb. At this rate she'd be here till Christmas. These people were angry, hostile, and frustrated.

After dialing the phone a third time, a man answered and Gloria cringed. So far she had spoken only to women, and while they were angry, they didn't shout or curse. She took a deep breath and told him who she was. There was a long pause, then a sigh.

"Are you finally going to fix the garage?"

Gloria glanced at the paper in front of her and hastily reread the list of complaints. There was no mention of a garage. "I'm . . . not familiar with that problem, Mr. Primavera. You didn't list it on your request form."

The man laughed. "That's what I thought."

"If you'll just tell me the problem, I'll see that it gets addressed."

The man laughed again. "How many times do I have to tell you people something? How many more forms do I have to fill out?"

Gloria heard the anger in his voice, but it was controlled, not even raised above a normal level of speech. This was someone with a deep grievance. "Would it be too much to ask you to explain your problem just one more time?"

"This really tears it. I've been fighting with you people for three months, and now I've got another one of you on the phone pretending you don't know what's wrong. Well, just forget it. Okay? Because now I'm going to get a lawyer. That's right, a lawyer. Maybe you'll listen when *he* talks."

"I'm sure there's plenty of paperwork on your problem. Only, I'm new and haven't come across it. If you'll only tell me what's—"

"The concrete floor in the garage is cracked. Big time. And beginning to separate from the walls. I think something's wrong with the foundation. If you ask me, I think the floor's going to go. That's why I don't park my cars in the garage. I'm afraid one of these days I'll wake up and find them both in a big pit under the house. I've been asking you people to pull off the concrete. Check the ground under the house. Make sure it's solid and not sinking, and if it isn't, to fill it, then shore up the house. But nothing ever gets done. I don't know what it takes to get your attention. Maybe the newspapers. Now, there's an idea. How about I call the *Eckerd City Review* or the *EC News?* Then everybody will know what kind of outfit you're running here."

Gloria promised to call back in ten minutes, then raced to the corkboard and checked the pouch marked Foundation. Nothing. Mason—nothing. Then she charged out of the trailer and scanned the premises for Don Blaster, ignoring the freezing cold wind that whipped her face and the dust that peppered her eyes. She finally spotted him by one of the backhoes, talking to two men. She waved, and when he saw her, he came over.

"Problem?"

Gloria nodded and quickly told him about the phone call. She watched his face redden.

"I told him we'd get to it."

"Then you know about it? About his garage floor?"

"Yes."

"There's no paperwork. And I wasn't sure—"

"It's a special case. Not a usual punch list item. We're on top of it, so don't worry about it." He kicked one shoe in the dirt, then pulled on the loops of his jeans.

"I don't know. He seems pretty—"

"Just don't worry about it. *Okay?*"

Gloria wished he'd stop kicking the dirt like that. Clouds of dust were mushrooming around her face and seeping into her mouth. She tasted grit and resisted the urge to spit it out. And Don Blaster was starting to annoy her, with his agitated expression that clearly spoke of his desire to be rid of her. Even now he was about to turn and head for the backhoe.

That's when she did it. Hurled a wad of saliva and dust from her mouth and onto the ground, missing one of his tan work boots by millimeters. Years ago, when they were little, she and Tracy used to have spitting contests to see who could spit the farthest. Gloria always won. It was one of the few things she could do better than Tracy, that and use a hammer. She never expected it to come in handy—never expected to apply this talent to anything worthwhile. Until now. It made big Marine Sergeant, Aryan Superman, manliest of men Don Blaster stop in his tracks. Her one little spit wad.

She pictured her beautiful Jesus raising an eyebrow and saying something like, "Maybe you could have found a better way," but she'd talk to Him about it later.

"I think you'd better go over and check out that garage again," she said, suddenly feeling cold and wrapping her arms around herself.

"Look, I take my orders from Mr. Mattson. Your job is to call these people and fill out forms. Everyone will get attention. In due time. I've got a schedule to meet, and right now I'm behind. We need to get those ponds dug. Plumbers are coming tomorrow to lay the piping and we just found—"

"I think you'd *better* go check out that garage. Mr. Mattson instructed me to give top priority to any situation that could lead to negative publicity. If you don't go today, I'm fairly certain this homeowner will either contact the newspapers or hire a lawyer, and I'll indicate that in my report to Mr. Mattson."

For a long time Don Blaster stood glaring at Gloria, his head looking like a bowling ball ready to flatten this ungainly pin in front of it. Finally, he raked his blond crew cut and heaved his massive shoulders backward, thrusting out his chest. "You have any idea the kind of pressure we're under? You're not the only one who has to answer to Mr. Mattson. And I've got my own set of instructions to take care of. My own priorities. But . . . okay, if you think it's going to cause a major stink, we'll go see it. I guess that's why you're the troubleshooter. But you'll see for yourself. It's not that big a deal. It can wait. A while longer, anyway. At least until we get some of these other important issues resolved."

❧ ❧

Gloria gathered her old cloth coat around her neck—the coat she had wanted to replace, which needed replacing desperately —and watched Don Blaster walk the floor of the empty garage . . . stopping here, running his fingers there. At one point he unclipped his retractable ruler from his belt, pulled it out about a foot, then slipped it through the large crack in the concrete floor that ran end to end sideways. When it went lower than eight inches, she saw the color drain from his face.

She followed him as he exited the garage and walked around the front of the house to the right. Then she watched him scan the foundation that jutted two feet out of the ground. Even from where she stood, she could see spiderlike settling cracks webbing the foundation. But she noticed Blaster didn't seem disturbed by these. But when he came to the large crack running perpendicular to the foundation, he stopped. The gash torn in the flesh of the concrete looked like a wound, with almost an inch of separation. When she caught Don Blaster's eye, she saw fear before he looked away. Then he slipped his walkie-talkie from his flannel shirt pocket and spoke in rapid, low tones she couldn't make out. She was sure he kept his voice low on purpose. But his eyes had already told her something was wrong. Very wrong.

In a matter of minutes, a mini-backhoe and truck showed up in front of the house. Then a man, wearing what looked like huge round earphones that totally obscured his ears, and rolling what looked like a giant saw on a dolly, began slicing up the concrete floor of the garage.

❧ ☙

"What do you mean, the foundation's sinking?" Tucker sputtered.

"Just what I said." Don Blaster sat behind his desk drumming his pencil on the large graffiti-covered blotter, the muscles of his jaw working back and forth.

Gloria sat near him, watching Tucker pace the narrow hall of the construction trailer, her heart thumping like one of those Salvation Army drums. She was a pro at spotting conflict way before it happened.

"It can't be sinking."

"Well, it is. You can't pour a foundation on fresh fill. I told you that. You should've let us pack it right. And . . . you should've used a better grade of filler."

"How many of the original fourteen are sitting on the filled section?"

"Five."

Tucker whistled. "How many are showing signs of sinking?"

"All of them. Only the one we checked today is the worst. We've got some time with the others. But this one is sinking faster than I expected."

Tucker stopped by Gloria's chair and tapped her shoulder with his fingers. "You've got to keep this man happy. He seems to like you. You were there for him." With each sentence, the tapping became more forceful. "You got him results. So he'll trust you now. He'll trust what you say. And you'll have to tell him what he wants to hear. You've got to tell him that

217

everything's okay. You've got to keep him from going to the newspapers or a lawyer."

Gloria slid down in her chair, trying to get away from Tucker's fingers. She knew what this was about. Jesus was testing her. Checking to see which side of the fence she was going to land on. She had yet to settle the question of how far she was willing to go on Tucker's behalf. And she knew that had Jesus worried. "What's going to happen to his house?"

Tucker shrugged and resumed pacing. She looked at Don Blaster, who started doodling on his calendar.

"How can I reassure this man when I don't know what's going to happen?" She stared squarely at Tucker. "And if something does happen? Empty words are not going to cut it. If you want me to keep him happy, I need to know the truth."

Don Blaster threw down his pencil. "The house is sinking. Unevenly. The garage is sinking faster and is starting to twist away from the rest of the foundation."

Gloria groaned. "Can you save it?"

"We can dig under the foundation and pour a new one. Only problem is we'd have to pour it on solid ground so it wouldn't sink again. That means we'd have to pour on original soil, dig below the fill."

Gloria shot a glance at Tucker and saw him standing quietly against the wall, gnawing his lip. "How deep is the fill?"

"Seven feet. We'd have to go below seven feet, support the house, then pour a new foundation. A lot like adding a basement to a house after it's been built."

It sounded expensive. "And this has to be done to all five houses?" Gloria asked, wondering what kind of lunatic would build a house on soft fill.

Don Blaster nodded, conspicuously keeping his eyes off Tucker. "Yep . . . all five."

Okay . . . at least there was a solution. Gloria felt relieved and knew it was because she could straddle that fence a bit longer. "So that's what I'll tell him. That we're concerned about his foundation and are going to pour him a new one, and that he'll end up with a free basement."

"You can't do that!" Tucker bellowed, almost rocketing off the wall and landing by her chair.

"Why not?"

"Because we don't want him to know there's anything wrong with his foundation."

Gloria pruned her face. "Don't you think he's going to know something's not right when you start digging seven feet under his house?"

Don Blaster started doodling again.

Tucker paced. "What about just filling the sinkhole in the garage with concrete?"

Don Blaster shook his head. "That's not going to solve anything."

"I *know* that. But our homeowner doesn't. It'll satisfy him until we can get to it. At least until Phase Three's finished. Then we can go back and fix all five houses. It'll buy time and get him off our back."

Gloria shook her head.

"What?" Tucker looked like he was ready to grab her by the throat.

It's just not fair, Jesus. It's just not fair. "I . . . don't think I can do what you're asking. You want me to tell this man that everything will be okay after you dump a little concrete in his garage when I know his house is going down."

If looks could kill.

"That's exactly what you *are* going to tell him." Tucker's face was like titanium. "And if you can't do it, then I'll find someone who can. I'm not going to lose everything just because your silly conscience might bother you."

Don Blaster glanced at Gloria, embarrassment written all over him, then looked at Tucker.

"I'm not joking, Gloria." Tucker bent low over her chair, his hot breath scorching her ear. "If you're not up to this job, then maybe you should pack your bags and go back to Appleton."

Gloria met his gaze, then watched him turn and walk out of the trailer. Maybe she wasn't up to the job, but one thing she knew—she wasn't going back to Appleton.

"Hello? Mr. Primavera? This is Gloria Bickford from . . . yes . . . you're welcome . . . yes . . . I know they're going to pour you a new concrete floor tomorrow . . . that's right, and fill in the hole . . . aha . . . yes, I'm happy too that you've finally gotten some attention . . . What? . . . Will this solve the problem? Ah . . . all I can say is that Mattson Development is committed to making it right, whatever it takes . . . I'm not trying to be evasive, Mr. Primavera. It's just that I'm not an engineer. Mr. Blaster will have to answer those questions. Just rest assured that Mattson Development will see it through, whatever it takes."

Had she lied without lying? Was that possible? Sure it was . . . by speaking half-truths, applying innuendos. But a lie was a lie. She had finally stopped straddling the fence and had come down on the wrong side. And all because her desperately wicked heart panted after an idol that didn't exist.

Oh, Jesus, sweet Jesus. I hope You're not sitting beside me right now, because I just couldn't stand the thought of how disappointed You must be.

That night, long after Perth had come home from her evening shift at Phil's Diner and the apartment was dark and quiet, Gloria continued to toss and turn in her bed. Finally, she flicked on the lamp next to her, propped the pillow behind her, and reached for her Bible. She opened the leather cover and unclipped the Paper Mate pen from the inch-thick strap that ran down the middle. Then she flipped to Isaiah 53:5 and began to silently mouth the words, "But he was wounded for our transgressions, he was bruised for our iniquities: the chastisement of our peace was upon him; and with his stripes we are healed."

She closed her eyes and pictured her beautiful Jesus' blood-soaked hair, His bruised face, the nails ripping through His hands and feet. She held this picture for a long time. Sin was so ugly. So vile. When she couldn't bear the sight any longer, she slowly uncapped the Paper Mate, put the date in the margin, and let her pen give voice to what her heart had been crying all night.

Create in me a clean heart, O God, and renew a right spirit within me.

Chapter Eleven

I SLEPT BUT MY HEART WAS AWAKE.
LISTEN! MY LOVER IS KNOCKING:
"OPEN TO ME, MY SISTER, MY DARLING,
MY DOVE, MY FLAWLESS ONE."
~ SONG OF SONGS 5:2 NIV ~

GLORIA COULDN'T BELIEVE how excited she was. Tracy would be here any minute. *Tracy.* Red-haired, green-eyed Tracy. Fire and Ice, the kids used to call her, and for good reason. And before the divorce, when Tucker still lived in Appleton, kids used to call the two of them TNT. That fit too.

Even though they had had their moments, oh, how Gloria missed her! You can't spend most of your twenty-eight years growing up with someone, going through all the angst of childhood with its playground fights and skinned knees, then puberty with its tampons and pimples and hormones that run up and down the full stairway of emotion, and finally womanhood with all the uncertainty, dashed expectations and fragile dreams, and not feel a void when that person is absent. Gloria knew about voids, knew all about feeling like a donut without a hole and rolling along the edge of a counter ready to fall off. She had done enough of that after her father died. And again, after Mother wouldn't let her see Grandma Quinn anymore.

Thanksgiving was going to be wonderful this year! She had been counting the days. And any minute now, Tracy would walk through that door, and it would be just like old times. Gloria's heart thumped in betrayal. Did she really think it would be like old times?

Yes.

Maybe.

No. *I've been wiping your nose forever.* She was different now, and that would make their relationship different. And the issue of Tucker was bound to color things too. He was like The Blob, growing and growing in Gloria's life, yet totally unrecognizable. Who was he, really? Every time she thought she had that figured out, he'd change shapes. That incident with Mr. Primavera certainly showed her a thing or two.

Mr. Primavera had watched with triumph as Don Blaster's construction crew filled the sinkhole, then poured a new concrete floor. His chubby pink cheeks looked like they stored walnuts every time he smiled, which he did a lot that day. But Tucker hadn't smiled. He had been quite upset with Gloria for telling Mr. Primavera that Don Blaster, as construction engineer, had to answer the question of structural integrity. And as other problems surfaced with more homeowners and Gloria fought to give honest answers, the tension between her and Tucker increased. And it was wearing them both out.

Gloria was sure that was the reason Tucker had refused her invitation to Thanksgiving dinner. He had mumbled something about "other plans," but Gloria couldn't believe he'd miss an opportunity to spend the holiday with his sister. She wondered how she was going to pretend that everything was "just wonderful" at Mattson Development when she saw Tracy. Perhaps Tracy already knew what was going on there.

Funny thing was, Gloria was sleeping better at night.

She glanced at the kitchen table, where three settings of white Pfaltzgraff dinnerware sat—the kind she had seen in Macy's—sixteen pieces for $129. Her set, the one Tracy was storing back in Appleton, cost $79.99—all 101 pieces of it. She readjusted a plate, then aligned the Cambridge flatware in neat Emily Post order. In the middle of the table was a Mikasa bud vase, holding three artificial pink roses. She fiddled with one of the cloth napkins—smoothed it down and placed it in the center of the plate. All this belonged to Tucker, and by blood and inheritance, she supposed to Tracy too.

She went to the stove and checked the pot of potatoes boiling briskly on a back burner. In the front, a saucepan of stock made from the turkey neck and giblets waited to be used for gravy. On another burner, nearly cooked broccoli lay hidden beneath a lid.

The kitchen steamed and sizzled with noise, and smells that Gloria hadn't smelled for ages filled the apartment with pleasant aromas. At least the food was hers. Or some of it, anyway. And she could offer it to Tracy with a loving heart. She thought of the turkey and suddenly felt embarrassed.

She heard the shower turn off and knew Perth would be out soon, bubbling with excitement. It was Perth who had insisted on buying and cooking the turkey herself. Now when Tracy asked, she'd have to admit she hadn't even bought that.

Why was that so important?

Gloria shrugged. Because when she found out that Tracy was coming, the first thing Gloria wanted to do was impress her with how well she was doing. She needed to get over that. This was Perth's first holiday without her father, and it would be difficult. Gloria knew that was one of the reasons Perth was so anxious to cook the turkey. It took Perth's mind off the fact she didn't have a father to share Thanksgiving with anymore. So Gloria had smiled while Perth spent two weeks poring through magazines for stuffing recipes and helpful "how-to" tips on turkey roasting. And she had smiled when she saw Perth's face after she told her company would be coming.

Some things were more important than you showing off, Gloria.

"I can't get over how much you've changed! How different you look," Tracy said, over and over, fingering Gloria's hair and making her turn this way and that. "Gosh, kiddo, you're a real knockout! Didn't I tell you? Didn't I tell you if you just stopped dressing like a geek and did something with your hair? Didn't I tell you? Just look at you!"

Gloria stopped showing off her new hairdo and hugged Tracy for the third time. "It's soooo good to see you. I've really missed you."

"Me too, kiddo. Me too."

Gloria thought Tracy looked tired, frazzled, but said nothing and led her into the living room, where Perth sat shyly on the couch, clad in a long-sleeve knit dress that hit her calves and made her almost look her age. Her freshly washed hair had a lovely sheen and was tied back by a green ribbon that closely matched the color of her dress. And she wasn't wearing all those silver pierced earrings, but only two small pearls—one on each ear.

When Gloria introduced Perth, she felt a sudden pride, as

though she were introducing a relative. It was an odd feeling. How had this waif, who was only two short months ago a stranger, suddenly become "family"? She watched Perth hug Tracy without reservation. Then she watched Tracy flinch and stiffen and resented her for it. Another odd feeling. Gloria had told Tracy of Perth's background, and it wounded her that Tracy couldn't be more generous with the girl after all she had gone through.

Gloria brought in hors d'oeuvres—a plate of Monterey Jack cheese, all cut up into cubes and surrounded by roasted garlic Triscuits—and passed them. Then she sat and listened to Perth chatter about New Field High and her boyfriend, Spike, who she just dumped. Perth seemed determined to make friends with Tracy, and that made Gloria proud. She had told Perth all about Tracy. How she was a Mattson, sister to the Mattson who had fired her father, sister to the Mattson who had taken away the medical benefits that would have made the last months of her father's life more bearable. And here Perth was, loving and generous and trying so hard to be friendly. Yes, Gloria was proud.

But Tracy . . . she was another matter. She sat cold, aloof. Hardly saying a word, seeming to resent Perth's presence, almost as though she were jealous. Oh, how ridiculous was that? It simply wasn't possible that the red-haired, green-eyed ruler of the world, indeed practically the owner of Gloria's whole world, could be jealous of the one priceless thing Gloria actually could claim in all of Tucker's apartment—Perth's friendship.

No, not possible.

Even so, Gloria found herself in the kitchen rushing the final preparation of the meal and calling them to the table a full twenty minutes early.

The dinner plates lay piled high in the sink, the remnants of gravy and mashed potatoes still clinging to them, and every inch of counter space was crammed with dirty pots and pans. But at least the leftovers were put away. The dishes, Gloria insisted, could wait until after Tracy's visit.

Now Gloria and Tracy sat at the table sipping coffee and picking at the pumpkin pie Tracy had brought. Perth had helped put the food away, then discreetly left the apartment for a walk.

Thoughtful girl.

"Well, kiddo, you certainly look like you've made a nice life for yourself. A great apartment, a great job with a great promotion. You've even added family."

"You mean Perth?"

"Anyone can see she's crazy about you, almost like you were her older sister or something."

Gloria shrugged. "She's just grateful. I was there when she needed someone. That's all."

"Gratitude's a rare thing." Tracy gave her a funny look. "Seems nobody has it these days. Seems people forget so easily."

Gloria pushed her coffee away. "Is that supposed to mean something? C'mon, Tracy, I know you too well. I know when you're trying to give me a message, when you're trying to sneak it by me like castor oil in a spoonful of jam. Why don't you just come out with it?"

Tracy swiped her bangs, exposing the deep furrow creasing her forehead. "I'm talking about Tucker, if you wanna know. I'm talking about the way you've been treating him lately."

"How well do you know him? Really know him?" Gloria said, dreading where the conversation was going, but knowing it had to go there.

"What do you mean? He's my brother, for heaven's sake!"

"But for years you lost touch. Things happen, people change. You know him now as a successful owner of a corporation, an older brother who is indulgent, generous, and of course you're proud of him, and maybe that's all clouding your perception."

"I don't get what you're trying to say. Yes, Tucker's generous. To a fault. And I am proud of him. Look around you, Gloria. I didn't hear many complaints when I asked him to set you up."

Gloria covered Tracy's hand with hers. "I'm not complaining, really. I have a lot to be grateful for. I know that. You and Tucker couldn't be any nicer to me. Don't you think I want to repay that kindness? Don't you think I want to do everything I can for you and Tucker? But there are some—"

"Then why do you fight him at every turn? Question his integrity? The way he runs his business? He says it's getting so he can't rely on you at all. You're not helping him, Gloria, and I just find that hard to stomach."

"Don't you want to know why?"

"It doesn't matter why. Tucker's under a lot of pressure these days. You know that. You should be doing whatever you can to make his life easier. You owe him that much. You owe us both that much."

Gloria removed her hand from Tracy's. Tracy had just asked her to take a cab down memory lane and pay the fare.

"You should be helping him," Tracy repeated.

"Even if it means I have to lie? Even if it means I have to convince a lot of people that there's nothing wrong with their homes when, in fact, they could sink right into the ground under them?"

"Yes!"

"Tracy . . . I don't know how to say this . . . but I think Tucker's in way over his head. Some of the things he does at the site—"

"Just shut up, okay! I don't want to hear any of your holier-than-thou garbage. This isn't church. You can't turn the other cheek in the business world. You have to fight all the way if you want to get to the top. Then you have to fight to stay there. And Tucker's in the fight of his life. You don't know what he went through after the divorce, after Mom and Dad split up. It did something to him. It's almost like he has to prove himself over and over. He needs this. He needs The Estates. It'll put him over the top. Maybe finally bring him some satisfaction, some peace. And he expected more from you. He expected you to be in his corner. You've disappointed him, Gloria, and you've hurt him."

Gloria took a long, slow sip of her coffee, then set her mug on the table. "I don't know what to say, except that I'm sorry. I'm sorry he feels that way. I never wanted—"

"He fired me."

"What?"

"Cutter fired me. Just like that. When he came back from Eckerd. I didn't want to tell you because I knew you'd blame yourself."

"Oh, no. He couldn't have. What are you going to do? How are you going to pay all those credit card bills?" Gloria narrowed her eyes. "That miserable worm! That jerk! I'm *so sorry*, Tracy. I don't know what else to say, except that I'm *soooo sorry*." She reached across the table and took Tracy's hand again. "And I do feel responsible. Only, I don't know how to fix it." *Oh, beautiful Jesus, what's happening here?*

"Forget it."

"I can't forget it. With all the debt you've got strung out on your credit cards, you can't afford to be out of work one day."

Tracy laughed. "You've got that right. Five of them already closed me down. And the phone calls . . . you wouldn't believe the phone calls. I swear they drag the bottom of the barrel for these people. They're all nasty baboons."

"Have you found another job?"

"Not in Appleton. Sent my résumé all over. Nothing." Tracy flipped her red hair over her shoulder. "But, kiddo, I did find a job right here, in Eckerd City."

"At Mattson Development?" Gloria didn't know why, but she hoped Tracy would say no.

Tracy nodded. "I'm taking the receptionist's place. She resigned yesterday."

"Jenny Hobart resigned?"

"Oh, you didn't know? Yeah. Something about her going into commercials. 'Course I won't be receptionist long. Only until Tucker finds a better spot for me. So you see, kiddo, we're going to be working together again. Just like old times. I had hoped we could also be roommates, but you've already got one." Tracy's eyes focused like lasers on Gloria.

"No, I can't . . . I absolutely can't throw Perth out," Gloria said, shaking her head. "She has no place else to go. No family. Nothing."

"What about Social Services? They can place her with some nice people and—"

"I said no." Gloria saw the look of surprise on Tracy's face, as though Gloria had just slapped her. "Perth's happy now. She's settled at school, has friends, a job. I can't disrupt her. I *won't* disrupt her."

"Okay. Okay. Calm down." Tracy's face clouded, making her look irritated, out of sorts. "No need to get huffy. If you'd rather room with a stranger than your best friend, okay."

❦ ❦

"I don't think she likes me." Perth crossed the living room in bare feet, her sterling toe rings catching Gloria's eye and making her smile. "I tried to be friendly, but for some reason we didn't click." She flopped on the couch.

Gloria was already lounging in the stuffed armchair nearby, happy to be finally sitting after doing all the dishes with Perth. "You shouldn't jump to conclusions." Gloria hoped she sounded convincing. "The problem is—Tracy's used to me. Generally, she does all the talking and likes it that way." It wasn't a lie. *Honest, Jesus. You know Tracy's used to being the only floor show and dislikes sharing the stage.* No point in telling Perth that Tracy was also ticked because she did not want to share the apartment. "I don't think she expected a chatterbox."

"Oh . . . I'm sorry. Did I talk too much?" Perth's face became a mass of regret.

Gloria laughed. "No. You were perfect. Just perfect. And by the way . . . thanks for giving us a little time to ourselves. That was very thoughtful of you. And I want that stuffing recipe. It was absolutely one of the best I've ever had."

"*Really?* Maybe we can trade secrets. I'll tell you what I did with that stuffing, and you give me pointers on how to put on mascara. Mine's never right, with all those black smudges on my lids. You're really so good with makeup. What do you say?"

"Well . . . sure." Gloria bit the inside of her mouth to keep from laughing.

"It was a wonderful Thanksgiving, Gloria. You made it special. I was worried on account of Dad . . . but you made it special. And I know Tracy didn't really like me. But that's okay. I have you. Only, I wish we were sisters. I wish we could be family, forever. I . . . love you."

Gloria smiled. "I love you too, kiddo." She leaned her head against the back of the chair and prayed that someday Perth would come to know her beautiful Jesus. Then they really would be family—joint heirs with the King, for all eternity.

⋘ ⋙

The first thing Gloria did Friday morning when she stepped out of the elevator and onto the sixteenth floor of Pratt Towers was to head for Jenny Hobart's desk. Jenny always got to work early. She told Gloria that a good receptionist should be at her post before the workday began, just in case. Gloria never understood what the "just in case" meant, but true to form, Jenny was already sitting behind her desk looking like a "10" and smelling like a bouquet of roses.

"I hear you got a job doing a commercial. Congratulations."

"Where did you hear that?"

"Ah . . . from somebody. It's true, isn't it? I mean you resigned because of—"

"Who told you I resigned?"

Gloria felt her face flush. "Well, I heard . . . and thought . . . Did I misunderstand?"

"This office!" Jenny waved her hands in disgust; a new shade of red slicked her nails. "They never get things right. When it comes down to it, I won't be sorry to leave . . . except for you, Gloria. I'll miss you."

"Well . . . thanks . . ." Gloria was strangely touched. "That's really sweet . . . but are you saying you didn't resign?"

"No. I was fired."

Gloria's hand went up to her mouth. "Fired! That can't be. I mean . . . what about the commercials?"

"There are no commercials. I don't know where you got that idea. And this is my last day. I wasn't coming in. I just wasn't going to show up, then I thought about it. Between you and me,

I could use the money. So here I am. The new girl starts Monday."

"I'm sorry . . . really sorry." Gloria was stunned. Why had Tracy lied about Jenny resigning? Maybe she didn't know. Maybe it was Tucker who had lied. "Something will come along. Maybe an opportunity to really do a commercial and—"

Jenny snorted with laughter, sounding uncharacteristically coarse. "I'm beginning to have serious doubts about that too."

"What about Jordon's connection? What about that agent who was going to help you?"

Jenny laughed even louder. When people began staring, she finally stopped. "There's no agent." She leaned across the desk. "Never was. It was all a lie. Spencer finally admitted it. Claims he told me that because he wanted to go out with me. The sleaze. He's the reason I got fired. Oh, what a sleaze!"

Suddenly, Gloria felt sorry for Jenny Hobart, for beautiful, poised, perfect-enunciator Jenny Hobart. And then something else too, that came right out of the blue. It was knowledge, the knowledge that physical beauty can be a burden. "I'm sorry about Jordon. I know how much you wanted to do commercials." She thought she saw Jenny flinch.

"Well . . . I guess we don't always get what we want, do we? But you stay clear of him, you hear?"

Gloria laughed. "No need to worry. I doubt he'll go to any trouble trying to get a date with me."

"Oh, stop teasing, Gloria."

Gloria shrugged. "Was he really that bad?"

"He's . . . what's the difference? I can't get fired all over again. He doesn't . . . well, Spencer has no respect for women, and he can get rough."

Gloria stared stupidly at Jenny. "I don't understand."

"He likes to smoke pot and wanted me to join him. I guess

234

he thought I'd be more agreeable to his other ideas if I was high. When I wouldn't, he'd get rough about it. Start pushing me around. A little shove here, a poke there. Once he actually hauled off and slapped me across the face, hurt my lip. But I covered it with makeup, and nobody noticed. Even after he has a joint he doesn't give up. I always heard you got mellow smoking pot, but Spencer, he gets aggressive, and even more nervous than usual, if that's possible. I hated it, just hated being with him. My stomach would be in knots for days knowing I was going to have to see him."

Gloria remembered Jenny's split lip, her distraught manner these past several weeks. It all made sense now. "What makes you think you were fired because of Jordon?"

Jenny twisted her face into a frown. "Spencer had been hounding me every day, calling, saying he needed more information for that agent. But inside I knew it was just a lie, but still I went. Imagine that. How stupid was I? Even after he hurt me that night, split my lip. It's amazing what you're willing to do sometimes when you want something so badly. But when I found out there was no agent, I told Spencer I never wanted to see or hear from him again."

"And what did he say?"

"He told me if I stopped seeing him he'd have me fired. I told him go ahead, but if he ever bothered me again, I'd have my very large Delta Force brother take care of him. I got fired the next day, the day before Thanksgiving. Happy Thanksgiving, Jenny! Mr. Mattson told me I could finish out the week, and like I said . . . I need the money."

"What are you going to do now?"

"I don't know. The creep really did a number on my head. It's still a little scrambled. I mean, I really did think this was going to be it. My big break. You know? And I so wanted a chance to do commercials. I thought I'd really be good at that. And time is critical. That old clock is ticking. Once the wrinkles come, well . . . forget commercials. Maybe that's why I wanted so desperately to believe Spencer. I still can't get over how naive I was. How I deluded myself into believing his lies, how I endured going out with him. And for nothing. All for nothing. When you want something so badly . . . but you won't know anything about that."

"Why not?"

"Because, anyone who came in that first day looking like you did has got to have it together. When I saw you walking in with that long khaki skirt and vest, that white shirt with the stain, I said to myself, 'Jenny, now here's someone who has it all together. You could learn from her. She's strong and doesn't care what people think.' Even when I had to go buy you clothes because Mr. Mattson insisted, you were so . . . cool about the whole thing. Oh, you were annoyed, I could see that. But so calm and cool and totally unruffled. Me, I would have been in the bathroom bawling my eyes out." Jenny glanced at Gloria almost shyly, then began inspecting her nails. "That's because I obsess about everything: a hangnail, a pimple, my eyelashes, positively everything. I want people to like me, so I try to make myself as perfect as I can. I know that sounds silly to someone like you."

Gloria moved around the desk and folded her arms around the receptionist. "I'm going to miss you," she said, hugging her tightly, all the while realizing, with shock, that nobody really had it together, not even someone as beautiful as Jenny Hobart.

Then she began wondering just what kind of hold Spencer Jordon had on Tucker.

~◈ ◈~

Chapter Twelve

I OPENED FOR MY LOVER,
BUT MY LOVER HAD LEFT;
HE WAS GONE.
—◉ SONG OF SONGS 5:6 NIV◉—

"YOU WON'T BELIEVE WHAT happened last night," Perth said, kicking off her covers, then dangling one pajama leg off the side of the couch.

"Well, good morning, sleepyhead," Gloria said, breezing into the living room. She had been up and dressed for hours. "I've already washed down the bathroom and kitchen. I thought I'd head for the bedroom closet, *our* closet, and attempt to organize it for the *third time.* I hadn't expected you up so early. It's not even noon yet."

Perth laughed. "You're sounding more like a nagging sister every day. You wanna hear my story or not?"

"Sure." Gloria took a detour and headed for the armchair, tousling Perth's hair as she passed.

"Well, this nice man, about forty maybe fifty—it was hard to tell—came in and sat in my section." Perth propped herself on one elbow. "Then he ordered a huge dinner: appetizer, soup, salad, the meat loaf special with mashed potatoes and extra sides, and even a piece of pecan pie with whipped cream. The works. I thought, boy oh boy, I'm gonna get some tip!"

Gloria felt pleasure watching Perth's animated face—the eyes like bright lanterns, the mouth wide with exaggeration—and her heart rejoiced over the precious changes taking place in Perth, subtle as a budding forsythia. "So how much did you get?"

"Not a dime. Not one dime. Just as I handed him the bill, these environmentalists came in, with their pickets and leaflets and—"

"Phil let them demonstrate in his diner?"

"No. They came to eat—eight of them, and Heidi, one of the waitresses, led them to a back table, I think to get them out of the way. They were pretty rowdy and noisy and dropped their leaflets on every table they passed. Everybody ignored them except my customer. He cursed and brushed the leaflet to the floor, saying he didn't want any of their blankety-blank propaganda. That's when this guy, the leader, I think, came over and asked my customer to repeat what he said. When I saw his neck veins bulge, I backed away. But my customer stood up and started talking about the ranch he lost because of radicals like them. And he started talking louder and louder, trying to draw in everyone around him, telling them to wake up and smell the roses while they still had roses to smell, because after these crazy environmentalists were through, nobody would have roses or anything else to call their own."

Gloria curled her legs under her and frowned. "Then what happened?"

"Pow! He socked him right in the jaw. Laid him out flat."

"*Who?* Who laid who out?"

"The environmentalist laid out my customer. I didn't know you could knock someone out like that with one punch. Pow!" Perth slapped her fist against the flat of her hand. "It happened so fast I didn't even have time to get scared. But by the time Phil came over, my knees were shaking, and my stomach felt like I had just eaten a pound of his three-day-old chili. I gave Phil the tab and told him the customer was knocked out before he could pay. I figured it was an owner's job to straighten out something like that. 'Course I knew there goes my tip."

"What happened to the environmentalist?"

"Phil had one of the girls call the police, and when they finally got the guy off the floor, he said he wouldn't press charges. I think he was intimidated—with all of them and their picket signs, glaring at him, and here he was just this one guy."

"I know, I've seen them."

"Yeah. They're so serious and look mad all the time. And two nights ago—I didn't tell you about this—but when I got off work, I spotted a bunch of cop cars down the street, their lights flashing, and naturally I go and see what the noise is all about. And would you believe it? Someone trashed a car—I mean tires slashed, windows broken, fenders dented, the whole bit."

Gloria leaned forward in her seat. "Aha. And?"

"Nobody knows who did it. Only . . . the car had a bumper sticker on back that said, 'Radical Environmentalists Are Terrorists.'" Perth shrugged, kicked the rest of her covers off, and sat up. "I really didn't think anything about it until . . . last night. Seeing all that anger and hate made me wonder if these same environmentalists didn't trash the car."

Gloria shook her head. "I just don't get it. What are they trying to accomplish?"

"I asked someone at the diner if there was any endangered stuff at The Lakes. You know, an animal or bird or a flower, something. Nobody seems to know. I even read their leaflet, and it doesn't say anything about The Lakes. It's just a bunch of stuff about saving the environment. Stuff I've already learned at school. So I don't get it, either. What do they have against The Lakes?"

Gloria sat quietly, letting Perth's statement roll around her mind like a dust ball gathering lint. "How about we try to find out?" she finally said.

Perth rose to her feet, her thin arms and legs already in motion as she whirled around the room. "Sure." She grabbed the pair of jeans draped over the end of the couch and headed toward the bathroom. One thing about Perth, once she got up she was sheer energy. "But how are we gonna do that?"

Gloria shrugged. "Maybe we should start at the library."

❧ ☙

"This is as far as I go, lady." The cabbie pulled to the side of the highway. "I'm not gonna wreck my tires and shocks over them ruts." He pointed to the dirt road in front of them. "It ain't far. Half a mile and you'll see The Lakes. One of them, anyway. You still want me to wait?"

Gloria nodded and slid across the seat toward Perth.

"It's gonna cost. Time's valuable. Can't sit here for who knows how long without some compensation."

"You'll be compensated," Gloria said, following Perth out the door of the car.

"Maybe you should pay me now."

Gloria laughed. "Do I look that dumb?" She slammed the door, then slipped her arm through Perth's and headed down the dirt road.

The first thing that struck Gloria was the foliage. Evergreens spiked everywhere, like green bristle brushes, and in between were large maples with some tenacious yellow, orange, and red leaves still clinging to their branches.

When they reached a spot where they could see the lake, Gloria released Perth's arm and just stood and stared. It took her a moment to take it all in. She had never seen anything so lovely. Maples, evergreens, and birch everywhere, but not like a dense forest where sunlight didn't penetrate. Tall brownish grass, looking almost like wheat, along with dried wildflowers covered the landscape that rolled gently downward toward a giant lake. Even with the dead underbrush, it was breathtaking. In the spring and summer and early fall, it had to be spectacular. It reminded Gloria of the stream a mile outside Appleton where she and Tracy and Tucker used to fish, the place Gloria had always called the most beautiful spot in the world. Until now.

The head librarian told Gloria the two crystal-clear bodies of water weren't lakes at all but one large stream that disappeared underground for half a mile before reappearing to form the second "Lake."

The librarian also told Gloria that Hugo Pratt's family had owned this whole area called The Lakes for the past three hundred years, and it had only recently been sold off after Hugo Pratt, the last of the Pratts still living in Eckerd, died. The heirs, scattered across the country, had no interest in anything other than what could be converted into cash and had liquidated the entire estate. The one stipulation in the will was that if the heirs chose to sell "The Lakes" then Hugo's doctor, Dr. Lawrence Braddock, had the right of first refusal. People had been trying to get their hands on The Lakes for years, and many in Eckerd were angry over the stipulation, Tucker Mattson being one of them.

The Lakes was a true real estate plum.

Dr. Lawrence Braddock had purchased The Lakes at a high but fair price and brought in two partners. The librarian knew one of them was another doctor at Eckerd Hospital, but she had no clue about the other. But Gloria knew. Cutter Press.

Now, looking around, Gloria felt her heart soar. It was beautiful, tranquil, picturesque, not far from a major highway, and close to Eckerd City. It put Tucker's Estates property to shame.

"Oh, how beautiful!" Perth finally said. "Can you just imagine living here?"

Gloria nodded, still taking it in. She watched the sun dance on the water, watched the breeze rustle the last stubborn leaves of the oaks. "It would be almost sinful if nobody could build here."

Perth bent down and plucked a dried flower and twirled it between her fingers. "I still don't get what those environmentalists are trying to do."

"I think I'm beginning to," Gloria said quietly.

"Yeah?" Perth nudged Gloria with her elbow. "C'mon, give. What?"

"Tucker Mattson could never compete with something like this."

Gloria's footsteps felt like lead coming out of the elevator and onto the sixteenth floor. Ever since seeing The Lakes, she had wondered how she was going to continue with Mattson Development. She had spent hours seeking God and ended by realizing that she didn't really want to hear from Him. What if He called her to take the hard road? What if He asked her to quit her job or move back to Appleton? She didn't think she could do that. How could she give up her hard-won freedom? It had cost her so much just to get this far. And what about her debt to Tracy? How could she leave her, just like that? Without repaying her? After all, what had she done for Tracy so far?

Gotten her fired.

And what about Tucker? He had been kind. Had gone out of his way to help her. He had even placed his confidence in her by giving her a promotion, a raise, and an opportunity to repay him.

He had also tried to use and manipulate her.

She had tried putting it all on a scale and weighing out her obligation along with her growing concerns. Could she continue working with Tucker and act as though nothing was wrong?

She was still trying to figure that out when she reached the receptionist's desk and saw Tracy sitting behind it, a big smile on her face. It felt strange and somehow disquieting not seeing Jenny Hobart there.

"Hey, kiddo. Isn't this neat? The two of us working together again?"

Gloria smiled and wondered at her lack of real enthusiasm. "Yes, great. Are you settled in at Tucker's?" She thought she saw Tracy's lip purse, but just for a second.

"Oh, sure. Tucker was a big help. You can always count on family. 'Course, I'll only be bunking with him until one of his apartments empties."

Strange how Tracy hadn't considered taking Jessica Daily's old apartment. "I'm glad you're settled. And it was great having you for Thanksgiving. Sort of like old times."

"Not quite."

Gloria was startled. "What do you mean?"

"I mean, not quite. Oh, I had a good time and all. But you're different, Gloria. Not the same sweet girl I knew. In a sense, I guess I'm to blame. I guess I helped create the monster."

"Create the *monster?*"

"Now, don't get uptight, kiddo. I said you're different. I didn't say I didn't like you. Only . . . I am disappointed I'm not staying with you. I had such plans . . ."

So that was it. Gloria leaned against the desk like a yardstick. "Maybe when Perth gets settled, or goes to college, if she's going, we can discuss being roommates. Only . . . I must admit I'm confused. You've always preferred being on your own. Back in Appleton when I was desperate to leave Mother and find my own place, you didn't want me to room with you. You said I'd cramp your love life. And I was fine with that. Only, what's changed all of a sudden?"

"I was just making a statement. You don't need to bring up the past and get—"

"You're my best friend, Tracy, and I love you like a sister. No one has done more for me than you. Only . . . don't you think sometimes you have a double standard?"

Tracy blinked silently behind the desk. "You're getting so thin-skinned I can't say anything. Tucker told me you were almost impossible to talk to. I just didn't believe him."

Gloria walked away without another word. She knew Tracy was watching her. She could almost feel her eyes burning a hole in her jacket, but she didn't look back.

❧ ❦

When Gloria got home, she was surprised to find Perth lying on the couch, her bed made for the night.

"What's the matter? You sick?"

Perth shrugged. "Sort of." Her ponytail brushed against the collar of her cotton floral pajamas, the ones Gloria had given her the first time Perth came and let her keep. "I had one of the girls at the diner take my place. I figured I'd come home and rest."

Gloria went over to the couch and placed her hand on Perth's forehead. "No fever. My mother never let me get out of anything unless I had a fever."

The two laughed, and when they were finished, Gloria tousled Perth's shiny, clean hair. "Tell you what, I'll spend a quiet evening in my room so I don't disturb you."

"You don't have to be quiet. I'm not that sick. I think I just needed a little time off."

Gloria was about to leave, but when Perth began picking her nails, she sat down on the edge of the couch. "What is it? What's really bothering you?"

Perth shrugged. "Nothing."

"I've got some chunky beef soup in the cupboard. Let's say we split it?"

"Can I have a piece of toast on the side?"

"Sure."

"And will you eat with me?"

Gloria caressed Perth's cheeks. "Sure."

Gloria sat curled on the armchair, blowing across her cup of soup and watching Perth stretch out on the couch and stir hers. After a while, Perth placed the steaming cup on the coffee table and begin twirling long strands of hair around one finger.

These days, Gloria was more relaxed about Perth. Social

Services had never shown up to take her away. And a recent article in the paper had convinced Gloria they were not likely to, either. According to the *Eckerd City Review*, Social Services had lost over three hundred children—had literally lost track of where these children had been placed. If they lost that many, the chances of them overlooking one teenager were extremely good. Still, Gloria kept it covered in prayer. She didn't want to get too cocky about the whole thing. Grandma Quinn used to say it's when you got cocky, when you stopped watching over the chickens as you should, that the fox came into the henhouse. Not that Social Services was the fox or anything like that, but it was wise counsel, just the same.

"The kids were talking about Christmas break. Everybody has something to do. Some place to go."

Gloria nodded. "I know it's hard for you, Perth. The holidays especially. Maybe we can do something together. Something special that doesn't cost too much."

"You'd do that?"

"If I can. Yes."

Perth's eyes widened. "You're great, Gloria. You really are. But I guess I'm not saying it right. I'm not making sense. It's not that I want to actually *do* anything during Christmas break. It's that I have no plans. No plans at all. Not for Christmas, not for beyond graduation, not for the rest of my life."

"Everyone's talking about college, is that it?"

"Yeah. Some of my friends even got their acceptance letters. And it suddenly struck me that I'll probably be working at Phil's Diner for the rest of my life."

In spite of herself, Gloria chuckled. "Why?"

"Well . . . what else can I do? What else is there?"

"There's the whole world," Gloria said, trying not to laugh outright. She remembered her senior year. Her feelings of inadequacy at facing the world and not knowing what to do with it. Except her mother had not sat down with her like this and talked.

If only she had.

"I've always wanted . . . now don't laugh . . . but I've been looking into physical therapy, the requirements and all. After Dad, I thought I'd go into some line of health care." Perth pulled the beige sheet up under her chin. She looked so young, so sweet. "And I think physical therapy is something I'd be interested in."

"So what's stopping you?"

"You need to go to college—about six years' worth. How could I ever pay for something like that?"

"Student loans, part-time jobs. I'm not saying it would be easy, but it can be done if you really want it. Hasn't your guidance counselor talked to you about this?"

"Yes . . . he went over some of it. But my GPA's low. This year really killed me. He doesn't think I'll get accepted. Especially not to Bristol. That's where I want to go. Bristol College. That's my first choice. I . . . actually sent away for their catalog and application. How stupid is that?"

"Dreams are not stupid, Perth. But they're never easy. If you want to go to college, then you have to apply. The worst that can happen is they say no."

"I don't know if I can stand that."

"What's worse? Trying and failing? Or not trying at all?"

"You really think I can do it? Go to college, I mean? For all that time, and make it?"

"I know you can. You're smart. You're a hard worker. There's financial aid, and there are part-time jobs to help with the bills. If you really want it, you can do it."

Perth ducked under the sheets, and Gloria heard her giggle.

When she poked her head out, her face was all smiles and light. "Tomorrow I'll talk to the guidance counselor again. Have him help me come up with a list of places he thinks I can get into and that I can afford. Then maybe we can go over that list together."

"Sure."

"And . . . it wouldn't hurt to ask God for help . . . to pray. Would it?" Perth said. "Only, I'd like you to do it because I don't wanna mess it up. It's just too important."

Gloria put down her soup, went over to the couch, and took Perth's hand. Then she closed her eyes and began praying, and for the first time her prayer flowed from her lips just like one of those church ladies in her old prayer group.

Chapter Thirteen

I LOOKED FOR HIM BUT DID NOT FIND HIM.
I CALLED HIM BUT HE DID NOT ANSWER.
SONG OF SONGS 5:6 NIV

"ARE YOU COMING HOME for Christmas?"

Gloria stared at the stack of Perth's college catalogs that cluttered the kitchen table and tried to think of what to say.

"Well?"

"I'm not sure, Mother."

"I don't see what the difficulty is. Either you're coming or you're not."

Her mother's tone told Gloria she still hadn't gotten over Thanksgiving. But what could Gloria say? It would be unthinkable to leave Perth alone for the holidays, and her mother still didn't know about her roommate.

"Well?"

Gloria took a deep breath. Maybe it was time to tell her. "I don't think I'll be coming, Mother. I can't leave my roommate."

"What roommate?"

Gloria quickly told her about Perth.

"And just when I thought you were developing some common sense. Honestly, Gloria, sometimes you don't have a brain in your head. What were you thinking? How could you let a perfect stranger come live with you? You don't know anything about this girl, about her people, her background. What if she's deranged? You want to get murdered in your bed? Is that it?"

"You're always trying to scare me, Mother. When I brought home birds, I was going to get parasites. If it was a kitten, I was going to get fleas. Now . . . I'm going to get murdered in my bed."

For a long time her mother was silent. "They have agencies for this kind of thing," she finally said. "You can't go bandaging all the birds with broken wings that come your way."

"I can try."

"I thought I broke you of that."

Gloria thought of Jessica Daily. "You almost did, Mother."

"Well, there's no use arguing with you. You've gotten so stubborn since you left Appleton. Seems I can't win, no matter what I say, so I won't say any more about it. But does this mean I won't see you for another holiday?"

"Why don't you come here for Christmas?" *Now why had she said that?* There wasn't enough sleeping room, and she still wasn't ready to face her mother.

"I don't know . . . I'll think about it. You know I hate traveling during the holidays. All those heavy coats and sweaty armpits and body odor that could choke a horse. And the pushing and shoving. The waiting in endless lines. Then there's Virginia. She's not feeling well and—"

"Mrs. Press is sick again?"

"Yes. The doctors are doing tests. Right now, no one knows what it is. I told her that's what happens when you have children and they grow up and disappoint you. Cutter's been miserable lately. Impossible, actually. I've never seen him snap at his mother like he's done this past month. It seems the two of you have more in common every day. I told Virginia that you've forgotten practically all your manners too, and can barely keep a civil tongue in your head."

Gloria pulled the box of Domino sugar from the cabinet, then glanced at her watch. "Mother, I have to get to work. We can talk about this later."

"That's what you always say, but you never call, even when I leave messages on that infernal machine of yours. I might just as well open the phone book and call the first person on the page. What would happen if there was a real emergency? I'd be in a pine box and covered with dirt before you'd ever get around to calling back."

"Mother, I'm going to miss my bus."

"Okay . . . okay. Go to work. I'll think about Christmas and let you know."

Gloria leaned against the receptionist's desk, armed with a smile and a steely determination to mend fences with Tracy. It grieved her that they were like two clouds being driven by the wind in different directions. "So, do you want to go to the movies tonight? We could go for a burger, then see a show. It'll be nice to spend time together."

"It sure would, kiddo." Tracy raked her fingers through red hair that fell in soft waves over her shoulders. "But not tonight.

I promised Tucker I'd go out with this guy. He's only in town overnight, and Tucker asked me to go to dinner with him after they finished their business."

Gloria felt her heart thump. "What's his name?"

"Spencer something. I don't remember."

"Jordon?"

"Yeah. That sounds right. How did you know?"

"Because Jenny Hobart went out with him a couple of times."

"That so?" Tracy opened her purse and pulled out a lipstick and mirror and began coloring her lips with Estée Lauder's Parallel Fire.

How could Tucker ask his own sister to go out with someone like Jordon?

"Maybe we can do the burger and movie thing tomorrow night," Tracy said, snapping her compact shut and dropping it and her lipstick back into her brown Gucci bag. "What do you think?"

"I think you should forget about going out with Jordon."

Tracy frowned. "Really, Gloria, I can't drop everything just because you want to go to a movie. Besides, I promised Tucker."

Gloria locked on to Tracy's wrist and pulled on it like she used to when they were kids and wanted Tracy to pay attention. "Listen, Jenny Hobart said this guy's a real creep."

Tracy laughed. "Spencer is Tucker's business associate. It's only for one night, and I promised. Besides, according to Tucker, Jenny Hobart was a flapdoodle. So don't go putting too much stock in what she said."

Gloria didn't know why Tracy's remark made her angry, but it did. "She's nothing of the sort. She's poised and thoughtful and conscientious."

"Well, Tucker said she was a bimbo. That's all I know."

Gloria was really steamed now, as steamed as when Tracy

called Sherry Laneer, Gloria's only other friend, a geek nobody liked, just because Sherry once wanted to spend the night at Gloria's house instead of Tracy's. "Maybe Tucker's not such a good judge of character."

Tracy shook off Gloria's hold. "Maybe. And maybe I'm not, either. We both misjudged you, didn't we?"

❧ ❦

Without knocking, Gloria went into Beth Price's office and closed the door. Beth looked up, calmly peeled off her silver wire-rimmed glasses, and gestured for Gloria to sit.

"I'm sorry for barging in." Gloria wiped her damp palms on her navy blue skirt. This was dangerous ground. Already ice was cracking beneath her feet. A little more strain, and her relationship with Tucker and Tracy could plunge into frigid waters. How had things gone so wrong? Gotten so out of hand? Until now, it never occurred to Gloria that her friendship with Tracy could become seriously damaged or even . . . end. But here it was, on the brink, and if she pursued this, it could be the final undoing. But if she didn't, and something happened to Tracy . . .

No. That was not acceptable.

"How can I help you?" Beth's expression remained blank, but her eyebrows raised a millimeter.

Gloria began picking at her nails, fighting the urge to nibble on one of her cuticles. Finally, she placed her hands on her lap, palm side down, and took a deep breath. "I was hoping you could tell me about Jessica Daily."

Gloria felt uncomfortable when Beth studied her, inspected her from all angles like a photographer might do before shooting his film. "Why?" Beth finally asked.

"Let's just say it's something I need to know."

253

"Troubleshooting?"

"In a manner of speaking."

Beth leaned forward, placed her elbows on her desk, and tented her hands. "How important is it?"

"Very. It might help me help someone I care about. Might help this friend avoid getting in over her head."

"How much do you want to know?" Beth didn't look happy.

"Everything."

"That covers a lot of ground. Why don't I keep it simple and just cover the last two years of her life?"

Gloria nodded and wondered why Beth's lower lip trembled.

"Two years ago, Jessica came to work here as a receptionist. She was fresh out of junior college with an associate's degree in Marketing—Associate of Business Administration——Marketing was her actual degree. Her parents wanted her to continue her education, but Jessica refused. She had met a man, a man she claimed to love, and wanted to work for him. The man was Tucker Mattson."

Gloria swallowed the lump in her throat. It landed in her stomach like a rock.

"Jessica's parents were not happy about her quitting school or about the relationship. Tucker Mattson was almost ten years Jessica's senior. He lived in the fast lane, had a bad reputation with women. And he was a maverick in business. None of these particulars made Jessica's parents believe this was a good match or that it had a promising future. The tension between Jessica and her parents became so bad Jessica finally moved out. Actually, she moved into one of Tucker Mattson's apartments."

Gloria closed her eyes and saw the slim, agitated body, the sad, haunting face.

"Is something wrong?"

Gloria opened her eyes. "Jessica lived next door to me. I met her the first day I moved in."

"I see." Beth gnawed her lip, then coughed into her hand. "Where was I? Yes . . . Jessica worked for a year as receptionist, then Tucker Mattson created a job for her, Marketing Strategist. I've never seen anyone so happy. For a while it looked like all of Jessica's dreams were coming true. She and Tucker were tighter than ever. He relied on her, asked for her opinion, gave her freedom to explore, experiment. She did a lot of the early PR for The Estates. It was going to be bigger than anything Tucker had ever done. It was going to make him a multimillionaire, and she was determined to help it happen. Then . . . Spencer Jordon came to town."

Hearing that name made the muscles between Gloria's shoulder blades tighten.

"Jordon was important to The Estates project. He was to be wined and dined in style. Tucker told Jessica that as Marketing Strategist it was her job to keep Jordon happy. She went out with him once. Then twice. Then it became a constant. Sometimes I would hear Jessica and Tucker fighting about Jordon in his office." She pointed to the ornate mahogany door that separated her office from Tucker's. "It's not as thick as it looks. You can hear everything when people raise their voices."

"What did they fight about?"

Beth shook her head. "I don't think you need to know that. But I'll tell you this. Jessica changed. She became depressed, withdrawn."

Gloria rubbed her forehead. "I feel so bad."

"Why?"

"I . . . thought it was just a fight, a silly squabble. I didn't know. I could see something was wrong. But I thought he was her boyfriend. I just thought they had a fight."

Beth leaned forward. "What are you talking about?" Her voice was as tight as dry rawhide.

"I think I was the last person to see Jessica Daily alive. She came over to borrow some milk, but what she really wanted was to talk . . . and I didn't make time for her." Gloria still couldn't defeat her guilt.

"And he was there? Spencer Jordon?"

Gloria nodded. "I feel terrible."

"How do you think her mother feels?"

"I can't even imagine."

"No. I mean she feels terrible too. She's the one who introduced Jessica to Tucker."

Gloria couldn't believe talking about Jessica Daily felt so terrible and yet so good, like taking Pepto-Bismol. "Keeping things buried inside always binds a person up," Grandma Quinn used to say, "but bringing it to the light sets you free." She was right. Gloria couldn't think of one good thing she had ever gained by bottling herself up. "What happened to Jessica? What did Spencer Jordon do to her?"

"Drugs, for one thing. But he was abusive too . . ." Pain warped Beth's face, making it look like a wrinkled sheet.

Gloria put her hand to her mouth. "You're Jessica's mother! No . . . sorry. Of course not. That was stupid. I mean that couldn't be true. You have different names."

"Jessica's father died when she was eight. I remarried two years later." Beth suddenly looked ten years older. "My husband couldn't have been a better father. He even wanted to adopt Jessica, to legally make his name hers, but she wouldn't. She said it seemed disrespectful to her dad's memory." She looked hard at Gloria. "It's not something that's common knowledge around here. Jess wanted it that way. Al Simms is the only one who knows, because he also does all the Human Resources stuff, and it came out in the forms."

"Don't worry. I'm usually the brunt of office gossip. I don't spread it. This will stay between us. Only . . . how can you still work for him?" Gloria suddenly felt anger rise up like acid reflux and wished for the millionth time she was more like Jesus. "How can you still work for Tucker?"

Beth replaced her wire-rimmed glasses and began shuffling papers around her desk. "My reasons don't concern you."

Gloria scattered the layout of the next *Mattson Newsletter* over Tucker's desk and watched his reaction. The angle of the desk lamp partially shadowed Tucker's face and made him appear drawn, perturbed, but the smile said otherwise.

"These newsletters are getting better and better. I really like this collage of the crew, how you're spotlighting the foreman and some of the others."

Gloria found it difficult concentrating. This whole newsletter critique seemed insignificant in the light of Beth's revelation. She only hoped her courage wouldn't fail her. "I think it'll heighten buyer confidence," she said in a monotone. "Your foreman has a good background—multiple degrees, a long list of recommendations, respected in the field. I think it'll go a long way in offsetting some of those rumors about The Estates."

"Great work, Gloria. And since you've been spending time at The Estates, the homeowners are happier. You and I haven't seen eye to eye lately, but I must admit you have a way with them and—"

"I know you intend to fix everything, to make good on all of it, but we're far from out of the woods. Some of these people are on the brink. If something else goes wrong, the dominoes could fall. There's talk of a class action suit. And if that happens, all the newsletters in the world wouldn't do any good."

The shadow seemed to plaster a brooding look over Tucker's face. "You cover your end, and I'll cover mine. Okay?"

Gloria nodded and took the pile of proofs from Tucker. "Just one more question." Despite her resolve, her voice shook, and her courage faltered just a bit. *Jesus, beautiful Jesus, be with me now.* "Who is Jessica Daily?" She had never seen Tucker turn white before. But here he was, standing in front of her looking like someone had dusted him with flour.

"What . . . makes you ask?"

"Tucker, please, *please* don't make Tracy go out with Spencer Jordon."

"What are you doing, Gloria?" Tucker's face had gone from white to red in a matter of seconds. "Just what do you know about Jessica and Jordon?"

"A lot." Gloria saw fear in his eyes.

"Does Tracy know you're talking to me about this?"

"No."

"Should I tell her to join us?"

"I wish you would."

Tucker flinched, then struck the desk with his fist. "If you don't beat all. I took you in because I felt sorry for you. Gave you the break of your life, and you have the gall, that's right, Gloria, the absolute *gall* to question me about things that are none of your business."

Because I felt sorry for you. Those words made her feel as if she had swallowed soap. Illusion. It was all illusion. This job, their friendship. She was nothing to him. Nothing at all.

"I was in love with Jessica. Okay?" he finally said, his voice crackling like aluminum foil. "Now I think you better get out."

Gloria was making some minor corrections to the news-letter when her phone rang. She was sure it was going to be Beth Price telling her that Mr. Tucker Mattson no longer required her services and that he had asked her to leave the building. To her surprise it was a voice she recognized as Don Blaster's new sec-retary.

"Gloria, we've got big trouble."

"What's wrong, Dot?"

"The garage floor of lot four just caved in, and the home-owner's car went with it. Her brand-new Lexus is now sitting in what looks like a ditch. The boss is there with a tow truck and crew trying to pull it out. He wanted me to call Mr. Mattson and tell him, but . . . I'd really appreciate it if you'd do that. Sometimes Mr. Mattson gets *so* angry. Do you mind?"

"Well . . . sure, Dot. I'll tell him."

Gloria hung up, then raced for Tucker's office, remembering the time Tracy first told Tucker she had overheard their parents discussing divorce. Right in front of Gloria. She'd never forget his face. Like one of Madame Tussaud's waxed figures—molded hate and fear. She had seen that look again when Don Blaster told him about the first garage floor problem.

Gloria quickly bypassed Beth's office, choosing access to Tucker's suite via the hall, instead. Taking a deep breath, she knocked once, then opened the door before being asked. "There's a problem at The Estates," she said, walking into the office and closing the door behind her. Without emotion, she told Tucker what happened and watched that paraffin look solidify into hatred and fear.

Gloria was sure the chain was going to break. It heaved and strained and made grinding noises as the tow truck's winch pulled the Lexus out of the hole, inch by inch. Someone had been able to get into the driver's side and put the car into neutral before the winch began its work. Even so, Gloria wondered if the car would ever be the same. To one side, Tucker shouted at Don Blaster, his hands waving in the air like weapons.

Outside, standing on the front lawn, was a solitary woman in her fifties, with a neat coiffure, brown linen slacks, and a tan cashmere coat, quietly crying into a monogrammed lace handkerchief.

Gloria walked up and introduced herself. The woman bunched the handkerchief in her hand and nodded politely, but her eyes remained on the Lexus.

"Mattson Development will take care of everything. They'll make everything right," Gloria said weakly, watching the woman dab her eyes.

Now, how in the world was Tucker going to get out of this one?

Gloria was utterly exhausted as she got off the bus and headed down Pratt Parkway. Tucker had offered to drive her home, but she couldn't stomach another white-knuckle ride, so she asked him to take her to the nearest bus stop, instead. He didn't press the point. He was already late for his meeting with Jordon at Pratt Towers. Neither of them mentioned Jessica again, though Gloria was sure she was just as much on Tucker's mind as hers.

But Tucker had his hands full with other problems now. She had overheard him talking to Don Blaster about a free basement for lot four—Gloria's idea for lot two redux. And she had heard them complaining about what it was all going to cost.

By the time he dropped her off, Gloria had stopped thinking about Tucker or Tracy, Jessica Daily or Spencer Jordon. She was wondering where God was in all this. Why things were going so badly. She thought maybe it was again time to remind Him of His promise and did so, right there on the crowded sidewalk. But nothing out of the ordinary happened. No voices or thunderclaps or lightning. People just continued to rush by her or close up shops, catch buses and cabs—all trying to get home.

Her feet moved rapidly over the sidewalk, rushing to get to her own apartment a few blocks away. Maybe then she would just sit down and have a talk with her Jesus. Ask Him what was going on. But she slowed her pace when she approached E-Z Printing. It looked dark and quiet; a shop already closed for the night, but through the window Gloria saw a light way in the back. She found her hand on the doorknob, found herself pulling the door open and walking in. She had passed this printer so many times she barely noticed it anymore. But she had always wanted to go in. Only, why was she doing it now?

A buzzer sounded, and Gloria realized she had stepped on something under the black rubber doormat. Footsteps came from the back, then an elderly man appeared.

"Can I help you?"

"Well . . . I don't know." She liked the man's gentle smile, the way his white curly hair hugged his ears, the way he tilted his head to one side while patiently waiting for her to state her business. "I was just wondering how much you charge for a photocopy." Gloria said the first thing that came to mind.

The man pointed to two machines in the corner where a large sign read "10 cents a copy."

Beautiful, Jesus, what am I doing here? She glanced in the back, where a portion of a duplicator could be seen through the doorway. "Who does your layouts?" she finally asked, pointing to the ugly green and yellow flyer still hanging on the window behind her.

"I do. Lost my girl a while back."

"Maybe you could use some part-time help?"

"I need full-time."

Gloria felt silly. She had no idea why she was standing here asking for a job. "Well, maybe until you get full-time help, you could use someone part-time?"

The man scratched his head. "Maybe."

"Okay, then. How about me?"

"You got any experience?"

"Uh-huh."

"You work your other job Saturdays?"

Gloria shook her head.

"Okay. Come around Saturday morning and show me what you got. I'm not promising anything. You give me two hours, I'll give you minimum wage. Then we'll see."

Chapter Fourteen

THE WATCHMEN THAT GO ABOUT
THE CITY FOUND ME: TO WHOM I SAID,
SAW YE HIM WHOM MY SOUL LOVETH?
~⦿ SONG OF SOLOMON 3:3 KJV⦿~

GLORIA COULDN'T BELIEVE how much she loved working at
E-Z Printing, or that it was her third Saturday at the little gnarly
desk in the corner. Her fingers flew over the keyboard as she
tweaked her clipping path, then scratched it and pulled up a new
one from an alpha channel. After a few frustrating minutes, she
scratched that one too and pulled up an embedded path previ-
ously saved with her picture file. For the past hour she had
worked on a collage for a Knights of Columbus flyer, and she
still wasn't sure which way to go.

The Knights had so liked the simple bulletin she did for
them last week they brought in their last year's flyer with a zil-
lion changes and new pictures and asked her to do something

"creative" for this year. Creative. She had liked the sound of that. It had made her heart soar. And if the truth be told, it was still soaring now.

The flyer, if it was good, could mean a ton of business. The Knights were well connected, and one member knew someone at the Chamber of Commerce who was looking for a new printer. And the Chamber of Commerce always needed lots of pamphlets, flyers, bulletins, and the like. And E-Z Printing needed a boost in sagging revenue. And she needed to continue working here, although she didn't know why, exactly, except it was linked to that word "creative."

Gloria finally scratched the embedded path and chose another option that contoured the image itself while ignoring nonwhite photo areas. She began playing with one of the pictures—a group of middle-aged men wearing suits and blue sashes over one shoulder and across their chests. Maybe she'd do runarounds and wrap the text around each picture.

"You gonna have that ready today?"

Gloria looked up at Harry Grizwald, his white curly hair coiling around his ears, his white beard obscuring half his face. She nodded, then smiled when she saw him staring at her rather than at the monitor. His lack of interest in what she was doing told Gloria he already trusted her. "Give me a few hours."

It had taken Harry Grizwald less than forty-five minutes to hire Gloria that first Saturday she was here. And since then, she had received plenty of customer compliments, which Harry was quick to pass along.

They had hit it off right away. Harry was intimidated by computers and happy to pass off all design to Gloria without offering suggestions or imposing limitations. That left Gloria free to experiment. And that left Harry free to do the steady repetitive work on the presses he so loved. It was a good match and already beginning to reap rewards. In three weeks, Harry Grizwald's little print shop had doubled its requests for original design, while the flow of incoming camera-ready work had remained about the same.

"Christmas is only two weeks away," Harry said, pulling on his beard.

Gloria tinkered with the stapler on her desk. She didn't want to think about Christmas. Mother had finally made the decision to come and spend Christmas Eve and Christmas Day in Eckerd.

"I know you're here to earn a little pocket money for the holidays."

The statement startled Gloria. She had never given a reason for wanting the job. That's because she wasn't sure of the reason herself. But the extra money would certainly help her get through the holidays, so she didn't bother correcting him.

Harry cleared his throat, then gave his beard another tug. "What I need to know is, will you be leaving me after the holidays?"

"I . . . hadn't planned on it. That is, assuming you still want me."

"Of course I want you!" Harry's feathery eyebrows, resembling white miniature wings, flapped up and down on his forehead. "Only thing is, the way you're going, the way you're pulling in business, I'm gonna need a full-timer soon. You think you'd be interested?"

"I can't afford to work here full-time, Harry. My pay wouldn't even cover the rent."

"Yeah. That's what I thought. 'Course, there's an apartment upstairs you could have, cheap. That is if you wanted to come. I could clean it up a bit. That is if you wanted to come."

Gloria thought of the mounting stress at Mattson Development. Even Tracy had begun treating her differently. And both

Tucker and Tracy had refused her invitation to Christmas dinner. *Was God opening a door?*

"I'm not ready to make any moves right now," she said, feeling something akin to panic over the prospect of yet another change in her life. "But there's one thing you could do for me—honor me by coming to Christmas dinner." Harry's eyebrows continued working up and down, making him look as though he were about to take flight. But Gloria was already used to this. In the past several weeks, she had learned four things about Harry. He was a widower, he was a Christian, he was lonely, and . . . he worked his eyebrows whenever faced with a dilemma.

"Before you say no," Gloria said, pushing her chair away from her desk and looking him in the eye, "I have to tell you I have an ulterior motive. My mother's coming, and she's . . . well, difficult. I thought having you around would make it easier. So you can see how selfish this invitation is. I'm really asking a favor."

Harry's eyebrows finally leveled off. "You don't know me well enough to ask for a favor. But just supposing I do come, supposing I do help you out with this problem of yours, then I think I got the right to ask for a favor too."

"Yes . . . you can ask."

"Okay, then. I want you to pray about coming to work here full-time."

Gloria tensed. How could she do that? Things might be strained with her and Tracy and Tucker, but she still owed them. Then there was the question of finances. How could she survive on Harry's pay?

"You gonna do it? You gonna pray?"

"Okay," Gloria said in a near whisper. *But if she prayed and God said yes . . .*

"What was that?"

Gloria swallowed hard. "I said, okay."

On Harry Grizwald's advice, Gloria had tried Blessed Redeemer Church. "You got praise and worship the way it should be, lively yet reverential, and you got sermons straight from the Word," Harry kept telling her. "And it's close by. Only half a mile past West Meadow Market." So she went, and after a few visits, she felt as if she belonged, even though Harry Grizwald had yet to show his face. She had wondered about that—his not attending church—and even questioned him once. "Got things to work out with the Lord," he had said. And she let him leave it at that.

But this morning, though she was looking forward to Sunday service, an inexplicable burden for Perth made her rethink going. All through her shower she had prayed. Perhaps she should ask Perth to go with her. Perhaps that was the reason for the burden.

Gloria toweled herself dry, slipped on her old white terry-cloth robe with yellowing collar and cuffs, then went to the living room. Perth was stretched, facedown, on the couch, her hair looking like tangled moss over her back and pillow. Faint snoring punctuated her otherwise quiet, even breathing. Perth had worked last night, then went with friends to a late movie. Maybe Gloria should let her sleep. She was about to walk away, when Perth turned and opened her eyes.

"Oh, hi," she said in a faint, drowsy voice. "You smell good. Like you just came out of the shower."

"I did."

Perth propped herself up on one elbow. "You going to church?"

Gloria nodded and saw a look of disappointment cloud Perth's face. "You want to come?"

"I can't." Perth fingered the satin edging of her blanket. "I've got to work on that financial aid stuff. It's a nightmare. And it takes forever. All those forms! And the waiting. I can't stand the waiting. Gloria, do you think it's *ever* going to happen? I haven't heard from one college. Not one! I knew I shouldn't have gotten myself excited. I knew I shouldn't have let myself believe I could do it."

Perth's clock on the end table told Gloria it was late. She'd have to hurry if she wanted to make that service. "How about we talk this over when I get back?"

"Sure," Perth said, her face suddenly looking like pulled taffy. She rolled over, dragging the tangle of hair with her like a cape.

"Or . . . I could stay," Gloria found herself saying. "We could go over those forms together, then when we're finished we could grab a hamburger. What do you think?"

In a flash, Perth was sitting upright. A wide grin replaced the sleepy look. "You mean it? Wow! That would be great. All week I've had a giant knot in my stomach. I was just dreading this. And I'm so nervous. What's going to happen if I get into college but can't get aid? Or if I get aid but don't get into college?"

"I've been praying for you." Gloria walked over to the couch, sat on its edge, then began brushing away the unruly strands of hair plastered against Perth's cheeks. "I've been praying that God opens just the right door and closes the ones He doesn't want you to walk through. And I do believe He's going to do it. But will you trust Him? Will you be content with the one He does open?"

"I don't know. Are you always content with what God does?"

Gloria shook her head. "Not always."

"It's hard, huh?"

"Sometimes."

Perth threw back the covers, almost knocking Gloria off the couch. "I guess I better hurry and get ready."

"For what?"

"Church." Perth was already by the bathroom. She stopped and glanced back. There was a smile on her face.

"What about those forms?"

"They can wait till we get back. I think I need to get to know this God I'm supposed to be trusting."

~�� ��~

Tracy hadn't looked at Gloria all day. Even when Gloria stopped by Tracy's desk first thing in the morning, Tracy hadn't looked up but only mumbled something that resembled "goo mornin'." Now all the lunch breaks were over, and Gloria was determined to see Tracy and find out what was wrong.

She walked toward the receptionist's desk, noticing Tracy's stooped shoulders, how she slumped in her chair, almost as if hiding. Funny how the wide, startled look in Tracy's eyes reminded Gloria of that small injured finch so many years ago. And when Tracy cupped one side of her face with her hand, then rested her elbow on the desk, Gloria saw a small bruise on Tracy's chin.

"What happened to your chin?" Gloria asked, dreading the answer but unwilling to pretend she hadn't noticed.

"Nothing." Tracy swiveled her chair away from Gloria.

"Did Jordon do it?"

"Who's been circulating *that* rumor?" Tracy's eyes frosted. Old Fire and Ice. She could still melt or freeze everything around her when she chose. Still, Gloria wouldn't be put off.

"No rumor. I've seen this before. With Jenny Hobart."

Tracy dropped her hand. "C'mon, Gloria, give me a break.

Stop tending everybody's garden. Get the weeds out of your own backyard, will you?"

"Tracy, *talk* to me. This is Gloria, your best friend. Remember?"

"No, I don't think I do. From where I sit, I'm reminded more of a one-way street. We give. You take."

"What are you talking about?"

"The Estates. Lot four. You told that woman we'd give her a free basement and now lot two—Mr. Primavera—wants one too. Tucker's got his hands full over there. You should have consulted him or the foreman before you went ahead and diverted his manpower and resources."

Gloria stood in front of the desk, wondering if she hadn't stumbled onto the stage of a mad comedy. "Tracy . . . I never told that woman anything of the kind. Tucker did."

"Tucker says otherwise. Now he's in a real pickle. Not only does lot two want to get in on the act, some of the other owners are griping about the soundness of their slabs. There's talk of them hiring an independent engineer. What's going to happen then? Huh? Is Tucker supposed to give them *all* basements?"

Gloria felt blood rushing to her face, heard what sounded like waves crashing inside her eardrums. She had never been so angry. "You believe what you want, but Tucker created this situation from the beginning. He's the one responsible, only he doesn't want to take any responsibility."

Tracy placed her hands on the desk and pushed upward, rising from her chair. "I fought Tucker on this, but now I see he's right. You're not cut out for the job. You're just creating too many problems. So, I'll save Tucker the time and effort by telling you myself. Starting tomorrow, I'm taking over Communications and PR. And starting tomorrow, you'll be sitting at this desk. With an appropriate reduction in pay. We're fairly confident that here is one place you can't make trouble. But if you do, Gloria"—Tracy pointed in the direction of the glass-and-brass door that led to the elevators—"if there's one more incident that hurts Tucker, your next move will be through that door."

Chapter Fifteen

WHO IS THIS COMING UP FROM THE DESERT
LIKE A COLUMN OF SMOKE,
PERFUMED WITH MYRRH AND INCENSE
MADE FROM ALL THE SPICES OF THE MERCHANT?
SONG OF SONGS 3:6 NIV

GLORIA HAD HOPED FOR a white Christmas, but the flakes were melting like butter in a hot pan as soon as they hit the ground. So instead of snow, it looked as though it was just going to be wet. The weather channel had dashed what remaining hope Gloria had by forecasting that temperatures would continue to hover above freezing for the next forty-eight hours —well into Christmas Day. Her father had always loved white Christmases, and she guessed she got that preference from him.

Mother thought snow was messy.

Gloria's boots moved rapidly over the sidewalk, rippling shallow puddles and kicking up sprays of water. On both sides, people rushed past her with their winter coats and steaming breaths, laden with bundles and expectations. Christmas. How she loved it. It was her beautiful Jesus' birthday. Even if it wasn't His real date of birth, as one of the Bible ladies at Appleton Full Gospel claimed, she didn't care. It was the one time of year when practically every store in the civilized world played music that praised her Savior.

Even the hustle and bustle, and nerves and pocketbooks strained by overspending never dampened Gloria's enthusiasm. Actually, she loved that part too. Especially the shopping, which she had been doing all morning. She was almost finished now. Perth's present, a *Webster's New World College Dictionary* and a *Roget's Thesaurus*, was tucked neatly into one of her shopping bags. Mother's present, *History of the Miss America Pageant*, was in another, along with a pack of tinsel, three Christmas stockings, a can of fake snow, wrapping paper, and bows.

Any more stuff and the bags would be a problem, but not nearly as much of a problem as what to get Tracy. It had to be special—no run-of-the-mill sweater or perfume—something that said, "I love you, let's make up." These days Tracy spent most of her time at The Estates, and Gloria rarely saw her. And that bothered Gloria. So did the way Tracy looked—drawn, thin. Tracy worked sixteen-hour days, and Gloria guessed it was because things weren't going well.

Gloria tramped through another puddle and pictured Tracy's pinched face. Tracy assured her Spencer Jordon was fun, intelligent, witty. That she enjoyed his company. Well . . . maybe it was true, but Gloria couldn't help feeling that somehow Jordon, as much as overwork, was the cause of Tracy's changed appearance.

So what could she get this overworked, harried best friend who wasn't exactly a best friend anymore? As Gloria readjusted her bundles, she was struck with an idea and turned and headed back to the bookstore. It was so obvious, so simple. She had seen it, with its colorful cover, in the back left corner of Book World, a perfect gift: *The One Year Bible.*

※ ※

"No, no. Wind the garland more this way." Gloria brushed wisps of stray hair from her face and smiled warmly at Perth. She hadn't had this much fun decorating a tree in years. "See that bare spot over there? We need to fill it in."

"Where did you get this sick-looking thing, anyway? Out of a garbage pail?"

"No, silly. From Honest Henry's."

Perth burst out laughing. "That crook! How much did he wrap you for?"

"Never mind." Gloria pulled out a little wooden snowman from the box of ornaments she had bought a few days ago and hung it on the tree. In the background a small clock radio played "Silent Night."

"Come on. How much?"

"Twenty dollars."

Perth howled. "He always could spot a sucker."

On the coffee table sat a bowl of popcorn waiting to be strung. Gloria picked up a piece and tossed it at Perth. It landed in her French braid and stayed.

"Hey!"

Gloria did it again.

Then Perth lunged for the popcorn, took a handful, and peppered Gloria with it. There was a tugging match for the bowl, and in a matter of seconds, popcorn covered Perth, Gloria, and the floor.

"It looks like we're having a white Christmas after all,"

Gloria said, and the two laughed and started picking popcorn from their hair, then laughed again.

"Too bad your mother couldn't come today," Perth said, looking sweet and joyful and full of Christmas cheer. "She would have liked decorating the tree with us."

Gloria's expression remained frozen. She had never once decorated a tree with her mother, only her dad, and when he died, Gloria did it alone. She was glad her mother was only coming for Christmas Day and not Christmas Eve too, as she had originally planned, and that made Gloria feel guilty. She was also glad her mother was spending Christmas night at a hotel. More guilt. Why was her mother still able to make her feel so guilty?

Conditioning, Gloria. Conditioning.

Perth's hand suddenly rested on Gloria's shoulder. "I guess a little sister isn't much of a substitute."

"Oh, Perth," Gloria said, squeezing the young girl's hand. "Don't you know that a little sister is just about the best thing in the whole world?"

Gloria couldn't believe how nervous she was. Her mouth was dry, her hands trembled, a miniature army marched around in her stomach. She had filled the morning with prayers and work. The apartment sparkled, the table was set, the rump roast was in the oven, and the spinach cooked. The little spindly Christmas tree was decorated and the presents wrapped and arranged neatly under it. Even the three stockings were tacked to the wall. And two of them were filled.

For Perth's stocking, Gloria had bought a new tube of Tangerine lipstick, a Hershey's with almonds, a pack of black Bic pens

—all of them Perth's favorites. For her mother's, three white linen handkerchiefs rolled into logs and tied with thin, white silk ribbons, a jar of Lancôme grape polyphenol moisturizer, and a pack of pink and white Carol Wilson stationery—all her mother's favorites.

The work, at least, had paid off because everything looked and smelled wonderful. But so far the prayers had failed to calm her down. Any minute her mother would be coming through that door. What would they talk about? How would Mother behave? Would she be kind to Perth?

Perth had helped cook and clean. Then she had showered and dressed and disappeared into the bedroom with her own packages to wrap. She was still there, and even through the closed door, Gloria heard the rustling of paper. It made her pray harder. Would Mother be caustic and spoil Christmas for Perth? And here, when Perth was trying so hard, trying so hard not to be glum or depressed or to talk too much about her own father and mother. But it was obvious from the minute Perth got up that it wouldn't take much to set her off. Twice already, Gloria had caught her crying.

Gloria opened the oven and inserted the meat thermometer into the roast for the third time in as many minutes. Mother hated beef well-done. Said it tasted like shoe leather. The thermometer registered 155 degrees. Gloria withdrew the thermometer and closed the oven door. A few minutes more—when it reached 160—she'd take it out, let it sit. Mother claimed cutting meat before it sat was barbaric—this from a woman who seldom cooked.

When she heard a knock on the door, Gloria almost dropped the thermometer, then composed one last prayer, wiped her hands on the dish towel, and answered the door. She felt relieved when she saw Harry Grizwald standing there, one arm extended, holding a box of Whitman's, his white hair neatly combed back and parted on the right, his beard trimmed short into a perfect U around his oval face. He wore a crisp, clean, blue shirt with navy slacks and highly polished shoes. Only his ink-and-grease-stained fingers reminded her of the old Harry.

"Merry Christmas," he said, breezing past her. "What's that you're cooking? It sure smells great. Gotta tell you, I brought a healthy appetite."

Gloria laughed and showed him into the living room just as Perth walked in, her arms full of wrapped packages. Gloria waited for Perth to slip the gifts under the tree and into the empty stocking before introducing her. And then it was sort of love at first sight. Perth fetched Harry a 7-Up and pretzels and immediately began telling silly jokes that seemed to delight him to no end. Gloria suspected it had been a long time since Harry had laughed or since he had had someone fuss over him. And Perth . . . she needed a father figure to help her get through the day.

⚜ ⚜

The roast had been sitting for twenty minutes, and Gloria was worried. *Where was Mother?* When the phone rang, she feared it wasn't going to be good news.

"Gloria?"

"Mother, *where are you?*"

"About thirty minutes outside Appleton. The bus broke down. There's all this black smoke coming out of the front . . . or there was, anyway."

"But, Mother, you left hours ago."

"Now you know why I hate traveling on holidays. You can't find anybody. No one's where he's supposed to be. And there were no extra buses to come get us, and almost all of the repair crews are off. I'm half frozen. I can't even feel my fingers. I'd be surprised if I didn't end up with pneumonia or something. Already my chest feels tight, and I'm starting to wheeze. It's been a nightmare. If you had come home like I asked, none of this would have happened.

"But never mind that now. This is the first time I've had a chance to call. I borrowed someone's cell phone. He finally got off. Had it stuck in his ear all morning. What a mess. Great way to spend Christmas, huh?"

"Oh, Mother, how awful. What are they going to do?"

"Two buses are on their way and should be here any minute."

"Two buses?"

"One headed for Eckerd City, the other back to Appleton for those who want to return."

"But you'll come ahead, won't you?"

"I don't think so. By the time I get there, it'll be time to go to the hotel and sleep. If you didn't have that roommate of yours, maybe I'd reconsider. Maybe I'd come. Anyway, I guess I won't see you this holiday either."

"I'm sorry it worked out this way. I think—"

"What are you having for dinner?"

"*Dinner?* I . . . that is . . . we're having rump roast and—"

"You didn't overcook it, did you?"

"No, Mother. It's a perfect 160." Gloria smiled as she pictured her mother by the roadside, cold, tired, annoyed, and still worrying about the roast. Strange how it didn't upset Gloria. Instead, it seemed rather sweet. Maybe because it was Christmas, and she wanted to feel goodwill to all.

"Are you letting it sit?"

"Yes, Mother, it's sitting. And I'm sorry you can't be here to eat it."

"Oh, here comes the bus. Doesn't that beat all? I finally got a chance to talk to you, and the bus comes. Okay, Gloria. Merry Christmas. And don't forget to call your mother once in a while."

"Merry Christmas, Mother. I'm really sorry you can't make it. Call me and let me know you got home okay. And . . . I love you."

❧ ☙

After Gloria told Perth and Harry what happened, she began taking the extra plate off the table but stopped when a name popped in her mind, as though she had just read it off a flash card. When it was followed by a tug on her heart, she knew her beautiful Jesus was trying to get her attention.

"I'll be back," she said, racing out the door. Maybe it was too late. Maybe she already had her dinner. And certainly Emily Post wouldn't approve of this brazen last-minute invitation. But that thought didn't stop Gloria from flying down the stairs, then knocking softly at the apartment closest to the front door. No answer. She rapped harder, making her knuckles smart, then continued knocking until the door opened.

Miss Dobson appeared in a blue floral blouse with navy linen slacks. Soft, perfect curls neatly hugged her forehead and ears. "Merry Christmas, child. What can I do for you?" She ushered Gloria into the apartment.

Over Miss Dobson's shoulder, Gloria studied the tidy living room. "Well . . . I was wondering . . ." A woman this orderly might be offended by such a rash, spontaneous invitation. Gloria began having second thoughts. "Actually, I wanted to wish you Merry Christmas."

Miss Dobson's face lit up. "Now, aren't you thoughtful. My

babies and I were having the best time. I just gave them their gifts. You want to see?"

Gloria nodded and watched Miss Dobson retrieve the rawhide toys strewn on the couch next to two sleeping dogs.

Miss Dobson held up something that looked like a pretzel, then something else resembling a small bone. "It took me forever to find the right size. My babies don't like it when their toys are too big. They have little mouths, don't you know?"

Gloria nodded again and glanced into the kitchen. On the counter sat a TV dinner still covered with foil. "Listen. I've got company upstairs and have to go, but we were all wondering if you'd like to join us. For dinner. I know it's terribly rude to give such short notice, but even so, I must insist and really won't take no for an answer." Before Miss Dobson had a chance to say a single word, Gloria led her out the front door and up the stairs.

The small, brightly lit spruce blinked red and green and white, and cast a strange glow over Perth as she sat on the floor pulling a thick gold ribbon off her present.

Gloria sat next to her, watching quietly. All day she had looked forward to this part. There were times, once over dinner and once while they were doing the dishes, that she wanted to stop everything and just give Perth her surprise. Not the books. The other surprise. The one she was sure Perth would love. She could hardly wait to see the look on her face when she opened it.

Gloria leaned, exhausted, against the side of the couch. It had been a wonderful day. Laughter had filled the apartment, Miss Dobson's and Harry Grizwald's especially. They were gone now, and the dishes were done, and there was nothing left to do but the one thing that had occupied a lot of Gloria's mind the past two days.

"Cool!" Perth flipped open the dictionary. "This is going to come in handy at college. I can't spell to save my life. The thesaurus is great too. Thanks, Gloria!" Then Perth dumped out her stocking and examined all her goodies. "These are perfect! Just perfect! I really love everything." With her right hand, she blew Gloria a kiss. "Now open yours."

Gloria looked down at the three neatly wrapped packages on her lap and picked up the one on top. Her mouth dropped when she opened it. *"How to Start Your Own Business.* What's this?"

Perth shrugged. "I don't know. It just grabbed me when I saw it, and I thought someday it might come in handy for you. Maybe it was stupid."

"No . . . it's very . . . original. And thought provoking. Thank you." Gloria opened the other two: a pair of red woolen mittens and a matching scarf. Then she shook out her stocking and found a new lipstick, a candy bar, and some pens and laughed. "Everything's wonderful. Just wonderful."

"You know, it's been a pretty nice Christmas. I was worried. I guess I can tell you that now. But Dad used to love Christmas, even more than Mom. He was like a kid. He'd be the first one up, then wake us. He was always excited about what he bought us."

Gloria fingered the envelope in her pocket and smiled.

"I really thought it was going to be much harder, but you made the day so great. You and Harry and Miss Dobson. Now, there's a sweet lady. Nice sense of humor too. 'Course, if she told me one more story about her 'babies,' I might have screamed, but she was cute. Too bad your mother missed everything."

Gloria shrugged, then pulled the envelope from her pocket. "I have just one more thing for you."

"Oh, cool." Perth took the envelope from Gloria's hand,

opened it, and pulled out a sheet of paper with pictures pasted on it. First there was a car with two people in the front seat. Next to the hand-drawn arrow pointing to the person on the passenger's side was Perth's name. Gloria's name was by the arrow pointing to the driver. Then there was a picture of a highway leading to a school. Over the picture of the school was written Bristol College. Perth screamed and threw the paper into the air.

"We're going? We're actually going to see it?"

Gloria nodded, hardly able to contain her joy. "I rented a car. I also spoke to Phil and told him you wouldn't be at work tomorrow. And I took the day off too. We're leaving early in the morning."

"I . . . I don't know what to say." Suddenly Perth's arms were around Gloria. "Except thanks, Gloria. Thanks. I can't think of a nicer gift."

~� ��

The round trip to Bristol had been long and tiring but, oh, so much fun. Gloria had never seen Perth so happy. And it was love at first sight for Perth when she saw the college with its red brick walls and ivy overgrowth, its large, modern, student union building, its massive library, and even its blatantly tired dorms with small, overcrowded rooms. Gloria's only fear was if Perth didn't get accepted the visit would make the disappointment all the greater.

Gloria listened to the shower running as she hung up her slacks. Perth would be a while. She always took long showers. Maybe Gloria would skip hers tonight and shower in the morning. She was wiped out. She had pretty much decided to call it a night when the phone rang. Only her mother would call at this hour. It had to be nearly eleven.

Normally, she'd have let the answering machine get it, but on Christmas night when her mother called to say she had gotten home okay, Gloria had to cut their conversation short because she still had guests. She just couldn't brush her mother off now.

"I've been trying to reach you all day."

It took Gloria several seconds to recognize the voice. "Beth?"

"I found something yesterday . . . when I was going through some of my daughter's things. I don't know why I picked Christmas Day. I guess I was missing her, and . . . well, I found myself going through one of the boxes. When Jess . . . died I couldn't even go to her apartment. My husband went and packed up everything. Most of the boxes are still sealed. It's too painful . . ."

"I'm sorry, Beth." Gloria didn't know what else to say.

"Yes . . . well, anyway, I want you to see what I found. I won't be at work tomorrow, so how's Saturday? But not at your place. I haven't been there since Jess died."

"Saturdays I work at a print shop. You could meet me there. I finish at five."

"Okay. But don't tell anyone."

Gloria gave directions, then hung up, feeling as if she had a boulder the size of Texas in her stomach.

Saturday seemed to have been fired out of a pistol. It went that fast. Gloria had spent the entire day laying out a prospectus for a midsize software company in downtown Eckerd. From that first awful *Mattson Newsletter* put out by Precision Printing, Gloria had learned that the best insurance against frustration and wasting time was *communication*. It seemed ironic that she of all people would have learned that lesson so quickly. But in keeping with this newly acquired knowledge, Gloria had been on the phone throughout the day with the software company, clarifying, asking advice. And it had paid off, because she was sure the proofs would get approved the first time around.

She was putting them into a marked folder when Beth Price stepped on the doormat by the front entrance and filled the room with a buzzing sound. Gloria waved and shouted from her corner desk that she'd be right with her, then brought the folder to Harry Grizwald, who planned to deliver it personally. Then she grabbed her coat and purse and, with a quick "good night" to Harry, walked out of the print shop with Beth.

"Where to?" Gloria asked as soon as they got outside.

"I noticed a little diner not far from here. We could go there."

Gloria thought a minute. The only diner nearby was Phil's Diner, where Perth worked. Did she want to go there? Have Perth possibly overhear something sensitive? Parade dirty laundry? Especially things about Tucker Mattson? She didn't think so.

But why?

Perth looked up to her. No one had ever looked up to Gloria before, and she didn't want Perth to overhear anything that might change that. Because then Perth would see she had clay feet. Great big ones. *Oh, Jesus, why am I so vain, so selfish? Why can't I be more like You?*

"I know the place," Gloria said reluctantly. "It's fine."

～❧ ❧～

Though Gloria had reconciled herself to Phil's Diner, she avoided Perth's section and chose a booth outside her territory. Even so, when Perth saw Gloria, she managed to square it with the other waitress and in a matter of minutes stood beside Gloria's table with pad in hand.

"Hey! What can I do for you?"

Gloria introduced Perth to Beth, then ordered the cheapest sandwich on the menu, a grilled cheese. Her job at the print shop had made it easier to get through the extra holiday expenses, but she was nearly tapped out. She saw Perth frown as she wrote the order.

"Is this supposed to be dinner?"

Gloria nodded.

"Not much of a dinner. You'll get hungry later."

"If I do, there's plenty of roast beef in the fridge." She ignored Perth's pinched lips, ignored the hand she suddenly put on her hip. "Anyway, I need to lose a few pounds."

"Ha! Around your earlobes I suppose."

Gloria gave Perth a dirty look, then jerked her head, as though telling Perth to leave.

"Obviously you two know each other," Beth said after Perth disappeared.

"My roommate."

"I didn't know you had one."

"Long story, which I'll skip, if you don't mind. Besides, I'd rather hear yours."

Beth looked around nervously and almost choked when she saw two picketers walk by and take a booth in the back. "Those people make me nervous. Did you hear the latest? Some woman came out of Patty's Palace and found one of them spray-painting 'gas hog' on her SUV. When she tried to stop him, there was a scuffle and the woman ended up with a broken collarbone. Can you believe that?"

Gloria remembered Perth's stories and nodded. "So what did you want to show me?"

Silently, Beth pulled a folded paper from her purse and slid it closer to Gloria. "I know why they're here," Beth said, jerking her head in the direction of the back booth where the environmentalists sat with their picket signs propped against the wall. "And I know why Tucker owes Jordon."

Gloria unfolded the lined yellow legal paper and smoothed it with her palm. It was full of neat, crisp longhand—Jessica's —Gloria realized without being told. According to the date on the top right-hand corner, it was written almost a year ago. Heading the page was the word MEMO. Beneath that were short bulleted statements: Reprice Phase II—Eckerd Estates, Step Up Marketing efforts, Mailing blitz to West Coast, replace S. McGregor.

Unconsciously, Gloria covered the page with her hand in case Perth came to the table.

Replace S. McGregor.

A single bullet. So tidy, so direct. Gloria wondered if Jessica had any idea what impact this little bulleted statement had had on S. McGregor. When she looked up, Beth was frowning.

"It's at the end of the page." Beth reached over and jabbed the yellow paper with her finger. "Look at the end."

Gloria's eyes scrolled down to the last two bullets:

Damage control—counter EPA land grab attempt.

Check out S. Jordon.

Gloria looked up at Beth and shrugged. "What does it mean?"

"About a year ago we began getting letters from the EPA asking us about our plans for preserving the groundwater and natural habitat at The Estates. Tucker had Jessica write up a detailed reply after sending her to the Town Planning Department to obtain a geological survey. Then he had an engineer draw to scale the position of cesspools, their depth, etc., showing them well above any groundwater repository. She detailed the plant and animal life and indicated the ratio of developed to undeveloped property that would remain after site completion. Since the position of the cesspools would be code, and since there were no endangered plants or animals in The Estates area, no one thought anything about it, other than all the paperwork being a royal pain. A month later Jordon showed up. That's when everything changed." Beth's eyes narrowed.

"Who is he exactly?"

"He said he was head of Special Projects at the EPA, that he reported directly to the Assistant EPA Administrator for Policy Planning and Evaluation. And that the EPA and National Park Service were concerned about Tucker's Estates, as well as what everyone called The Lake, Hugo Pratt's tract of land stretching along the outskirts of Eckerd. All of it privately owned, by 'inholders,' a name given to people who own land surrounded by a national park. Though it's a loose fit here, since The Estates and The Lakes are only surrounded on three sides. Anyway, Jordon said the EPA, as well as the National Park Service, had serious concerns over the development of this land. They were especially concerned about groundwater, which they said might be polluted by overuse of the lakes.

"Then he and Tucker had a *huge* argument. Tucker told him this was privately owned land, and since there was no endangered anything involved, and since they were not violating any building codes, and they had all the necessary permits to continue building, the EPA should just butt out. I don't think I've ever seen Tucker so mad."

Gloria absently fingered the edges of the legal paper. "What happened then?"

"Nothing."

"I don't get it."

"Jordon wanted to declare the entire Estates and Lakes area in need of protection so that no one could build on it."

"But that didn't happen."

"That didn't happen to The Estates. Jordon's still trying to tie up The Lakes. Keep it from being developed."

Gloria raked her fingers through her hair. "All this time I thought Tucker put Jordon up to targeting The Lakes so he wouldn't have competition."

"Not true. Jordon, or I should say the EPA, came up with that one all on their own."

"How did Tucker escape?"

Beth pulled an envelope from her purse, held it a minute as though having second thoughts, then slid it across the table. "Read this."

Gloria opened the envelope and drew out several pieces of folded white paper. She tensed when she saw it was an undated letter from Jessica to her mother. "You sure?" Beth nodded.

Gloria read silently, wanting to shield Beth from having to rehear words that Gloria instinctively knew were going to be unpleasant.

Dear Mom,

This is a letter I needed to write, even though I have no intention of mailing it. So if you're reading it now, it's because I finally did it . . . finally put an end to the last chapter of my very messed-up life. I hope I don't. I hope I can find a way clear of this. Because if I can't that would mean I failed. I failed you, Tucker, but most of all myself. But it's funny about mess-ups. You never see them coming, or maybe you do but never actually believe they will catch up to you. Other people yes. But not you. You believe that somehow you'll beat the odds and that what you actually sow is not what you will actually reap. A lie. Like everything else I see around here.

Right about now your eyes are tearing. If the tears are because you're going to miss me, I thank you. If they're because of some misplaced guilt, don't bother. You have nothing to reproach yourself for. I only have myself to blame. You tried to warn me about Tucker. But your warning was not entirely correct. You said he was too old for me. The truth is I was too old for him. But by the time I figured that out, I was already in over my head.

The problem is that when you hook up with someone younger than you, emotionally speaking, you begin to take responsibility for things. Things you shouldn't. You try to protect, to nurture. I'm sure there's some psychological mumbo jumbo that explains all this, but it really isn't important now. It's enough for you to know that this is what I tried to do, and this was my undoing.

But I don't want you to blame Tucker or try to hurt him in any way. I loved him, love him even now as I write this. So if the dead can be granted one request, I ask that you try to help Tucker in every way you can. And if you can't do that, then I ask you not to hurt him and try to be as kind to him as possible.

But Spencer Jordon is another matter. If my hand can reach up from the grave to point an accusing finger at the one who has done me the most harm, that person would be Spencer Jordon. Jordon would have ruined Tucker, used the courts to hamper his building efforts, or kept him entangled in so much bureaucracy he'd never build another thing for the rest of his life. That bunch Jordon works for can do just about anything they want, and nobody can stop them. Even so, Tucker wasn't about to take it lying down. He and I put our heads together and came up with a plan. The only logical course of action was to pay Jordon off, first with bribes, then favors. Somehow I entered that mix. Oh, it was innocent at first. Though innocent is hardly the correct word when used in conjunction with bribery. Anyway, I was going to soften Jordon up. Take him out for a good time. Send him back to D.C. with warm and fuzzy thoughts of Mattson Development.

And that's how it started. I actually had fun playing Jordon, stroking his ego, building him up, trying to make him like me and Mattson Development. It must have worked because he began coming to Eckerd more and more frequently. Sometimes he'd even bring friends—members of various environmental groups, but not associated with the EPA directly. All they wanted to talk about was the environment.

Like I said, it was fun at first. But as Jordon and his friends became more comfortable with me, their conversation changed. It was still about the environment, but suddenly it was about a letter bomb, or killing someone's pet to send a message. Then there was talk of how to stop the spraying of herbicide 2,4-D in the western forests to save their friends' marijuana crops. And marijuana itself was a big topic of conversation.

That's when I became uneasy. For the first time I saw the scope of their power as well as their deep anger and hatred. They hated technology and people most of all—blaming both for ruining the environment. I decided I wanted no part of them, that I would end my relationship with Jordon, which was no relationship at that time in any sense of the word. I pulled away, discouraged Jordon from calling, and when he did, I refused to see him. But Jordon is a man used to having his way. The more I tried to get out of it, the more insistent he became.

He threatened to open up an EPA investigation, bury Tucker with tons of paperwork. He threatened to send a swarm of environmentalists down here and make it impossible for Tucker to continue construction. He threatened to close Tucker down completely by having the environmentalists file an injunction and tie Tucker and his assets up for years. He could have done any of these. Tucker and I talked it over, actually argued about it, and I told Tucker I'd start seeing Jordon again. Tucker didn't want me to. I told him there was no other way, and that I'd watch my step.

The next time I went out with Jordon, he brought some of that marijuana he talked so much about. He insisted I try it. I refused. He hit me. That was the first time, but it wasn't the last. Jordon was not opposed to using force to get what he wanted. It wasn't long after that I began accepting Jordon's joints. At first to keep peace, then to block out what was going on between us, what I was allowing to go on. What was worse, I couldn't tell Tucker. He would have severed his relationship with Jordon, to his own hurt, and then make what I had done, what I had been putting up with, all come to nothing.

I don't know how much longer I can keep this from Tucker. Part of me actually suspects he already knows. Our relationship is beginning to feel strained. And that's largely my fault. Because if Tucker knows about Jordon and is letting me do this anyway, what does that say about him? And what does that say about me? How can a person love someone like that? Anyway, I don't have the strength anymore to deal with this or to fight with Jordon. This whole thing is swallowing me up alive. I've been depressed lately and can't seem to shake it. They say depression is anger turned inward. I don't know. All I know is that sometimes I find it hard to come up with a reason to get out of bed, and a person should have a reason for getting up in the morning. This whole thing has torn me apart. I don't know where it's heading. If I don't get a grip soon, I fear it will all end badly. I can't face being with Jordon one more night, but I can't face being the instrument of Tucker's ruin either. And I can't deal with my growing suspicion that Tucker knows and remains silent. I'll have to figure all this out. It's something I'm going to give a lot of thought. And if I decide the fight's just not worth it . . . well, there'll be this letter to hopefully help you understand why.

I love you. You've been a great mother, always there for me throughout all my problems. But this is one problem you can't solve.

Jessica

Gloria bit her lip. *If only she had told her about Jesus.* Even now she could picture the lifeless body strapped to the gurney. "Why have you shared this?" she asked, her voice cracking.

Beth removed her olive car coat and folded it neatly on the seat beside her. "I'm not out to hurt Tucker, if that's what you're thinking. I have to admit that I've stayed at Mattson's hoping to find an opportunity, some opening where I could do him harm.

But now—after this—I can't. Not without ignoring my daughter's last wishes. Tucker's had a lot of time to think about why Jess killed herself and probably already knows about her and Jordon. If not, it's up to you to caution Tracy. I know that you've been worried about her. So I'm giving you permission to tell her about this letter and to . . . warn her."

"I'm not sure it'll do any good. Tracy can be stubborn. Hates to admit when she's wrong. And I've already tried to warn her about Jordon."

"Well, try again! She's your friend, isn't she?"

Gloria sighed and nodded. "And Jordon?"

"There's nothing we can do."

"What about going to the police?"

Beth picked up the letter and carefully folded it along the existing folds, as though it were a relic to be preserved. "What can the police do? I'll not drag Jess's name through the mud, air her dirty laundry when all I'll end up with are a few sleazy head-lines."

Gloria frowned. "How can we let Jordon get away with this? What about the right to own property without having someone try to take it away? What about the powerful victimizing of others for their own agenda? What about . . . Jessica?"

Beth's fingertips brushed her damp eyes. "That's the only one I'm thinking about now."

Chapter Sixteen

MY LOVER IS RADIANT AND RUDDY,
OUTSTANDING AMONG TEN THOUSAND.
~◉ SONG OF SONGS 5:10 NIV◉~

WHEN GLORIA WALKED INTO the construction trailer and saw the angry look on Tracy's face, she knew her mission was going to be more difficult than she anticipated. They used to call themselves the Lone Ranger and Tonto—a team that would never break up. That seemed so long ago.

"What are you doing here?" Tracy's voice sounded snarly.

"It's my lunch hour, and I wanted to spend it with you."

"You took a cab all this way to have lunch?"

Tracy's fingers drilling the desk told Gloria she wasn't buying any of it. "No. To talk."

Tracy pointed to the mound of papers on her desk. "I'm swamped. You should have called first."

"Well, kemosabe, this can't wait." Gloria looked for the smile that always appeared on Tracy's face whenever she called her that. Instead, she saw the thin jaw clamp shut. "We can talk here or somewhere more private if you want."

"Give me a break, kiddo." The jaw relaxed. "I'm buried with work."

Gloria shrugged and pulled a metal chair close to Tracy's desk and sat down. "Okay. I guess it'll be here."

"Man, this better be good. I'll give you five minutes to tell me what's so important."

"You are. I'm worried about you, Tracy. I know about Spencer Jordon."

Tracy grabbed a manila folder and started pulling out papers. "Make sense, will you?"

"I *know*. That's what I'm saying. I know about Jordon trying to shut Tucker down. About Jordon's crazy friends. About the marijuana. About his abusive ways with women."

Tracy shot up from her chair and pulled Gloria into a small cluttered office, then closed the door. "Are you crazy! Coming in here like this and spouting off about Jordon. I swear, he's got people everywhere. I don't know how he finds out about things, but he does. And look at you with all this nerve! Nerve and no brains! You have no idea what's at stake here. Tucker's overextended—his offices at Pratt Towers, his home, his car—all window dressing, bait, so he can catch the big one. Eckerd Estates. He's put everything on the line. *Everything*. If The Estates don't make it, he's going down."

"And you? Did you put everything on the line?"

Tracy looked away. "He's my brother."

"Oh, Tracy . . ."

"Don't sound so shocked. It's done all the time, people giving and getting favors. What's so wrong with it?"

"You tell me," Gloria said, pulling on Tracy's wrist.

Suddenly, Tucker opened the door and entered. "What's going on?"

"We're talking about Jordon," Tracy said, breaking free from Gloria's grasp. "She knows."

Tucker quickly closed the door behind him, and Gloria watched his face chalk, then wondered what he'd say if he knew about that picture she carried around in her wallet—like an idol. Funny thing about idols, eventually they all ended up like Dagon, their heads severed and lying in the dirt of their own temple floor. Tucker was only a man—pained, striving, frail. Why had she tried making him more? And why had it taken her so long to see that she wasn't the only ugly, misshapen creature in the world?

We're all ugly without You, Jesus.

"Look. Whatever you think you know, you better keep it quiet," Tucker snapped. "At least if you still want to work for Mattson Development."

"I'm not out to hurt you. I'm only thinking of Tracy."

Gloria felt Tracy's hand on her shoulder. "If that's true, then you can't tell anyone about this. Tucker's crews are working around the clock to finish The Estates ahead of schedule. Once it's completed, Jordon can't hurt us anymore. He won't be able to stop construction or drag us through the courts on some pretext."

Gloria eyed Tucker. "Just tell me one thing. What was all that business in the newsletters? Those articles on the environment and The Lakes property?"

Tucker shrugged. "A trade-off. Partial payment to Jordon for leaving The Estates alone. I was supposed to help him create a grassroots movement against development at The Lakes."

Gloria shook her head, love and pity and anger all rolled up in her eyes, and Tucker saw it too.

"As soon as we're out of the woods, we can try to make that right with The Lakes' owners," Tucker said. "We *will* make it right. You'll see. Just as soon as we're out of the woods."

Gloria grabbed Tracy's wrist again. "Walk away from this now before you get hurt."

"You're not doing any good here, Gloria. Go home," Tucker said, moving closer to his sister. "You have a decision to make. Either you're with us 100 percent, and that means keeping everything under wraps and doing whatever is necessary to finish The Estates, or you're out. Out of the company. You decide."

Gloria went straight home from The Estates. She was too upset to go back to Pratt Towers. Everything was wrong. Nothing was as it should be. Tracy was ruining herself. Tucker was nearly bankrupt. And Jordon manipulated the two of them like marionettes.

And they wanted her to be part of all that?

The whole thing broke her heart. It also put her into a panic. If she left Mattson Development, she'd have to go home, a failure.

Back to Mother.

How could she bear that? Yet how could she remain and be party to what was going on?

Not even bothering to change, she headed for the nightstand and her Bible. She needed her Jesus now. Needed to feel His presence. Needed to lay these problems at His feet because they were too much for her.

Gloria slipped off her heels and carried her Bible to the living room. Suddenly, there was a knock on the door. Miss Dobson must have seen her come home early. It would be impossible to pretend she wasn't in. She padded across the apartment in her stocking feet, trying to push away the feeling of irritation at being interrupted.

"Hi, Miss Dobs—" A tall woman, wearing a drab gray suit under a black cloth overcoat stood in the doorway. "How did you—?"

"That lovely woman downstairs, Miss Dobson, I believe, let me in. My name's Sasha Morgan. I'm from Social Services—Special Cases Division."

Gloria didn't think her heart could sink any lower, but as soon as she heard the words "Social Services," it plummeted to her toes.

"May I come in?" Sasha Morgan's melon face looked pleasant enough, like the face of a reasonable person. So why was Gloria's heart still thumping around in her feet? "I can't believe my luck. I was in the neighborhood and thought I'd stop by. But I never expected to find you home. I thought you'd be at work." She walked past Gloria. "Nice place. How many bedrooms?"

"One."

Sasha Morgan made clucking noises. "We like our wards to have their own room." She stopped and smiled. "That's my own name for them. They're really called clients." Then her eyes scanned the apartment. "I understand Perth's going to be legal in a few months."

"April tenth." Gloria placed her Bible on the end table and followed the social worker.

"Right. Less than four months." Sasha poked her head into the bathroom. "That's what makes me want to bend the rules just a bit." Then she walked into the kitchen. "Mind if I check the fridge?"

Gloria shook her head and nervously picked her nails while Sasha bent over and opened the bins. In one were half a dozen apples. In the other, a stalk of celery and a slimy head of Romaine. "I . . . go shopping tomorrow. Food shopping. There's usually more food in the refrigerator but—"

"No need to explain. About average for two working girls. Perth has a part-time job. I already checked that out. Was there today. They like her and said she's a hard worker. Checked on her school, same thing."

Gloria felt herself relax.

"Where does Perth sleep?"

"Ah . . . on the couch." Gloria was having trouble keeping up with the woman. One minute her head was in the refrigerator, the next she was counting beds.

Sasha Morgan walked out of the kitchen and carefully inspected the living room. Her eyes rested on the neatly folded bedding at one end of the couch. On top of the pile were Perth's flannel pajamas. "Tidy, isn't she?"

"Yes. She's a good kid and—"

"That's what I hear. And she seems happy. All her teachers and her employer said so. Even Perth says so."

"You talked to Perth?"

"Interviewed her today."

"She didn't tell me she was doing an interview with you."

"She didn't know. That's how I operate. I like everything au naturel. Surprise them so they have no time to prepare, no time to put up smoke screens. But Perth seemed happy enough. And I can spot the fakers. That's the other reason I'm going to make an exception. No use in pulling the child out of school and relocating her when she's happy and doing well. Not for this short of a period. If it were longer . . . but I just got this case four days ago. It was hung up somewhere . . . Anyway, you're not a relative, and normally this wouldn't be allowed. Not unless you signed up as a foster parent, and that would take months for the paperwork and background check, and even then there'd be no guarantee that you'd get Perth. So . . . because I like what I've heard and seen today, I'm going to twist the rules just a bit and let Perth stay."

Unexpected tears filled Gloria's eyes, taking both her and Sasha Morgan by surprise. Miss Morgan studied Gloria, then smiled. "I see you hate heels as much as I do. That's the first thing I take off, too."

Gloria pressed her sweaty palms together. "So, it's settled? Perth stays?"

"I don't see why not. So far, everything checks out. The only thing I've got to wait on is your employment verification. I sent it out yesterday with a little questionnaire. Once I get that, it'll be official."

The words "employment verification" rolled around like a loose bolt in Gloria's mind.

"Good thing you have such a nice-paying job."

As soon as Gloria was able to close the door, she picked up her Bible and carried it to the armchair in the living room. Bright afternoon sun streamed through the lace curtains and created a filigree pattern on the floor by her feet. How could everything outside look so cheerful when her own world was becoming a holocaust? She sank into the chair and slowly opened to Psalm 27.

"'The Lord is my light and my salvation; whom shall I fear? The Lord is the strength of my life; of whom shall I be afraid?'"

But she *was* afraid. And nervous and upset. God had brought her to a new city, a new job, and instead of getting the desires of her heart as He promised, she faced the possibility of losing the little she had—her best friend, her job, her apartment, Perth. And if she did, then she'd deserve the name that everyone had called her all her life.

Loser.

Chapter Seventeen

PLACE ME LIKE A SEAL OVER YOUR HEART,

LIKE A SEAL ON YOUR ARM;

FOR LOVE IS AS STRONG AS DEATH,

ITS JEALOUSY UNYIELDING AS THE GRAVE.

~ SONG OF SONGS 8:6 NIV ~

GLORIA STRUGGLED FOR DAYS over whether or not to leave Mattson Development. Finally, everything came to a head. It happened in the predawn hours, when things seemed especially clear. Like Jacob, she had wrestled with God all night. And just before dawn, when her heart ripped in two, when her swollen eyes couldn't cry another tear, when surrender finally came and she felt herself float into the bowels of a deep crypt, she sensed the hand of Jesus not upholding her but covering her with a shroud.

Now she lay on her back, staring up at the ceiling. No bright future filled with opportunities skipped happily before her. No dreams played merry tunes in her head. Empty. All empty. And for a moment, she thought she'd just lie in bed forever and never get up. But finally, when she was sure Perth had gone, Gloria did get up and showered and dressed in Boris Karloff mummylike fashion.

And when she entered the living room, the first thing that caught her eye were Perth's folded pajamas, and she had to look away.

What was going to happen to Perth?

Gloria eased herself into the stuffed chair, then watched her hand move along the large tufted arm, watched one foot cross the other at the ankle. Her hands and feet seemed as if they belonged to someone else. Not hers at all.

She sat a moment listening to the silence, remembering how she had given away her future. *Still . . . if she wanted to, she could change her mind.* In a strange way, that pleased her.

She stared down at her cuticles and realized she had not chewed them in a long time. *How odd.* That this was her only triumph, her one achievement.

But she could still change her mind.

Gloria closed her eyes, listening. Maybe . . . maybe God would change *His.* Last night she had heard His voice, soft as a breeze—making requests and breaking her heart. He had asked her to give Him back His promise, give up her dream, give up her job, give up everything and allow Him to do with her life as He pleased, with no promises of what that life held in store. And she had said, "yes." Yes to disappointment, disgrace, and loneliness. And she had written it down in her Bible—written her name in a blank front page with the date, and next to it the words, "How painful it is to die to self." Maybe now that voice would say it had all been a mistake. Or it had just been a test. A test of her willingness. Perhaps that's all God required.

"Yes," she heard herself saying, knowing in her heart that

God wasn't going to change His mind, and needing to reaffirm what she had done, needing to remind herself that her decision was set and that she wouldn't go back on it now.

"Yes," she said one last time before dropping to her knees.

❧ ☙

Gloria didn't take the bus as usual but walked to the cab-stand around the corner. She clutched her beige cloth coat, wrapping it around her like a bathrobe to try to better insulate herself against the wind. The weatherman called for icy rain today. Gloria dreaded that because it made everything so slick, made her walk on toes in ducklike fashion and look foolish. Why had she always been frightened of falling? She laughed. Landing on a sidewalk seemed preferable to the fall she was about to take.

The howling wind penetrated the thin cloth coat and lay against her chest like an ice pack. She shivered and thought of the black-hooded lamb's-wool jacket with velvet trim she had seen in The Everything Shop, a place with prices she could afford. She had planned on buying it next week. My, how fast things could change.

At the cabstand, six yellow cabs, with little checkered stripes running along their sides, lined the curb. Gloria picked one and got in. She gave the cabbie the address, then settled back in her seat. In a few hours she would begin a new life.

Oh, beautiful Jesus, help me deal with all this.

❧ ☙

Gloria refused to allow the scowl on Tracy's face to intimi-date her and walked briskly to the little desk in the back of the construction trailer. It looked as cluttered as it had the last time she was here.

"Why aren't you at Pratt Towers?" Tracy looked at her watch. "It's way too early for lunch."

"I'm not going to Pratt Towers."

Tracy frowned. "Taking the day off?"

"I'm not going in today or any other day." She heard Tracy gasp. "I'm sorry. But I've prayed about it. I've got to leave. And I was hoping you'd come with me, get away from all—"

Tracy's laughter silenced Gloria. It was loud and shrill, almost hysterical and so much like Jessica's the day she . . . Gloria hugged herself and shuddered.

"You think I'd walk out on my brother? That I lack gratitude or loyalty?"

"You mean like me?"

"If the shoe fits."

"Look, I know I owe you both a lot. And I appreciate—"

"Appreciate? What's that? A word you can use so you sound, oh, so nice? You think that's going to cut it? Make me feel all warm and fuzzy?"

"The guilt thing isn't going to work this time."

Tracy's green eyes widened, making them look like sliced kiwis, then slowly a smirk appeared on her face. "And to think I was worried about you being a doormat, always letting everyone walk all over you. When did you start walking over others, Gloria? When did you stop caring about anyone but yourself?"

"I care about you."

"If you did, you'd stay and help us—Tucker and me."

"I can't do that. And in your heart you know I'm right."

Tracy sat twisting her fingers like paper clips "You're going to have to move, you know that. You can't stay in Tucker's apartment."

"I know."

"Will you go back to Appleton . . . to your mother?"

"No." Gloria didn't know why she said that, because until this second, she really didn't know what she was going to do. She was leaving that up to the Lord. But now she felt a boldness she hadn't felt before. God had drawn back the curtains of her spiritual eyes, revealing the first step He wanted her to take. "I think I'll stay right here in Eckerd. For the time being."

"Poor little Gloria. You're finally going to be out on your own." Tracy reached up and squeezed Gloria's hand. "I'm sorry it had to happen this way, kiddo."

Gloria studied Tracy's hand, the small pink nails and delicate fingers, and wondered how she had ever expected this hand to uphold her. "Can I call you after I'm settled?"

Tracy shrugged. "I suppose. But we have fences to mend."

"You always said I was good with a hammer."

Tracy slowly rose from her seat and the two hugged and wept.

Now that she was unemployed, Gloria would have preferred taking a bus instead of the cab, but no buses went from The Estates to Pratt Parkway. Throughout the ride, she sat in the back putting stickers on each emotion, as though trying to tag the feelings that were spinning inside her like clothes in a dryer. Sadness over her strained friendship with Tracy. Anger at Tucker and Spencer Jordon. Concern for Tracy. Joy that the Lord was allowing her to stay in Eckerd. Unexpected excitement over her future. And profound relief that she had finally, finally given God full control of her life.

Before she even stepped on the black rubber mat that would send a buzzing sound throughout E-Z Printing, Gloria saw Harry Grizwald's head, with his mop of white curly hair, bobbing next to the pile of boxes along one wall.

When Gloria's foot finally sounded the alarm, Harry straightened from his stooped position and looked up. Instantly, a smile appeared on his face.

"Hey! Looks like the cavalry's come."

Gloria walked over and flipped open one of the boxes. "What are you doing?" She saw Harry's eyebrows rise. Saw his eyes inspect her thin cloth coat that was opened and exposing her gray Ann Taylor suit. "So, what are you doing?" she repeated.

"Maybe I should ask you that. Kinda fancy schmantzy, aren't we?"

"This is what I wear to work." Gloria bent over and poked through several boxes marked AB Dick, pretending to be interested in what was inside. "Electrostatic solution, cleanup blades, DPM cassettes, oh . . . I see you got your new cylinder."

"Yeah. Lot of good it'll do me. This stuff's kept me from even looking at the presses. I still have to sort through all these boxes, then there's a pile of bills needing attention. I got three calls on the machine I haven't even returned. Then the collator needs fixing. When Lily was alive, she'd do all this . . . this *busy* work. It's all gettin' too much for me. I outta just sell the place and be done with it."

When Harry pulled the jaw cylinder cam out of the box, his expression changed. He carefully removed the packaging around his new part, then looked at Gloria with doleful eyes. "I suppose you've come to tell me you're quitting. Been expecting it since the holidays. Just hoped it wouldn't be so soon."

"Actually . . . I've come to ask about full-time work, because

I need a job. You offered me one once and . . . an apartment, remember?"

Harry's white bushy eyebrows took a nosedive. "What happened to your other one?"

"I quit."

"Just like that?"

"Just like that."

"You gonna tell me why?"

"Maybe someday."

Harry placed the new cylinder carefully on top of the box, then wiped his hands on his shirt. "I can't pay you what you were making."

Gloria laughed. "How do you know what I was making?"

"I know expensive clothes when I see them. Used to buy Lily things like you got on for Christmas or her birthday or our anniversary." He smiled, as though picturing his wife in one of his gifts. "I liked seein' her in good things." He squinted at Gloria. "Your coat's ready for Goodwill, but your suit, now that's quality. Don't expect to be buyin' any more like that once you work here."

Gloria pressed her hands together. "You mean I have the job?"

"I see no need to break in anybody new. Got used to you already."

Before she could stop herself, Gloria gave Harry Grizwald a hug.

"Now . . . none of that . . . none of that."

She let Harry go and noticed he had a big smile on his face. "And the apartment? Is it very expensive? Big enough for two?"

"Two? For you and who else?" Harry's face pruned. "Not some boyfriend?"

"No, silly. For Perth." Gloria watched Harry's eyes brighten and remembered how well he and Perth got along Christmas Day at her house.

"Well . . . seeing it's for you and Perth . . . come on." He grabbed her arm and led her to the back, past the duplicator, the three presses, the collator, the testing equipment, the ultrasonic cleaners, the encoder, and racks and racks of supplies and spare parts that had all been in full use during E-Z Printing's heyday. He took her through a door that opened to a narrow stairway, flipped on a light switch, and told her to hold on to the banister. Slowly, they climbed the stairs.

"The private entrances are outside, to the left of the store. But this here's a shortcut. Takes you right up to the apartments—two of them, plus mine. Used to rent them. But no more. Not since Lily died. It's just too much trouble, that and I don't much like bumping into strangers in the halls anymore. Not since Lily."

When they got to the landing, they stopped in front of a brown wooden door. Harry turned the knob. "Got two apartments here, and a storage room for my extra supplies. Kinda small, but nice if you fix them up. My place is on the third floor." Harry's chin jerked in the direction of the stairs that continued rising through the bowels of the brownstone. "Got that whole floor to myself. It's too big now. Since Lily. I've been meaning to move down to one of the smaller places but never seem to have the time."

They stepped into a dingy hall. At the far end of the hall was the storeroom. On either side were the two apartments. Harry opened one—it wasn't locked—and flipped the light switch by the door, turning on a small end-table lamp. It didn't give much light, so it took a while for Gloria's eyes to adjust. The living room was a decent size, but dingy with caramel-colored walls and cluttered with too much furniture that left barely enough room to walk. There was a musty smell and large stains on the rug.

The bedroom was small. A queen-size bed dominated the room, and what looked like a toy dresser stood in one corner. The bathroom and kitchen were also small but more than adequate. With a little paint and some personal touches, she and Perth could turn this into home.

Please, God, let the price be right.

"So . . . what do you think?"

"It's nice."

"The other apartment's pretty much like this. I figured you could have one, and Perth the other."

Gloria gulped. There was no way she could afford two apartments. "I don't know. Two apartments. That's double the expense, double the—"

"I figured two hundred a month would do it. Cover the cost of the extra electricity."

Two hundred a month. She could do that with her eyes closed. And if Perth put a few dollars of her own money in, Gloria could cover her rent too. They would both have their own place to stay. Wasn't God amazing!

"Yeah. Since I don't plan on paying you anything close to that big salary of yours, I figure this is what you'd call a fringe benefit. And the apartments are just going to waste. Doing nothing. So what difference if you use them? Just as long as it doesn't cost *me* anything. Two hundred a month should do it. A hundred from each of you."

Gloria's hand went to her mouth. *A hundred dollars.* She couldn't be hearing right. "Ah . . . that's a hundred for each of us?"

"You don't expect me to pay the electricity for you?"

"No." Gloria shook her head in disbelief. "No . . . I wanted to clarify, that's all. Make sure I had it right."

"So . . . you gonna take them? You and Perth?"

Gloria nodded, hardly able to keep from jumping for joy. "Fine. Now let's talk salary."

~⟡ ⟡~

Gloria felt a slight ache creep from her knees down her shins to her ankles. She had been kneeling by her bed for close to an hour. But she didn't move. She didn't want to. Her heart was too full and soared within her.

"Truly my soul waiteth upon God: from him cometh my salvation. He only is my rock and my salvation; he is my defense; I shall not be greatly moved."

She repeated the opening of Psalm 62 for the umpteenth time. Then wept with joy. God had been her rock today. He had saved her from disaster. And He had defended her and enabled her to stand and not be moved. She had seen His greatness. She had tasted and seen that He was good. Oh, how His mercy and goodness had followed her! What an enviable position she was in, to have experienced such love, His love. All morning she had felt her hand in His, as He led and guided. And she had felt a steadiness and boldness she had never felt before. No matter what the future brought, today Gloria learned beyond a shadow of a doubt that she could trust God.

"Oh, beautiful Jesus. How I love You!" she whispered into the still bedroom. "I know my love's still a scrawny, spindly thing, more like a dandelion than a rose, but please accept it." Her heart trembled within her as she felt His sweet presence engulf her like an embrace. "Only, please don't ever leave me. I don't care where we go, just as long as we're together."

~⟡ ⟡~

Chapter Eighteen

HE HAS TAKEN ME TO THE BANQUET HALL,
AND HIS BANNER OVER ME IS LOVE.

—◈ SONG OF SONGS 2:4 NIV◈—

GLORIA HEARD THE METALLIC scraping of a key being inserted into the lock. From her position on the couch, she watched the knob turn and the door slowly open.

"You still up?" Shock covered Perth's face.

"I've been waiting for you."

"Uh-oh. What's wrong?"

The December cold had its teeth in Perth's coat and seemed to hang on for dear life until it snapped at Gloria when Perth sat beside her. "Take that worried look off your face. It's *good* news."

"I got into Bristol!"

"Now, silly, how would I know that? I'd *never* open your

mail. Besides, nothing came in the mail today." Gloria watched the worried expression on Perth's face change to disappointment. "It's not about college. It's about your sleeping arrangements. You're finally going to have your own room."

"*No kidding?* How?"

"Actually, you're going to have your own apartment."

"Now you've got my head spinning." Perth wiggled out of her coat, making her hair crackle with static. "What's the deal?"

Gloria told Perth what happened at Mattson Development and left nothing out. Not even the part about Tracy, Spencer Jordon, and Jessica Daily. Then she told her about Harry Grizwald, the job, the two second-floor apartments, and then how much they cost.

"A hundred dollars? We can have our very own apartment for a hundred dollars each? You *sure?*"

Gloria nodded, getting pleasure from the joy on Perth's face. How easily it could have been otherwise. How easily both she and Perth could have been out on the street.

"You really, really sure?" Perth asked, her eyes wide with excitement.

"*Yes.*"

Perth jumped to her feet and began dancing around the room. "This is too cool. This is just too, too cool. Wait till I tell my friends. They're gonna be oozing green. I'll be the only one with my very own apartment. And I haven't even graduated!"

Gloria sat quietly on the couch watching Perth jump and spin and twirl, her heart soaring.

The Lord's goodness touched even those who didn't know Him.

❦ ❧

Snowflakes the size of quarters were piling up fast on the streets and sidewalks. It had begun snowing early that morning and continued while Gloria and Perth packed their things, then scrubbed down the apartment at 352 West Meadow Drive. It had taken most of the day, but neither of them minded spending New Year's Eve this way. Tomorrow was the beginning of a new year and a new life for Gloria. And it was the beginning of a new adventure for Perth.

They had worked hard, taken few breaks. Both of them wanted to get to E-Z Printing before dark. Harry Grizwald had called three times, wondering where they were, and told them he had a pot of hot soup waiting.

Now, standing outside E-Z Printing, with vapor curling from their mouths like steam from a teapot, Gloria and Perth hauled four suitcases and three double-layered black garbage bags out of the cab.

The front door of E-Z Printing was open, and Harry Grizwald, wrapped in an old gray sweater with a patch over one pocket, stood in the entrance, watching. As soon as the bags were deposited on the snowy sidewalk, he left his post.

"Gimme the heavy stuff," he said, already grabbing the two biggest suitcases and heading back to the store. He placed the bags inside the shop, just past the black rubber mat. Gloria followed behind with two suitcases, and behind her, Perth dragged the plastic bags over the snow.

"Let me," Harry Grizwald said, taking the bundles from Perth, who hesitated for a second, as though concerned for his age. "You're not one of those sassy women libbers who resents a man for being courteous, are you?"

Perth laughed and relinquished her bundles. "No. Knock yourself out."

Gloria couldn't help smiling as she scraped her snow-encrusted shoes against the mat, making it buzz and buzz, and thought how wonderful of God to give Perth the added bonus of a surrogate father.

Harry, hardly conscious of his new role, set the garbage bags on the floor, and along with it a goodly amount of snow. Already, snow deposited by their shoes and gear was melting into small puddles all over the hardwood. Gloria worried about the mess, about upsetting Harry, but he hadn't noticed it at all. He was too excited, fluttering around like a mother hen, gathering the newly arrived chicks into the nest. When everything was in, he closed the door of the shop and pressed two keys into Gloria's palm—one marked A, the other B.

"What are the letters for?"

"Oh, Lily did that. She was the organized one. Always had everything just so. They match the apartment. If you look on the doors, there's a letter A or B right above the knob. Kinda faint now, but you'll see it. You two can figure out who gets what." Harry picked up the three black bags. "Right now, let's just get this stuff upstairs. I've got seven-bean soup waiting for you."

Both Gloria and Perth shook their heads.

"What? You turning down a free meal?"

Gloria laughed. "No. Just postponing it. We've got to get to the hardware store before it closes and buy paint, rent a carpet cleaner, and—"

"Okay. Okay." Harry chuckled. "Suit yourself. Soup'll still be here when you get back. One thing Lily taught me, there's no arguing with a female once she's made up her mind about something."

❧ ☙

It was several hours before Gloria and Perth were sitting in Harry Grizwald's kitchen eating his homemade seven-bean soup. It had taken that long to pick out paint. They had deliberated, discussed, agonized, and finally made their choices. Perth chose her favorite color, powder blue, for everything, and Gloria picked peach for the walls, and white for the doors and trim. They both picked Benjamin Moore latex because the salesman at the hardware store said it was more forgiving and made for easier cleanup than oil.

Now Gloria sat devouring her bowl of hot soup and listening to Perth talk excitedly with Harry.

"We're gonna do my apartment first. Gloria *insisted.* First thing tomorrow morning, we start painting. Oh, you should see the beautiful blue I picked! Every day when I wake up, I'm gonna think I'm in heaven."

Harry laughed. "Never thought of this place as heaven."

"I can't thank you enough, Harry!" Perth's eyes were moist. "I don't know what would have happened to Gloria and me if you hadn't rented us these apartments. I don't think I could have gone back to the street . . . ."

"Lily always said I was a shrewd businessman. And don't this situation prove it? I got this here old asset going to rack and ruin, and then along come the two of you, willing to fix it up for nothing. You're gonna make me worth more when you finish. Guess there's no doubt which one of us got the better end of the stick."

Gloria watched Perth give Harry a hug. Watched Harry blush and hug her back.

Jesus, You do the most amazing things!

Gloria had never worked so hard in her life. It took her and Perth five fourteen-hour days, from Wednesday morning, New

Year's Day, to Sunday night to finish both apartments. But they did it. And both apartments looked fresh, clean, with painted walls, shampooed rugs and couches, polished furniture, washed windows, scrubbed kitchens and baths.

"Looks like a different place altogether," Harry Grizwald said, sticking his head in Gloria's doorway. She had chosen the apartment Harry had first shown her. "And you rearranged the furniture. Looks real nice. Not so crowded."

"I put one of the armchairs in the bedroom. It works better in there."

"Lily was tidy and organized but never had a flair for decorating. Didn't have an eye for color, either. I like what you did. It's soft and happy."

Gloria could tell by the look on Harry's face it was a genuine compliment. She followed him into Perth's apartment, where Perth was tacking dark blue gauzy material to the ceiling, then draping it against the wall behind her bed, making it look like something belonging to royalty.

Perth turned when she was finished. "So, what do you think, guys?"

Harry scratched his head. "It's different."

"It's perfect," Gloria said, picking up a piece of discarded fabric from the floor and liking how it felt between her fingers.

"I once saw this in a fairy tale, over a princess's bed." Perth pinked with embarrassment. "I guess it's silly, but I've always wanted one. Always wanted to feel like a princess when I crawled between the sheets."

Gloria smiled. Maybe someday Perth would come to the Lord and become a child of the King and know what royalty really felt like.

<hr/>

Monday morning Gloria started working full-time at E-Z Printing. The first four hours were so busy she didn't even take a break. She emptied all the boxes piled on the side of the room, had Harry show her his filing and bookkeeping system, then organized and paid his bills. Then she ordered more black ink and ink additives, some hand cleaners, and cleanup sheets. Afterward, she notified AB Dick about the roller covers missing from their last order. Finally, she opened a pile of mail that was more than a week old, chucked most of it, then put the bills in an accounts payable file and anything Harry had to handle himself into his personal in box, which she had set up. Being on her own in Appleton had made her an expert at organizing paperwork and handling bills. She was glad she could now apply these skills to Harry's advantage.

By lunchtime, Gloria and Harry had fallen into a comfortable pattern that suited them both. Gloria as OM, office manager, and graphic designer. Harry as master and maintainer of the presses he loved. They were also exhausted. Gloria had driven them both without mercy. So when Harry pulled out two liverwurst and onion sandwiches and offered one to Gloria, she took it and the seat next to Harry with gratitude. Their chairs faced the Schriber, a metallic-looking monster that was actually a six-station continuous collator Harry had been working on.

"Finally getting that baby to purr." Harry loved doing all the repairs himself. He had manuals as well as catalogs, with complete lists of spare parts for all his equipment.

And Gloria could tell by the way he sat now, by the way he cocked his head to the side and looked at his Schriber, that he was pleased with his morning's work.

"Never thought I'd get to it. Not with all those boxes . . . all them bills. I think it's gonna work out fine having you here. Yep. I made a good bargain. Mighty good bargain. Lily always said I had a head for business. You're a hard worker, Gloria. Don't mind telling you I was prepared to pay you fifty dollars more a month, if I had to. But you'll be earning that in no time in raises." He looked at Gloria out of the corner of his eye, then back at the Schriber, all the while resembling the Cheshire cat.

Gloria nibbled her liverwurst, watching him, hardly able to keep from laughing. Finally, she couldn't help herself and started to giggle.

"What's so funny?"

"Nothing. Only I was prepared to take fifty dollars *less* a month."

Then the two howled.

⚜ ⚜

Midafternoon the mailman came to the shop and dropped a bundle of mail on the front counter. At her first opportunity, Gloria sorted through the envelopes and magazines. Three of the envelopes plastered with yellow address correction stickers were for Perth—all of them from colleges.

One of them from Bristol.

⚜ ⚜

"What's going on? I called your apartment and got a recording saying your number was disconnected, then got this number."

Gloria groaned. She was exhausted and had just this second come up from downstairs for the night. "Hello, Mother. I've . . . been meaning to call and tell you—"

"Even Cutter called his mother on New Year's Day."

"What do you mean Cutter called his mother?" Gloria

320

kicked off her shoes, then walked barefoot across her spotless kitchen floor. She opened the refrigerator and peeked in. "He lives there."

"Not anymore."

"You mean he left?"

"Virginia . . . Mrs. Press and Cutter had a falling out. And you're partially to blame."

Gloria closed the refrigerator. *What else was new?*

"Cutter simply refuses to settle down. Refuses to even look for another wife since you left. Told Virginia flat-out that he wasn't ready to get married, and he wasn't going to marry anyone just to please her. He told her if she didn't like it she could fire him and that would be fine with him. Then he moved out! Can you believe it? But of course you can. Look what you did. I must say, you two have really put us through the wringer. We almost had it set . . . then . . . well never mind that now. You haven't told me why you changed your number."

"I moved. I quit my job at Mattson Development and couldn't afford to keep my old apartment. My new apartment's right over the print shop where I work. It's really convenient and—"

"You work at a *print shop?* You mean like Appleton Printers?"

"Yes."

"Gloria, I can't believe it! You moved out of your town, the town where you've lived all your life, a town where you know practically everybody and practically everybody knew you, so you could work for a *printer?* How could your sights be so low? At least when you worked for Mattson Development, I could hold my head up. I could tell people you worked for a big corporation. That you had a good job. Now . . . now what am I supposed to tell them?"

"The truth—I'm happy and I love my work."

"Well . . . I hardly know what to say. Except that I'm disappointed. Really disappointed in you."

After Gloria hung up, she opened the cabinet where she kept the Domino sugar but didn't reach inside when she realized she didn't want any. She didn't have that vinegary taste in her mouth that she usually did after talking to her mother. *Oh, beautiful Jesus. Only You could do such a thing.* She didn't know how He did it, only that He had. And the whole thing had caught her by surprise—like a child might be surprised to find that pony she had dreamed of, had desired with all her heart but knew it was impossible, tied to a tree under her window.

And Gloria was surprised about something else too. She didn't feel anger over her mother's unkind words. Just sadness. Sadness that her mother couldn't rejoice with her. Rejoice over the fact that her daughter was actually happy. But the greatest blessing of all was the realization that it was her mother's failing and not her own. There was something liberating about that knowledge. Something that made her feel free, made her spirit soar. Gloria couldn't make her mother proud of her. No matter what she did, Gloria could never make her mother proud of her. Her mother would always find something to be disappointed about, to be unhappy about. And that's because *her mother was unhappy.*

Oh, what joy! What freedom to know that the only One she ever needed to please was Jesus. It made her dance, like a child, right there in her kitchen, right there in her bare feet.

Gloria reached behind the gallon of milk and pulled out the jar of seven-bean soup Harry had given her. She was too tired to cook tonight, too tired even to make an omelet. Her first day at E-Z Printing had knocked her out. She poured the soup into a large bowl, and while it was nuking, she scribbled a note, then took it and the three envelopes to Perth's apartment and slipped them under the door. The note asked Perth to come to her place after she opened the college letters.

Gloria would wait up.

The soup felt good going down, soothing and relaxing, and delicious. Harry sure could cook. Tomorrow, Gloria would go to the grocery and stock up. She'd get a few things for Perth too, some nibbles like apples and granola bars. Things Perth could grab for breakfast on the way to school. Maybe make some hard-boiled eggs and put them in Perth's refrigerator. They never locked their doors. Even tonight Gloria could have gone into Perth's apartment instead of slipping everything under the door, but she didn't want to. She was determined to respect Perth's space whenever possible.

Gloria drained the last of the soup and thought about having Harry over for dinner Saturday. By then she'd be used to the apartment, have her pantry stocked, and maybe feel like cooking. It was only fair that she reciprocate his kindness. After all, Harry had been feeding her since she got here. Feeding Perth too. Feeding both of them, and that could not be taken for granted.

Harry was a gift. Pure and simple. Part of God's bountiful provision, His love. Now if only her mother could experience that love. Or Tracy.

Tracy. She hadn't talked to her since leaving Mattson

Development. She should call, begin that fence-mending business Tracy said was needed. They hadn't exactly parted on bad terms. But it wasn't exactly good, either. Even as she thought about it, Gloria's fingers dialed Tucker's number.

"Hello?"

Gloria recognized Tucker's voice. It was hard, cold, like an icicle in her ear. "Oh . . . hi, Tucker. This is Gloria."

Silence.

"I wanted to let you know I left the key to the apartment with Macy Pierce."

Silence.

"I tried to leave the apartment the way I found it."

Silence.

"It was a lovely place, and I want to thank you again for letting me have it."

Silence.

"Is . . . is Tracy there?"

"She's resting."

"Can I talk to her? Just for a minute?"

"I think she's asleep."

"Well, okay. Would you tell her I called, and would you give her my new phone number and address?" Gloria rattled off the data but doubted if Tucker was writing it down. "Did you get it all?"

Silence.

"Okay . . . just tell her I called."

"She's hurt. You really hurt her. You hurt both of us. You really let us down. We expected more. We're really disappointed in you, Gloria."

Before Gloria could answer, the phone went dead.

Oh, great. Now Tucker and Tracy and Mother could all be disappointed together.

Gloria kept dozing off in the chair. When her head suddenly snapped forward, she awoke and sat up. An old Gloria Swanson movie flickered across the TV screen, and for a second, Gloria was mesmerized by the star's dark, expressive eyes. She pictured her mother watching the same movie and smiled, then turned it off. She was exhausted but had promised Perth she'd wait up. What time was it, anyway? Gloria stumbled into the kitchen and checked the large apple-shaped clock above the sink. After twelve. Perth was usually home from the diner by 11:30. And since their understanding, Perth never went out after work on a school night.

Gloria rubbed her face with her hands, then ran her fingers through her hair. She was sure she looked a sight, but she didn't take time to make repairs. Instead, she opened the door and looked out. From where she stood, Gloria saw light coming from beneath Perth's door. She took a deep breath and walked over. Even before she got there, Gloria heard the sound of crying and paper ripping.

Gloria knocked, and when Perth didn't answer, she opened the door and found Perth sitting on the blue floral couch shredding something in her hands, her face wet with tears.

"Did Bristol reject you?" Gloria asked softly, walking over to the couch.

"They all rejected me! These were my last three colleges and they *all* rejected me!"

Gloria sat down and put her arms around Perth.

"I feel like such a loser!"

"Oh, Perth, you're anything but a loser. You've had a rough year, and your grades have suffered. We always knew your GPA would be an issue."

"Nobody wants me. Nobody has any confidence in me." She buried her head in Gloria's shoulder. "I'm such a loser!"

Gloria stroked Perth's hair. She knew all about feeling like a loser. She also knew there was only One who could take the most insignificant life and make something out of it.

And He was no respecter of persons.

Chapter Nineteen

MY LOVER IS MINE AND I AM HIS;
HE BROWSES AMONG THE LILIES.
~⊘ SONG OF SONGS 2:16 NIV⊘~

GLORIA HAD TROUBLE concentrating as she sat at her desk. In the back room, Harry Grizwald worked the Ryobi 640K, filling the air with the sound of spinning rollers. But it wasn't the noise that distracted Gloria. Rather, it was thoughts of Perth and Tracy that ping-ponged back and forth in her mind.

Perth was so disappointed over her college rejections, rejections that left her future up in the air. Then there was the question of Social Services. What would they do when they found out Gloria no longer worked for Mattson Development?

And Tracy? Tough, in-control Tracy was being shamelessly manipulated by her brother. Gloria hoped Tucker wouldn't let Tracy whoosh full speed down a slide, with only hard ground to catch her.

But enough of this. She had two business cards and a four-color poster to design before the customers came in later to approve them. The cards were easy. One was for Trudy Hudson, owner of Hudson Florist about a block away. Gloria planned to take the H and F in Hudson Florist, enlarge them to four times the size of the other letters, then use them as arbors by entwining them with green ivy. All the lettering would be mauve printed on cream 80-lb-coated cover stock. She had thought of using flowers instead of ivy, but that would make it more than a two-color job and too pricey. Trudy had told her to hold the cost down.

The other card was for a hardware salesman. He told Gloria flat-out that he didn't want to spend much, so she planned on making the card one-color, process blue lettering on 60-lb matte, book weight. In the top left corner she'd put a pile of tools: hammers, screwdrivers, wrenches; whatever she could find in their vast database of clipart.

But it was the poster for the Eckerd Performing Arts Center that would take more thought, and Gloria simply couldn't concentrate. Harry had told her this was the first time the Center had given them business, and he naturally hoped it would lead to other jobs. So . . . she couldn't afford to mess up.

She opened QuarkXPress, set up a document, set up guides, created multiple text boxes, removed item runarounds, then began working on the simplest project first: the business card for the hardware salesman. Maybe by the time she got to the poster, her brain would be functioning.

❧ ❧

By lunchtime, Gloria had both business cards done, and Harry was pleased.

"Nice job," he said while handing her a tuna sandwich.

Gloria took the baggie from Harry and smiled. "Thanks. And thanks for lunch. But you shouldn't have. You can't keep feeding me like this."

"Why not? I figure if you're well fed you'll work harder."

Gloria pulled out the tuna sandwich and took a bite.

"'Course, you don't seem so alert today. Not that I'm complaining, mind you, 'cause I like what you did with the cards, but that poster, that's a whole other ball of wax. You got to be focused. You got to give them something that's gonna knock their socks off."

Gloria nodded and continued chewing.

"So, what's wrong?"

"Nothing," she said between bites.

"Don't give me that. I know when someone's head is disconnected and floating in outer space. Is it Perth? She got rejected, right? Those colleges turned her down, and you're worried what's gonna happen."

Gloria sighed and told Harry about finding Perth ripping up her college letters.

"She's been through a lot. Oh, don't look at me like that. I know a wounded deer when I see one."

Harry Grizwald waved his sandwich in the air with such force Gloria was sure all the tuna was going to fly right out of the bread and land on her shoes. She relaxed when he placed his sandwich on top of the baggie.

"But she's young and she's smart, and she'll come through. Mark my words, she'll come through. She just got the wind knocked out of her, that's all."

Gloria finished her sandwich without saying a word.

"But that's not all, is it? Your mind's still whirling around up there in space. You must be near Jupiter by now."

Gloria laughed, then stopped when she saw the look in his eyes. There was no way she was going to get away saying "nothing" again. "Know anything about radical environmentalists?"

"Some." A peculiar look came over him. "Why?"

"Friends of mine have . . . well, they've gotten mixed up with some, and now they're having all kinds of grief."

Harry was quiet for so long Gloria thought the conversation was over. "Yeah," he finally said, his face twisted. "It's been known to happen."

"My friends have gotten in over their heads and don't see a way out. To be honest, at this point they're not even looking for any. They just want this whole mess to be over. Right now, they're just trying to survive."

"Trouble is . . . sometimes you don't survive no matter how hard you try."

"What do you mean?"

"Sometimes a person doesn't have enough clout, doesn't have enough money or connections to fight the bully with power. If the bully's big enough and powerful enough, he can take anything he wants."

Gloria twisted around to see him better. "Harry, this is America."

"America's changed. It's full of unscrupulous bureaucrats and wealthy foundations and crazy environmentalists who can get together and take away your land, if they want to. They can take away anything they want. Even a business that's been in a family for generations."

Gloria sank lower in her chair. "You sound like you had a friend who got hurt too."

"No. A relative. My brother-in-law. And he's dead."

"Dead?"

"From a spiked tree. Nearly killed Lily too, when she found

330

out. Took the heart right out of her. We never had a family, so Lily's family meant a lot to her. Especially her baby brother. She loved that boy. She was never the same."

"I'm . . . so sorry."

Harry shrugged. "Know what spiking is?"

"No."

"That's when environmentalists put long nails into trees to stop the loggers from cutting them down. The nails break their saws. Sometimes cause injury. My brother-in-law, Chip, hit a sixteen-inch spike with his chain saw, and the blade broke, snapped back and hit his neck. Severed his carotid artery. He bled to death before they could get him to a doctor." Harry leaned his arms against his thighs and hung his head. "I didn't help. He told me about the trouble. And he fought them . . . the environmentalists for a long time. But I didn't help. I didn't even try. Maybe if I had, things would have been different."

"We all have our regrets."

Harry nodded. "They spiked a total of thirty trees in Chip's section. The other loggers found them later. But they were on the lookout, so no one else got hurt. But the environmentalists had been after Chip's outfit for a long time. Chip had a contract to thin the western ridge of Too Tall Mountain, as part of the forest management program to keep the forests from becoming tinderboxes. He was to cut down all the dead or dying trees and remove all the fallen trees and branches from the forest floor.

"But the marijuana growers didn't want Chip's crew near that section because just south of it, where all the trucks and heavy equipment would have to travel, were the areas used by guerrilla growers—marijuana growers using federal lands.

"Some years back there was a big fight over the use of 2,4-D —a herbicide used on newly planted forests to control the brush. Only problem is in addition to killing the brush, it kills the marijuana plants. Well, the growers had a fit and did everything they could to stop the brush control, stop the use of 2,4-D by sabotaging equipment, cutting down trees, and creating road blocks, attacking Forest Service crews while they were hand-spraying. Some eco-radicals even came in to help the growers. The radical environmentalists and guerrilla growers have had a loose partnership for over thirty years. They both have the same goal—to close off all national forests, but for different reasons —one to save nature, the other to save their marijuana farms. Anyway, it got so bad, and there was so much vandalism the Forest Service gave up and promised the growers they would suspend brush control for a while.

"So when Chip got the contract at Too Tall, the hassling started all over again. Neither the marijuana growers nor the environmentalists wanted Chip in the area."

"And they stopped him."

"Nobody ever paid, either. Not one person was convicted. If the truth be known, the authorities are a little afraid of the environmentalists."

Gloria remembered the bold way the environmentalists had walked into Perth's diner, remembered the story Perth told her about the rancher who had confronted them and then backed down with fear.

"So, Gloria, this is your America now—a place where people kill others to save a tree or a marijuana plant."

Gloria stared silently at Harry. *What had Tracy and Tucker gotten themselves into?*

"His name was really Ken, but they called him Chip."

Harry rose to his feet, his ink-stained fingers running through his white hair, and Gloria half expected to see him leave a trail of black.

"They called him Chip because of how fast he could make

the chips fly when felling a tree. Left a wife and three kids. Patsy, his wife, tried running the business for a while but went belly-up because of all the hassle. Finally remarried and moved away. The kids are all grown now. Not one of them's in logging. Three generations of loggers—gone. Just like that. All gone."

﹏ ﹏

For the next several hours, Gloria worked on the poster for the Performing Arts Center. They had not given her much guidance, only told her what it was for—to herald the celebration of their 100-year anniversary marked by a fund-raising cocktail party. And they told her to make the poster different, exciting. She had the local library e-mail the lithograph bitmap of the Performing Arts Center as it looked a hundred years ago, complete with horses and buggies hitched outside. She had asked the library to convert it to a CMYK.TIFF file so she could separate the colors. Once she got the picture and manipulated it the way she wanted, she created a huge 100 in embossed Century Gothic that covered the entire poster, then layered it on top of the picture box, making it resemble a watermark. The finishing touch was the poster's border. Gloria created it entirely of musical notes.

While she worked, Gloria couldn't get Harry's story out of her mind. And even when the assistant to the director of the Center came in and saw the proof and told Gloria how much she loved it, told her how beautiful and perfect it was, Gloria was still thinking of Chip and the end of three generations of loggers.

﹏ ﹏

The little black Elgin on Gloria's desk told her it was almost closing time, so she began pushing all the scattered papers into neat little piles. Tomorrow would be another busy day. Already she had two flyers, two more business cards, a bookmark—honoring the recent completion of the new wing of the Eckerd Library—and the invitation to an Eckerd Chamber of Commerce annual dinner to design. Maybe she'd come in a little early and get a head start.

"The Center loved your poster. You did a great job," Harry said, stopping by her desk.

Gloria nodded and smiled. She felt embarrassed taking any credit. With her mind being distracted most of the day, it was only by God's grace she had come up with anything original at all.

"I see you got plenty of work for tomorrow."

Gloria looked down at the order forms that formed a pile in the center of her now tidy desk. "I think the word's getting out. Who knows? Maybe before too long I'll be looking for an assistant."

"Maybe."

Gloria studied Harry's knotted face, watched him wipe the same two ink-stained fingers over and over on his rag. "What's wrong?"

"Been distracted all day. Ever since I told you about Chip."

"Me too."

"What I've been thinking is that maybe we shouldn't let them get away with it. Maybe we should make some noise. Kick up some dust—for Chip and Lily and your friends. For all the other Chips and Lilys. Whaddya think?"

"I . . . don't know. I mean, how much dust can two people like us kick up?"

"They been walking around this town like they owned it.

And everybody's afraid, afraid of not being politically correct, afraid of saying the wrong thing, afraid of sounding like they're greedy and selfish and care more about protecting their business than protecting their environment. And those not afraid don't really understand what's going on. They just don't get it. Even if they don't like the tactics, they think all this picketing and shouting and screaming is because the environmentalists are trying to do something good. And I think we got to tell them otherwise."

Gloria shook her head. "It's not going to bring Chip back."

"I know that. Don't you think I know that?"

"But knowing it up here," Gloria pointed to her head, "and knowing it in here," she pointed to her heart, "are two different things."

Harry shrugged. "You wanna do something or not?"

"I don't know. I'll have to pray about it."

Just before Harry Grizwald turned out all the shop lights, Gloria quickly sorted through the pile of mail the postman had delivered earlier. This was the first chance she'd had to check it. It was mostly junk mail with a few bills mixed in, and she was about to leave it for tomorrow, when she spotted the last envelope in the pile. A yellow change of address sticker was plastered across the middle, and on the top right-hand side in bold black letters the words: *Do not deliver if address incorrect.* It was addressed to her.

Gloria ripped open the envelope and quickly read the letter that was on official Department of Social Services letterhead and that detailed Sasha Morgan's last visit and authorized Perth to remain with Gloria, pending her employment verification. It was only by God's grace Gloria had received it. By rights the post office should have returned it to Social Services. What happens if they sent another letter? Or tried to call? Or found out that Gloria no longer worked for Mattson Development? Would that make them rethink their position? In about three months Perth would be of age.

If only they could squeeze by until then.

—◈ ◈—

Chapter Twenty

O DAUGHTERS OF JERUSALEM, I CHARGE YOU—
IF YOU FIND MY LOVER,
WHAT WILL YOU TELL HIM?
TELL HIM I AM FAINT WITH LOVE.
~ SONG OF SONGS 5:8 NIV~

"A NEWSLETTER? That's your idea?"

"Yes." Gloria stood beside the gleaming American Eagle press, nodding at Harry Grizwald like one of those little toy dogs stuck on a dashboard. She had talked to Jesus about her idea for over an hour, then walked the floor like an expectant father in some maternity waiting room. What did she think was going to be brought forth? Something of genius? The look on Harry's face told her how foolish that thought was. Well, maybe a newsletter wasn't the answer—but at least it was a place to start. Besides, what was the best way to expose something that *sounded* good? That most people believed in, at least to some extent? Because just about everybody with the feeblest sensitivity was an environmentalist at heart. They cared about their world, wanted to be good stewards of it and preserve it for their children and grandchildren. Now she was suggesting that she and Harry write something for the whole of Eckerd to read, something that would make them both sound like nut jobs—namely, that environmentalism wasn't at all what people thought it was. It wasn't this benign, do-good hippie thing. Rather, some environmentalists wore pin-striped suits, occupied important positions in Washington, and behind them, pulling the strings, were wealthy foundations with their own hidden agendas.

Gloria could feel the scathing criticism already. Hear the angry words of rebuttal. And it made her uneasy. She was loath to dive into controversy. It was still too much like bungee jumping. But her research made her even more loath to abandon the project. It wasn't like being between a rock and a hard place exactly, but more like being between a giant cactus and a rattler.

Sometimes, Gloria, you don't have a brain in your head.

No . . . that wasn't true. She had the mind of Christ, didn't she? And she was sure He had given her this idea.

"I thought we could tell Chip's story, and maybe others would write us. Then we could tell theirs." Gloria absently tugged on the edges of her blue sweater, trying to read Harry's expression. Right now, it resembled a bowl of bland vanilla pudding. "I think by telling these stories, people will come to understand what's really happening. Of course, we'll need to do more digging—find out everything we can—and what and who's behind the movement and where the money really comes from."

Harry Grizwald scratched his head. "I . . . think I like it. Follow the money. Yeah. That's always a good place to start."

"I thought we'd call it *Conservation and Common Sense.* We have to show we're not anti-environment but pro-common sense.

And Chip's story will kick it off." Gloria didn't tell Harry she hoped to track down that cattleman Perth had told her about and get his story for the second issue, just in case there was no second issue. Just in case this whole thing bombed.

"I suppose we could test the waters. Put something out, something small, a flyer maybe rather than a newsletter, and see what we get. But what about distribution? How you gonna get it to people?"

"The best I could come up with is we hire a couple of teen-agers to hand them out at every food store in town."

"People just gonna toss them."

"Maybe. But they toss junk mail too, and this won't cost as much, since we don't need addresses, labels, postage, or the time to put it all into a database. Let's just fling it out there like bait and see what we catch."

Harry began rummaging through his shelves. "Now, where's that stock I've been trying to get rid of?" His hand finally rested on several reams of green 50-lb offset, and he turned to Gloria with a frown. "Okay. But let's just hope your bait doesn't catch any sharks."

~~◐ ◑~~

The next three days were a blur for Gloria as she filled the mounting volume of new orders. In between, she drafted the first issue of *Conservation and Common Sense (CCS)* in flyer format.

Chip's story covered the entire front and half of the back. Gloria filled the remaining space with a Part I article about the Endangered Species Act. She had not liked what her research revealed. And she highlighted this revulsion by exposing how sweeping the Endangered Species Act was, how it outranked all other laws in U.S. courtrooms and was the means by which both private and public lands could be shut up tighter than a drum against any use. In Part II, Gloria planned on covering how the Act has been used to destroy rural economies.

The last remaining space in their first issue of *CCS* contained contact information, which included a post office box Gloria had opened for that purpose. She had also included her phone number. Harry had not liked her putting her number on the flyer, but Gloria couldn't think of any other way. They had already ruled out using the shop phone. "We need to give them *someplace* to call if we want them to contact us," Gloria had retorted and won the argument—all the while harboring her own misgivings.

Gloria had been thinking a lot about love lately. Her mind had started along this route after reading 1 John 4:19: "We love him, because he first loved us."

He first loved us.

Those words had bounced around in her head like oil in a hot skillet, then slowly made their way down into her heart, where they coated and warmed and healed. Gloria knew she loved Jesus. The first time she got hold of the vision of Him bleeding and broken and hanging on that rough-hewn cross for her sins, she couldn't help but love Him, couldn't help but whisper, with trembling voice, her pledge of love into His ear.

He first loved us.

But there was another reason she loved Him. She hadn't even understood that reason until those words had dropped into her heart and opened the eyes of her understanding. And that reason was this: *Jesus first loved Gloria*—silly, foolish Gloria, lacking beauty of face and form, lacking in almost every quality—

Jesus *loved* her. Even before He had touched her with His grace and power, even before He had taken the poorly formed clay and began shaping it into something useful and perhaps even pleasant to look at—He had *loved* her. And that revelation had taken her breath away, just as surely as a handsome suitor takes away the breath of his beloved. And it had made her swoon with love and joy.

Gloria loved Jesus because He first loved her.

Even now, as Gloria stepped into the dimly lit diner, it gripped her—a consuming fire that consumed her heart and flowed beyond it, out to those He had placed in her path. It was the very reason she was here. It was the very reason she knew the days of walking passively through life without trying to touch others were over.

Gloria squinted her eyes, trying to accustom them to the shadows, the dark vinyl seats and tables, the dark paneled walls. Only half a dozen people were in the diner. That was good. That meant Perth would have free time. Gloria spotted her, idly leaning against the wall, wedged between two other waitresses. The little mauve uniform with black trim, hitting Perth above the knee, made her look childlike. Gloria smiled and waved, then watched as Perth made her way to the front, slowly, and a little labored as though she carried a giant tray on her shoulder.

"Anything wrong?" Perth asked, anxiety in her voice.

"No. Just thought it would be nice if we had dinner together."

Perth looked around and shrugged. "Sure. Why not? I don't think anyone will mind. It's dead tonight. And I haven't eaten yet."

Perth directed Gloria to a booth in her section; a section Perth always claimed was the busiest. Except for tonight. *Thank God.* Because Gloria had something she needed to say. She went over it in her mind while Perth left to clear it with her boss.

Minutes later she returned carrying two menus. "Okay. It's all set."

They both took time deciding what they wanted. Perth picked the stuffed flounder dinner. Gloria chose a tuna melt and didn't even want that because she wasn't hungry. But she had to order something, or Perth would wonder why she came. While Perth went to the kitchen to place their order, Gloria went over again what she was going to say. She had to be tough. No feeling sorry for the girl. Perth was sitting on a fence right now, ready to drop down the wrong side.

Oh, how much Perth reminded Gloria of herself.

When Perth returned, she slid into her seat and slumped forward, leaning her elbows on the table. "I love having my own place, but sometimes . . . I miss you. I'm real glad you came."

Gloria smiled. It felt good to be missed. "How have you been?"

Perth shrugged and picked her nails.

"Have you given any more thought to college?"

Perth threw up her hands. "You forgot? I've been rejected."

"So that's it? Just like that? No more trying?"

"Cut it out, Gloria. Stop pulling my chain."

"Kind of overdosing on self-pity, aren't you?"

"What do you *want* me to do? Can I force them to let me into their crummy college?"

"You can go to Eckerd Community. Work hard for two years, earn a high GPA, then transfer to Bristol."

"Gloria, I'm tired of getting rejected. How many more times do I have to get hit over the head before I get the message?"

"What? You don't think you're college material?"

"I'm marginal. I've always been marginal. Mom used to tell me I should learn a trade. Maybe become a beautician."

"And you?"

"Dreams are nice, but then you wake up. It's hard for you to understand. You always get what you want. Everything seems to work out for you. Just look . . . you lose your job, and the same day you get a new one. And not only that but an apartment that's practically free. How could you understand what it's like to want something so bad and it not happen?"

Gloria suppressed her urge to laugh. "You listen to me. Go to Eckerd Community. Work hard. And in two years, Bristol will be calling you."

"Oh, stop it." Perth sat up a little straighter.

"Seriously, it's worth a try, isn't it?"

"I don't know. I did think about community college but figured why bother. I don't know if I can take any more rejection. I mean . . . what if they don't accept me?"

"What if, what if . . . you just apply and see. Okay?"

Perth sighed. "Community college *is* pretty cheap. Between this job and a student loan, I could probably hold on to most of my savings—you know, the money I got at Dad's funeral. And then I could keep the apartment at Harry's. And two years isn't so long."

"That's right." Gloria saw color creep over Perth's cheeks, saw excitement flit across her eyes like fireflies. "You're on the right track now."

"And if Bristol doesn't take me in two years, some other college will."

"That's right."

For the first time since the discussion began, Perth smiled. "I feel kind of stupid that you had to come here and tell me the obvious. I guess I was so focused on my dream, on Bristol, that I didn't want another way. Pretty immature, huh? But I was so *disappointed.* I wanted it so badly, Gloria. Still do. It's hard giving it up. Even now."

"I know. Sometimes we have to give up our dreams."

"Yeah. And maybe . . . maybe sometimes they're just delayed."

⥱ ☙

No sooner had Gloria closed the door to her apartment than the phone rang. She thought perhaps it was someone calling about the flyer and let the answering machine take it. But when she heard the name Sasha Morgan, Gloria yanked it from the cradle.

"Miss Morgan . . . sorry about that. I just got in and was screening calls."

"Aha. I don't like answering the phone when I first get home either. Of course, I'm still at the office. Trying to catch up." She cleared her throat. "Which brings me to the purpose of this call. It seems you've left your place of employment."

"Yes, that's right. I'm working for E-Z Printing on Pratt Parkway now. I've moved too. Have an apartment above the shop." She figured she'd beat Sasha Morgan to the punch on that one.

"I thought as much, after I called your old number. I'm assuming Perth is still with you."

"Oh yes!" Gloria returned, a bit too loudly. She squirmed at the silence on the other end. "She has a lovely apartment. We fixed it all up and—"

"Perth has her own apartment?"

"Yes." Gloria cringed. The chill in Sasha Morgan's voice told Gloria she had just made a mistake. "It's right across from mine and—"

"How can she afford it?"

"Because Harry Grizwald is very kind and generous and—"

"A *man* is paying her rent?"

"No, Miss Morgan. Harry Grizwald owns E-Z Printing. He has two apartments he rents out on the second floor. His is on the third. And he has graciously given us the two second-floor apartments for a nominal—"

"Has it occurred to you that you may have put Perth in a compromising position? By all indications you seemed stable and desirable—a good influence, and since the time was short before Perth came of age, well, naturally we wanted to allow Perth to remain in that stability. Now it appears I . . . that is, Social Services may have been wrong. The stability we assumed existed . . . in reality does not. On top of which there now seems to be a man in the picture and—"

"Miss Morgan, I'm afraid you've gotten this all wrong. Harry Grizwald must be over *sixty*. He's kind, considerate, and has become a father figure to Perth. To suggest—"

"We know how it is with young, impressionable girls. Believe me, Miss Bickford, we've seen it before. Girls like Perth are hungry for fatherly attention, and unfortunately there are all too many men who will capitalize on this. Perhaps we need to reevaluate Perth's case. You'll be notified of any change." Then Sasha Morgan hung up.

Gloria stood beside the kitchen counter looking at the dead phone in her hand. *You'll be notified of any change.* No, that couldn't happen. No change. Not now. Now when they were so close to Perth's eighteenth birthday.

~◑ ◐~

After Gloria calmed down, she walked up the stairs to the third floor and knocked on Harry Grizwald's door. The smell of fried steak oozed from his apartment and filled the hall. *Must be having a late dinner.* She was about to leave when the door opened, and Harry stood in front of her, looking curiously like the Pillsbury Dough Boy with a white apron wrapped tightly around his slightly rounded middle.

"You're just in time! I had two steaks in the fridge and had to cook them before they went bad. Help me eat one."

"Harry, don't you believe in freezers?"

"Hate frozen meat." Harry pulled Gloria into his apartment. "You gonna help me out or not?"

Gloria eyed the two huge T-bones lying across the platter like oven mitts. "I've already eaten—with Perth."

"Then stay and keep me company."

It was another two hours—after Harry ate, and after they did the dishes—before Gloria finally told him about Sasha Morgan's disturbing phone call.

⋙ ⋘

Gloria watched Harry Grizwald slowly button his sheepskin jacket, then pull a black wool cap so low over his white curly hair he almost covered his eyebrows. "Be back later," he said, nearly tripping over the big Ryobi press as he passed.

He looked sweet, even with that stern expression on his face, and she wanted to ask him if he prayed first but didn't. But she had prayed. She had asked Jesus to keep Harry from making the whole mess with Social Services worse. Not that she blamed him for going to see Sasha Morgan. According to Harry, he had to set the record straight. How could you stop a man who felt that way? "If you're not back by lunch, mind if I close the shop and do an errand?" she asked, trying not to look too disapproving or worried.

"Sure . . . whatever."

"I'll probably take an extended lunch hour, but I'll make it up. I'll work a little later and—"

"Since when have you started punching in?"

Gloria was really getting worried now. The look on his face was as frosty as the ice-cream sodas she used to have with Tracy at Tad Bick's Parlor, and his words felt like the raw edges of a tin can. She watched Harry walk to the front of the shop, adjust his hat, then open the door and step out into the freezing January morning.

Oh, Jesus, don't let Harry say anything to upset Sasha Morgan.

By noon Harry Grizwald still hadn't come back, so Gloria locked up the shop, hailed a cab, and headed for The Estates. She had been calling Tracy for days, but either she got no answer, or Tucker answered and wouldn't put her through to Tracy. She needed to see Tracy, tell her about the flyer. She didn't want Tracy to find out from someone else. She didn't see how the flyer could have any effect on Mattson Development, one way or the other. Still . . . she wanted Tracy to know.

Even before the taxi rolled to a stop by the construction trailer, Gloria saw a cloud of dust mushroom over the far left of the construction site, where three yellow dozers ripped and pulled the earth. They were clearing Phase II lots. How could that be? Wasn't it too cold to pour cement?

Inside, the trailer was empty except for Tracy. Gloria could see the top of her red head bent over the little desk in back, looking like the tip of a burning match. "Hey, there," she called out, not wanting to take Tracy totally by surprise.

"Gloria! Gee, kiddo, it's good to see you."

Gloria walked to the desk, thinking how much her life had

changed since coming to Eckerd. How much *she* had changed. And these changes had leached into her friendship with Tracy, had altered it somehow. And even though it made her sad, Gloria knew it was a good thing too. In a way it was like when a child goes to camp for the first time. There's a painful tearing away, but later the child returns home more grown-up.

"Tucker says you're all settled in and found a job. I'm glad you're doing okay."

"I wasn't sure Tucker was giving you my messages."

Tracy looked embarrassed. "I've . . . been meaning to call. Just been so busy. Tucker's . . . pretty stressed, not himself right now, so I try to stay close. Actually, Gloria, he has me pretty worried. Everything puts him on edge. And he's starting to get reckless. Do stupid things."

"Like preparing to pour the foundations for Phase II?"

"How did you know?"

"I saw the dozers and figured it out."

"I tried talking him out of it. We've just finished all those garages, you know, the ones that had problems. But the weather's gotten too cold now, only he won't listen. He said there's cement with admixtures that can be used in freezing temperatures. But Don Blaster claims using a mix of chemical and mineral admixtures, like Tucker's doing, could create incompatibility and compromise the cement's integrity. I just wish Tucker would listen. But enough of my problems. What about you? What brings you here?"

Gloria pulled the flyer from her pocket and placed it on the desk in front of Tracy. "I wanted you to read this."

"Terrible—really sad," Tracy said after breezing through it. "Hard to believe something like this could happen. But . . . why was it so important that you came all this way so I could read it?"

"Because of Jordon and what's going on here, and . . . because I wrote it. I don't see how it could hurt you, even though—"

"I like that you brought out the drug connection—between the pot growers and the environmentalists." Tracy bent over the desk and lowered her voice, even though no one else was around. "Spencer's talked about it. He talks a lot when he's high."

"I was hoping you weren't seeing him anymore." Gloria watched Tracy pull on her eyelashes. She seldom did that, and only when she was nervous.

"He's not so bad. That's because I've finally figured out how to play him, figured out what makes him tick. And why shouldn't I? If it helps Tucker? Spencer and the people he knows are really connected, Gloria. You wouldn't believe the big foundations that fund them." Her voice was almost a whisper. "I'm talking *big*. Spencer brags about it all the time."

Gloria couldn't help thinking that in a perverse way Tracy was bragging too, and suddenly she was reminded of Jessica Daily. For a while, Jessica had thought she was playing Jordon too.

"Spencer says the environmentalists aren't small potatoes anymore. That foundation money flows like the Ganges to those environmentalists who play ball, who line up with the foundations' agenda. And we're talking millions." Tracy sighed and sank deeper into her chair. "Spencer once said that before too many more years the foundations—those pulling the strings behind the scenes—will be making most of our domestic policies. They have PR firms that can create artificial grassroots, sway public opinion, create media blitzes, and make it all look like the work of John Q. Public."

There was always someone who wanted to rule the world. Who wanted to push and shove and snatch away the things that belonged to others. Gloria knew it had everything to do with that first act of disobedience way back in the Garden of Eden. And the rest was history.

"Of course you could stop seeing Jordon anytime you wanted to, right?" Gloria was pushing the envelope. "I mean . . . in case things got out of hand."

Tracy pulled a black scrunchy from her desk drawer and tied back her hair. "Sometimes, Gloria, you say the silliest things. People in business wine and dine each other all the time. They do favors and get favors in return. I've already told you that. That's how it's done. And if you weren't so naive, so . . . so small-town Appleton, you'd understand it."

"So you're saying if things really got bad you could get out?"

Tracy pulled on her eyelashes. "Sure. Anytime I wanted."

Gloria's lunch hour turned into three by the time she left Tracy. And when she got back to E-Z Printing, there was a message on the answering machine from Harry Grizwald: "Gloria, I'll be getting back later than I expected. I'm downtown, at the fifth precinct. They're giving me an appearance ticket—a summons to go to court for disturbing the peace. I guess I got a little riled when I was talking to Sasha Morgan."

Chapter Twenty-One

LISTEN! MY LOVER! LOOK!
HERE HE COMES, LEAPING ACROSS THE MOUNTAINS,
BOUNDING OVER THE HILLS.
MY LOVER IS LIKE A GAZELLE OR A YOUNG STAG.
SONG OF SONGS 2:8 NIV

GLORIA HAD DISMISSED THE IDEA of warning Perth about
Social Services. Why get her upset? Worry her for nothing?
Because it may never come to anything at all. Still . . . Harry had
not helped their case, and if Social Services did come and take
Perth . . . These thoughts harassed Gloria as she went about her
Saturday chores. Washing down the kitchen and bathroom, they
bubbled. Dusting and vacuuming, they churned. While doing
laundry, they boiled. By midmorning, this stew of anxiety forced
Gloria to her knees, and after she prayed for Perth, Sasha Morgan, Harry, herself, she left the entire matter in God's hands.

She was in that comfortable position when the phone rang,
and Sasha Morgan's voice shattered it. "Hello, Miss Bickford?

I'm across the street. Mind if I come up? We're still considering Perth's case. I find that surprise visits work best, so I won't apologize for the intrusion."

A soft answer turneth away wrath. She'd be civil, try to walk in God's love. *But, oh, Jesus, please straighten this woman out!*

"Miss Bickford? Are you there?"

"Yes," Gloria said, choking down her anxiety. "Mine is the first entrance on your left. I'll be right down."

Within minutes Gloria escorted Sasha Morgan up the dedicated staircase that led directly into the kitchen, all the while listening to her chatter about how much she loved the shops along Pratt Parkway. Once inside, Sasha Morgan said little. Instead, she scurried around the apartment, making notes in her little yellow spiral. Finally, when the inspection was over, Sasha Morgan tapped her notebook with a number-two pencil. "It's smaller than your last apartment. But nice. Very nice. And Perth? She has the same accommodations?"

Gloria nodded.

"Of course I need to see them."

Gloria looked at the kitchen clock. Ten to eleven. Perth would be asleep, and her apartment probably a mess. On top of that, her refrigerator was sure to resemble the floor model at PC Richards—empty—because most of her meals were eaten at the school cafeteria or the diner. Gloria wondered if she should point this out, then decided against it, and walked quietly to Perth's apartment.

Sasha Morgan followed.

Gloria had to bang on the door several times before any sounds of life were heard.

"Yeah . . . okay . . . okay I'm coming." Even through the door, Gloria heard the sleep in Perth's voice and cringed. Sasha Morgan was not going to be treated to the image of an alert, mature, and self-sufficient young woman. Gloria hoped Sasha Morgan was in a good mood. She tried to assess her out of the corner of her eye but couldn't.

"What's all the fuss?" Perth said, opening the door in a pair of gray thermal underwear and gray sweatshirt, hair sticking out in all directions. Then her mouth dropped in surprise. "Ah . . . hello Miss Morgan . . ."

"Mind if I come in and look around?"

"Sure . . . okay." Perth's fingers tried combing through the tangle on her head. When that failed, she attempted to press it down with her palms. "Ah . . . you gotta excuse the mess. I don't have much time during the week with my job and homework . . ."

But Sasha Morgan was already gone, scurrying from one room to the other, her pencil flying over her yellow notebook. When Gloria heard the refrigerator door open and close, she groaned. "Anything in it?" she whispered to Perth.

Perth shook her head.

"What about men?" Sasha Morgan said, emerging from the kitchen. "Any come to the apartment?"

Perth looked stunned. "No . . . of course not. Gloria wouldn't allow it. She said I can have my girlfriends anytime but no guys because—"

"And Harry Grizwald? He ever come to see you?"

"Well, last weekend he stopped by and brought me some stew. Why?"

"How long did he stay?"

Perth shrugged. "I don't know . . . half an hour . . . we got to talking and—"

"Does he come often?"

"I . . . don't understand."

Suddenly, Gloria stepped between Perth and Sasha Morgan. "I know you're only doing your job. But somehow you've gotten a wrong impression. Harry Grizwald also brought me stew. It's what he does. He loves to cook, and he has nobody else, and well . . . it gives him a lot of pleasure. In fact, two nights ago I had dinner at his apartment. Not dinner . . . exactly. He had an extra steak and—"

"You're not the minor, Miss Bickford. She is." Sasha Morgan pointed her pencil at Perth. "I've come with an open mind, hoping to convince myself that Perth hasn't been placed in a potentially compromising position. But I remain unconvinced. For one thing, there's no supervision. Perth could come in anytime, day or night, and you'd never know it. For another, an unsupervised vulnerable female should not be placed in a position of indebtedness to a man, especially an older man."

"Perth and I have an understanding." Gloria struggled to keep her voice calm. "I always know where she is in the evenings, and if she goes out after work—which she doesn't do on a school night—she always calls me." In spite of her effort, Gloria's voice began to sound shrill. She tried once more to subdue it. "And as far as Harry Grizwald is concerned, you're way off base!" No use. Even to Gloria's ears, she sounded like a boom box.

Sasha Morgan snapped her little yellow notebook closed. "I know you think I'm the enemy, Miss Bickford, and I can't help that. My only concern is for Perth. I will sit down with others and review the case." She turned to Perth and pointed the notebook at her. "But off the top of my head, I'd say you better start packing, because you won't be here much longer."

~◉ ◉~

"I don't get what the big deal is. What does she think is going on here, anyway?" Perth stomped around the apartment venting. "How can she expect me to just pick up and go? It's so *unfair*." Finally, she stopped and crumbled onto the couch. "I can't start all over again. I *won't!*" Perth swiped at her eyes, but her cheeks were already wet. "How can I leave my school . . . how can I leave you and Harry?"

Gloria's eyes rested on Perth's toe rings. It wasn't that long ago Gloria thought them ridiculous; thought Perth annoying, a bother. Now . . . her heart was breaking. "I think we must pray, and I'm going to pray a strange prayer. What I'm going to ask God to do, as long as it doesn't violate His perfect will, is to allow all Sasha Morgan's paperwork pertaining to your case to be misplaced for the next three months. That's all the time we need, three months."

"Cool!" Perth smiled and wiped her face with the back of her hand. "And can we pray about me getting into Eckerd Community College? I mailed in the application yesterday."

Already? God had done so much in Perth's life. There was no reason for Gloria to think He'd stop now.

After Gloria finished praying with Perth, she went to see Harry. She found him in the shop with his presses. Since Gloria came to work at E-Z Printing full-time, Harry could spend Saturdays puttering with his machines, which generally put him in a good mood. Even now, there was a big grin on his face.

"You got a pile of new orders this morning. I put them on your desk."

"Is that why you're wearing a grin the size of Rhode Island?"

Harry chuckled. "No. I'm smiling because of you. I heard you all the way down here. 'Course, when I saw Sasha Morgan come out your front entrance I knew why."

Gloria guessed Harry had deliberately kept out of sight. Only yesterday the fifth precinct called and told him the charges had been dropped. He obviously hadn't wanted to tempt fate.

"So, what did she want?" Harry asked as he continued to work on his press.

Gloria quickly told Harry what happened.

"You and Perth are the best thing that's happened to me since Lily . . ." Harry kept his eyes on the gleaming Ryobi, rubbing it down with his rag, focusing on nonexistent dirt. "Never realized how empty . . . how lonely this old place was until you two came. I'm back to cooking too. I love to cook. Haven't done much since Lily . . . haven't done a lot of things since Lily. Now some old prune comes along and wants to spoil everything. Wants to hurt Perth. Wants to put an end to it all . . ."

"I think Sasha Morgan really wanted to let Perth stay. But she must have seen too many abused kids. That's had to taint her, made her suspicious of everything. Made it easy, somehow, to get the wrong idea. However misguided, I think she's only trying to protect Perth."

"Well . . . I'm not gonna let her hurt Perth just because of some stupid notion that's lodged in her brain," Harry said, stopping his work and looking Gloria straight in the eyes.

"You want another appearance ticket?"

"You got a better idea?"

"How about praying?" She quickly told Harry about how she and Perth had asked God to hide the paperwork. He started laughing.

"Now, that I'd like to see! Yes sir. I'd really like to see that. Might even make me think of going back to church. Now wouldn't that beat all? Harry Grizwald sitting in the front pew of Blessed Redeemer Church? Haven't been there since Lily."

"Maybe we could go together."

Harry's face clouded. "Don't go jumping the gun. I said I'd *think* about going if I saw that prayer of yours answered."

"You can't stay mad at God forever."

"Who says I'm mad?"

"I do."

Harry sighed. "I believe in prayer. Pray all the time. Only . . . when it came to the big one, the one that counted, well, don't mind telling you I felt let down. He coulda healed Lily, just as easy as snapping His fingers. I know He's got His ways, and they're higher and all, but it makes it a little hard for me to sit in church and listen to how He's our healer and all. I just need a little more time, to get over things."

"You're mad at Him."

Harry shrugged. "If He answers this one, about Perth, I'll consider going back."

"I don't think it's right, putting conditions on God like that. But okay, that's between you and Him. Only, I must tell you I don't like sitting in the front pew. I prefer the third or fourth row. But we can work all that out. Maybe one week I'll sit up front with you, and the next week you sit where I want." With that Gloria left Harry Grizwald standing beside his Ryobi with his mouth open.

Instead of returning to her apartment and getting ready to go to West Meadow Market as she had planned, Gloria stopped by her desk, thinking she'd read through the new orders Harry talked about so she could give her mind a chance to percolate some design ideas over the weekend. She had just gathered the mess of papers into a pile when the buzzer went off. By the time she looked up, the cold air pursuing the newly arrived stranger had reached Gloria and made her shudder in her navy sweats. She was about to call Harry from the back but stopped as she watched the woman close the door. Her coat collar was pulled high around her ears, a beige muffler wrapped her neck and chin, and a beige cap was pulled low over her forehead. It was impossible to see the woman's face. Even so, there was something familiar about her.

Gloria continued staring. *"Tracy!"* Gloria shouted when recognition finally hit. Then she flew to the front and embraced her friend. As she did, her leg brushed against the suitcase in Tracy's hand.

"I . . . didn't know where else to go," Tracy said, not moving a muscle while Gloria pulled off her hat and muffler as if she were a child.

"I'm glad you came. Let's go upstairs, and you can tell me what happened over a cup of nice hot tea." Gloria took Tracy's bag, then led her through the shop, past Harry Grizwald, who was still polishing his Ryobi, then up the stairs into her apartment. After Gloria showed Tracy around, she took her coat, hung it in the hall closet, and settled Tracy in one of the kitchen chairs.

"Nice place. Nicer than I expected. You must be making good money." Tracy rubbed her hands together nervously. "I'm glad you landed on your feet. I mean that. I never wanted you to get hurt."

"I know," Gloria said, pulling mugs and tea bags from the cabinet, then putting a kettle of water on the front burner. "You've always been my best . . ." Gloria stopped and felt her heart soar with joy. No, she knew who her best friend was. It had taken her so long. But now that knowledge was deep inside her, ingrained into her very being. He loved her—her best friend —and He was never going to leave her or forsake her. And because of that love, because of that sweet, wonderful, penetrating, healing love, she could love others. Even now her heart was bursting with love for Tracy as she sat so helpless and childlike before her. It was as if God was taking Gloria's puny shriveled heart and stretching it, enlarging it so that it could accommodate others.

"You've always been a very, very dear friend. I hope I don't have to tell you how much I love you. How much I want to help. What happened?"

"I don't know. I woke up this morning feeling like my life had slipped out of control." Tracy rubbed her hands together, like one of Grandma Quinn's friends with arthritis used to do. "All of a sudden I found myself in a place I didn't want to be, didn't know how I got there, or how to get out. Does that make sense?"

Gloria nodded. It was like reading Jessica's letter all over again.

"I thought Tucker would understand. But he didn't. He only got mad when I told him I didn't want to be part of this whole Spencer thing anymore. I know he's stressed, so I've been making allowances, making a lot of excuses for him, but when he started calling me names, when he actually started cursing at me, well . . . I knew there wasn't going to be any meeting of the minds. I figured I'd give him a chance to cool off. Come to his senses."

"So you ended it with Jordon?"

Tracy nodded. "Never expected Tucker's reaction. I always thought we were so close. It hurts. You know?"

Gloria quietly prepared the tea and brought the steaming mugs to the table and sat down. *Jessica Daily, Jenny Hobart, and now Tracy.* What had changed Tucker—the kind, sweet, fun-loving boy—into Tucker—the manipulative, selfish man who thought nothing of using others for his personal gain? Was it the divorce? Or had Tucker made his parents' divorce a blanket excuse for his own poor behavior? "Maybe it's time you got away from here. Went back to Appleton," Gloria said softly.

"Leave Tucker flat? Just like that?"

"It's not a question of leaving Tucker. It's a question of getting away from this mess, before it drags you down. Tucker's in a fix, and by the look of things, he's not going to follow any sound advice. Did he start pouring concrete?"

Tracy nodded.

"See what I mean? He's not going to listen to you or anyone else. So there's nothing you can really do, except get yourself over it. You've taken the first step. You've come here. The rest will be easy."

"If I go back to Appleton, I'll have to live at Mom's. My credit cards are killing me. I owe so much and never seem to get ahead."

"It would only be temporary. After you get a decent job, whittle down some of that debt—"

"I don't know. I hate leaving Tucker. But he really is *impossible*. And getting a fresh start . . . that sounds tempting." Tracy worked her hands, as if they were sponges in need of wringing. "Being with Spencer was making me go nuts, and then being with Tucker . . . he was making me nuts too."

"Explain this to Tucker. Tell him how you feel."

"He won't talk to me right now."

"Then write him a letter. Eventually, he'll see the truth. Eventually, he'll understand why you couldn't stay."

"It seems so wrong . . . so disloyal." Tracy continued pulling on her hands.

"Right now, I think you need to get yourself together. Sort things out. You can stay here as long as you want."

"Really?"

"Really. Only . . . there's something I need to know. That business with the marijuana . . . you finished with that?"

"How did you . . . ?" Tracy smiled disdainfully and shrugged. "If I wasn't, would you let me stay?"

Gloria thought for a minute, then slowly shook her head and told Tracy about Perth and Sasha Morgan. "So . . . no drugs, right?"

Tracy's hands wrapped tightly around her hot mug. "No, I'm finished with all that."

That night, after Tracy had finally fallen asleep on the couch, Gloria pulled her wallet from her purse, removed Tucker's picture from its hiding place between her driver's license and VISA, and ripped it into a million little pieces.

Sunday afternoons were meant for occasions like this, Gloria thought, as she watched potato water splash and hiss over the edges of the large front burner. A sharp knife plunged into one of the tumbling potatoes told Gloria it was time to turn off the burner. She did, then grabbed pot holders and drained the water. Sunday dinner would be a feast: mashed potatoes, chicken Parmesan, asparagus, tossed salad. She hadn't made a meal like this since Christmas.

Perth, Harry, Tracy, and even Miss Dobson—by special request from Harry—were sitting in the living room chatting and eating cheese and crackers. Perth and Harry were making jokes and laughing. Tracy and Miss Dobson were quieter but not antisocial by any means.

Gloria was sure Tracy's reticence was due to the fact she had a lot to think about. Had some tough decisions to make. They had talked most of the evening the night before. And Tracy had told her more about her relationship with Spencer Jordon than Gloria really wanted to know. And Gloria had tried telling Tracy about Jesus, about His wonderful forgiveness and healing touch, but she would have none of it.

~◉ ◉~

Harry Grizwald put the last forkful of chicken cutlet Parmesan into his mouth and smiled. "Where did you learn to cook like this?" he said after swallowing. "One of the best I've ever had. Next to mine, that is. Lily never liked cooking. So we made a deal. She kept the shop and apartment clean, and I shopped for groceries and cooked. It worked for us. And after a while I got to be a pretty good cook, if I do say so—" Harry suddenly stopped talking and looked around, as though he were embarrassed. "Don't know what's been making me run at the mouth all afternoon. Can't seem to stop talking. Haven't talked this much since . . ." Harry shook his head. "There I go again. Yak, yak, yak. Ever have so much hot air in one room?"

"NO!" Perth said. "I was going to tell Gloria to turn off the heat and save some money."

"No respect. No respect for their elders. That's the trouble with the younger generation." Harry sipped from his water glass and winked at Miss Dobson. "Isn't that right, Dorie?"

Gloria watched Dorie Dobson blush, then giggle. "What's an old spinster like me know about young people?"

"Now, Dorie, you told me earlier you're only two years older than me, and I'm practically in my prime. Which makes you *prime* yourself."

Dorie, Perth, Gloria, and even Tracy giggled, and Gloria couldn't help wonder how awful it must be for those who had no one to laugh with or spend a Sunday afternoon with. And suddenly she found herself thinking of her mother.

"Sorry for calling you so late, Mother, but I had company, and they just left." Gloria heard her mother clear her throat, then sigh, then silence. "I just wanted to say hello, but if this is a bad time, I'll call another day."

"No . . . it's okay."

"I just wanted to tell you I was thinking of you. And that I . . . missed you."

"Oh . . . well . . . thank you. That's really sweet, Gloria, even at this hour."

"It really *is* late. I shouldn't have called—"

"No, it's all right. I'm glad you did. I'm touched. Really. I don't think you've said that before. About missing me. I'm touched."

They talked about the weather; about all the tests the doctors were doing on Virginia Press; about Gloria's job.

"Well, I won't keep you, Mother. I just wanted to say you're in my thoughts and prayers. And that I love you. Good night." Gloria hung up the phone and smiled. She was still utterly amazed. She actually *missed* her mother.

Chapter Twenty-Two

I AM MY LOVER'S AND MY LOVER IS MINE;
HE BROWSES AMONG THE LILIES.
—◈ SONG OF SONGS 6:3 NIV◈—

GLORIA WOKE UP WITH A SENSE of foreboding. It was hard to describe, to actually put her finger on, but if she were pressed, she'd say she felt a little like she was about to do aerobics with a vile of nitroglycerine in her pocket. She had tried to shake this feeling by prolonging her morning prayers, by reading extra pages of her devotional, by meditating longer on Scripture. But in spite of them all, the feeling persisted.

Now she scurried around like a hamster on a wheel trying to get ready for work. This feeling would pass, she told herself. It was silly. It meant nothing. She tiptoed into the living room to retrieve her brown pumps and passed the couch, where Tracy lay sprawled, a blanket over her head. She didn't feel good about leaving Tracy. Maybe that was the root of her uneasiness. Tracy was fragile.

When the phone rang, Gloria scrambled to get it before it woke Tracy up and glanced at the clock. Why did Mother always call at the most inopportune times? "Hi, Mother. How are you?"

"I read your flyer," said a strange man's voice. "I didn't like it. You made us look like a bunch of weirdos. You made it sound like all environmentalists are crazy."

Gloria's chest tightened. The anger in the man's voice had been unmistakable . . . and frightening. "I told a true story. I'm sorry you didn't like it. But sometimes the truth hurts."

"Yeah? Well maybe you're the one who's gonna get hurt—if you keep writing stuff like this."

After the phone went dead, Gloria hung up and looked over at the couch, where Tracy was still buried under blankets. And for a second, Gloria felt like going back to bed herself, felt like pulling her own covers over her head. Instead, she walked to the door, took a deep breath, and headed for the shop downstairs.

Noon couldn't come fast enough. As soon as Gloria's desk clock said twelve, she headed for the back stairs to her apartment and took the stairs in twos. All morning, when her mind wasn't on the strange caller, it was on Tracy. She had left a note on the kitchen table telling Tracy to come down to the shop if she got lonely. She didn't know what else to do.

When Gloria stepped into the apartment, she half expected to see Tracy sprawled on the couch. But all she saw were covers piled in a heap. For a second she panicked, until she heard the shower being turned off. She'd wait for Tracy. Spend some time with her.

She walked over to the couch. Unlike Perth, who was generally neat when time permitted, Tracy was a slob. Gloria used to tease her about her apartment looking like a bargain basement and that Tracy would rather buy new clothes than wash and iron her old ones. Like most exaggerations, it held a kernel of truth.

Absently, Gloria pulled at the bunched-up covers and folded the top blanket. When she pulled the second blanket off to fold that, a plastic sandwich baggie fell to the floor. Gloria stooped to pick it up and wondered what was inside. At first glance it looked like dried oregano. She unzipped the baggie and sniffed. *Oh, Tracy.*

Quickly, Gloria brought the baggie into the kitchen and dumped the marijuana down the drain. Then she turned the faucet on high and let it flush the pipes. She spun around when she heard Tracy scream.

"Stop it! Stop it!" Tracy shrieked, looking like a madwoman in Gloria's old bathrobe, her wet hair plastered to her face. Tracy clawed the air, jostled and pushed, and scratched Gloria's arms until she was finally able to rip the baggie from Gloria's hand. But she dropped it as soon as she saw it was empty. Then she just stood in the middle of the floor wringing her hands. With little effort, Gloria forced Tracy onto a kitchen chair.

"It . . . wasn't yours." The veins in Tracy's neck bulged. "You had no right."

"How *could* you bring that into this house? I told you what was happening with Perth and Social Services. Suppose Sasha Morgan decided to make another surprise visit?"

"Stop sounding so sanctimonious. It was just a little. Nothing to sweat about."

"Did you even consider what could happen if anyone found out? To you? To me? To Perth? To Harry?"

"I was . . . going to wean myself off. Just use it a few more times."

Gloria stood over Tracy, her hand on Tracy's shoulder as if holding her down. "And what now? How am I supposed to trust you after this?"

"I don't have any more. I don't even know how to get more. That was from Spencer's private stock. Stuff he gets from his guerrilla-grower friends. He's the only source I have."

Gloria's hand dropped from Tracy's shoulder and she sat down. "Maybe you should get some help."

"You mean like see a shrink?"

"Or a pastor. You've done some things . . . and you don't like yourself right now and—"

"Look who's talking! The queen of insecurity. You have a short memory, kiddo. When I think of the times I tried to build up *your* self-esteem. Believe me, I got tired of it too. You were always my timid little shadow, needing to be propped up before you could do anything. Where would you be if it wasn't for me?"

"You were a good friend, Tracy. Now I want to be one. You need to—"

"You want to be my friend, then *back off.*"

Gloria stared at Tracy for a long time, then sighed and settled in her seat. "Okay, Tracy—for now. But you can't stop me from praying."

Gloria didn't know how she managed to get through the afternoon. Most of the time her thoughts were on Tracy. The other times they were on that strange man who didn't like her flyer. She didn't tell Harry about the call. And she knew why. If she told him, he might not let her do another one. Maybe she should just forget about doing another flyer. That man's angry phone call and threat made her realize this whole thing could get personal. And it resurrected her old fears, made her feel insecure. Something she hadn't felt in a while. It had even made her want to chew her cuticles.

Still . . . when she thought of Tracy and Tucker, of Jessica Daily and Beth Price, of Jenny Hobart, she felt she had no choice. There was such a thing as the sin of omission.

She was still thinking about it when Perth called.

"Hey, Glory." This was something new. Just recently, Perth had started calling Gloria, Glory. And Gloria didn't mind. In fact, she liked it. Nobody had even taken the trouble to give her a pet name before. Not even Tracy, other than "kiddo," which Gloria hated and would eventually get around to telling her. "He's here. That guy you wanted to talk to. You know . . . the rancher who had a run-in with those environmentalists. He just got here. I'll stall him as long as I can, but if you want to talk to him, you better get down to the diner quick."

Gloria groaned. What was she going to do with Tracy? She didn't want to leave her alone, not after their run-in about the marijuana.

"Glory? You coming?"

"Yes," she said after she settled on a solution.

Gloria splashed cold water on her face, then patted it dry with a white hand towel while Tracy paced in the hall outside the bathroom.

"I don't think I want to go. I'd rather stay here and have a sandwich."

Gloria stuck her head out the door, the white towel in her hands. "You've been in all day. Don't you want to get some fresh air? Besides, it's my treat. Come on. You'll enjoy it."

"I don't know. I'm not sure I want to sit around all night and hear about how some poor guy got taken by the environmentalists. It's too close to home. I mean, the wounds are still fresh."

"It might be good for you. To hear what happened to someone else. To know you weren't the only one."

"Why?"

Gloria playfully brushed the towel against Tracy's nose. "Because—"

"Because misery loves company?"

"No. Because we can use this information for good. To help someone else."

Tracy turned her back on Gloria and walked away. "What makes you think I'm interested in signing on for some crusade?"

"It's not a crusade," Gloria said, following her. "It's a way of turning something that wasn't good into something good. It's a way of using what happened to you to help someone else."

Tracy laughed, and for a second, she sounded almost like her old self. "I'm not the one with the halo. You go meet this rancher. When you come back, tell me all about it. If I like what I hear, maybe I'll even help you with that flyer."

***

Gloria stepped into Phil's Diner and scanned for Perth. The perky teen was by one of the back booths, standing over a customer who was wearing a tan trench coat. They were laughing. Gloria waited patiently in the alcove as Perth finished with the man, then watched Perth take an order from four elderly women at one of the center tables.

"Tan coat, back left booth," Perth whispered as she passed, looking like a 007 wannabe, her mouth barely moving. "What took you so long? He's almost half finished with dinner."

Gloria shrugged. She didn't want to get into the issue about Tracy and blew Perth a kiss, then walked toward the back. She fingered the flyer in her pocket, then slowly pulled it out. It was in her hand when she reached the table. In a low voice, she introduced herself, told him what she wanted, then handed him the paper.

He was younger than she expected—fortyish was her guess —and well-groomed. She didn't know why she expected him to look grungy. She guessed it was the association with hard times or unfortunate circumstances that set the improper stage. She watched as he quietly read the flyer and noticed he moved his lips. At different intervals, he'd stop and look up with a troubled expression, then return to his reading. He read slowly, methodically. Finally, when he was finished, he folded the flyer in half.

"I'd like to put your story in our next flyer."

"What makes you think I've got a story?"

"Someone in the diner witnessed your run-in with the picketers and told me about it."

"Mind if I keep this?"

Gloria shook her head, then watched as he carefully slid the paper into his coat, as though it were a list of secret Zurich account numbers.

"Sad business, this Chip story. Tough break."

"I understand you've had a tough break too."

"Maybe. But even if I had, what makes you think I'd want to share it?"

"For the same reason Chip's story kept you reading, even when you didn't want to."

"How did you . . . ?" The man looked up and frowned. "Maybe you better sit down."

Gloria slid onto the cushioned vinyl seat and pulled a small notebook, just like the one Sasha Morgan carried, from her purse. "Mind if I take notes?"

"Didn't say I was gonna tell you anything." The man took a bite of his steak and chewed carefully. "The meat's not prime," he said, after swallowing. "Hard to get a good steak nowadays."

Gloria sat quietly, watching the man take another bite. Finally, he put his fork down and extended his hand. "The name's Jonah." Gloria shook it, then waited quietly for him to open the discussion. After three large swallows of iced tea, Jonah did. "I've always been the kind of guy who looked out for others. So my natural instinct is to want to help you. But truth is, I can't afford to. I've got a good job now. Took a long time, and I don't want trouble."

"I'll conceal your identity. No one will know it's about you."

"You don't know who you're dealing with. If you had any idea, you'd leave this whole thing alone."

Gloria thought of the angry male voice over the phone. "I guess it could make some people mad."

"Mad? It could get you into a heap of trouble. A lot of them love the earth but *hate* people. Doesn't make sense, does it?"

"No."

"I don't want to be responsible for any more bloodshed. I can't go through that again. And ever since that night here in the diner when I had that run-in with the environmentalists, I've been trying to keep a low profile. Like I said, I got this good job now and—"

"What bloodshed are you talking about?"

When Jonah twisted in his seat, then folded and unfolded his hands, rearranged the knife and fork on his plate, Gloria knew he was waging an internal war. Finally, he let out a sigh, and Gloria knew the battle was over.

"Ever hear of Intelligent Conservation?"

Gloria shook her head.

"It's a group that believes in conservation but not at the cost of hurting people or destroying lives and livelihoods. A friend of mine started it. He believed both sides of the issues should be addressed intelligently, that that was the only way answers could be found. He started the group after me and some of the ranchers on the other side of Too Tall Mountain started having run-ins with environmentalists.

"One morning, he received a package, the size of a shoebox, in the mail. And that was that."

"What do you mean?"

"Seems he was on an eco-hit list. When he opened it, it exploded. They had to pry his body out of the wall. One arm and both hands were missing and—"

"Okay . . . okay . . . I get your point."

"I don't think you do. The point is, do you want to have to look over your shoulder every time you go out? Do you want to have to take the postal inspector's mail bomb detection course just so you can open your mail? Because if you continue with this, you just might have to."

Gloria suddenly felt nauseous as she envisioned herself on the eco-hit list. She folded her hands on her lap and stared down at her cuticles. She had lived with fear all her life and had finally believed she had overcome it. But if what Jonah said was true, she'd have to deal with it on an entirely new level. Was she up for that? Did she even want to try? Even now, Tracy was in her apartment, probably sprawled on the couch, uninterested in what was going on here. And Tucker? He didn't want to stir up any pots. He just wanted to finish The Estates and make his millions.

Gloria looked into Jonah's eyes. They looked older than forty. Much older. What right did she have coming here and making him relive the pain of his past? Drag up things he was trying to forget? Who did she think she was, anyway? Some crusader like Tracy had said? Some holier-than-thou plaster saint? Why do this? Why bother? If things were as bad as Jonah said, it would take more than a few flyers to make a difference.

But there was such a thing as the sin of omission.

"I don't know if I really want to go any further," Gloria said carefully, "and I don't know where this will go even if I do use your story, assuming you'll even tell it to me. And then I can't be sure it'll do any good, anyway. Maybe I need to think about all this some more."

Jonah nodded. "I like your answer. Shows you're sensible. Shows you got some intelligence. That you're not just someone looking for cheap headlines. Maybe you're the kind of person I want to tell my story to."

Slowly, Gloria flipped open her notebook and uncapped her Bic and once again felt like she was about to do aerobics with a pocketful of nitroglycerine.

When Jonah opened his mouth, the words that came out sounded like dry, brittle toast grinding against his teeth. "At first I'd find one or two lying dead among the herd, but that number went up to a dozen or more after a few months. A dozen cows shot every day by the same .270 caliber rifle, and sometimes their calves too, lying right beside them. That left us with the job of collecting all the dead carcasses, and the ones we missed we'd always find by following the swarm of flies in the pastures. 'Course that always brought another problem— the possibility of disease from the rotting flesh."

Gloria's pen flew across the page, shaking slightly as she wrote the words "dead," ".270 caliber rifle," "rotting flesh."

"The same thing was happening to other ranchers in the area. We went to the sheriff and reported it, individually, then collectively. But there was nothing he could do."

"What about posting guards over the herd?"

Jonah laughed softly. "My ranch covered over five square miles, and the grazing range many more miles. There wasn't money to buy enough manpower to guard that kind of acreage. Anyway, after I went to the sheriff, I began getting the post-cards."

Gloria stopped writing and looked at Jonah, at the pained expression on his face. "What postcards?" she finally coaxed, fearing he wouldn't continue.

"The ones that threatened to 'blow my head off.' My wife took that real hard. Made her cry every time one of them showed up. I tried getting the mail before her, just in case, but most of the time she'd beat me to it. Ranching is a full-time job. Doesn't leave much time for sitting around waiting for the post-man. But maybe I should have made more of an effort, because that's when she began to change. Guess the stress started getting to her. Guess she started worrying that maybe the crazy gunman would try for the kids too. At any rate, it was kinda downhill after that. Every year at least one cow camp would be torched. One year both the cookhouse and bunkhouse were burned to the ground. In between times, corrals and fences were damaged, water facilities destroyed. It was a real strain on our finances, our nerves, our children, our marriage. And then came the straw that broke the camel's back." Jonah's voice cracked and he stopped.

Gloria held her breath. Did she want to hear any more? His story was fantastic, frightening . . . but true. She could see the truth of it etched like trenches across his forehead, could see the truth of it from eyes brimming with sorrow. *Don't tell me any more!*

Oh, please don't say another word. What was she going to do with it all? She watched him lean over, then gulp air.

"Hercules, our prized Brahma bull, was shot ten times. It took him twenty-four hours to die. My kids helped raise him as a 4-H project. They showed him at fairs. They loved that animal. When he died, they were more than devastated. And me. I had had enough. Enough of seeing my family terrorized. Enough of all the financial drain. Enough of working hard and seeing it all come to ruin. That's when I decided to quit ranching. It was a tough decision. I've never quit anything in my life. And I didn't want to leave my kids with that kind of legacy. But I could see what it was doing to Beth—my wife. She had started shutting down emotionally. I could see what it was doing to all of us, and it just wasn't worth it anymore."

Gloria bit her lip. *Oh, Jesus, don't let me lose it. Don't let me start crying.* Tears would embarrass Jonah, make him angry even. This wasn't about self-pity. This was about getting his story out. This was about truth. But it all seemed so unfair. How had this decent, hardworking man lost the livelihood he loved? What was he doing now? Selling shoes? Cars? She didn't have the heart to ask. "How do they get away with it?" she finally asked, the injustice of it burning her like acid.

Jonah sighed a heavy, painful sigh. "They've infiltrated government positions, the environmentalists, and use their power to further their own agenda. For years, the Bureau of Land Management, the Bureau of Reclamation, and the Forest Service have used technicalities and regulations to purge the land north of Too Tall Mountain of all ranchers and farmers by attempting to cancel out their water and range rights. They've bombarded the ranchers with regulations at every turn in hopes of driving them off. I can't tell you how many times I'd find my fences cut and my cows grazing forbidden zones, then be slapped with a huge fine by the Forest Service. They can cut your vein and slowly bleed you to death, and there's no one to stop them. They just have too much muscle."

Gloria watched Jonah settle back in his seat, saw the edges of his mouth relax and knew the interview was over. She also knew something else. She had to run the story, no matter the cost.

Gloria was eager to share what she had learned with Tracy. She hoped it would fire Tracy up, motivate her and pull her out of that pit of depression she was in. But when she got home, Tracy was on the couch with the blanket pulled over her head. In the kitchen, Gloria found part of a six-pack of beer sitting on the table. And when Gloria crept closer to see if Tracy was okay, she nearly tripped over three empty bottles. Gloria didn't keep beer in the house. That meant Tracy had gone out. She wondered why Tracy had lied about wanting to stay home. She also wondered if the beer had been Tracy's dinner and checked the refrigerator. Nothing had been touched. Maybe Tracy ate out. Gloria hoped so. She'd talk to her about it tomorrow.

The next morning when Gloria tiptoed to the couch to see if Tracy was awake, she found the covers rolled into a ball and the couch empty. On the coffee table was a note.

Thanks for the hospitality. I've decided to go back to Appleton. I'll bunk with Mom until I get a job and back on my feet. Call me sometime, although we don't seem to have as much to say to each other as we used to. Tracy.

Chapter Twenty-Three

SEE! THE WINTER IS PAST;
THE RAINS ARE OVER AND GONE.
FLOWERS APPEAR ON THE EARTH;
THE SEASON OF SINGING HAS COME.

~❧ SONG OF SONGS 2:11–12 NIV❧~

LIFE DIDN'T GET BETTER THAN THIS. Gloria sat crammed between Harry Grizwald and one of the girls who worked with Perth, a tall, friendly waitress who was obviously pleased by what was going on. Bodies pressed all around the large rectangular table that filled much of the diner's private back room, making elbows collide with elbows. Overhead, helium balloons hovered like a flock of overweight birds, and colored streamers rustled softly whenever someone jumped from his or her chair or moved suddenly. Perth stood at one end, pink with pleasure, and grinning so wide it made Gloria's cheeks ache just to look at her. It also made her heart soar.

"Come on, make a wish!" someone shouted.

"How does it feel to be an old woman?" someone else teased.

Perth bent over the two-foot sheet cake, decorated with red, yellow, and blue roses, and covered with white butter cream frosting. In the middle of the cake stood two large paraffin number candles, a one and an eight. Gloria watched Perth make little ladylike blowing motions before the candles extinguished, then watched tiny wisps of smoke curl above the wicks.

As the smoke dissipated, so did the last of Gloria's trepidation. Perth was finally of legal age. Sasha Morgan no longer posed a threat. Only a week ago, Miss Morgan had called and said that something unexpected had happened. That somehow, Perth's file had been lost along the pipeline at Social Services and only that morning had resurfaced. She said since Perth was so close to her eighteenth birthday she was closing the case. And that neither Gloria nor Perth would be receiving further correspondences from them. Even so, Gloria's nervousness had lingered. It was gone now. Extinguished with the candles. Perth was free. Free to pursue her new life, which would begin at Eckerd Community College in the fall.

"I still don't know how you guys pulled this off," Perth said, holding a knife in one hand and licking butter cream from the other. "Not one of you slipped. I can't believe it."

Voices rose higher than the balloons as half a dozen people tried talking at once.

"I almost told you yesterday."

"I avoided you like the plague."

"I thought for sure I'd be the one to spill the beans."

"Yeah, me too."

"Don't expect this next year."

"You shoulda seen the look on your face!"

"Come on, open your presents."

Gloria smiled, then thought of something and leaned over and tapped Harry's arm. "Sunday, you can have your turn first. We'll sit in the front pew."

Harry nodded. "Gotta hand it to you, the prayers worked."

From the corner of her eye, Gloria saw Harry slip his hand over Dorie Dobson's. He'd been seeing a lot of her lately.

"Guess it's time for me to let Lily go. Five years . . . time to let go. Time to get back to church. Time to get back to a lot of things . . ." His voice trailed off, and he was no longer looking at Gloria. Dorie Dobson had his full attention now.

"Open your presents!" someone shouted again, then someone else, until a clamor filled the room.

Perth's face turned a deeper shade of pink as people began piling gifts in front of her. "All right. All right." She took the one closest to her and pulled at the ribbon. "It's from Miss Dobson . . ."

Gloria sighed and settled comfortably in her chair. Her present to Perth wasn't among the others. Perth would get that tomorrow when Gloria took her to Elegant Affairs for a prom dress . . . and shoes and panty hose and whatever else Perth needed to complete her outfit. She watched Perth pull a new backpack out of Miss Dobson's box, then covered her ears as Perth shrieked with joy.

No. Life didn't get better than this.

~◉ ◉~

Gloria sat curled on the couch, her apartment quiet. She felt mildly weary from the evening's activities. It was the pleasant fatigue one feels after a job well done. She had worked on Perth's surprise party for over a week. And the look on Perth's face tonight told her it had all been worth it. But it did suddenly strike her as strange that she was the only one in the group of merrymakers who now sat alone. Perth and her friends were continuing the party at her new boyfriend's house. And Harry Grizwald had left with Dorie Dobson.

Gloria rarely thought of God's promise anymore. Not since she gave that promise back to Him. Once she had believed she'd find the man of her dreams. Instead, she had found so much more—a love deeper than anything she had imagined.

She had fallen in love with Jesus. Really fallen in love.

Jesus had shown Himself to be provider, protector, a faithful friend, the lover of her soul. She was both humbled and awed by His love. And He had given her so many other things to love . . . Eckerd, her life here, her new friends. But already Gloria knew she wouldn't stay. She'd see Perth graduate from New Field High, then help Perth over the summer get ready for college. And during that time she'd train someone else to take her place at E-Z Printing. And . . . she'd continue her flyers. She had told Harry about the threat. He received his own threat when the rancher's story came out. Someone had discovered that the flyers came from E-Z Printing. But nothing had come of either threat. And she no longer felt frightened by the environmentalists. A little nervous sometimes but not frightened. She was in the everlasting arms. She knew that just as surely as she knew her name.

She thought of Appleton and smiled at the prospect of going back with a Bible full of notations—of things she had learned here in Eckerd—just like those church ladies back home at Appleton Full Gospel. Well . . . not exactly like the church ladies. She still had a lot more notations to make before it would really be like theirs. But it was a start.

But when she went back, it was nice to know she'd go back different. And go back she would. To make peace with her mother, with Cutter Press, with Tracy. And she knew her willingness to return pleased Jesus. And that gave her pleasure as well. She didn't know what awaited her in Appleton. But she did know her walk with the Lord was deeper now and made her secure. And He'd be with her and help her share the love He had placed inside her once timid little heart, a heart He had enlarged to where it was big enough to hold the entire town of Appleton itself.

Even Mother.

As Gloria sat with her head resting against the soft back of the couch, she suddenly heard a still small voice and sat up to listen. No, it wasn't her imagination. She recognized that voice. And there it was again . . .

Arise, My darling, My beautiful one, and come with Me.

Author's Note

Dear Readers:

I enjoyed writing Waters of Marah. *The character, Gloria Bickford, intrigued me. Her insecurities and need for love reflect basic issues residing within most of us. But what I liked best was how God can take the most insignificant life and make something beautiful out of it. It's a spiritual truth that should lift any downcast heart.*

Just as in my previous books, when doing research for Waters of Marah, *I was shocked and disturbed by what I discovered. Radical environmentalism is a vicious form of advocacy and should be called by its real name: domestic terrorism. Most conscientious people care about the environment and believe efforts to save it are benign and useful. Unfortunately, this is often not the case.*

I hope you'll join Gloria Bickford next year in the sequel, Return to Appleton, *as threats, resulting from her anti—eco-terror flyers follow her back to her hometown. And in the midst of it all, she'll try to repair her relationship with her mother, Tracy, and Cutter Press. And who can tell? Maybe she'll find that special someone in the process.*

Blessings and love,

Sylvia Bambola

Web site — http://www.sylviabambola.com
e-mail — sbambola@tampabay.rr.com

Discussion Questions/Study Guide

1. In chapter 1, we learn that Gloria dislikes both the color green and frogs—the two somehow being connected in her mind—because of the teasing she endured when she was younger. What are some of the things people carry over from childhood into adulthood? And how does Scripture tell us to deal with them? In Gloria's case two Scriptures can be readily applied: 2 Corinthians 10:5: "Casting down imaginations, and every high thing that exalteth itself against the knowledge of God, and bringing into captivity every thought to the obedience of Christ." And also 1 Corinthians 2:16: "But we have the mind of Christ." What are some others?

2. When Gloria sets out in search of her heart's desire—someone to love her—do you think she's really capable of loving anyone in return? Or is she like so many people who want to be loved without actually being capable of real love themselves?

3. The disappointment Gloria feels after her failure to get involved with the neighbor who committed suicide seems to have made Gloria more open to helping Perth when she needed it. How does God use our failures to reinforce our resolve when we are given another opportunity to repeat the situation? How has this happened in your life?

4. There are many references to beauty in the book. Gloria's mother is an ex-beauty queen. Gloria is named after a beautiful film star. Gloria herself desires to be beautiful. She uses the perfume, Beautiful, and tries to emulate the beautiful Jenny Hobart. She even calls Jesus her "beautiful Jesus." Yet, all her life, Gloria has felt unworthy, unloved, and ugly. What does this say about sin or the sin nature?

5. In chapter 4, after Gloria meets Perth for the first time, she is mentally critical of Perth's mother. Gloria's criticisms reflect her own mother's attitudes (i.e., What was she thinking?). How many times do we find ourselves doing or saying the same things as our parents even after we swore we never would? Give some examples. And why do we do that?

6. In the same scene with Perth, Gloria makes a mental note of what her own mother would do (make sure she had on a warm coat and mittens, etc.)—all things done by a parent who loved her child. And this coming on the heels of Gloria mentally accusing her mother of not loving her. How many times have we overlooked the acts of love performed by our own parents and concentrated on the negatives? How many times have our own children done this to us? How many times have we done this to God?

7. Perth tells Gloria that she likes Gloria's new hairstyle and that the old hairstyle made Gloria look as though she didn't care about her appearance. This is when Perth herself looks a mess. How common is it to see the faults of others but not see these very same faults in ourselves?

8. Gloria likens Tucker to an idol—something she had installed on the throne of her heart as an object of desire, when only One has the right to sit there. How can people and things become idols in our lives? What can we do to guard against that?

9. There are times when Gloria makes notations in her Bible—times when she has reached a milestone in her life. What are some of the milestones in your life? Situations that changed you? Brought about profound growth? Were most of these changes brought on the heels of pain and adversity? If so, why do you think that is?

10. What do Perth's comments in chapter 11 about Gloria being so good with makeup and Jenny Hobart's comments about Gloria in the same chapter having it all together say about human nature? About how easy it is to misjudge others?

11. In chapter 18, Gloria disappoints her mother, Tracy, and Tucker. Sometimes obedience to God means disappointing others. How has obeying God created negative reactions or situations in your life?

12. In chapter 20, Perth says Gloria could never understand someone like Perth, someone with frustrated dreams, because Gloria gets everything she wants. This, of course, is a huge misconception. How common is it to believe that the next guy has it better? or easier? or doesn't suffer as much?

13. How different is Gloria's concept of God from chapter 1, where her flashback reveals that Gloria believed God punished her disobedience for being in Clive McGreedy's barn by letting Cutter Press humiliate her, from her concept of God in the last chapter?

14. Has a shift occurred from chapter 19, where the heading is: "My lover is mine and I am his"; and chapter 22, where the heading is: "I am my lover's and my lover is mine"? The focus of these Scriptures is totally different. The first is focused on self rather than the beloved. The second is focused on the beloved rather than self. How is that reflected in Gloria's life? What has changed?

15. In chapter 21, roles have reversed. We see Gloria removing Tracy's hat and muffler as if Tracy were a child. And things come full circle when Gloria counsels Tracy to "leave town," much like Tracy counseled Gloria in chapter 1. How many times have roles reversed in your life? in the lives of some of your family members? of friends? And why?

16. Do you think Gloria is strong enough at the end of the book to go back to Appleton and accomplish everything she plans to? Why or why not?

WATERS OF MARAH TEAM

ACQUIRING EDITOR:
Michele Straubel

COPY EDITOR:
Terry McDowell

BACK COVER COPY:
Julie-Allyson Ieron, Joy Media

COVER DESIGN:
UDG| DesignWorks

INTERIOR DESIGN:
Ragont Design

PRINTING AND BINDING:
Dickinson Press Inc.

The typeface for the text of this book is
Centaur MT